3-23

IN THE TIME OF OUR HISTORY

IN THE TIME OF
OUR HISTORY

SUSANNE PARI

THORNDIKE PRESS
A part of Gale, a Cengage Company

Thorndike Press® Large Print Basic.
The text of this Large Print edition is unabridged.
Other aspects of the book may vary from the original edition.
Set in 16 pt. Plantin.

LIBRARY OF CONGRESS CIP DATA ON FILE.
CATALOGUING IN PUBLICATION FOR THIS BOOK
IS AVAILABLE FROM THE LIBRARY OF CONGRESS.

ISBN-13: 979-8-88578-485-6 (hardcover alk. paper)

Published in 2023 by arrangement with Kensington Books, an imprint of Kensington Publishing Corp.

Printed in Mexico
Print Number: 1   Print Year: 2023

For Shahram

And for all the writers, artists, and
thinkers who have been silenced

PART 1

■ ■ ■ ■

SISTERS

In the time of our history when the Song-writer Who Imagined was murdered in New York and the dictator Saddam invaded Iran, there was a girl who wanted to be as free as a boy in choosing her future. Her father, however, cared only that she marry a suitable young man. Her mother wanted peace all around. Despite his relentless nagging, the daughter refused an audience to any suitors who inquired. Soon it came to pass that the girl's younger sister, who was demure and obedient, and to whom the elder sister was supremely devoted, fell in love with a suitable young man of her own and wanted to marry. The father, recognizing this as an auspicious opportunity, pronounced that he would allow the marriage of his younger daughter only when the elder daughter consented to marry as well. Much to everyone's surprise, the elder daughter swiftly and dispassionately chose the next suitor in line. With great aplomb, the father sent invitations far and wide for a grand double wedding, at which point the elder daughter secretly visited a surgeon and had herself made barren — and therefore unmarriageable. The father, apoplectic with rage and determined not to lose face entirely, allowed the younger daughter to marry, but he disowned the elder one, who happily moved far away to pursue her desires.

PROLOGUE

As a matter of coincidence, the American Embassy hostages were released on the same day that Mitra Jahani had her tubes tied. January 20, 1981. She saw the men on a wall-mounted television screen when she woke up from the surgery. The volume was low, but she heard their hoots and hollers, saw one punch the air in triumph, another one kiss the tarmac at the bottom of the mobile stairs. Fifty-two of them, long-haired and bearded, looking fairly decent for having spent more than a year in the clutches of a group of young Iranian militants. *Either I'm still zoned out and dreaming,* Mitra thought, *or I'm hallucinating.*

Mitra closed her eyes, counted to five, opened them tentatively, and kept her gaze away from the television screen. Here was the top of her hand, covered in a mess of clear tape, sprouting a needle and IV tubing that snaked beyond her peripheral vision.

9

Here was her body covered in a flimsy white hospital blanket, her big feet down there like two molehills. Her other hand, she realized, rested under the blanket on a thick strip of gauzy bandage taped to her lower belly. She turned her head slightly, and here was Olga, sitting next to her like Luca Brasi on a job for the Corleone family.

The caption on the TV screen read: RHEIN-MAIN AIR FORCE BASE, GERMANY. With an oversize smile, President Jimmy Carter — actually, former President by just a few minutes — was greeting the hostages for whom his administration had finally negotiated a release.

"This is surreal," Mitra muttered.

Olga bolted up from her chair and bent forward. "What you say, Mitra-joon?"

Mitra pointed weakly at the TV, coughed, then winced. Amazing how many stomach muscles were involved in a simple cough.

"You have pain," Olga pronounced anxiously in Farsi. She hurried into the hallway, her rubber-soled orthotics squeaking on the linoleum. " 'Scuse me, 'scuse me! I need nurse here. My girl, she need medicine for pain. You coming now? Now you coming? Please. Right 'way, please! Oh, t'ank you, t'ank you." A pill came to Mitra in a plastic cup. Olga's thick dishpan fingers tilted a

10

glass of water to her lips. She swallowed and let her head fall back against the pillow.

Now the caption read: HOSTAGES RETURN AFTER 444 DAYS IN CAPTIVITY. Okay, she wasn't hallucinating.

"Number four very bad luck," said a voice to Mitra's left. A Chinese woman in the other bed was shaking her head at the screen. "Four-four-four. *Triple* bad luck."

"Ignore her," said Olga in Farsi. "Bad luck is more complicated than one number. Anyway, she is nosy, asking why a young girl such as you had a woman's surgery. She thinks you had an abortion, and she wants to disapprove. You should have a private room."

Mitra smiled thinly at the woman. To Olga, she shrugged and responded in Farsi, "It's only one night." She gestured at the television. "Why aren't you joyful, Olga-joon? No more yellow ribbons or 'Bomb Iran' songs." Mitra thought people would slowly forget the whole miserable crisis. Maybe they'd even revert to thinking of Iran as Persia, an exoticized place whose inhabitants lived in silk tents and rode camels. To think that such ignorance had once pissed her off, that she'd tried to correct people about where her parents originally came from, even to show them a map sometimes.

11

She never thought she'd want that back again, that anonymous heritage.

Olga said, "I do not care anymore about the hostages or the new President Reagan or Iran, may God castrate its mullahs. I am worrying about you, Mitra-joon. How you are and what you have done." She looked away. "How I have helped you do this terrible thing."

Olga knew about operations. Eleven times in her youth she had let the surgeons cut her. Operations to "correct" her. Of no use. She remained infertile. This was what happened when girls were married off at twelve and pregnant by thirteen. A body too small to nurture another body. Death before life. A full-grown baby boy — gray as a dead tree — cut out of her like a useless goiter. The look of her bloated belly still told the story: the first cut — from breast to mound — like a river on a map; the other cuts like silvery moonlit tributaries.

Mitra had said her belly would not look like that. Just a small incision that would fade to a nearly imperceptible line, like a kitten scratch. The golden-haired doctor at the institute in Manhattan had said so, his smile made stupid by the lie Mitra told him about an inheritable disease and by his guilelessness about young women who say they do not ever want children anyway.

Over the last weeks, Olga had begged Mitra: *Don't do this. Run away, just run away.* But Mitra always did what she wanted with the single-mindedness and impatience of a teenage boy with an erection. From the moment Olga set eyes on her at the New Jersey house just over ten years ago, she knew that this girl — then just thirteen years old — was a force: rebellious, stubborn, determined. *Takes one to know one,* Mitra later taught her. Yes, Olga had seen herself in Mitra; herself as she once was.

"Are you hungry?" Olga asked, sitting like a Buddha (America had made her fat), hungry herself, but not wanting to eat.

Mitra shook her head, eyes opening and closing. "No." She blinked slowly. "What time is it?"

"Night."

Mitra's eyebrows shot up in surprise. "Go back to the hotel now, Olga-joon. Call Maman at eleven o'clock and tell her that the show was wonderful and we're safe in the room. You remember the name of the show?"

"The one about the cats."

"*Cats,* that's what it's called. *Cats.* Remember."

Olga nodded and wrung her hands like a

13

murderer about to confess. "I don't want to leave you," she said.

"Tell Maman I'm in the bathroom. Tell her I'm tired and we're going to bed. She won't need to talk to me."

"But you will be alone here."

"Olga," Mitra said sharply. "Have I ever minded being alone?"

Olga jerked her chin up and smacked her tongue against the roof of her mouth: a forthright Persian no.

"Go then," Mitra said. "You have money for the cab, right?"

Olga rose and pulled a crumpled wad of dollars out of her raincoat pocket. "I am going," she said, but she stood still, her vision suddenly blurring.

Mitra smiled through her discomfort. "Don't look like that. Everything is good. I am satisfied."

"You are strong, azizam. Too strong."

Mitra shook her head. "No," she said in English. "I'm free."

14

CHAPTER 1

She came to the East Coast for the first anniversary of her sister's death. It was the Shia way, to mark the Death Day — first at seven days, then at forty, and finally at one year. Not that Mitra was a believer. She came because she felt sorry for her mother, still crestfallen and clutching tightly to the traditions she'd been trying to instill in her two daughters since they were born at Bergen County Hospital. Mitra had fought hardest against those rituals — Persian New Year parties, Zoroastrian festivals, Ramadan fasting — but now Mitra was her mother's only child.

Dawn at Kennedy Airport. Round-edged melamine furniture, miles of burgundy carpet, burnt coffee smell — the air of a banquet hall the morning after a raucous party. A janitor harpooned candy wrappers and dirty napkins from the floor. Mitra heard the drone of a vacuum cleaner as she ordered an espresso from a café cart, then took a seat at the end of a bank of bucket chairs facing the windows. She was in no hurry to escape the boundaries of transit. On the tarmac sat a gaggle of airplanes tinged pink in the daybreak.

From a distance, say, from the point of view of the logy barista who had served her espresso, Mitra looked unapproachable. This was not only because the barista was a young twentysomething and Mitra just over the cusp of forty. Despite her jeans, plain white shirt, and tight-fitting leather jacket, Mitra exuded the self-assuredness of a power-suited executive. And there was strength in her face: the olive skin, chocolate eyes, long arched eyebrows, and especially the angular nose — not exactly hooked, not exactly humped, but definitely a feature that would have inclined most girls to opt for a slight surgical correction.

Mitra scalded her tongue on the coffee, and her eyes watered. One of the airplanes trembled at the strain of its full-on engines, and she remembered tramping across the tarmac all those years ago in the shadow of her parents, little Anahita clasping her ears and squinting against the noise of the rush of air, while Mitra jumped and giggled in the thrilling vortex of mechanical energy.

Mitra belched softly, rubbed two fingers over the heartburn behind her sternum. Espresso and anxiety — well behaved on their own, rambunctious as urchins together. She dropped her coffee into a trash can. Transit was just another word for limbo, and there was no such place. Except maybe death.

She got up, kicked her carry-on to a wheel-perfect slant, and made her way toward the moving walkway. Nearing the edge of transit, she quickened her pace, focused on the resolute *clip-clop* of her heels on the terminal's stone floor and on a faraway Exit sign, not once eyeballing the small crowd of impatient, neck-craning welcomers straining at the stanchions and barrier ropes. And yet, she caught a whiff of Anahita's Chanel No. 9, a glimpse of little Nina's pink hair ribbons, a snatch of Nikku's pubescent belly laugh. Phantom memories. The car crash had taken all three of them — sister, niece, nephew.

At baggage claim, Mitra stepped outside and bummed a cigarette from an oily-haired businessman with a French accent. She hadn't smoked in fifteen years.

The rental car was appliance white. A Ford

something. Itchy seats. Bad radio. Mitra's mother had offered to pick her up, but Mitra said it was too early in the morning. The truth was, Shireen was a terrible driver, the kind who kept the steering wheel in constant motion as if the mechanism needed second-by-second readjustment, who overcompensated on every turn and used the brake pedal like a pogo stick. It never occurred to her to wonder why her daughters got carsick only when she was at the wheel.

Mitra adjusted the seat to accommodate her lower back, which ached from transplanting a manzanita bush in her yard the day before. The September sun splashed onto the parking lot, making the concrete shimmer. She dug into her purse for her sunglasses. The air already felt humid, and she longed for the cool fog of San Francisco.

She merged into rush-hour traffic on the Van Wyck Expressway. She hoped it would take her a long time to get to New Jersey; it was hours before she was scheduled to pick her mother up for lunch. She could first drop her luggage off at her cousin Nezam's apartment in Manhattan, where she would be staying, but she felt too sluggish to deal with his five-year-old twin boys. Besides a short, openmouthed nap on the flight, Mitra hadn't slept. She was a bit numb, as if only half of her had landed in New York. She tuned in to the NPR station and was struck, as always, by the flood of news and commentary on the Bill Clinton–Monica Lewinsky affair, its salacious details gravely analyzed by politicos and journalists while they ignored the massacres in Kosovo, the embassy bombings in Africa, and the Rwandan genocide trial.

In the Holland Tunnel, Mitra was ready when the memory of Anahita came to her. They were children in the back seat of her father's Cadillac, the tunnel like the inside of an animal's throat, yellow beams of light sweeping and flickering over their party dresses and lace-ruffled anklets, Anahita moving her rose-petal lips in silent child-prayer to keep the Hudson River from crushing them, and Mitra leaning over to whisper in her ear, *Omigod! I just saw a leak!*

The wicked memories; wicked because Mitra had been wicked in those early years. Until later when Anahita was Sweet Ana, red-licorice-smelling and cheeks like cool pillows and eyes that said tell me what to do — baby sister, unlucky sister; breakable to break Mitra's heart. Anahita, who wanted and needed everything Mitra did not.

Despite the traffic, Mitra arrived at the turnoff for Devon in an hour. The vehicle seemed to know its way: past the golf course at the country club where her father used to play tennis (trees hinting at the gold and red of autumn), through the condominium development that had caused such a ruckus when her father's company built it ten years before, over the plank bridge (now reinforced with steel), past the grammar school where Bobbie Dowd had thrown a rock at her forehead from the top of the jungle gym and Nancy Goldberg had lost a chunk of her red hair in Mitra's fist, and then into the town of Devon, named for the dairy cows, lowing ghosts now.

Three days short of a year ago, Nezam had driven Mitra here from the airport. Her brain had registered nothing of her surroundings; she'd felt numb since the phone call came that her sister was in serious condition from a car accident. Anahita and the children were already dead, of course, but this was the Jahani family way. News of death was not imparted over the phone, in a letter, or even in person, until it was absolutely necessary, like on your way to the morgue. To take this tack was thought of as being sensitive, being careful not to shock the person, but that night when Nezam turned the car, not into the hospital's parking lot but the mortuary's, Mitra grabbed the collar of his jacket, yanked and shook, and screamed *Coward!* over and over. Poor guy, he was as devastated as she. No. He was better off; everyone was. Only Mitra knew the accident might have been prevented. Worse, that she might have caused it. She and a man she'd never met.

There were no empty spaces in front of the Starbucks, which had obliterated the Dairy Queen two years before. The main drag of downtown Devon still boasted a kosher deli and Kleinfeld's Fine Jewelry, but where the Woolworth's used to be was a market that advertised fresh eel and Korean videos — a testament to the influx of Asian immigrants. There was a different nail salon every two or three stores, each offering mani-pedis at bargain prices. In every one, Mitra saw the ghost of her sister, hands and feet stretched out for painting.

She parked in one of the diagonal spaces next to the train tracks. Even when she was a child, no trains came through here; the tracks had been left intact to lend a certain small-town quaintness to Devon. The old stone station was now Café Buon Gusto! Like so many suburban cafés, it was a restaurant, not a place where you could drop in for coffee, a pastry, and the newspaper.

Mitra crossed the street, reminding herself with pleasure that jaywalking was generally ignored on the East Coast, and headed toward what used to be the corner candy store, where her father had forbidden them to go *because only bad American children hang out there.* Inside, it had been close and hot all year-round, the floor-to-ceiling shelves packed with useless but gotta-have items that suburban children spent their allowances on: baseball cards, glitter, fake mustaches, comic books, spinning tops, Mouseketeer hats, warm Pepsi in a glass bottle. Mitra had never liked candy, but that hadn't prevented her from stealing a great many jawbreakers from the grizzled owner and his dwarfish wife, standing guard behind a peeling Formica counter no bigger than a foot square.

As Mitra went into the store now, two crimson-lipped matrons stepped around her, accents Jersey-nasal, a plethora of tinny *t*'s and yawning *i*'s. The store had a bright and roomy 7-Eleven look, with a smiling Bengali clerk behind the counter ("Register has no more than $30 cash"). Mitra averted her eyes from the shelves of primary-color candy and snacks (*Skittles!* Nina squealed in her ear) and from a small toy section where she'd once bought Nikku a balsa airplane. She walked swiftly to the tall counter and asked for a pack of American Spirit Blues, forked over the bills, and was glad to find herself back on Main Street.

She craved a latte but headed toward Devon's vintage diner, a Sterling Streamliner that she wished someone would restore. Two cops sat at the counter, hunched, silent, ignoring the squawk of the radios weighing down their belts. The lone waitress, reddish-gray hair twisted into a small tire on the back of her head, refilled their mugs. Mitra slid into a booth.

She remembered the waitress. Tammy. That was her name. Her hair had been copper red back then, and Ana was mesmerized by it. "I bet it's down to her knees," she'd said. The bulbous configurations Tammy sculpted on the back of her head had run the gamut from donuts (several à la Jo Anne Worley) to stiff ringlets the size of Slinkies.

"Who cares?" Mitra had said.

"Why doesn't she ever wear it down?"

"Because, stupid, it's against the law."

Eyes wide. "Why?"

"She's serving food. She has to wear it up so it doesn't get in the food."

"Oh."

Their mother used to drop them off at the

23

diner sometimes when she had errands to run, order them a banana split to share. Mitra wouldn't let Ana touch the chocolate ice cream, would shove the nuts onto Ana's side of the bowl, even though Ana hated the nuts as much as she did and painstakingly ate around them. The waitress had always been nicer to Ana and had once brought her a scoop of chocolate in a little dish. Mitra was livid, and she quickly drummed up a story: *Chocolate is more fattening than vanilla or strawberry, so chubby kids like you shouldn't eat it.*

Tammy served Mitra a cup of coffee that tasted like a blend of instant and yesterday's grounds. Mitra looked at her watch: eight thirty. Time was not flying. She thought about reading the paper and glanced at a much-fingered tabloid sitting on a stool across the aisle. *STAINED!* it shouted, referring to Monica Lewinsky's dress. She shook her head slowly and realized with sudden disgust that it was a gesture her father made when he was feeling contemptuous, which was often. She clenched her jaw. Being back meant she would have to deal with him.

She contemplated the sticky menu. She could order some eggs, even pancakes. *Why don't you ever get fat, Mitti?* Her finger grazed a rip in the vinyl cushion next to her.

24

She looked down. A long slit and yellow stuffing. *I'll sit on the rip, Mitti. You sit on the other side.* Short, pudgy legs, white sandals dangling inches above the speckled floor.

Mitra left a five for the one-dollar coffee. On the way out, she leaned across the counter to Tammy. "Your hair's beautiful. Do you mind me asking how long it is?"

"Just under my braw strap now," Tammy said, eyes gleaming to life. "Used to be down to the backsamy knees, hon, but that was a lawng time ago."

Downtown Devon was too small. And flat. Going for a walk in San Francisco was an aerobic workout no matter how leisurely you strolled. Mitra got back into the car and reached for her phone, stopped herself before dialing Julian. She didn't want to wake him; he'd been on call last night. She imagined him taking up the whole of her bed, half of his face on her pillow, his long legs spread to the bottom corners. It wasn't that she missed him really, she just craved the whispery baritone of his voice, the slur of his British accent. It might help her to step back from the gray swirl of Devon before it sucked her in, but she dropped the phone back into her purse.

She drove out of town, up the long hill

the school bus used to take, and veered off into a neighborhood of houses on one-acre plots. Many had been renovated, but they bore the remnants of the extra-tall double-entry doors and wrought-iron railings of midcentury fashion. She took several streets — left, right, down, around — driving by rote the way she applied lip gloss without a mirror. She parked and walked, stepping over cracks and avoiding potholes that had grown wider and deeper but remained childhood markers. At the edge of the school playground was a bench she didn't remember. She sat and closed her eyes, let the sun hit her face.

Anahita had been three years behind Mitra in school. The first day of third grade — Ana's first day of kindergarten — Ana ducked under Miss Callahan's outstretched arm, ran straight for the third-grade class lining up in the hallway, and tried to hug her sister. Mitra gritted her teeth and pushed Ana away. "Go back to your class!" And later, on the school bus: "You sit in the front and I sit in the back. And don't come up to me at school!"

Anahita had obeyed, as she always did. Not once after the first day did she look toward Mitra. Not when she was teased and taunted for her frizzy hair, not even when she broke her arm falling from the slide. Not until Ana was twelve, when suddenly everything changed between them, when it was too late for Mitra to expunge those callous acts, at least not in her own mind.

Mitra startled as the gymnasium door burst open and regurgitated a gaggle of exuberant children. She stood, gathered her purse, and noticed a metal plaque screwed into a lower slat of the bench:

Nikku & Nina — Gone Too Soon

Eyes stinging, careful not to stumble, she headed for the car.

The old residential part of Devon had experienced a madness of boomer remodeling, what Mitra thought of as a reawakening of postwar nuclear family idealism. She made a K-turn and parked across the street from the bungalow Anahita and her husband once owned. After the accident, Bijan had taken a month's leave of absence from his bank job, spending most of it in bed reacquainting himself with his collection of bongs. The bank had finally honored his request for a transfer to their London office. Mitra had spoken to him once before he departed, a short conversation that left her feeling cold. She knew they might not talk again for a long while; he couldn't bear it. She missed him now, especially his Jimmy Stewart stutter and his dry jokes about impotent bankers.

She opened the window and lit a cigarette, promising herself to drive off when she finished it. A breeze whisked the smoke out the window. Sun glinted off the side mirror. She lifted her gaze to study the house.

Same, same — only different. Anahita would notice the film of dust on the black shutters and the faint brown spots on the lawn. She would hate that the wooden screen door had been replaced by a cheap metal one, that the front porch where she'd had Adirondack chairs and hanging plants was now a parking spot for two adult bicycles and a half-dead, left-leaning ficus.

Did the new owners know the sad story of their predecessors? They must, Mitra decided. Neighborhoods owned the tragedies of their inhabitants. The new people were no doubt solid American white people, not immigrants like her parents who weighed every story for bad luck — and bought a different house.

Mitra turned the car off to hear suburbia: a distant lawnmower, barking dogs, a woodpecker knocking itself out on a telephone

28

pole, the faraway chatter and laughter of the playground — sounds of her childhood, sounds Anahita loved and Mitra hated.

She broke her promise and lit another cigarette from the butt of the first one. Anahita would have scolded her; she'd never smoked, never done anything their parents would have disapproved of. Mitra's opposite.

A maroon minivan pulled into Anahita's ex-driveway, and a young woman in gray sweats jumped out, opened the back door, and reached in to tug a towheaded toddler out of the car. The child wore a pink sundress and white sandals. Mitra saw, even though she was too far away to see, each of the child's pink toes with their moon-shaped nail beds and pliant white cuticles. Her throat swelled. She turned the key in the ignition, turned it again, and the mechanism grated. With a jolt, she drove off.

She'd been holding her breath, it seemed. She was on the shoulder next to the golf course. Gasping, she inhaled the odor of fresh-cut grass and fertilizer. The digital clock on the dash read 9:15. She cursed herself for avoiding Libby and Nezam's apartment; she could have dropped her luggage off, taken a shower, skipped the tour of Devon altogether. A year goes by and you think you're strong, and then you're not. She rummaged for her cell phone and dialed her mother's number.

"Hello," he said.

Stunned at the sound of the wrong voice, Mitra clenched her jaw. She couldn't remember her father ever leaving for the office later than eight thirty. Then again, it had been seventeen years since she'd been witness to his schedule.

She swallowed dryly. "Hello, Baba."

Silence. Would he hang up?

Go ahead, Mitra thought, *hang up.*

And he did.

CHAPTER 2

His hand tingled from slamming the receiver into its cradle. A chip of plastic had flown off the machine and been swallowed by the nap of the bedroom carpet. The one morning Yusef Jahani had slept in, had not set his alarm for 6:00 a.m., and had indulged in the sight of the news anchor's sleek legs while he looped the ends of his silk tie, was the one morning that the telephone rang at 9:15 and his wife was not the only person home to answer.

He shouted into the hallway: "That was your daughter!" But Shireen was already down in the kitchen. Scowling, he donned his suit jacket in one swift motion, snapped on his gold watch, swept up his briefcase, and descended the stairs at an age-defying clip.

"That was your daughter," he barked across the kitchen at his wife's back.

"Oh!" She pivoted from the sink, an eager

31

smile lighting up her raccoon-eyed face. He glanced at the table — an omelet, warmed lavash bread, feta cheese, honeycomb, waiting for him. Shireen's smile evaporated, her mouth twitching with remorse. "Yusefjoon," she pleaded. "I'm sure she thought you were at the office."

"Thanks to you, Shireen, I am not."

She took a tentative step forward, wiping wet hands on her apron. "Did you speak to her?"

He snorted, shook his head in disgust, and strode for the door that led to the garage. The woman was impossible. After all these years, she still held out hope that he would reconcile with their diabolical daughter. How had he tolerated such a simpleminded woman for more than four decades? He slid into the tumescent seat of his Jaguar. She appeared at the door then, her hand raised timidly for him to "wait" or "stop" or "please," and he put the car in gear, watched her worried features grow dimmer as he backed out into the sunlight, and exhaled with satisfaction as he pressed the button to close the garage door, making her disappear.

She deserved it, he thought, coming to a brief stop at the bottom of the driveway, then turning leisurely in front of a car that was, he felt, traveling far too speedily, driven by a pimply-faced teenager. This was what happened when a man spoke to his wife about business matters. Last night he'd been more irritated than usual, and he'd made the mistake of complaining about a young Irish painting crew who had stolen the Westchester project's only fourteen-foot ladder. Instead of merely listening, she started in with her pampering: *Oh, but, Yusef-joon, you've worked so hard all of your life and now is the time for you to rest a little.* He reminded her that he was never going to be like an American husband who spent his final years grazing on a golf course. *At least go in a little later to the office, Yusef-joon. You deserve it.* Right. Her suggestions were always idiotic. Furthermore, if Shireen were a properly loyal wife, she would not be speaking to Mitra either. She was lucky he hadn't forbidden it over the years. But what did he get for being nice? Disrespect, that's what. And that gleeful look on her face when she heard that Mitra had called — aah!

He glanced in the rearview mirror. Why, the pimply-faced punk was tailgating him! Not only that, the boy was craning forward, scowling, and giving him the middle finger. Yusef snorted and put his foot on the brake. At the busy Pilgrim Avenue intersection, he stopped and waited for a school bus to lumber up the hill before turning, which allowed him a few moments to gaze appreciatively at the condominium complex he had built, with its brick veneer, white Georgian columns, and double-story sunburst windows. The yuppies had bought them all.

On the main road, the school bus flashed its lights and slowed to take on a group of children. Yusef peeked into the rearview mirror and chuckled at the teenager's angry contortions. When he looked back at the bus, a glint of pink caught his eye: a shiny backpack, the likes of which he remembered well, on the back of a little girl with dark silky hair so familiar to him that he could feel the strands slipping like bird's feathers through his fingers. His throat constricted. He would never again experience that. This was how the ghosts of his lost grandchildren came to him — suddenly. An ambush, an attack, a weakening of his bladder. A gasp filled his chest. And then the life of his precious Anahita unfolded before him . . . the tiny baby who gripped his finger for however long he held her, the chubby toddler who crawled into his lap to feed him a rice cookie, the girl whose delicate feet walked on his back, whose dark eyes gleamed when he came home at the end of the day, the woman who never challenged him, always respected him, and who gave him those beautiful grandchildren.

The school bus extinguished its red light, and a plume of gray exhaust ballooned from its tailpipe. Yusef pulled the Jag onto the narrow shoulder. He didn't notice the triumphant fist of the tormented teenager thrust like a periscope above the car as it passed. His eyes were fixed on the back window of the school bus, looking for another glimpse of pink.

The spell began to pass in less than a minute, which was as long as it took him to dial his office. "Any messages?" he demanded when his secretary answered.

"Good morning, Mr. J."

He sighed. Vivian would not give him his messages until he returned her greeting. It was impertinent, but she'd been with him for thirty years; more important, she had the sharp mind and quick skills of a master bookkeeper but required only the salary of — what did they call it these days? — an administrative assistant.

"Good morning, Vivian," said Yusef. "Any messages?"

"No messages, Mr. J."

"Did you track down those punk paint-
ers?"

"No such address, Mr. J. The phone
number's wrong too. It's a pizza place in
the Bronx."

He slapped the steering wheel with his
palm. "I will be there in fifteen minutes."
He hung up, peered into the side mirror,
and peeled out, raising a cloud of gravel.
He was himself again.

As far back as anyone remembered, the Jahani patriarchs were landowners. Khans,
they were called, gentry. Even after the
Shah's White Revolution in the 1960s when
massive plots of private land were distributed
to the tenants of these khans, the Jahanis
continued to profit from land-related projects. And now, in America, it was the same,
though not as filthy lucrative as it had been
in Iran. Over the years, Yusef had slowly
bought up land with an intuition for how
the suburbs would grow and sprawl, and
with an imagination that saw housing tracts,
apartment buildings, and strip malls where
forests and dairy farms had once been.

Yusef pulled into his usual parking space
and hung his illegally procured handicapped
tag from the rearview mirror. The Jahani
family offices occupied the fourth and top

36

floor of a stucco building fashioned in a faux Mediterranean style — teal-colored trim, arched portico, and pathways of tessellated pavers. The building was flanked by two twenty-story 1960s brick apartment houses, their air-conditioning units sticking out like tongues dripping saliva. Yusef rather liked the apartment houses, had in fact considered purchasing them, evicting their fixed-income widows and bubblegum-chewing single mothers, and converting the units into condominiums. But Nezam, his sister-in-law's son, who now took care of the legal department, talked him out of it. "It's not worth the hassle with the city or the bad publicity," he'd said. "Besides, the buildings are ugly, Uncle." This new male generation, Yusef thought, with its power-bar lunches, vibrating pocket gadgets, and diaper-changing skills, had no sense of architectural aesthetics. Sourly, he recalled how he'd allowed Nezam and the others to persuade him on the Mediterranean design of this, his own building, when he'd wanted to erect an elegant glass rectangle evocative of the Hancock Building in Boston. It had been one of his weak moments.

The "others" were the twelve or fifteen (he could never remember exactly) boy children of his various half siblings and relatives who had fled the Islamic Revolution in 1979 with little more than the clothing in their Louis Vuitton luggage and the jewels hidden in the heels of their wives' shoes. Suddenly, the America he'd thought of as his alone, where he played gracious host to visiting kin, transformed into a melting pot for his extended family. Some of them, thank God, had moved to Los Angeles, where they marinated in a false revival of the bourgeois decades before the fall of the Shah. But the others had, to their credit, obsessed over the education of their children, sent them to Ivy League schools, and proffered them up to Yusef. He took them, of course. He'd shown his family the benevolence that their common patriarch had never shown him.

Pressing the elevator button, he chuckled slightly. Who would have imagined that he — son of a minor wife, orphan of a madwoman, ignored burden-child — would end up being the family patriarch? As the metal door slid open to admit him, Yusef smiled. Just for a moment.

As soon as Vivian heard the familiar click of Mr. J's heels in the hallway outside the elevator, she beelined it to the galley kitchen to pour his glass of tea. By the time he made it past the marble reception area, with its faux-painted wall of a Persian rose garden, and wove his way through the maze of office cubicles (acknowledging no one), she was stepping carefully, silver tray in hand, past the gargantuan blueprint copier, conference room, restrooms, and her own office, where she quickly grabbed her steno pad and skittered out to fall in behind her boss as he entered his corner office.

The immense space was suggestive of an outmoded hotel suite; lots of chrome and tweedy orange fabrics, a sitting area with a long velour sofa and wet bar, a glass desk as large as a twin-size mattress. His employees called it the Retro Room.

He placed his briefcase on the desk, clicked it open, removed a pile of papers, and turned to unlock one of the oak cabinets in a bank behind his black leather executive swivel chair. Vivian laid his tea to the left of the blotter and took a seat on the other side of the desk, her pen poised over the steno pad.

"Where is Nezam?" he asked, his back still to her.

"At the project upstate," she said. "Something about a failed electrical inspection in the kitchens."

"And Kareem?"

"In Westchester at the Tarrytown building."

"What is he doing there? Ali One and Ali Two are responsible for that."

"He didn't say, Mr. J."

"Did he leave me a copy of the punch list on the Bergen duplex?"

"Not that I'm aware of, but I can ask Jane."

He turned. "Jane? Who's Jane?"

She paused slightly. She'd introduced them several times, but he never remembered the flat-chested ones. "A new secretary."

He reached for the tray, popped a lump of sugar in his mouth, and slurped at his tea. Vivian could never get used to the sound; in her house, food noises were bad manners. Over the years, she'd learned to accept some of Mr. J's incongruities, his "immigrant ways" — an afternoon nap on his sofa, slimy discarded sunflower seed shells in his ashtray, the waft of enough cologne to hide the odor of a postgame football team, and the fact that he never used his wife's name. After all, no matter how long a person lived in the United States, there were bound to be certain things they were incapable of assimilating. Her Scottish mother had never been able to look at a banana as anything less than a prize. And her neighbor from Bombay, a computer engineer, had been blowing his snot into the flower beds for fifteen years. It took a generation for people to become true Americans. Mr. J's kids were a perfect example. Correction: Mr. J's kid. Vivian cringed as if she'd made the mistake aloud. Why couldn't she go through a day without thinking about Anahita? He never mentioned it, but she was sure he grieved. What parent wouldn't? Sheri in the billing department, who'd been with the company for ten years, thought Mr. J was made out of concrete. *Not one tear at the funeral,* she often reminded Vivian. *He even smiled and thanked the rich suits for coming.* Sheri could say what she wanted; Vivian understood stoicism. Besides, this was the man who had paid for her husband's kidney transplant.

Yusef topped off his tea and leaned back into the desk chair. "Get Kareem on the phone and tell him I want the punch list on my desk by this afternoon. Have Nezam report to me as soon as he gets in. Take a letter." Vivian flipped to a fresh page in her steno pad. "*Attention: Mr. Francis Fogarty, Fogarty Investments* — send it to his home address, Vivian." She nodded. "*Dear Frank,*

41

It was a pleasure to run into you and . . . uh — find out the wife's name — *last weekend at the country club,* period, new paragraph. *As per our conversation, I am very interested* — correction, I *am* extremely *interested in viewing your family property in Maryland,* period. *While the market in the area is very depressed, a rural property is something my wife and I are considering for our retirement,* comma, *a place for our family to gather,* period, new paragraph. *Please call me at your convenience so we may arrange a meeting* — period. *Looking forward,* et cetera. *Sincerely,* et cetera."

"Would you like this on your personal letterhead, Mr. J?"

"Yes, the Joseph Jahani one. And tell Pirooz to research the demographics of Cambridge, Maryland, with the idea of putting a golf resort on that property."

"Pirooz isn't in today, Mr. J. His wife had the baby last night."

"He's taking the whole day off?"

"I believe so."

Yusef shook his head disapprovingly. "What did they have, then?" he asked.

"A boy. Ali."

He sighed. "Jesus. Another Ali." He dis-

42

missed Vivian with two fingers and reached for the *Wall Street Journal.*

Vivian sighed and slipped her shoes off under her desk. Her boss was particularly antsy this morning, and she knew it was because Mitra had come to town. There was nothing more irritating to him than his eldest daughter. She propped her bunioned feet on the extra chair, the one her part-time clerk used, the one a teenaged Mitra had used twenty years ago when she worked at the office during the summers. She'd often sneaked away from the reception desk to peer over Vivian's shoulder at the ledgers and to complain about her father, imitating his accent and mannerisms so perfectly that Vivian dissolved into paroxysms of laughter. Once, she took Vivian's eyebrow pencil and drew herself a thin mustache so she could better act the role; stiffening her back, expanding her chest, pointing a finger in the air, she delivered a speech on the merits of stenography according to her father: *Eighty vords a meenute; a girl is vorth nossing widout dat. Vhat happens if your husband loses his job? Eighty vords a meenute and polite phone answering vill save you.*

That girl had no fear of the man; and the other one — Anahita — all she had was fear.

43

She'd worked at the office only one summer, answering phones in the sweetest way, tolerating every snobby secretary who called and every brash salesperson who walked through the main door, in a way that made her father proud. But being perfect took its toll, and Vivian had found Ana sniffling in the restroom several times. Mitra, on the other hand, had once told a flirtatious union official that if he didn't smell like a sewer in ninety-degree weather, she might consider thanking him for staring so blatantly at her breasts. Another time, Mitra told the mayor's secretary — a consistently rude person — to call after her PMS was over. She would beg anyone to take her place at the reception desk so she could prowl the firm's nooks and crannies; examining blueprints and schematics; shuffling through bidding contracts; memorizing the names of floor tile samples, concrete textures, and roofing material. On her lunch break, she often persuaded one of the general contractors to take her along to walk a project; she kept a yellow hard hat and work boots in the trunk of her Fiat Spider. Once in a while, she sidled her way into the conference room, sat in a corner to listen as her father and the subcontractors battled with the architects over how to bring their designs in line with the reality of costs. He allowed this only because he didn't want to risk her sassing him in front of the other men, but the rest of the time, he went out of his way to speak down to her, show her how inconsequential she was; he was determined to break her spirit, or at least to mold it into one of a conventional girl, a fifties throwback, like her mother. But she was unfazed. She kept coming back every summer, and sometimes after school if she wanted to learn the details of a new project. Mr. J wouldn't let himself see how involved she was, how she could have been his natural successor, far more capable than any of the boys who came later, some of whom were a drag on the business, but secure in their jobs because they were family and, of course, male.

Vivian poured a fresh cup of coffee from her thermos into her #1 Grandma mug. She'd grown old in this office, watching the Jahani soap opera, at first envious of their money and then buoyed about her own simple life as their tragedies piled up. The Revolution in Iran came first, the losses from it — notably the confiscation of the Italianate mansion whose enlarged framed photograph hung on the wall in the conference room; apparently, it had been turned into a sanitarium — and the dubious gains: men, women, and children without a country. She couldn't deny that Mr. J and his wife had risen to the occasion, helped find homes for the displaced, doctors for the traumatized. And when they came, those cousins and uncles and in-laws, it was hardest on Mitra, who was no longer the only eager disciple in the office and found her place as self-appointed apprentice to the contractors, the subs, and the architects quickly usurped by foreigners. But Vivian had to hand it to the girl; she'd found a solution, she was her father's daughter. First she went to his rival in Manhattan, Manny Hourian — "the Filthy Armenian," as Mr. J called him, though Vivian had heard only good things about the man, who wasn't an immigrant at all, and had been in the business since his grandfather started it a century before — and learned everything she could there. Then, halfway through her graduate studies in architecture, there had been a terrible fight between father and daughter, in his corner office no less, one day seventeen years ago when Vivian was out with the flu. No one heard what was said, but when the two emerged, the look of rage on his face and of determination on hers left little to the imagination: those two might never talk again. Which was exactly what had happened.

Over the years, Mitra had called Vivian once in a while from San Francisco or when she was in town visiting, and they'd chatted about this and that, mostly personal stuff like Tom and his kidney problems; in fact, it had been Mitra who urged Vivian to talk to Mr. J about helping pay for her husband's transplant. *There are some things he's soft on,* she'd said. *Sick people is one of them.* Vivian knew that Mitra had started her own design and construction business in California (forgoing graduate school), that she'd bought a little run-down house, renovated it, and sold it for a profit, only to do it again and again. She didn't know if Mitra was wealthy now — the girl wasn't the type to brag about that sort of thing — but she assumed she was doing all right.

The click of the intercom came through the phone speaker. Vivian picked up the receiver and pressed the blinking button. "Yes, Mr. J?"

"Call my wife, Vivian. Tell her I have an early-morning meeting in Manhattan and I'll be staying at the St. Regis tonight."

"Yes, Mr. J."

Vivian began dialing Mrs. J's number but decided to wait until afternoon when she

47

knew Mrs. J would be out with Mitra; then she could leave a message on the answering machine, avoid telling the lie in real time. Unaware that her lip was curling, she wondered if her boss had found a new girl or if he was still balling the blond word-processing temp from two months before.

CHAPTER 3

It was a rare morning when Shireen did not wake to the fresh memory of her daughter's death and the death of her two grandchildren, but today she'd woken in glorious anticipation of Mitra's arrival and had not shed the usual tears. Now she was crying because of Yusef's infuriating behavior. No amount of concealer could hide the raw redness of her nose, and she had redone her mascara twice. Mitra should not see her like this. Poor Mitti; she had called and her father had probably hung up on her. It was all Shireen's fault for suggesting that Yusef sleep late this morning. Even the small goodnesses she performed seemed to end up hurting people. Olga, dear Olga, used to praise Shireen for her guilelessness — *You are such a pure woman, Madame* — but Shireen knew what a fine line there was between pure and stupid.

After all these years, Shireen still hadn't

adjusted fully to Olga's absence. Just last week, she'd woken from her nap and nearly called for Olga to pour tea so they could have their usual afternoon chat. She thought about phoning her now and resisted; they'd already had their weekly conversation. Anyway, the telephone was never as intimate as a person's presence in the house. How odd she still found it that she'd become so reliant on a servant for companionship. Children were apt to do that with their wet nurses or their nannies, but it was unseemly in an adult, which was why Yusef had finally thrown her out and sent her back to Iran. No, she should never have been a housemaid at all, being literate and multilingual and modern thinking, but it had been the least complicated strategy for coming to America at the time.

Shireen gave up on her makeup and went into the bathroom to wash her face. Mitra would not arrive until noon to collect her for lunch; she had two hours to tame her tears and lift herself out of this ugly mood. She went into her closet, still redolent with Yusef's lime-scented shower gel, and pulled on her usual ensemble: black below-the-knee skirt, black blouse, black sweater, black-tinged pantyhose. The color of mourning, but Shireen had never worn bright colors. She slid into her leather slippers; she would come back for her pumps later. In the floor-length mirror, she inspected the lay of the fabric on her body, looked for wrinkles, snags, stains. She'd long ago stopped being critical of her figure; it was well-proportioned for her average height. Never a beauty, not willowy or voluptuous like her husband's mistresses, she was aware that having less prettiness to miss as it crumbled was a blessing. At family gatherings, she wanted to scream at her friends and relatives who talked endlessly about the maintenance of youth and beauty. It was a game that a woman ultimately lost badly. Best not to participate at all. As Olga used to say (and Olga had experienced more in the way of men and lust than anyone else Shireen knew): *In the end, a woman is better off being admired for her dignity than for her appeal to men or the appraisal of women.* That was a road taken by fools. And with a husband like Yusef, Shireen had had to grasp the straws of dignity early. It had taught her appreciation, she thought proudly. Appreciation for her home and her garden, for her children and grandchildren. Tears welled up again, and she turned her face from the mirror, rearranged several of Yusef's hanging suits so that the grays and blacks were together.

Back in the bathroom, Shireen unpinned her dark hair and ran a large-toothed comb through the wavy tresses that reached the middle of her back. She always pulled her hair into a bun, but when Anahita was a child — even when she was older, bless her heart — she would sit behind Shireen in the evenings and braid it while they watched TV. What joy and comfort that touch had brought her! Anahita had frizzy hair that she could not stand to grow out long enough to braid. All through adolescence, she kept it at chin-length and ironed it so that when Shireen kissed her cheek the odor of singed hair struck her. Mitra had inherited Shireen's hair, and she let it fly free, no buns for her, and certainly no sense of responsibility where lusty men were concerned. *That's their problem,* Mitra would retort. Shireen still wondered where her oldest daughter had learned to think like that. Anahita had innately understood that it was a traditional woman's responsibility to refract unwanted male attention, a concept Mitra once denounced as a direct offshoot of the idea of hejab, invented and perpetuated by men who didn't want to take responsibility for their own lust. Not that Mitra flaunted herself. She simply had no use for such values; she was too busy with what was going on in her mind. *They have opposite natures,* Olga used to say when Shireen would fret about her daughters. *Nothing you can do, Madame, but accept it.*

It was Anahita who had begged to hear the stories Shireen had heard in childhood from her own mother and grandmothers. *Tell me the* andaruni *stories,* Anahita had pleaded, and though Shireen would sigh with exasperation because she had no time to engage in such frivolities, she was secretly delighted to talk about the days before Reza Shah forced men to bring their women out into the open unveiled. Shireen's family had been large and traditional, an established clan of textile manufacturers whose forebears had traded along the Silk Road, and who, when Shireen was a child, lived together in a compound behind ten-foot walls in the center of Tehran. Of the several buildings in the compound, one housed the women's quarters — called the *andaruni,* or inner chambers — where many women spent their whole lives, cloistered from the outside world. Surrounding them was the *biruni* — the outer chambers — which was the domain of men, including those who were trustworthy enough to act as liaisons between the outside and the inside. Shireen barely remembered this bifurcated world; in fact, soon after she was born, the *andaruni* became part of the main house, and by the time Shireen was a young girl, it had disappeared altogether. Her younger sister, Golnaz, couldn't imagine it. All that remained were two distinct parlors for entertaining female and male guests separately on the infrequent occasions when the elderly and old-fashioned came to visit. Still, an Iranian home carried the suggestion of the *andaruni* — its communal warmth, its safety, its collective industry — and these were as alluring to Shireen as the Hollywood films she saw in Tehran's movie theaters. And later, Anahita's fascination with that bygone era gave Shireen a connection with Iran that helped to soften her homesickness and her sense of otherness in America. Oh, the *andaruni*! Its floor strewn with intricate Isfahani carpets, its purring samovar lit with a flickering flame visible through a cloudy little window next to the spout, its neat piles of rolled mattresses against the walls. The doughy arms and breasts of its mothers and aunties, their rosewater scent and sibilant murmurings. The tangy aroma of slivered orange peel awaiting transformation into marmalade, the *shoo-shoo* sound of uncooked rice against a metal tray. Winter days gathered around a quilt-covered brazier, toes brushing calves, napping and waking like the tides. Games never played alone, kisses and food shared like secrets, herbs and tinctures prescribed for every ill, prayers offered for good fortune. Advice never from just one. Such a safe life! A hidden life untouched by strangeness. A sheltered freedom.

Shireen reached into the wicker laundry bin and collected a small bundle of dirty clothes: two pairs of Yusef's briefs, plaid pajamas, a sleeveless undershirt, four gold-toe black socks, her own underwear. Certainly not enough for a load, yet she took the bundle down to the basement laundry room, her backless slippers slap-slapping against her heels in the quiet house, and arranged the smelly light-colored fabrics evenly in the machine. Her nose was still leaking, and she dabbed at it daintily with the corner of a napkin she'd already ironed, then dropped it into the machine as well.

For a moment, she stood staring at the wall, mentally going over the long list of necessary tasks for the One Year gathering on Friday. The final shopping for fruits and vegetables could not be done until Friday, but everything else food-wise had been prepared; her freezer and refrigerator were stocked neatly with Tupperware containers of eggplant *khoresh,* lima bean and lamb polo, saffron rice pudding, dolmeh, Russian potato salad, green stuffed peppers, and two cheese casseroles. She'd cooked all this last week. The walls had been washed, the bathrooms disinfected, new shell-shaped soaps and scented candles purchased, the grout between the foyer tiles bleached with a toothbrush, the carpets vacuumed and fringes tucked under. She couldn't think of a thing that hadn't been done or that could be done just yet. She looked at her watch: 10:25. Time slithered like a snail.

Upstairs in the kitchen, she poured herself another glass of tea, very light, the color of American honey, so as not to risk the jitters that would surely make it impossible to apply her eyeliner smoothly. She resisted a piece of fattening halva and gathered a handful of white raisins to sweeten the tea in her mouth. In the family room, she sat in the middle of the long sofa and turned on the television. She jumped at the sudden loudness; Yusef's hearing was definitely going. She donned her reading glasses so she could see the markings on the remote control, then lowered the volume and found her channel: HGTV, a bathroom remodel — such marble! Ana sometimes used to come over and they would watch together, Ana with her yellow writing pad making lists of decorating ideas for her house; then they would go buy fabrics or paints or hardware — and once some castoff outdoor chairs — to work on at Ana's house, transforming areas large and small into what they had seen on the television.

Yusef rarely allowed Shireen to make any adjustments to their house that didn't involve professionals. It had always been like that. Before they moved to New Jersey almost forty years ago, Yusef and Shireen lived in Manhattan in the East Sixties in a two-bedroom apartment Yusef had begun renting in 1953, before he married Shireen, who came over from Iran three years later. Just remembering that place made Shireen roll her eyes and slap her cheek. Terrible. All big brown furniture smelling of pipe smoke. It had taken her a whole week after her arrival to work up the nerve to ask Yusef if they could use some of her dowry money for drapes to "complement" the Venetian blinds, and perhaps an understated quilted bedspread and maybe a set of drinking glasses that were not tinted a masculine gray. She was eighteen. He was thirty. The second time she'd laid eyes on him was on their wedding day (the first was when he came *khastegari* with his two aunts and she'd served tea as was expected of her when a suitor visited). To her redecorating requests, all Yusef had to say was no in a mild voice and the matter was closed. Luckily, Shireen became pregnant quickly. Still, Yusef insisted that the crib and changing table match the dark wood and bulgy style of the guest room headboard and bureau; nothing Shireen purchased, including the baby's layette from Bloomingdale's, was left to Shireen alone. This was Yusef's way, and Shireen told herself that she was fortunate to have a husband who cared so deeply for his home. Marriage could be much worse.

Mitra had spent her first year in that apartment. Shireen often thought this was why her eldest daughter preferred to live in cities and was unperturbed — actually lulled, it seemed — by the background noises of traffic and sirens. But Mitra's arrival had cluttered the second bedroom, and it became ever more difficult to accommodate friends and family who visited from Iran. And there were many, some who stayed for weeks to sightsee or shop or install their children in boarding schools and colleges. Yusef, as gracious and effusive a host as he was an aloof and restrained husband, finally proclaimed to his young wife that it was time to build a house.

Shireen pressed the remote for the Food Network. Another pasta dish. She sat back and sighed. Her nose was finally dry and clear; she felt her eyelids with the tips of her fingers; still a bit swollen. But no more crying, she ordered herself. It was always an effort. If Olga were here, she would help, tell a joke from her repertoire — about the cuckolded Rashti husband, about the miserly Turk, about the lecherous Arab — or she would shower Shireen with compliments, sitting cross-legged as always on the floor with her back against the sofa (despite Olga's more modern upbringing, she liked the floor as much as any servant), and state a case for Shireen's measured goodness as a mother, a wife, a friend, an employer, as if she were a vizier defending the virtues of a slandered empress at court. Shireen had drunk Olga's praise and respect like a suckling infant, but of course the quench was never permanent. Like a barren woman — like Olga and poor Mitra — Shireen couldn't make her own milk.

Abruptly, she stood and walked toward the dining room. It was pointless to torment herself with such thoughts. She opened the bottom drawer of the mahogany credenza and removed a pile of tablecloths. Setting the pile on the table for twelve, she went back down to the laundry room and lugged the ironing board up to the family room, pulled it squeakily up to waist height, and went to retrieve the iron. Yes, the tablecloths had been ironed after the last washing — a year ago, the funeral — but the fold lines needed to be pressed out. How had she forgotten to place this important task on her list? But she knew how; Olga had always been in charge of the ironing. Shireen looked at her watch again, with clear intent now, determined that if she worked swiftly on the tablecloths, she would have time to do her toilette and finish dressing before Mitra arrived.

OLGA

In the time of our history when the Soviets retreated from an untamed Afghanistan and the terrorists in the news were Irish and Italian, there was an Unconventional Woman who returned unwillingly to the country of her birth. She settled in the capital and pined for her adopted family in America, praying for its patriarch's absolution that would take her back there, even to the monotonous suburbs she loathed. Soon, however, her watery eyes could not ignore the misery wrought by the dictator Ayatollah and the dictator Saddam during eight years of war. For the nation, nothing was gained and nothing lost — the borders remained intact. The cost, however, was borne by the wailing women robbed of their sons, husbands, fathers, brothers — hundreds of thousands returning, not in glory, but in burial shrouds. Those who survived trickled home, maimed, traumatized, wheezing from the gas.

The Unconventional Woman did what was in her nature. She cooked.

Aromas wafted from her apartment, flooding the hallways and elevators with the scent of basmati rice softening in boiling water and belching its floral scent, of saffron and dill, of mutton and mint. The neighbors were lured, and she welcomed them with piroshki and eggplant omelets and noodle soup; halva and chickpea cookies and saffron ice cream. Food was a balm, and to it she added her flair for telling stories from the old days when the people could dance in cabarets and buy Coca-Cola and watch a French film in a movie house. Stories also of America, of the children there she still pined and prayed for. There was hope, she told them; the war was over. She felt useful and appreciated.

But then the Summer turned Bloody. The dictator Ayatollah sent his guards to Purge the disloyal, the US Navy launched a Mistake missile that plunged three hundred innocents into the Gulf, and the militia marked and followed the artists and intellectuals. Now the scent of Suspicion took the place of everything else in the air. The Unconventional Woman wanted to fold inward, to surrender to old age and aloneness. But it was not to be. The chefs and the storytellers become known to the Underground through whispers. Writers, artists, filmmakers, journalists, teachers — their soft, desperate knocks came at her door. She fed them, and more.

CHAPTER 4

Mitra couldn't believe a hearse was tailgating her. In the cemetery. What's the hurry? At the crest of the hill, the lane plunged down, then climbed and flattened as if it might go on to the horizon; way in the distance, looking like Tonka toys, were two orange trucks spewing the sour-smelling smoke of hot tar, paving the way for death. A year ago, at the funeral, this lane had ended a few yards after the crest. There had been a silent bulldozer, its cab window splattered with dried mud, its serrated shovel propped in the air like a giraffe's neck.

Mitra pulled over and stopped. It took a pound of willpower not to flip off the hearse driver as he passed. In her sideview mirror, she saw a conga line of cars with their headlights on. She was glad for the excuse to linger in her seat for a while.

To her left, a mound of dirt for a new

grave rose above the tombstones. Mitra remembered the grit in her fist, the spatter of it hitting the caskets, the look of her palm cobwebbed with clinging soil, and the ugly job-finished gesture of rubbing her hands together.

She remembered the mullah her father hired to preside over the service. Shireen had insisted, pleading until Yusef agreed. He detested the clergy, called them parasites, but rather than listen to Shireen's keening, he procured the services of an Iraqi mullah from Washington, DC.

Mitra was sent to pick him up. She was grateful for the task, any task away from the houseful of mourners, away from her broken brother-in-law and her mother wrapped in black to her chin. The mullah stood by the baggage carousel wearing a white skullcap and a brown robe down to the laces on his Thom McAn's. It was a sight Mitra would never have seen growing up in the America of the sixties and seventies, and she had to remind herself that the costume was probably as easy for people to ignore as it had been for her to ignore nuns' habits and Hasidic garb. For her, the mullah was a representation of revolution and autocracy and loss. He bridled when she introduced herself, livid that a female had been sent to collect him.

She made him accompany her through the parking lot. It was drizzling, a mist that caused his skullcap to wrinkle and his beard to become a frizzy mess. The animal smell of wet wool billowed from his robes. They were a strange pair, she in her beige slicker and thick-soled rain boots, long hair flying, and he in his desert garb.

He asked Mitra one question in his thick-accented English: "Is it your sister who has passed away?" When she said yes, ignoring the burn behind her eyes, he bowed his head and said, "May peace be upon her." Mitra thanked him, and neither of them said another word until she dropped him off at his hotel in Fort Lee. Two hours in traffic. If Mitra ignored her peripheral vision, the only telltale sign that he was sitting beside her was the blinking red light on the dashboard indicating that his seat belt wasn't fastened, a fact that lent all kinds of vengeful images to Mitra's imagination.

The following day at the graveside, the mullah tipped back and forth on his heels, rolled his eyes heavenward, and chanted Qoranic suras in minor tones. The non-Moslem attendees put on forcibly interested expressions, as if watching a strange tribal ritual on the Serengeti. *How quaint!* they

66

must have been thinking. To Mitra, the mullah was as tedious as any minister or priest or rabbi, matching them dogma for dogma.

She checked her sideview mirror again. The funeral procession had passed and the lane behind her was empty. She got out of the car and picked her way across the tombstone-spotted area. She had no trouble finding the graves; Shireen had told her she'd planted a purple petunia border around the plot in June. Purple had been Anahita's favorite color. *Of course you wouldn't pick a primary color,* Mitra had said when Anahita announced this at age seven.

Mitra stood before the plot, eyes lowered. Slowly, she went down on her knees, on the sparse grass and dry dirt outside the petunia border. Clearly, her mother had been watering the plot, because the wide rectangle of grass was thick and green. She picked up a few twigs and leaves and tossed them aside without letting her eyes stray to the tombstones. She wondered how her mother could visit the cemetery four times a week. She felt like her chest was on fire. She ground her teeth and forced herself to look at the stones, at the simple monument to her younger sister — *stupid crybaby, ugly fatso, goody-two-shoes, Baba's little pet* — and at the two smaller stones flanking Anahita like seedlings. Nikku on her left, Nina on her right. It was the years, engraved in the stone forever, that got to her. *1960–1997, 1986–1997, 1989–1997.* People would count, on their fingers, in their heads, moving their lips — they would count and know how very young they all were.

She would not think of them dead. She would not think of the kids at all. For the millionth time, she remembered their last days together at the saltbox house they rented every Labor Day weekend near the shore out on Montauk. Ana, Bijan, the kids, Nezam and Libby and their twin boys — five days that always proved raucous, hectic, and to Mitra thoroughly enjoyable. *That's because you get to go back to your quiet single life,* Libby would say. Perhaps she was right. But during that last trip, Mitra's mind had been fraught with suspicion and frustration.

As usual, she'd flown in the night before and stayed at Ana and Bijan's house in Devon because she got a kick out of all of them piling into the car the next day for the long drive. Despite her jet lag, she'd woken earlier than usual the next morning. Padding down to the kitchen from her bedroom in the converted attic, she poured a cup of coffee and peered into the backyard to see

Nikku and Nina blowing up beach balls, checking for leaks, and Bijan attaching the bike rack to the top of the car. Ana, she knew, would be in the master bedroom fretting over how to fit all their stuff into one suitcase.

Maybe if Mitra had been wearing her slippers, Ana would have heard her shuffling down the hallway. Maybe if Mitra had knocked on the half-closed bedroom door, if she'd announced herself, if she hadn't heard Ana, hidden in the walk-in closet, say four words: *"I love you too."* Common words for Ana, uttered easily to her family. Mitra used such endearments sparingly, as if they would mold or rust in the open air. Still, Mitra knew her younger sister's every inflection. Even now, the echo of those words — the unmistakable lilt of romantic passion — twisted her intestines.

The closet door had swung open and Ana collided with Mitra, bounced back, and dropped the cordless phone and an armful of tank tops. "Mitra! Jeez, you scared the shit —"

The horror on Mitra's face scorched Ana's smile away. Neither moved. Ana was wearing her high-heeled mules, so the two of them were nearly the same height. Her caramel-colored skin, naturally a shade lighter than Mitra's, had taken on a sickly olive cast that reminded Mitra of a time they'd donated blood and Ana grew faint and weak.

Mitra took a breath, but before she could speak, Bijan appeared noisily in the bedroom. "Ready to get on the road?" he said. "Car's packed up."

She and Ana separated and the tension vanished. They'd long ago learned the skill of dissimulation.

Throughout the long weekend, Ana avoided being alone with Mitra, and Mitra tried to indulge as she usually did in the nonstop craziness of preparing ten peanut butter and jelly sandwiches at once, putting on and taking off little bathing suits whose crotches were weighed down with sand, tugging boogie boards through the rough Atlantic waves, building sand castles that looked more like warehouses, refereeing Candyland and Monopoly games, straining her eyes on jigsaw puzzles and bedtime books. Nikku, then eleven, had wanted to talk about the sex act (he was too shy to ask his parents): *Is it something that people do even when they don't want to have a baby, and if yes, ick, why?* Nina was unhealthily attached to her Glamour Barbie, asked Mitra whether she thought God would make

70

her hair blond if she prayed hard enough. The twins, well, they'd just turned four, and were mostly intent on clasping a Matchbox car in each hand, even while they slept.

Mitra did everything with one eye on her sister and a lump in her throat. Not once did Ana seem at all distant or different with Bijan; she was as loving as always. They'd been married for sixteen years. Madly in love from the start. Mitra began to doubt what she'd heard in Ana's voice in the closet, but then she recalled the words and the sound of her voice, and the doubt evaporated. Over and over, she asked herself the same question: If someone — a god or a blue genie or Buddha himself — offered to erase what she'd accidentally learned about her sister, would she say yes or no? Yes, yes, yes. And no. Now that she knew about it, she had to fix it. It was what she did.

In the evenings after the kids were asleep, bottles of wine were uncorked; Libby and Ana attempted handstands and giggled through Downward-Facing Dog, gossiped and reminisced about people Mitra had forgotten or never known, debated the nuances of creating Persian dinners, and complained about their husbands' long work hours. Mitra joined Nezam, Bijan, and their fat cigars out on the deck to babble about the collapse of the ruble, the Y2K scare, and Al Gore's claim on the Information Superhighway. Later she lay in her bed, staring at the ceiling, her imagination spewing out heart-wrenching scenarios that included an emotionally crushed Bijan — devoted to Ana since their teens — face in his hands at the kitchen table in shock and grief, while Nikku and Nina sobbed as their mother left in a cheap sports car driven by a tanned tennis pro.

When finally, on their last evening at sunset, Mitra contrived a sisterly walk on the beach while Libby was in the shower, there wasn't an iota of equanimity left in her; she was in full-tilt bully mode.

"Talk, Anahita. Now."

"There's nothing to talk about."

"Who is this guy that you would risk *everything*?"

"Look, Mitti, I'm sorry you overheard what you did. It puts you in a bad position. I know you love Bijan; I love him too."

"Then why are you cheating on him?"

"Please don't say those words, Mitti. I don't see it that way. I wish you would just forget about it."

Mitra grabbed Ana's arm and turned her so they faced each other in the sand. "Forget? You're kidding me, right?" The ocean breeze whipped her hair across her face. "After everything we went through so that you and Bijan could be together? I'll forget, Ana, when you end it."

Ana didn't pale as Mitra expected, nor did she look down in contrition. In fact, she held Mitra's gaze, tilted her head slightly, and frowned. "I'm sorry, Mitra. I can't do that."

"Excuse me?" Mitra swept the hair off her face and held it back behind her ear. She felt like she was talking to a stranger, and she tightened her grip on Ana's arm. "Don't be stupid," she said. "Don't jeopardize your family for an infatuation that'll fizzle out in a few weeks!"

"It's not like that. It's already been a long time." Ana wrenched her arm free and lifted her chin. "And don't yell at me, Mitra."

They stood seething for a long moment, a stare down accompanied by the raucous calls of seagulls. Ana's face flushed with defiance and she spoke first. "I'm surprised at your outrage, Mitra. You're the one who's so liberal and liberated. When it comes to me, though, you have a double standard."

Mitra cringed now as she remembered her response. "Because you're different from me!" she'd said, like an impetuous child stomping her foot.

Ana's expression turned derisive, another first. "Maybe not," she said, veering toward Nina as the child ran toward them in meltdown mode about the twins using her new Barbie sleeping bag as a dwelling for the crabs they'd collected. Pulling on Ana's arm, they began to walk away.

The wash from a large wave rushed over Mitra's feet, and she caught her breath. "Ana!" she yelled. "Ana!" But for the first time in their lives, Anahita hadn't turned around at her sister's call.

Back in the house, amidst half-packed suitcases of soiled clothing and the screeches of overtired children whose summer vacation had come to an end, Mitra simmered with frustration, watched her sister behave as if nothing was amiss, and realized she would have to wait until they could speak by phone after she returned to San Francisco.

Now, she touched Ana's headstone. She didn't like thinking about those calls.

Two sparrows alighted on the graves and poked about for seeds and worms. Mitra would always remember the yawning pit, so deep it seemed like a punishment.

This was grief: sudden and unbidden thoughts — minutiae, really — and unexplainable emotions.

She'd been furious at the dough-faced undertaker with his motorized coffin-lowering device and at the gravediggers she was sure were waiting with their shovels behind a mausoleum nearby. Furious at the expensive caskets in which her sister and the children were buried — the ultimate constriction, the opposite of deliverance — but Shireen had refused to consider cremation, gasping at Mitra as if she'd grown horns. Yes, she'd been furious at herself most of all.

She stretched her arm out and rested her palm on the warm grass. The sparrows fluttered away. She wondered, as she had at the service, whether the undertaker had wrapped the bodies in the white shrouds her parents had given him, or whether he'd said fuck it and simply stuffed the mutilated bodies into the shiny boxes.

She squeezed her eyes shut and willed herself to remember the last moment she'd seen her sister alive — when they dropped her off at the airport on their way home to New Jersey. What had Ana been wearing? Her red sweater? The ruby earrings Bijan gave her for their tenth anniversary? Had she and Mitra embraced? They must have; they always did, no matter if Mitra was angry. But she couldn't remember. Their walk on the beach overrode all her other memories of that trip. Or was she just trying too hard to recall the details — Ana's perfumed neck, the tickle of her wiry hair against Mitra's cheek, the pillowy compression of their breasts meeting, the light warmth of Anahita's small hand on her back?

What Mitra did remember, too clearly, was the last of several tense phone conversations they'd had the following week when Ana was driving the kids home from a piano lesson. She was trying to keep her voice down; Mitra could hear the kids quarreling in the back seat — Nikku's irritable tone, Nina's defensive high pitch. It was raining hard, and Ana had suggested they talk later, but Mitra refused to let her off so easily. Oh, Mitra knew how to badger her baby sister, how to persist with a singular goal until Ana could be persuaded to do what Mitra thought best. Mitra had no patience when it came to Anahita; even after her childhood contempt had evaporated and been replaced by an equally intense desire to protect her sister, she'd bullied her.

She slumped at the foot of the graves, her upper body curled like a comma, her legs tingling beneath her. She would remember now, an unbidden memory that ended with the crunch of metal, the deafening smash of breaking glass, the vertiginous roll of the car.

Mitti, please. Let's not talk about this anymore. I'm sorry you found out.

Sorry I found out, but not sorry you're cheating on Bijan. And the kids, Ana. You're betraying them too.

That's not true. They have nothing to do with this, and —

All because of a foolish infatuation. Believe me, Ana, once you end it, the lust will evaporate.

No, I told you, Mitti. It's already been a long time. Please, can't you just forget?

You end it and I'll forget.

No. I can't. I . . . I won't.

Ana! Don't be stupid.

Please, Mitti, don't yell at me.

Don't start crying now. We have to talk about this.

I'm sorry. I never wanted to disappoint you, Mitti. I'm —

And the connection was lost.

Mitra dropped her face into her hands. "Oh, Ana," she whispered. "What did I do?"

Back in the car, Mitra pulled the phone card out of her wallet and dialed — an 800 access number, a ridiculously long pin code, then thirteen numbers — and here was the solid tone of Olga's ring, then her low, raspy voice.

" 'Allo?"

And Mitra let loose: "I told you coming to New Jersey was a bad idea."

"Mitra-joon?" Olga asked, clearing her throat.

"No," Mitra growled, "the boogeyman." So annoying how Olga often seemed to be checking whether it was really Mitra calling. Or if Olga phoned, how she announced herself in the Farsi way — "I am Olga" — as if Mitra wouldn't know her voice. It was a mark of the older generation, some sort of ingrained Iranian etiquette, and Mitra teased her for it.

"Hah," Olga chuckled. "What is wrong, Mitra-joon?" Olga insisted on speaking English on the phone, as if this could impede the Islamic government wiretappers in their mission to detect dissenters and blasphemers. Mitra thought this was ridiculous — they never spoke of anything incriminating — but she secretly enjoyed it after years of Olga's Farsi-only rule. Now it was Mitra who had the advantage.

"Where you are?" Olga asked.

"The cemetery."

78

"Ach. This very hard, I know." She sniffed. "I wish I be there with you."

"For what? To cry over a square of dirt and stones? It's sick. And another thing: I called the house and Baba hung up on me."

"I sorry. I sorry, but why you yell at me? You mad at him. This not nice. You always doing this."

"Fuck," said Mitra. "Now he thinks I'm trying to make up with him. He's such an asshole. Stop laughing."

"I sorry. You know American cursing make me laugh. I sorry."

"Stop apologizing," Mitra snapped, gritting her teeth.

"Okay," Olga said. "What I can do, Mitra-joon?"

"Nothing! Just stop apologizing."

"Okay. I be quiet."

"I can't believe this. I hate him. I'd gotten to the point where I just felt indifferent toward him."

"What?"

"Indifferent . . . like a feeling in between hate and love, like a nothing feeling."

"Uh-huh."

"I hate hating him."

"She your father."

"He," Mitra corrected. He, she — in

79

Farsi, there were no gender-specific pronouns.

"Sorry. He your father," Olga said. "Natural to have feelings."

"He never misses a chance to humiliate me."

"Maybe he just not know what to say."

"Come on, Olga! You're defending him?"

"No, not defending. Trying to make you feel better."

"Well, you're not."

"Okay. He is bad father, I know. But you still do right thing, going there for One Year, right thing for your mother, for yourself."

"Why? All that crying and wailing. People coming to pity us and gossip about us. Having to deal with Baba. It doesn't do anybody any good."

"Don't think about him; then he control you. Think about Ana-joon; he always control her. Forget about your father. You and your mother will comfort each other. This is reason for One Year. Why you crying?"

"How do you know I'm crying?"

"You silent, let me talk. Not usual when you are angry. So you must be crying."

"Right. Well, there's nothing comforting about this One Year ritual."

"Don't be like American girl, trying to

forget death, forget pain. Feel pain and get comfort. Honor your sister. You will feel better."

"No, I won't. I don't."

"Ach, Mitra. You stubborn as donkey. Go have Dairy Queen ice cream. You feel better."

"The Dairy Queen is gone. Anyway, it's eleven in the morning, Olga."

"Sorry. Is time for dinner here, and I missing Dairy Queen soft ice cream with chocolate dipping sauce. Ach, I die for that."

A bubble of laughter escaped through Mitra's tears.

"See?" Olga said. "Now you laughing."

"Okay, okay. I just needed to get mad."

"I know, azizam. I wish I being there so you can maybe hit me or kick me if you want to."

Mitra snorted. "Yeah, that would be fun."

"Bad girl. So disrepting."

"What?"

"Sorry. Disreptful."

"What?"

"Ach! *Porroo,*" Olga said, finally using the Farsi word.

"Disrespectful," Mitra enunciated.

"Yes, that is word."

Mitra sniffed. "I wish I could hug you. I wish you were here."

81

"Don't say it, azizam." Olga's voice trembled on the endearment. "Go now. See your maman. Give her big kiss from me."

"It's still too early to go there. Let's talk more. I don't want to hang up."

It exasperated Mitra that Olga couldn't get used to the fact that phone calls across the world weren't so expensive anymore; all their conversations were rushed, clipped; it was like speed dating — the intimacy left for later, in a quiet place, face-to-face, as if such a future were possible. Olga could never return to the United States. Letters were impossible; neither were literate enough in the other's primary language, and anyway, Olga said the post office was filled with government spies who read everything.

"What's the weather like over there?" Mitra asked in Farsi, waving an errant mosquito away from her face.

It took Olga a few seconds to switch gears, to swallow, Mitra knew, a flood of tears she'd been expecting to let loose in the aftermath of their conversation. "Weather?" she echoed, unmindful that the language shift had rocketed them into a sentimental past. "Sun. Warm. But the nights are growing colder."

"We liked that, when the nights were cold in New Jersey," Mitra said.

"Yes, we always open window, even during snow."

"Especially when it snowed. Baba used to get so mad. *You're wasting electricity!* Remember?"

"He was angry for more than that, azizam."

This was true. Mitra had often gone in the night to Olga's small basement room, dragging her duvet and pillow to nestle into the corner on the floor. Olga didn't sleep more than two hours at a time; the light was always on, the window cracked, a half-finished crossword puzzle from an Iranian women's magazine at the ready. There was no need to talk. Mitra slept best when Olga was awake, as if her primal self needed to know that someone was standing watch. That Mitra seemed to feel such security in a servant's room rather than her own infuriated her father. This, despite the truth that he himself, as a child in Iran, had surreptitiously crawled onto his auntie's pallet for years after his mother died, and was able to quit the habit only when his half brothers discovered it and taunted him. Maybe for that reason he hated it even more to find Mitra with Olga, the room a fresh, cool island away from the luxe, secure, centrally heated home he provided.

"So how is your lover?" Olga asked in English.

"I'm waiting for him to make me angry so I can kick him out."

Olga laughed. "Crazy girl."

"He's not that important. It'll be over soon."

"You are lying. You are saying this for almost a year."

"Not that long."

"Almost. He is a British boy, no?"

"Yes, a British boy. A boy for sure."

"The British are not good in sex; they have dry tongues." Olga choked on her laughter, coughed, sighed.

"Half British," said Mitra before she could catch herself, and continued quickly in order to avoid the question about the other half, which she had no intention of revealing to Olga. "Anyway, he's young, which makes up for other things."

"Oh ho! Young is very good, Mitti. Is the right balance — older woman, younger man. The energies are equal. And he wants to please you; you can tell him what you want." In Farsi, she asked, "Is he in love with you?"

"I hope not." Mitra's back itched from the car seat's rough fabric. "It would be a mistake." She reached around to scratch between her shoulder blades.

"Because he is younger?"

"Partly."

"But of course he loves you. He would not stay so long if he did not."

"I don't want him to love me. It's not fair."

"Why not fair? Is his decision."

Mitra paused. "He doesn't know everything."

"I see. Then you must tell him."

"Yes. I know, Olga. I know."

CHAPTER 5

Mitra drove slowly along Maple Street toward her childhood home. More than half of the Jahanis' neighbors had been Jewish, so at Christmastime there were displays of menorahs and blue lights. But now there were more Asians and Indians, which irked her father because he considered them ugly, passive, and smelly; he had no idea that he fit better in this neighborhood than he ever had in the past.

Here was Barbara Ferber's house, which had once sported a brick façade on the lower level and was now painted all white with a red door. Barbara was a year younger than Mitra, and they played regularly until Mitra snipped at her long braids with a safety scissor and the hair fell out in her mother's hands later that night when she went to brush it. Across the street lived Eddie Shapiro, the token neighborhood slob, whose family owned a Saint Bernard unimaginatively called Bernie, always with a slimy rope of drool hanging from his chops. The pink house had belonged to Rick Jones, who one day, together with Eddie, mixed up a Flintstones glass of water and dirt, put a spoon and straw in it, and told Mitra it was chocolate milk. It wasn't for nothing that she'd learned, from all the time spent watching her father deal with construction workers, that when boys were extra nice to you, something was probably amiss, and after smelling the liquid, she slugged Eddie so hard his nose bled. Next door, the Helmans had a pool, but the Jahanis were never invited to swim in it, not even in the hottest weather; Ana and Mitra would peek through the slats in the wooden fence and watch them swim, eager as starving children not invited to the barbecue.

Hideous, Mitra thought as she pressed on the gas to make it up her parents' steep driveway to the double front door. She hated this house. A "contemporary," it was called: gray-stained wood, narrow windows, sharply angled roofs. A 1960s experiment in right angles. A Frank Lloyd Wrong. She yanked up the parking brake and waved at her mother, who stood in the middle of what Mitra called the not-garden, a series of terraces paved in geometric patterns of stones and pebbles that covered the whole front yard. This so-called rock garden, spotted with a smattering of sorry-looking plants and struggling ground cover, would have been a perfect slope for sledding, and therefore it was one of Mitra's most profound childhood frustrations. Every other house up and down their street had a lawn where kids rolled and played catch and romped with their dogs, where daddies raked leaves, set the sprinkler up in summer, and hired teenagers to mow. Not the Jahani family. Iranians didn't live their lives for outsiders to see; if there couldn't be a ten-foot wall around the property, a rock garden would do. Passersby could tell they were aliens right from the edge of the driveway.

Shireen waved exuberantly and quickly poured what remained in a plastic watering can onto a sickly jasmine vine that Mitra had purchased for her two years before. Jasmine grew beautifully in San Francisco and in Esfahan, where her mother had spent her childhood vacations, but certainly not in New Jersey, and Mitra, on one of her devilish whims, imagined using the flowering plant — or its lack of flowering — to tempt her mother to come to California for a visit, at least once.

Before Mitra could emerge fully from the car, Shireen was reaching for her. Mitra stooped to rest her chin on her mother's shoulder, taking in her Estée Lauder scent, dabbed on her pulse points even before she had her tea in the morning. "My daughter, my daughter," Shireen whispered in Farsi. She pulled back, cupped Mitra's face in her palms, and kissed her cheeks lingeringly. "You have become too skinny," she said.

"I'm the same as the last time you saw me," Mitra replied in English. That was how they often spoke: Shireen in Farsi and Mitra in English, though each peppered her sentences with words and phrases from the language of the other.

"You do not eat well, I know," said Shireen. "Come. Come inside for some halva."

Mitra made a point of looking at her watch. "What about lunch? I made a reservation at the Pilgrim Inn."

"Oh!" Shireen said with a little jump. "Yes, of course. I just change my shoes." She turned to walk back toward the door, and Mitra stifled a snort at her red plastic gardening shoes. Ana had called them Mom's Ruby Slippers.

The Pilgrim Inn Restaurant irritated Mitra:

Sunday nights at The Pilgrim, as if the Jahanis had been a normal American family after a day of church and football. They had a standing six o'clock reservation, despite the fact that they never ate before eight every other night of the week. The men in their navy-blue jackets with gold buttons, the women in white blouses and pearls, the kids with slicked-down hair and patent-leather Mary Janes. And then the Jahanis, their caramel skin and inky hair setting them apart like cacti in a lily pond. Her mother greeting people with a hand over her heart, bowing slightly. Her father strutting ahead, his pipe resting like a cocktail in his hand, responding only if someone greeted him first, and never if anyone called him Joe instead of Joseph: *Nice to see you, Ted. Nice to see you, Bob. Nice to see you, Ed.* At the table, Shireen picking imaginary lint off the tablecloth, tearing bread into bite-size pieces, cutting Anahita's steak. *The Woodards brought their new baby. She's very cute.* Yusef grunting, mumbling: *Vice-President, Chase Manhattan.* And then to Mitra and Anahita: *Chew with your mouth closed. Use your napkin. Sit straight.*

An elderly hostess led Shireen and Mitra to a table next to a maroon-draped window.

90

Mitra peered at the faded ink on her menu. A waitress in a colonial-style barmaid's uniform — square neck and ruffled apron — brought them water. Mitra glanced at a bow-tied gentleman who was wrestling with a wedge of iceberg lettuce smothered in Russian dressing. If Anahita were still alive, the three of them might have ventured to an Italian bistro in Tenafly or a fish place on 9W. But there seemed no point in that now.

The waitress was having trouble taking Shireen's order. She wanted oil and vinegar with her salad — *weenager* — so Mitra interrupted and enunciated the word, trying not to show irritation, either at her mother or at the waitress. When Shireen emigrated to the States in 1956, Yusef hired a private English language tutor to come to the apartment three times a week, a ponytailed blonde from Ohio who worked as a secretary at the UN. Shireen didn't know how Yusef had made her acquaintance, but when it became obvious that he was coming home from the office earlier on tutoring days, she told him she had learned enough English to get by and why waste money when she could learn the rest from her soap operas. She figured this would appeal to his stinginess, but when Yusef didn't agree and one evening offered to drive the young woman home to Manhattan, Shireen fired the woman herself, telling Yusef she had quit to elope with her Italian boyfriend.

Mitra once asked Shireen why she hadn't taken an ESL class at Hunter or Berlitz. She laughed and shook her head. "You know your father. He wanted me home." Mitra knew, but she asked questions like this because she hoped they might inspire Shireen to defy Yusef.

Shireen sipped her water and blotted her mouth with a yellowing napkin, leaving a maroon lipstick mark. "I am sorry about the telephone call with your father this morning. It was my fault; I persuaded him to go later to the office today."

Mitra shook her head. "Why do you do that, Mom? Take responsibility for his bad behavior?"

Shireen looked away and patted at her bun; this was an old discussion she wouldn't have. "So," she said. "You still like California." It was not posed as a question, but with resignation, to let Mitra know that while Shireen hoped her daughter might one day say she'd grown to hate San Francisco and would be moving back east, she was not counting on it after all these years.

"Yes," Mitra said. "You should visit me. You'd like it there too."

"I can't leave your father."

"Just for a week or so."

"I can't leave your father."

Mitra looked straight at her now. "You can't or he won't let you?"

"He needs me."

"You need some time off, Mom. All servants get time off." The sentence was out of her mouth before she could swallow it. Wasn't she too old to make sarcastic remarks to her mother? Shireen's eyes filled with tears. They were real, Mitra knew, but also a manipulation. "I'm sorry, Mom. Forget I said that."

Shireen blinked and dabbed her eyes with a corner of the napkin. She looked sallow, age-spotted, older than her sixty years, like she was trying to keep pace with her seventy-two-year-old husband. "I know you are angry with him, Mitra-joon, but it is not fair to turn your anger on me."

"You're right," Mitra said, now just wanting the subject to change.

"I wish, Mitra-joon, that you would make up with him. He is an old man now. He is your father who loves you. Make up with him. Do it for me, my daughter."

Mitra avoided her mother's pleading eyes and dug her nails into her palms. More manipulation. Why did she always forget how crafty Shireen was? She remembered only her mother's meekness, her softness. "Let's not talk about this, Mom." She reached across the table and covered her mother's hand with her own.

Shireen swallowed and forced a smile, lifted up her thumb and wrapped it around Mitra's, squeezing. They parted as the waitress delivered their lunches. Mitra stared at her club sandwich and remembered that The Pilgrim Inn's turkey was usually so dry and the lettuce so limp that she was going to eat only the fries, which were crispy and shiny with oil. Shireen drizzled more oil than vinegar onto her salad, a wilted mound of spinach sprinkled with bacon bits and sliced egg.

Mitra picked up a fry. "I spoke to Olga this morning. She sends you her love."

Shireen chewed and swallowed what was in her mouth — Mitra had never seen an errant fleck of food on her mother's lips or teeth — and finally, she said, "How is she? I do miss her."

Mitra shrugged. "She's lonely. I wish I could visit her."

Shireen jerked her upper body toward Mitra, her face suddenly pale. "Never do that. I have told you this; Olga has told you. It is not a place for a girl like you, unable to hold your tongue. Even under the Shah, that summer we sent you, all your criticisms of the poverty and the SAVAK police. Imagine now! You would not even be able to stand the wearing of the hejab. I know my own reckless daughter; you will want your wine and be jailed in no time." Pink blotches had appeared on her cheeks.

"Okay, okay!" Mitra said. "I didn't say I was going, just that I wished I could visit her. Calm down, Mom."

Shireen took several sips of water and patted her bun again. Finally, she said, "So, is Olga well? Last time we spoke, she complained of a tremor in her arm."

Waving her fork, Mitra said, "That's gone. She thought it was Parkinson's. One of her neighbors has it."

"You know how she exaggerates." Shireen smiled and shook her head. "Whenever I took her to the doctors, they said she would live a long time." In English, she added, "She is healthier than a mule."

"Horse," Mitra corrected.

"Yes, right." Shireen expertly folded several large spinach leaves onto the back of her fork and directed them carefully into her mouth. Mitra decorated her fries with more ketchup.

"Olga was difficult to manage when she

was sick and complaining," Shireen continued. "Perhaps it was best that she returned to Iran. I'm afraid she might have become a burden."

Mitra bit back a retort, as if Anahita were throwing her a pleading look. This was Shireen assuaging her guilt and salvaging her dignity. Any "burden" Olga might have brought to Shireen's life in old age would have been eclipsed by devotion. Olga had been Shireen's champion, standing up for her honor as no one ever had. Yusef called it meddling, and it finally became too much for him. Mitra didn't know the details of the last brouhaha ten years ago that had compelled her father to put Olga out of the house with a one-way ticket to Tehran. She knew it had to do with one of her father's infidelities, a subject she had always, very methodically, refused to think about. Unlike Anahita, she could do that. Compartmentalize. Anyway, Mitra hadn't found out Olga was gone until after she was gone. And while Mitra was upset and angry about it, her emotions were blunted by the twenty-five hundred miles she'd put between herself and the family. Did she blame Shireen for Olga's banishment? A little. She blamed her for deferring to her husband so completely, but she'd watched her mother do this all of her life. She couldn't imagine Shireen being any different.

"Anyway, Mom, I've managed to bring a little bit of Iran into my house in California."

"What are you talking about?"

"I've got these two women — a mother and a daughter — staying in the apartment downstairs."

"Iranian? Which family?"

Mitra shook her head and picked at the turkey meat along the rim of her sandwich. "You wouldn't know the family; they're village people from Gilan Province."

Shireen bridled. "Village people? Goat herders?"

"They're sort of like refugees. The mother's even illiterate, and she wears a chador. The daughter is a teenager."

Shireen was silent, struck dumb. Finally, she asked, "How did they get here? Where did you find them?"

"A relative of theirs is a doctor, and he sponsored them. The woman is a widow."

It had been Julian who'd taken Mitra to the bungalow in Fremont, a city across the Bay that had become, through the infinite global family network, an island for Near Asian immigrants. The sponsor, whom Julian knew from the hospital, begged him to

97

find another place for the two women; he'd gotten in over his head with refugee family members. To Mitra, it had seemed like the morally right thing to do at the time. Maybe she'd thought it would lift her spirits after Anahita's death, though now she couldn't imagine how she'd been so naïve as to think that. It was Julian's way of thinking. It didn't hurt that her tenant — a computer geek with five cats whose dot-com company had been bought by Microsoft for an obscene amount — had just moved out.

"Amazing," Shireen said.

"No, really, Mom. Things have changed a lot since you and Baba were bringing maids over from Iran."

"These women?" Shireen asked. "They are working for you?"

"No. I don't think either of them would have much to contribute at a construction site. Besides, I don't have any active projects going right now."

"I mean, they work in your house?"

"As maids, no. I don't need them. Carmen, my manager's wife, comes once a week to clean."

"The widow surely knows how to cook."

"I'm sure she does, but I don't want her messing up my kitchen. She's not exactly the cleanest, and I'm not sure she'd know how to use my appliances."

"You must teach her. They must all be taught when they first come over."

"Mom, I didn't take them in to be my servants. They need a place to live for a while."

Shireen's eyes were wide, pupils like pencil points. "You are making a big mistake, my daughter."

"Don't worry, Mom. I told you, it's just for a little while. Just until her sponsor finds a rental near him." Mitra pushed her plate away. "So," she smiled. "Dessert?"

"Dessert at home," Shireen said.

Her father's cologne — Paco Rabanne — assaulted Mitra the moment she stepped over the threshold into her parents' house. He didn't have to be home for it to permeate the air like horse dung in a stable.

Mitra followed Shireen through the dining room toward the kitchen. She was glad to ignore the biliously decorated living room with its brass tabletops carved with lions, its overstuffed sofas, divans, kilim pillows, and iron filigree lampshades that cast prisms of light onto the ceilings, its walls covered with framed carpets and paintings of women in balloon trousers, chiffon veils, and sable unibrows holding trays of tea for men with pointy gold shoes to match their pointy, long beards.

At the kitchen threshold, Mitra halted, speechless. Gone were the pistachio-green appliances, speckled linoleum flooring, and knotty pine cabinets with wrought-iron handles. Where there had been a solid wall adorned with Persian brass trays, a bay window looked out onto the backyard.

Shireen twirled to face Mitra. "You like it?" she almost squeaked, smiling ear to ear. She stood next to a granite island where an oak table and chairs used to sit. The cabinets were lacquered white and topped by a heavy cavetto-style crown molding; several had glass panels behind which Shireen had displayed her Waterford crystal. The floor was Denizli ivory travertine, one of Mitra's favorites: Turkish, expensive, and elegant. The appliances, alas, were General Electric, but her father always skimped (and bought American) on those.

"Wow," Mitra said. "It's beautiful, Mom. I feel like I'm in a different house."

"Your father finally let me do it, after all these years."

"How in God's name did you convince him?"

Yusef's answer to any remodeling suggestion had always been to scold Shireen for

100

being ungrateful and remind her that superior architecture and construction never went out of fashion.

"Remember that Mr. Kasagian who was the architect for this house?" Shireen said. "He lives in Tehran now and he came to visit last year. He was astonished to see his old work, and he began laughing at it, especially the kitchen, in the way that a person makes fun of what he once foolishly considered fashionable. Then he began bragging about how his designs in Tehran contain precious stone and marble with Italian tile backsplashes, and the most modern German appliances. You know, Mitra, the same I have been telling your father about for years now."

"So Baba was embarrassed."

"Of course. It is necessary for him to hear it from someone he respects."

"And that's certainly not you."

"That is not what I meant, Mitra. Mr. Kasagian is an architect."

"Okay. Well, it's beautiful. Congratulations."

Shireen twirled again and walked over to the stove to pour tea. "Look," she said in English. "Six-burner gas. Oven big enough for two rice pots." She handed Mitra a glass of tea and a small plate of two diamond-

101

shaped cumin-spiced halva pieces dusted with confectioner's sugar. "Come," she said, lightly pressing her hand into Mitra's back. "We sit at the table; there is still some nice sun shining in the window."

The table — glass and spotless — was in the bay window nook. Mitra imagined her mother cleaning it, sitting on the floor to wipe the underside. "I always thought there should be a window here," Mitra said.

"Yes, you did. You drew it once."

"You remember that?"

"Of course. I remember all of your drawings of buildings. Well, maybe not all of them, not the ones that were strange like triangles or with windows only in the ceiling —"

"Skylights."

"Yes, right. But the drawings you did of our house, I have them all in storage."

Mitra smiled. "That's so sweet, Mom."

Shireen waved the statement away and angled her chair so she could watch her daughter fully. Elbows on the table, she leaned in and said, "So, my daughter, eat!"

Mitra laughed. The halva melted on her tongue, an exquisite nostalgia of late-night snacks with Olga. She sipped her tea and looked at her watch. "I shouldn't stay too long, Maman. I don't want to get stuck in rush hour traffic on my way to Libby's."

"It is still a long time until traffic starts. You need a nap, joonam, after your long trip. Your eyes are crossing."

Mitra popped another quadrangle of halva into her mouth, chased it with hot tea. She did feel suddenly sluggish; that was what sugar and a mother's voice — not to mention a red-eye flight — could do. "All right," she said. "A nap sounds good. A short nap."

Shireen's face brightened. "You can go upstairs to your old bed. I had Maria prepare it in case something like this happened."

"Who's Maria?"

"New housecleaner."

"What happened to Raquel?"

"She vacuumed one of your father's cufflinks."

"Oh, dear. How utterly abominable of her."

"My daughter, if you use words I am unfamiliar with, I will not be so kind to you when I speak Farsi."

"Sorry." Mitra stood up. "I'll lie down in the family room on the couch. Will you wake me up in an hour, Mom? One hour, okay? I don't want to chance running into Baba if he decides to come home early."

Shireen's face fell and she looked away. As

she rose heavily from the table, she muttered, "An embarrassment that my daughter cannot stay the night in her own mother's house."

The smell of fresh herbs woke Mitra. There it was, at eye level on the coffee table: a bowl piled with dewy mint and basil leaves, radishes, and green onions — the condiments of every dinner she'd ever had in her parents' house. Her lids closed, and she felt her eyes rolling up into her head.

All-nighters used to be easier, she thought. A vaguely familiar *rat-a-tat* sound came from the low-volumed television. She let her mind begin to sink back into a dream when the *rat-a-tat* came again and she realized what it was: the spin of the *Wheel of Fortune.* Her eyes flew open. Vanna was turning an *E.* Mitra jerked up onto her elbows; the coffee table was covered in a smorgasbord of cheeses, breads, grapes and figs, and a cold eggplant casserole.

"Shit!" Mitra spat as she leapt to a sitting position. It was nearly dark outside. "Mom! What time is it?"

Shireen appeared in the doorway leading to the kitchen. "Be calm, my daughter. It is all right. I had a message from Vivian," she said, clasping her hands together and lifting her heels in a little hop of excitement. "Your baba is staying in Manhattan tonight, so you can stay here!"

Mitra swallowed. "Oh," she managed, feeling a twinge in her temple that was the sign of a headache. "Okay." She forced a smile.

"I called Nezam and Libby to tell them you will not be there until tomorrow. I have eggplant soufflé, your favorite, and we can watch *Everyone Love Raymond* and that funny blacked-skinned man after that."

"Great," said Mitra, willing her voice to sound more enthusiastic. She rubbed her eyes and suddenly noticed that her mother was wearing a flowered muumuu that she'd bought in Hawaii when Mitra was ten or eleven years old and had worn only on nights when Yusef was out of town. The house would take on a different ambience when her father wasn't there; Shireen would let them eat omelets in their pajamas in front of the television, and the maids would join them for *The Tom Jones Show.* The first time Shireen wore the muumuu, Anahita and Mitra screeched with laughter. Ana made a beeline for their mother's thighs and tried to wrap herself in the multicolored material. Shireen grinned, her hair miraculously loose to just below her shoulders.

"You look like Gidget, Maman," Mitra

said, expressing the ultimate compliment.

"Who is that?"

"A surfer girl on television."

"What is this surfer girl?"

"She rides waves on a board."

"Waves?" She pronounced it *vawes*, switching the *v* and *w* to create the most unintelligible and universally mispronounced English word uttered by Farsi speakers.

"In the ocean, Maman," Ana said.

Unbelieving, Shireen pinched Ana's cheek. "Silly!"

"I mean you look pretty," Mitra remembered saying, and now repeated that line. "You look pretty, Mom."

Shireen smiled. "Don't be silly," she echoed.

Shireen's white leather slippers peeked out at the bottom of the muumuu. She had removed her makeup, and Mitra noticed her swollen eyelids. "So what's in Manhattan that Baba has to stay overnight for at the last minute?"

"Why do you ask me such questions? It is business." Shireen turned back toward the kitchen.

"Really." Mitra couldn't contain the sarcasm in her voice.

"Please, Mitra, do not start that. It is business. He does not discuss it with me. And I do not frustrate him with a simpleton's questions."

"Don't put yourself down."

"I am not. Now go bring your luggage from the car."

Mitra sighed but did as her mother asked.

They sat on the couch and ate, laughing at the predictable humor of the sitcom until Mitra flopped back, rubbing her stomach. "I'm stuffed. Thanks, Mom."

"Dessert?"

"Please, no."

"In a little bit?" Shireen winked.

"Uh-oh. Why do I know that wink means hidden chocolate?"

Shireen laughed and got up. "Toblerone. I will take it out of the refrigerator."

While Shireen was in the kitchen, the phone rang. Mitra muted the television to listen. It wasn't her father; Shireen was speaking in full sentences, and there was a smile in her voice. "Yes, azizam," she said. "Of course your baba can stay overnight on Friday. It is a good idea; he will be tired after the gathering. But you will bring him, right? You will be here for the afternoon. I have not seen you, darling, in such a long time. . . . Good . . . No, joonam, everything is taken care of; you are a good boy to ask. . . . Yes. All right." And she ended the call with the usual Farsi sign-off, which translated roughly to *I would die for you.*

"Who was that?" Mitra asked when Shireen returned.

"Your cousin Kareem." She avoided looking at Mitra and walked to the corner of the room to place a thin blanket over a small parakeet's cage. "He has an appointment the evening of the One Year, so he can't take Uncle Jafar back to his apartment." She lifted an edge of the blanket to blow a kiss good night to the bird, the latest in a long line of parakeets, all named Tootie. "He wanted to know if Uncle could spend the night here."

Mitra pressed the off button on the remote, and the room filled with a tense silence. Shireen shot her a quick glance, then busied herself rearranging the bird's blanket. "Now, Mitra-joon, let's not ruin a good night together. It was just a phone call. He is not such a bad boy, really. Just a little spoiled, like all only sons with dead mothers. But he is a helpful son since the glaucoma took his father's sight, poor thing."

"Baba takes care of Uncle Jafar, not Kareem. Everybody knows that."

"Your father provides for him, which is

what brothers do for one another. Kareem looks after him. And he calls me often too. In fact, he has become spiritual — can you imagine? He wants to be a Sufi."

"That's impossible, Mom. Don't be so naïve. He's vile. You don't know; you just don't know."

"No, I guess I do not." Shireen returned to the couch and curled her legs under her, still avoiding eye contact, but Mitra detected an almost imperceptible hint of annoyance, even of insult, in the way she picked at and straightened the fabric of her muumuu. "You are always telling me how I do not know, as if I am not worthy of knowing, not smart enough to understand. For years you have called Kareem wicked, and you expect me to accept this without explanation. He always was the most helpful of all the cousins, taking care of the elders, running errands. Have you forgotten how attentive he was to the younger cousins in the old days? Taking them to the movies, the park, the shopping center? Minding them when the adults were busy? All the other kids his age were out and about or hiding in their rooms listening to the rock and roll."

"Oh yes, I remember perfectly," Mitra said through her teeth.

"You judge him because he is not so smart

as you, not so self-sufficient. Perhaps he seems insincere in the way he flatters people too much —"

"Ass-kisser is the word," Mitra interrupted.

"— but that is because the insecure thirst for love."

"Jesus, Mom, you should go back to school and study psychoanalysis."

"Mitra!" Shireen's dark eyes were wide with anger and tears, brimming with frustration. "You are just like your father!" Mitra winced. Shireen stood up, tugged two Kleenexes out of the box, and walked over to the window to stare out at the night.

Mitra turned her palms up. "What did I say?"

"You degrade me," Shireen said in a lower tone, speaking, it seemed, to her reflection in the window. "I am not stupid. I have lived a life, and I have wisdom from this living. My opinions of others are valid." She turned to face Mitra. "Perhaps I have a more trusting heart than you or your father with all your stubbornness and your black-and-white deductions about people. Look at you, you cannot even forgive each other! And you dare to go on about the flaws of others —"

"Stop," Mitra snapped, coming to her

feet. "Just stop, Mom. Come back here and sit down." She pointed to the sofa. "It's time I told you a story."

"What story? This is not the time for stories. You think I am a child who can be so easily distracted?" Shireen stood her ground, and Mitra realized that she better soften her tone if she wanted her mother to stay in the room, let alone sit down and listen.

"Mom, please. The way I feel about Kareem isn't trivial. There's a *reason*," and as she stressed this word, Mitra heard a whisper of warning from her cautious inner voice: *Don't tell her. Don't hurt her.* But it was too late. Shireen had heard the gravity in her daughter's tone.

"What reason? What do you mean?" Her voice was smaller, her expression of determination melting, turning to trepidation.

There was no going back, Mitra thought. "Sit down, Mom, and I'll tell you. But promise me you won't blame yourself." She pressed her fingers into her mother's forearm. "Promise me."

Shireen was frowning intensely, searching Mitra's eyes for clues, for reassurance. Quietly, she said, "All right. I promise. Now tell me, my daughter, tell me quickly."

111

CHAPTER 6

Mitra found Kareem and Anahita in the unfinished part of the basement behind the blustering metallic dragon of the boiler. Ana was twelve, an immature twelve. She still watched cartoons, played with her dolls, sucked her thumb in her sleep. She wouldn't get her period until she turned fourteen. Kareem's back was to Mitra. He had long hair then — his pride — and combed his fingers through it constantly. At the moment, he paid it no mind as it fell forward, exposing the back of his neck to Mitra's view, a sliver of gold chain catching her eye. Anahita was propped on an old barstool against the wall. All Mitra could see of her sister were her white-stockinged legs from the knees down, swaying to the rhythm of Kareem's grind. He was nineteen.

The collar of Kareem's flannel shirt in Mitra's fist was a sensation she will never forget; his strangled gasp as the front of the shirt slammed against his throat, his head snapping back, and the skitter of popped buttons on the concrete floor as she yanked the collar harder, mercilessly. He went to his knees. Still she yanked, then let him fall onto his back. The contour of his erection pressed at his jeans. She kicked him in the side, stepped over his leg, and kicked his testicles. She was wearing Frye boots.

His sweaty face was constricted in pain, and yet he kept from crying out. Self-preservation.

Anahita covered her face with her hands. Frozen. Mitra held her trembling wrists, talked to her dimpled fingers. "Upstairs. To our room. Act normal. Pretend. Can you pretend? Everyone's in the living room. Take your hands off your face! Let's go now! Ana, nod. Do you hear me? Nod. Take your hands off. Pretend."

Mitra lifted her sister off the stool. Shaking. Face ashen. Eyes wide and frightened at Kareem writhing. "Hold my arm. Pretend. You can. I'm with you. I'm here."

Words she'd never spoken.

Upstairs, they sat on the floor with their backs against Mitra's bed, the side near the wall as if they were hiding.

"We have to tell Mom," Mitra said.

"I already told Mom," Anahita said.

"What? What did you tell her?"

"I told her that Kareem kissed me all mushy like in the movies. She laughed and said he was playing with me. I told her no, it wasn't like playing, but she doesn't understand."

"Then we should tell Baba."

"No! I can't tell Baba something like that. I'm embarrassed. Please, Mitra, don't make me tell Baba."

Mitra knew Ana was right; she knew it before the suggestion came out of her mouth; it would never do to talk to Baba. Sex was a subject he only alluded to, and always in the context of their purity. The very idea of uttering sexually descriptive words to their father was unthinkable. Anyway, he wouldn't want to believe such filth had happened, not in *his* family. He would want to investigate, like he always did, whenever they told him something disagreeable that he didn't know about. Tattling. A million questions, all intended to trip them up, all with the intention of dispelling an incident that might prove uncomfortable to address or damaging to his image of the family.

"That bastard Kareem," Mitra said.

"It's not his fault. He loves me. He thinks I'm beautiful."

"Is that why you let him kiss you and touch you? You think you owe him for loving you and thinking you're beautiful?"

"No," Ana said, her eyes downcast, then suddenly looking into her sister's face. "I can't believe you kicked him, Mitra. He's going to be mad."

"Fuck him."

"He's going to be mad at *me.*"

"So?"

Ana shrugged and looked down. "But he loves me and —"

"And he thinks you're beautiful. Dammit, Ana. Did you like him kissing you and touching you?"

"No." Her eyes filled with tears. "I let him do it."

"You let him do it because he wanted it, because you thought if you didn't let him do it, he wouldn't love you anymore."

"Well, he won't."

"So?"

"I don't want that. One time I told him I didn't want to and he stopped talking to me; he didn't invite me to go to the movies or play charades with Mariam and Bita and Majid. I hurt his feelings."

Mitra grabbed Ana's arms roughly, brought their faces close. "Listen to me, Ana. It's not your job to make Kareem

115

happy or to keep him from feeling hurt. You understand me? If he really loved you, he wouldn't make you do something you didn't want to. Besides, he knows you're just a kid; he's not supposed to be doing stuff like that to you."

"But he didn't take my clothes off. He didn't try to have sex with me."

"Believe me, Ana, he will; he definitely will if you keep letting him do what he's doing, which is part of sex."

"He probably won't talk to me now anyway."

"Good."

Ana began to cry, the usual stifled hiccoughs. "What if I can't stop myself?"

"Are you kidding? Why do anything you don't like doing?"

Ana looked Mitra in the eye and sniffed. "But I always do things I don't like doing. I'm not like you, Mitti."

Mitra's lips trembled with anger and frustration, but she said nothing. Anahita hung her head and sobbed softly. Mitra saw the part in her hair, the fine wiry waves falling away from it like a paper fan to the bottom of her neck. Her hands were suddenly against those waves on either side of her sister's head, and she gently pulled Ana to her chest, where she nestled her face and

116

wet Mitra's shirt with hot tears that seeped into her skin, and deeper.

"Don't worry," Mitra said. "I won't let you do anything you shouldn't do." And Ana's arms went around Mitra's waist.

If Shireen had given her a choice, Mitra would've spent the night on the couch in the family room. Not in here, certainly not after telling that story.

The pink shag rug had been replaced by a cream Berber, but the rest of her childhood bedroom was the same, though a bit faded. Pink walls with a picket fence ceiling border, the ceiling itself also covered in wallpaper — a sea of roses that had spun Mitra's head when she was stoned. White ruffled curtains swagged across the windows, sills adorned with Delft statues of children. Furniture white with gold trim, twin beds with brass headboards. A framed poster above Ana's bed: the lower legs and slippered feet of a ballerina on point, ribbons perfectly crisscrossed up white-stockinged calves. Anahita's dream: to be a ballerina.

Twice a week until she was eleven, she attended Mademoiselle Valerie's Ballet School in Alpine, where she practiced harder than any of the other girls, most of them skinny and supple, and present only because their mothers insisted. It was the opposite in the Jahani family: Yusef thought the performing arts unseemly for proper girls. But Ana was a dancer. She could imitate any kind of movement. Mitra cringed when she did the splits, but was impressed; she dared her to perform all kinds of bodily contortions, hoping she'd get stuck. When Olga came to live with them, she indulged Anahita's dancing, encouraged her to learn Persian and Arabic movements, which involved a great deal of wrist-twirling and hip-thrusting, and Azeri dancing with its quick Cossack-like knee bends — *Up! Down! Up! Down! Hey!* — that Ana's muscular thighs were made for. In the evenings, Ana could often be found in the maid's room dancing to a cassette player, mixing the different styles and movements to make Olga drop her knitting and laugh like a hyena. Yusef would stand at the top of the basement stairs and growl at her to come up and do her homework.

Everyone but Anahita realized that she did not have the body of a ballerina. Yusef's pet name for her was "my little fatso," meant as a compliment. Shireen dubbed both herself and Anahita full-figured — *fool-figoorrd like Lizbet Taylor.* But Ana eagerly sought the approval of the prune-faced Mademoiselle Valerie until at last the Frenchwoman blatantly informed her that she was too short and *shunky* to be a ballerina and she should stop wasting her time. *I sujeste that you take up field 'ockey, my dear.* Mitra could close her eyes and remember the stifled sobs coming from Ana's bed during the night. She had felt sorry for her sister, but that was before she knew how to admit it.

She sat on her old bed and touched her finger to a cigarette burn on the bedside table. In the top drawer, Mitra had kept a copy of *Our Bodies, Ourselves,* along with a stash of rolling papers under a pile of *Architectural Digest* magazines. The bottom drawer had been Ana's, and Mitra was surprised to find several of her sister's charms and keepsakes stowed there: a rabbit's foot, a pillbox holding a few of Ana's baby teeth, a Russian painted wooden box containing a black-and-white photo of a young Olga wearing enormous hoop earrings. Shireen must have gotten these things from Ana's husband, Bijan, before he left for London. It was eerie, like a shrine at which offerings of centuries past remained untouched and decaying. Mitra was surprised that her mother had known and remembered where everything belonged.

She slid open the closet to hang her jacket.

The shoe shelf was lined with vintage Barbie dolls, each carefully suffocated in thin plastic; the last time Mitra saw them, they were living on a shelf in Nina's bedroom. Against the back wall leaned an easel blackboard Mitra had gotten for her ninth birthday. Shireen had saved so many of their toys for her grandchildren. Mitra ran her palm over the slate surface; it was slippery, and she remembered spraying it with Pledge, hoping to make it shiny. She'd ruined it, of course, which was a boon for Ana, who no longer had to act as Mitra's student, made to sit and be taught arithmetic, her worst subject, ushered up to the board to write out the answers to problems far beyond her level so Mitra could frown and snort disgustedly at her. And when Ana could no longer hold in her tears, Mitra would stop — *You're no fun, such a sissy* — and find something else to occupy herself.

Wincing at the memory, Mitra turned quickly and unzipped her suitcase, changed into pajama pants and T-shirt. In the bathroom, she heard the flush of her mother's toilet on the other side of the wall. She imagined Shireen, still bewildered and stunned, going through the motions of brushing and washing, her thoughts all about how she had failed to protect Ana

120

from Kareem, how she would never be able to apologize. Mitra felt terrible about telling her the story. Once again, she'd let her anger trump everything. She was still the shock jock in her family. Wasn't age supposed to mellow a person? And Shireen, she realized, had acted with uncharacteristic spunk tonight when Mitra first challenged her about Kareem. *You are just like your father,* she'd said. Mitra groaned. And then: *I am not stupid. I have wisdom.* Mitra smiled.

Back in the bedroom, she peered at herself in the mirror, rubbed her bloodshot eyes, then lifted the top of a jewelry box on the dresser, a gift she'd received at one of the annual Christmas parties at the Faridi family's house in Teaneck. What was weirder than a group of Iranian immigrant families using a Christian holiday as an excuse to dress up and give presents to one another's children? Mitra had never been interested in jewelry, so she'd grudgingly given the box to Ana, who loved jewelry so much she'd swallowed one of Shireen's pinky rings when she was five. The box still tinkled out "The Blue Danube," but the pop-up dancing ballerina was headless; Mitra couldn't remember if she'd been the one who perpetrated that crime. Probably.

She absent-mindedly opened what used

121

to be her underwear drawer. Empty save for a gnawed-at pencil and a small picture frame lying facedown. She picked up the frame and turned it over, sucked in her breath: a photograph of her and her father, taken when she was twelve, the two of them standing like conquerors on a mound of excavated earth, his arm around her shoulder, brown fingers obscured by her thick waves, both of them smiling identically at the camera, she in a yellow sundress, suddenly too tight around her blossoming chest, he in his usual weekend khakis, and between them they held — equally possessively — the rolled-up tube of blueprints for the new apartments in Fort Lee. More like father and son, like patriarch and scion, like mentor and protégé than like father and daughter. The last time they were together like that.

With trembling fingers, Mitra removed the photograph from its frame and ripped it into tiny pieces that fell into the drawer. In the mirror she saw her lips pressed into a line, and a flash of pain leapt to her temple from her clenched jaw. She slammed the drawer closed, peered at her angry face, and knew she wasn't really seeing herself, but rather using the mirror, as she had so often as a teenager, to spit venom at her father

122

for casting her aside, and at her mother for pretending that it hadn't been a big deal. Her hot breath created a fleeting circle of fog on the mirror, and Mitra drew back as if waking from a trance. She turned and reminded herself that she was here for only a few days, not long, just a few days.

She climbed into her childhood bed and switched off the light, burrowed into the pillow that smelled like her mother's lavender sachets. She breathed deeply to calm herself and imagined the fog rushing silently through the Golden Gate, the muffled foghorns you could hear all over the city, and before long she was drifting and Ana was behind her on the floor, pasting teen magazine cutouts of Bobby Sherman and David Cassidy into her scrapbook, humming off-key. Mitra's eyes snapped open, and it was all she could do not to jump up, dress, and leave the house quietly. No. It wouldn't be fair to her mother, not after telling her that story. She closed her eyes and visualized Ana in the other bed, older and miserable, daydreaming about a marriage that their father forbade. And then she let herself smile through tears, because hadn't she, Mitra, found a way to redeem herself for all her sibling brutality, almost eighteen years ago when she'd made it so that Ana got what she wanted? It's okay, Mitra, she told herself, it's okay; at least you did one good thing for her.

Shireen threw the bedcovers off and gazed into the dark. She could take a sleeping pill . . . but she didn't deserve such an easy solution, did she? She wanted to cry, but that also seemed improper. She had a terrible urge to beat her chest the way the public mourners did on the Death Anniversary of Saint Hossein. God help her, she wanted to bleed, to be in some kind of physical pain. Was this how the young people who cut themselves felt? Guilty? Ach, how could she do penance for what Mitra had told her?

She had no memory of little Anahita telling her that Kareem was kissing her "like in the movies." There was so much she had forgotten about those long-ago days when the house teemed with visitors and Kareem was the quiet one who was such a willing babysitter. Perhaps she had blocked it out. And what if she did eventually remember it? Would she also remember that she had dismissed such a thing? Oh, yes, she thought, pressing her face into the pillow and moaning, she would have dismissed it! Wasn't that how such things were handled?

She remembered the touch of hot fingers beneath her party dress, the smell of cigar smoke close enough to make her eyes tear, the burn of the molten shame that filled her veins; she remembered nothing else — not the man, not the place, not her age. Such things happened. They were meant to be forgotten. Mistakes. Lessons a girl learned about propriety, modesty, and the compulsions of men.

She sat up, leaned back against the headboard, drew her knees up to her chest. *Forgive me, Ana-joon. I was not the kind of mother who would have saved you. I preferred to avoid family feuds — your humiliation, Kareem's denial, your father's doubts, people talking.* But Mitra had rescued her sister. Thank God for that! Mitra had done so much. And yet her life was incomplete. Shireen got up and put on her robe and slippers. She took two certain steps toward the door, then stopped and retreated to sit on the edge of her bed. Finally, she went down the hall to the room her child-daughters had shared so long ago.

Mitra was on her side, facing the wall. Shireen sat carefully next to her and laid a delicate hand on her shoulder. "Mitra-joon, forgive me," she whispered in Farsi. "My intentions have always been good."

Mitra rolled onto her back and looked up at Shireen's silhouette against the weak hallway light. She gently squeezed her mother's arm. "There's nothing to forgive, Mom," she said. "Everything worked out. I didn't mean for you to feel responsible, just to understand how I felt about Kareem. Please forget about it. I'm the one who should apologize."

Shireen's eyes glistened and she smiled sadly. "Mitra-joon, you know that all I want is for my children and my husband — for you and your father — to be happy. I want to give you what you need. But I am not a very clever person and I am easily confused by which side is right or wrong. I am a mother; I want to be on all sides. Please never think I am against you. I am just trying to do what is right for my family. It was the way I was raised. It is the way I am."

"I know, Mom. You don't have to explain." A yawn overcame her. "It's okay. Go on to bed, Mom. It's late."

Shireen wiped her tears. "Turn over, my daughter. I will play with your hair like when you were a child."

Mitra thought, *That was Ana, Mom,* but she turned her cheek into the pillow, closed her eyes. Shireen ran her nails lightly through Mitra's hair and along her scalp;

Mitra shivered with pleasure and found herself relaxing.

"Shall I tell you a little gossip I heard?" whispered Shireen. "A bedtime story?"

Mitra sighed amicably.

"At the hairdresser last week, my friend Gitti — you remember Gitti who almost married the Shah until he found out she did not speak French fluently, or so she claims, and she married the uncle of your father's cousin who had a very successful textile business until —" Shireen's sibilant words began to fade in and out.

"So Gitti has fourteen grandchildren . . . always showing pictures . . . bragging . . . overly fat . . . some cross-eyed, poor things . . . I pretend they are cute, but it is —"

Mitra was headed for the edge of sleep.

"Another grandchild coming," Shireen's far-off whisper rustled. ". . . her daughter . . . same age as you, Mitti . . . two grown children, tubes tied ten years ago, but the doctor was able to reverse. . . . Mitra, my daughter, have you heard me? He was able to reverse the procedure."

Mitra had heard very well, but she didn't move.

"Just a little gossip for you, Mitti, something to think about. Mitti? Are you asleep?"

CHAPTER 7

Mitra let Libby wrap her in a hug as she came off the elevator into the apartment's marble-tiled foyer. She felt the bulge of Libby's abdomen and stepped back, incredulous. "You're pregnant again?"

"Shit no," Libby said, rubbing her palm over a significant paunch. "I'm still nursing." She scratched at an orange stain on her raggedy sweatshirt. "Sorry, I'm kind of a mess." Seeing that Mitra's stunned expression hadn't changed, she threw her head back and laughed. "Oh, Mitra, you are such a space cadet. I just had another kid. I sent you an email? About a month ago?"

"I . . . I—"

"Oh, shut up," Libby said, giving Mitra's sleeve a tug and grinning magnanimously. "This is me you're talking to. Elizabeth the Putrid. Haven't I always forgiven your weirdness?"

Mitra snorted. "Elizabeth the Putrid.

That's from, like, the last century."

It was what Mitra had named Libby when she and Anahita were nine, when Libby had just discovered her love of running, when a swampy odor wafted from her armpits, her neck folds, and, most profoundly, from the gray-tinged tube socks she was forced to expose when Shireen made her remove her Keds before she and Ana sequestered themselves in the basement playroom to stretch, leap, strain, skip, roll, and contort their bodies into endlessly revised gymnastics routines, all performed to "Nadia's Theme."

Libby pushed her stick-straight blond bangs off her forehead. "Put your luggage down and come into the kitchen. I'm cooking." The bangs fell back over her brow. "And wipe that stunned look off your face."

As Libby turned, Mitra said, "I'm so sorry, Libs. I don't remember getting the email. Shit. My mother didn't say anything. Or maybe she did. I can't remember. I'm so sorry. Um . . . what did you have?"

"A girl. Katy. Katayoon to your family. Thank God she's finally napping. We can have some quiet time before my neighbor brings the twins back from the park. Lucky me, she's got one their age who's starved for playmates."

Mitra followed Libby through the high-ceilinged living room with its hotel-size furniture the color of café au lait, and through the dining room with its fingerprint-smudged glass table. Just before reaching the kitchen, Libby said over her shoulder, "I know clutter insults your sensibility, Mitra, but with the kids, minimalism is not an option, so the place is a mess."

It sure was. Spaghetti sauce gurgled like a lava pit on the stove; liquid orange missiles leapt up to splotch the white cabinets. The sink was full of dirty dishes. On the counters was a mishmash of incongruous items: cereal boxes, crayons, a bowl of peeled potatoes in water, six Matchbox cars in bumper-to-bumper traffic, several empty beer and wine bottles, an orchid plant devoid of blooms, a box of rigatoni, and the largest plastic container of dried basil leaves Mitra had ever seen. She scooted into the banquette behind the kitchen table, and when she lifted her palms off the cushion, they were dotted with crumbs. Libby covered the spaghetti sauce, put a trivet under it, and turned the heat down. "They say the longer it simmers, the better it tastes."

"Who says?"

"I don't know. Italian grandmothers." She reached into the refrigerator and held up a bottle of wine. "White?"

"Sure."

"Wish I could join you, but it's apple juice for me. I swear, if I wasn't nursing, I'd be on my second bottle of the day. As it is, I have fantasies about disappearing to a Caribbean island for the rest of my life."

Libby said things like this, but she never meant them. In college, she had been an obsessively devoted mother's helper every summer for a family with four kids, a job she kept after graduation while everyone else worked at Bloomingdale's or Condé Nast — everyone except Ana, who was already married. No one had to ask Libby what she wanted in life. She and Ana were peas in a pod. But Libby's boyfriend, Jonathan, a mild-mannered guy whom no one found offensive (or anything else, for that matter), wasn't keen on tying the knot until he had a few years of work experience behind him. *Sound logic,* Mitra thought. Sadly, Jonathan was sucked into the hedonistic lifestyle of 1980s Wall Street. Libby broke up with him after finding a vial of cocaine in his briefcase, not two weeks before his boss was indicted for insider trading. At around the same time, Ana had to put off getting pregnant after suffering a rare ovarian cyst rupture, so the two friends

131

were able to comfort and amuse one another through it all. That Libby had ended up marrying their cousin Nezam years later was a surprise to everyone except Olga, who wasn't as myopic as most people when it came to "husband being younger than wife," and said she'd known Nezam was "crazy 'bout Libby-joon" since before he grew tall enough to look her in the eye.

"Have you seen the *Bryson Bulletin*?" Libby asked, pointing to a pile of mail on the table.

"Mine goes right into the recycle bin," Mitra said, sifting through the pile.

"I thought so. There's a nice memorial dedication to Ana. Page fourteen."

Mitra lifted an eyebrow. "Took them a while," she said, extricating a glossy periodical with a cover photograph of several schoolgirls in preppy dress.

"It's an annual publication," Libby said as she unwrapped a wedge of Brie. "The one before this came out about a week before the accident. I remember because there was a photo in it of Blanche de la Babineaux wearing a hat made of at least ten dead chinchillas."

Mitra rolled her eyes. "The fake French girl from Kentucky?"

"Yeah. Ana and I laughed about that for

hours." Libby reached high up into a cabinet for a box of water crackers.

Mitra flipped through the *Bulletin* slowly, as if each page contained something mildly interesting, which it didn't. The usual kudos and photos of alumnae fund-raisers, elderly women in short silver haircuts and pearls. An article on the new Head of School, who used to be called the Headmistress or Headmaster. Pages twelve and thirteen were devoted to the Science Department's annual ecological field trip to a remote Caribbean island, a badge of honor for girls who wanted to prove their ability to live for three weeks out in the open, washing their bodies in the sea, sleeping in tents, examining slimy creatures, and sometimes eating them. Finally, Mitra reached page fourteen.

In Memoriam

Anahita Jahani Markarian, Class of 1978, is fondly remembered for her dedication to Bryson's 130-year-old tradition of academic excellence and its commitment to diversity. Anahita's special devotion to the Art Department is exhibited in the Main Hall Mural, painted in 1976 by the Art Club, of which Anahita was President in her senior year. Anahita was also an outstanding Bryson gymnast and a fine mezzo soprano in the Bryson Chorus. We offer our deepest condolences to her parents and to her sister, Mitra Jahani, class of 1975.

Mitra hated it. They'd managed not to use the word *death* or even the phrase *passed away*. Reality was still too harsh for their sheltered community. And that word: *diversity*. A euphemism for non-WASP, for minority — a politically correct advertisement for the school. What a sham.

But she wouldn't let it get to her. She wouldn't give them that. With a shrug, she said, "I'm surprised the mural is still there."

"Why?" Libby asked. "It was beautiful. A forest in honor of Earth Day. Ana's birds were amazing. As if she'd pasted real feathers onto the wall. I wish she hadn't stopped painting."

"That's all she ever painted: birds. I think she got sick of them. I sure did. Anyway, she said she didn't miss it." Mitra looked at the photograph the *Bulletin* had used — of all things, Ana's graduation picture. "They couldn't have contacted my parents for a more current photo?"

"You know how they are. Bryson girls are preserved in time." Libby uncorked the wine with a flourish. "Like body parts in formaldehyde."

"Gross," Mitra said automatically, still staring at the photo of Ana at eighteen — her sweetheart neckline, a single pearl on a delicate chain resting in the hollow of her neck. And the white parasol. Mitra smiled. Olga had made it. Well, not exactly made it. Shireen had bought a white umbrella, and Olga had decorated it with lace on the handle and the spokes, and white organza flowers and butterflies on the outside of the canopy. The parasol had been inspired by Mitra, not because she meant it to be, but because of a sarcastic remark she made about how Bryson girls lived in the Dark Ages with their virginal white graduation gowns, and how they might as well wear corsets and carry parasols. Ana loved her parasol, not least because it helped her to keep her posture erect so that Baba couldn't poke his finger into her backbone: *Stand up es-traight!*

That day, as Ana and Libby took their places in Bryson's East Courtyard under the hot June sun to receive their diplomas, Mitra had briefly left her parents sitting primly in their white folding chairs on the grass and found Ana in the procession line. She pulled her aside. "You need some lip gloss." Ana frowned. "Baba will kill me,

135

Mitti." Her frizzy hair was pulled back and sprayed into a stiff little bun, her eyelashes brushed with Vaseline, her eyebrows subtly and secretly tweezed by Olga over the previous few weeks. Mitra's spine prickled as the ancient moment returned: Ana's sweet bowed lips, her deceptively mischievous smile that boys often took for flirtation but that Mitra saw as her guilelessness. The damp feel of Ana's dimpled cheek between her thumb and forefinger. "Hold still or it'll smear onto your face." A warm puff on her knuckles as Ana stifled a nervous giggle. The palest pink. Beautiful.

Mitra caught the tears in her throat and slowly covered the photo with her palm. She kept her head down to collect herself privately, but Libby had already come over to the table; she squeezed Mitra's hand, then slid a glass of wine toward her. Mitra lifted the glass and met Libby's watery eyes.

"To Ana," Libby said, lifting her glass of apple juice.

"To Ana," Mitra echoed hoarsely, touching her glass to Libby's. They sipped. Mitra sipped again.

Libby placed a plate of cheese and crackers on the table and sat across from Mitra. "I'll never forget what *you* wore for your graduation."

Mitra managed a chuckle, remembering her rebellion. Throughout high school, she'd staged at least one rebellion a year. As a freshman, she circulated a petition to abolish the school uniform, an ensemble of gray flannel skirt, white blouse, navy blue blazer, and matching knee socks. As a sophomore, she brought a copy of the newly published *Joy of Sex* to health class with the suggestion that it be used as a textbook. Her junior year, she refused to attend morning chapel on the grounds that she was not a Christian, which prompted twenty-two Jewish classmates to follow suit. Her senior year, it was the implementation of the Metric Conversion Act, with Mitra relentlessly reminding teachers and students to convert miles into kilometers, pounds into kilograms, Fahrenheit into Celsius, and so on. This rebellion hadn't earned her the same kind of admiration as the earlier ones, but she was unfazed. She made up for it at graduation.

"Yeah," she said as Libby proffered her a cracker and cheese. "I wore pants."

"Excuse me," Libby said in mock admonition. "Not just pants. You wore a white pantsuit. A three-button jacket and bell bottoms. Sewn expertly by Olga from one of your mom's white linen tablecloths."

Mitra smiled and popped the cracker and cheese into her mouth. Buoyed by her change of mood, Libby continued. "Seventy-five girls filing out to that stone patio dressed like brides. Except, of course, for you, with that high-and-mighty walk of yours, as if nothing is out of the ordinary. I swear, every graduation program that was being used as a fan came to a halt in midair. The old lady alumnae contingent?" Libby struck a nose-in-the-air pose. "They were, like, who is this swarthy girl, this likely *foreign* student whose father might not even be a *diplomat,* but rather an upstart Third World merchant, barely *civilized,* who dares sully our alma mater's traditions. It was like Gloria Steinem herself had crashed the party, or worse, that traitor Jane Fonda."

Mitra was laughing hard now. Cracker crumbs spewed from her lips and she clamped a napkin over her mouth.

"And your *parents*!" Libby continued, thrilled that she was making Mitra laugh. "Your mom was mortified; she just looked down at her lap. Your dad — I was one seat away from him next to Ana — I swear I could see the tiny hairs of his mustache lift away from his skin. And you got away with it! Any other girl would've been picked off that patio by the scruff of her neck."

It was true. Mitra had caused a bit of a scandal with the Bryson conservatives. But she was left to play out her rebellion, and she sat in her alphabetical seat and collected her diploma with the air of a suspect who's been assured of immunity. After all, she was the class salutatorian, accepted at Barnard, daughter of a generous donor to the annual fund, and a favorite of the headmaster's difficult wife, whose passion was the school theater, a place Mitra had transformed with her creative set designs, particularly the multi-tiered wooden stage for *Hamlet.*

"Speaking of necks," Libby said, "the red ribbon chokers you and those other girls wore, *now* will you tell me what special meaning they had?"

Mitra's eyes sparkled. She washed down the last of her cracker and cheese with a gulp of wine. "I told you and Ana a million times that it was a secret; we had a pact that we wouldn't ever tell."

"Come on, Mitra. It's twenty-three years ago. Jeez."

Mitra sighed, reached for the wine bottle. "You're right. It's no fun being coy without Ana around to do that hysterical doggie begging thing." She paused. "The girls who wore the ribbon weren't virgins. That's all."

"Oh my God," Libby said, flinging her

hands up to her cheeks. "That's exactly what Ana thought."

Mitra bridled. "I wouldn't have put it past you, Libs, but Ana?"

"I know. But that's what she whispered in my ear that very day. She knew you so well, Mitra."

She did? It was a question Mitra had never asked herself. "I didn't talk to her about my sexual adventures. I mean, you guys were such goody-goodies!"

"Give me a break, Mitra. You always underestimated our maturity; we weren't so naïve."

Libby was right again, Mitra realized. The proof of it was Ana's affair. Did Libby know about that? And if she did, wouldn't they find some comfort in talking about it? In deconstructing the day Ana died? Mitra studied Libby's profile, as if her features could reveal the memories stored in her head. She knew that Libby didn't know about what Kareem had done; Ana had told her that she wanted to pretend it never happened, and Mitra had accepted that. But the affair?

"So you guys had secrets too, huh?" Mitra made a point of lightening her tone. "Do tell."

Libby got up to stir the spaghetti sauce.

140

"Yeah, secrets like sneaking Oreos from the pantry and using your makeup. One time we put your bras on and stuffed them with scraped-out grapefruit halves."

"You did what?"

"Well, they had a nice conical shape. We let them air-dry first, of course." Libby put the lid back on the pot and began loading the dishwasher.

"What about later? Secrets you had later, when you were older?" Mitra prodded.

"Not me. You know I can't keep my mouth shut. As for Ana . . ." Libby looked up at the ceiling, thinking. "Huh. I can't recall anything." Mitra felt a pang; that Ana hadn't confided in Libby saddened her. "I mean, there was Bijan, when she first met him and didn't want your parents to know."

"Besides that. That wasn't really a secret. You just had to look at her rapturous expression to know she was in love."

Libby's face fell. "Shit," she said. "I forgot to tell you. Bijan called this morning."

"Is he here yet?"

Libby shook her head. "He's in London. He's not coming."

Mitra ran her fingers through her hair. "I guess I don't blame him. It's not like he needs a reminder that his wife and kids are dead." Libby stiffened at Mitra's blunt

141

language. "If it weren't for my mom, I wouldn't have come either."

"It's not such a bad thing, Mitra, people coming together for comfort. I mean, Americans have the funeral, the burial, and it's over. If you need anything else, you're supposed to go to a support group."

"Americans? You've been hanging around my family too much. We're all Americans now."

The remark stung, and Libby stood still, looked down at her peeling nail polish. It was easy to fall into the Iranian banter, the self-segregation, when you were around it all the time, when you wanted to be accepted into the clan. But Mitra, despite her blood ties, didn't approve of it. Even during the Hostage Crisis, she'd never lied about her heritage like so many others who called themselves "Persian," as if the exoticized word weren't a synonym for Iranian. And she could get belligerent sometimes, glaring at people with a steely look that said, *We're Americans, just like you.*

Libby blew at a stray wisp of hair and looked at her watch. "The twins'll be back from the park in a few minutes."

"I can't wait to see them," Mitra said.

"Yes, you can. Believe me."

"All right, I can, but tell me about my

favorite cousin. Is he treating you right?"

"He's been working late a lot, a residential community in upstate New York. I could strangle your father for putting him in charge of it. He comes home and complains about my bad housekeeping."

"That's not like Nezam. He's supposed to be our token feminist."

"Well, you know these Iranian men. They get more like their fathers as they get older." Libby raised an eyebrow.

Mitra chuckled. "In that case, expect him to turn into a househusband."

Libby nodded. "True. I do adore my father-in-law. Truth is, Mitra, Nezam's just frustrated, wishes he could spend more time with the kids."

Mitra shook her head slowly. "Not while he's working for my father."

"You know that won't change. Duty to family and all that."

"I'll talk to him," Mitra said, finishing off her wine.

Libby waved her hand dismissively and opened the dishwasher. "Oh, you don't have to do that, Mitra. We'll figure it out. We always do." But Mitra knew she didn't mean it.

"You cheated!"

"You cheated!"

"Did not!"

"Did too!"

"Eight and two don't make eleven!"

"It was an eight and a three! And that makes eleven! Right, Auntie Mitra?"

"Right."

Pedram stuck his popsicle-purple tongue out at his brother. Of the two, he was the tough one. Mitra rubbed at her foot, which had fallen asleep from her sitting cross-legged on the floor at the base of a bunk bed in the boys' Lego-themed bedroom, playing a Persian card game called *pasoor,* which involved matching cards that added up to eleven. Nezam, like his father, was fond of using cards to teach the kids how to add and to strategize.

"But it was a two, Auntie Mitra," Kian whined, giving her a puppy-innocent face.

"Was it?" she asked.

"She said I was right," interjected Pedram.

"I said you were right about eight and three equaling eleven." Mitra was certain that Kian was speaking the truth. "I didn't see whether you picked up a two or a three, Pedram. You did it fast, and I'm not very quick. Why don't you start this hand over?"

Pedram was sneaky, like Mitra had been. It wasn't only about winning with him, it was about bothering his brother. Mitra wondered if this was the way it was with most siblings: one angel and one devil, one bully and one victim.

Pedram slapped his cards down in anger. Kian gathered the deck up and handed it to Mitra for shuffling. Although the decision was not in his favor, he showed no sign of dissatisfaction. Mitra knew what he wanted: no conflict at all, no winning or losing. Same as Anahita. This was what she had finally understood when the Kareem incident happened. She hoped for Kian's sake that it wouldn't take Pedram that long, or be that traumatizing. She gently squeezed Kian's cheek between her knuckles, and he smiled; his joy came from approval.

Mitra dealt and watched as the boys tried to fan the four cards they each had. Pedram failed and dropped his facedown, but Kian kept trying with twisted fingers, the tip of his tongue fiddling at the corner of his mouth. Finally, Mitra said, "It's your turn, buddy." He looked from the cards in his hand to the four cards on the carpet and back again; he whispered numbers to himself.

"Go-o-o!" Pedram demanded. "You're so slow, Kian."

Finally, Kian's face lit up and he pulled a

six from his fingers and laid it beside a five on the carpet. "Six and five equals eleven!" he pronounced, then looked at Mitra for reassurance.

"Excellent," she said. "Go on, take the cards. They're yours." He tucked them under a scraped knee, and Mitra thought of the childhood scars she could still make out on her own knees, the faded chronicles of falls from bikes and stairs and rocks, the memory of being fearless, of braving the blood-red iodine wick.

Pedram flopped over on his stomach and with a breath of irritation picked a card from the stacked pile, obviously having no card in his hand with which to make eleven. Mitra did the same. Then Kian, with a smile as wide as a sparkling river, made eleven with a two from his hand and nine on the carpet. Pedram dropped his forehead to the floor and let the cards in his hand fall. "This game is boring. I'm not playing anymore." He rolled over, reached for two olive-green combat soldiers, and began making those throaty, saliva-bubbling fighting noises only boys' mouths can make.

"That's okay, Kian," Mitra said. "We'll play just the two of us." This was unlike her. She was once a firm auntie. A no-nonsense, tell-it-like-it-is grown-up to whom a kid could pose any question, even, say, the meaning of fuck. An adult who wasn't a mommy (and didn't know all the mommy rules), who wouldn't talk in a kid voice or ask dumb questions like "Can you spell your name?" or frown instead of giggle when somebody farted. That old Mitra would have taken a stern position with Pedram: *Finish what you've started, buddy. You don't quit in the middle of the game just because you're not winning.* She would've had just the right tone too. A little harsh, but not like a scolding adult's; more like a big kid with the power to choose who got to belong in the gang. That was how she would have reacted. But she realized that she'd become a softy. She treated all kids as if they were on the edge of tragedy.

Kian and Mitra finished the game and he won. She kissed his forehead and he blushed. Pedram released a loud, wet explosion from his mouth and sent his soldiers flying to their plastic deaths.

Libby peeked into the room. "Dinner's ready. Time to wash up, boys." She managed to fold down the collars of their matching white polo shirts as they shuffled by her to the bathroom. Squatting to help Mitra collect the cards and put them back in the box, she said, "Only you would have the patience to play cards with my five-year-old brats."

"Kids are easy when you don't have them all the time."

Libby shook her head. "Don't be modest, Mitra. Ana had good reason to designate you guardian to her children."

Libby had put Mitra in the baby's room on the daybed. Katy still spent the night in the bassinet in Nezam and Libby's bedroom, but her room smelled like everything baby: powder, Desitin, baby moisturizer, the slightly curdled scent of breast milk, and a faint mixture of urine and Lysol. A softly glowing night lamp on the dresser created wispy shadows on the faux-finished pink walls. Mitra felt like an oafish intruder.

At the crib, she caught her breath. In the corner, nestled against the daisy-patterned padded bumper, was a stuffed yellow dinosaur hardly bigger than a tea cup. She hesitated to pick it up, the thought coming to her that her hands weren't clean enough even though she'd just washed them. But she reached for it, gently squished its fleece skin and felt the nubby grains inside, heard the quiet swish that sounded like windblown sand. So soft. So unlike the synthetically rough stuffed animals Ana used to place above her head on the pillow every night, among them a gray one-eared squirrel that she later kept snuggled in a basket by her bed along with paperback child-rearing books. Mitra wondered what had happened to it. Why had she told Bijan and her mother that she didn't want any of Ana's things? At the time, it had seemed almost traitorous to need something to remind her of her sister.

The baby dinosaur had red and blue felt triangles sewn into its spine; a brontosaurus, Mitra guessed. She'd bought Nina a Beanie Baby mouse that had floppy felt ears like this, one of those Beanie Babies that had sold out from most stores in all of five minutes. She'd discovered it in a shop in Noe Valley and had FedExed it to her niece. She remembered Nina's scream of glee over the phone.

Thankyouthankyouthankyou, Auntie Mitra!

It was in her lap when the Verizon truck smashed head-on into the Range Rover's left bumper and crushed Anahita's legs, still in her lap when the Rover careened over the guardrail, still in her lap when the speed limit sign impaled her chest. The night before the funeral, Shireen had soaked the mouse in OxiClean over and over until the bloodstains looked more like stuffed animal eczema. Mitra had sat on the floor in Ana and Bijan's laundry room for an hour blow-drying the little thing. They'd directed the mortician to tuck it in Nina's casket.

A soft knock came at the door. She turned quickly, the dinosaur clasped to her neck as Nezam poked his head into the room. "Hey," he said quietly. His smile disappeared when he realized her condition, and he strode forward to embrace her. She cried silently into his chest, inhaled his particular black tea and lemon scent. "Aw, Mitti," he said, his voice swollen with a pity she wouldn't have tolerated from anyone else. "I guess we didn't think about how this room might upset you. Sweetie, I'm so sorry." He kissed the side of her head, pressed his warm hand into her nape.

"It's okay," she finally said, wiping her tears on his shirt. "I'm fine." She squirmed out of his grasp and put the dinosaur back in the crib, smoothing the sheet with her palm. "Now don't go telling everyone that I'm a mess. No pity shit. You know I hate that."

"Do you want to sleep in the living room?"

"Of course not. I just had a moment of weakness —"

"It's not weakness, Mitti."

"— and I'm happy to be near all these baby things. Aw, Nez, Katy is so cute. Con-

150

gratulations."

He grinned. "I know. It's so different to have a girl; it's really *shireen,*" he said, using the Farsi word for "sweet." He sat on the bed. "Sorry I couldn't make it home for dinner," he added. "It's a brutal commute."

"I can imagine. And the job stinks." She sat next to him.

He shrugged. "It's not what I went to law school for."

"For God's sake, Nezam, quit already. Stop feeling like you owe my father. You don't."

"It's not that simple, Mitti." He squeezed her thigh and smiled, composed as always, even-keeled. "I don't want to talk about it now. I've got to get some sleep." He looked at his watch. "I need to drive back there in about nine hours." His eyes lit up. "Hey, you want to come with me? See what your father's up to these days? We can catch up."

She hesitated.

"Don't worry. There's no chance he'll be there. He hardly visits the sites anymore. Come on. We can hang out. I miss you."

She'd never been good at saying no to him. And the distraction would be good; a brief respite, before the One Year gathering, from this painful reimmersion into all things Anahita. He left with a smile and soon the apartment took on the quality of a slumbering household — heavy, hushed, and lonely. Mitra swallowed an Ambien, changed into her night shirt, and slid under the quilt.

She dreamt a memory: of Nina as a baby, the meningitis scare. Nina's feverish cry — a weak bleating that seared Mitra's heart — the scald of Nina's neck as it rested in the crook of Mitra's arm. She and Ana sharing the vigil, walking the baby through the house, humming Persian and English lullabies until the fever broke. But when Ana turned around, Mitra's memory spun away and the baby in Ana's arms was pasty and lifeless. She gasped and opened her eyes. It wasn't the first time since the accident that she'd had a nightmare like this. How many different ways could the children be killed in her dreams? It was always one of *them,* not Ana. Was this what Mitra would've wanted if given the choice? Ana suffering the death of her own children so that Mitra could still have her? Why did she contemplate such unfair moral dilemmas? Was it a kind of survivor's guilt? She felt the weight of the darkness, the emptiness of the night, and the yearning for the childhood sound of her sister's breathing. Would she ever be able to feel as if she could exist without Ana also existing?

She flung the covers off and left the room. A glass of milk, some television. But in the unlit living room she found Libby pacing with Katy in her arms, the two looking like ghosts of Madonna and Child in the dim amber glow of the city lights. "Can I help?" Mitra whispered.

"Sure," Libby said. "She's asleep, but I've got to pee." She put the warm bundle in Mitra's arms and adjusted her nursing bra.

Katy, all twenty inches of her, fit against Mitra like the proper jigsaw puzzle piece. It had been a long time since she'd held an infant. Nina. Katy's eyes were closed, her lashes like wet feathers. Flakes of dry skin speckled her sparse silky hair, and her lips sucked at an imaginary nipple. Mitra brushed the side of her thumb against Katy's cheek; the softness was electric, a zap of sheer pleasure that made her feel as if her heart would beat clear through her chest. Then Katy's lips trembled, and she issued an exhausted, hoarse wail that sliced through Mitra like a drill. She wanted to pull Katy inside, under her skin, next to her organs, where she could be safe, and saved.

CHAPTER 8

"You look like hell," Nezam said, handing Mitra a Starbucks latte across the console of his SUV.

"Thanks, and I don't mean for the coffee. It's five a.m. where I'm from, you know. You're lucky I'm conscious."

"Take a nap. We have a ways to go."

"I might, if the caffeine doesn't work."

Once they were out of the city and on the thruway, Mitra said, "So, give me some gossip."

Nezam glanced in his sideview mirror and swung into the left lane to pass an Asian woman so low in her seat that she looked at the road from beneath the top of her steering wheel. "Gossip? In the family or at the office?"

"What's the difference?" Mitra said.

Nezam chuckled and finished off his cappuccino.

"Start with your parents," Mitra asked.

"How are they?"

"Doing well. My dad's teaching part-time now — basic physics to undergrads. I don't think he'll ever retire completely; he loves those kids. And my mom's still managing investment portfolios — quietly."

Mitra laughed at *quietly.* Her Auntie Golnaz's clients were mostly Iranian exiles, overproud men who'd been unable to find work that was anywhere near as prestigious as their jobs in Iran. Even those who took jobs — in banks or engineering firms — wound up leaving them; their egos incapable of bearing the diminished status. Twenty years later, these men spent most of their time in front of cable news, letting headlines propel their hopes that the mullahs would fail and their previous lives would be restored. Auntie Golnaz had tapped those very men who wouldn't work, whose wives had swallowed their pride and gotten sales jobs in Neiman Marcus and Madison Avenue boutiques, and offered to help them invest the money they'd managed to get out of Iran before the regime confiscated everything.

"Hard to believe our moms are sisters. Sort of like Ana and me, huh?"

"Nah, I just think my mom had more choices because she went to university, and our grandparents were less strict by then."

"Yeah, lucky her." Mitra pointed out the window. "Wow, some of the foliage up here is already changing color."

"Last October, we brought the twins to a farm near here and picked apples. Your old friend Layla invited us. Remind me to show you the photos. I've never seen the colors so vibrant and varied."

Mitra smiled. "Well, Layla; she can take photos."

"Did you see the ones she took of the renovated ceiling in Grand Central? I can't remember which magazine they're in."

Mitra hadn't. She'd completely forgotten about the renovation that had been going on for five years, a project she once would have dreamed of being a part of, when those dreams had seemed realistic. She felt a pang of regret and anger. If she'd waited one year more before pissing her father off, she would've completed her architecture degree. Everything would have been different. "I'll definitely go see it soon," she said. And she meant it, because she knew that regret could grow into a poison. She'd seen too much of that in the people around her who'd come out of Iran and spent their days and nights so absorbed in their regret that they couldn't do anything but go to parties, even death anniversary parties.

Nezam leaned in to change the radio station, which was playing Elton John's "Candle in the Wind," only to light on LeAnn Rimes singing "How Do I Live Without You." This was why Mitra had taken a hiatus from listening to music altogether. Nezam settled on a jazz station. "Oh," he said, "Pirooz and Melinda had a baby boy a couple of days ago. Almost ten pounds."

"Jeez. Ouch."

"And Rana's pregnant again. The fourth. Like she wasn't already losing her mind."

Mitra yawned. "What you get for marrying an Irish guy."

"Take a nap, Mitti. We still have a ways to go."

"Yeah," she said. "The caffeine's wearing off." She reclined her seat and closed her eyes.

She woke when the motion of the car slowed. Nezam was taking an exit called Marvelous Lake, the name of the company's newest suburban project. Mitra rubbed her eyes; she'd slept deeply but had no idea for how long. They merged onto a two-lane road, recently paved and marked with a sharp yellow line down the middle. It cut through dense woods and reminded her of the Saturday trips her parents used to arrange with the few Iranian immigrant families in the area (before the Revolution) to the Bear Mountain picnic grounds, a caravan of cars, trunks packed with heavy pots of precooked rice and marinated kebab, baskets of fruit, charcoal, and blankets to be used as tablecloths and for playing cards.

"I thought this project was in the suburbs," Mitra said.

"The suburbs," said Nezam, "are wherever people are willing to commute from. In a few years, this place will look like Devon when your parents first bought there."

"Who buys this far from the city?"

"Cops, teachers. They can't afford anything closer. And they want the American Dream for their kids."

Mitra shivered. "So isolated."

"I'm with you," he said. "No way I'm ever moving out. Your father thinks I'm crazy, makes jokes about us living in the 'inner city.' As if Manhattan hasn't changed since the seventies."

"He doesn't have a clue. Honestly, Nez, you need to move on. This job was supposed to be temporary."

About ten years ago, Nezam had quit his job at a multinational law firm to work for her father. It was the late 1980s, and their enormous family, which had fled Iran soon after Khomeini took over in 1979, had finally come to terms with the idea that they weren't going back to Iran anytime soon. Many of them were stuck in other countries, in Istanbul, in Hamburg, in Stockholm, some even in the Emirates. Visas to the US had slowed to a trickle. Not only were Iranians pariahs because of the Hostage Crisis and the mullahs' Death to America bullshit, but once Iraq invaded Iran and a full-blown war broke out, any male family member under the age of thirty-five would have been immediately drafted in Iran. There was no going back, and money was running out. Yusef, basking in this chance to exhibit benevolence, needed a full-time attorney to fill out asylum forms, present the cases, deal with the INS and the courts. Nezam already had his green card because of his law firm job, and Yusef knew how to woo his nephew: Was it fair to abandon the others to some cheap, shitty attorney? Nezam, like Ana, was easy to guilt.

"Don't you miss the law?" she prodded.

"I'm still practicing law, Mitra."

"Right. The company's taxes, contracts, leases, and petty lawsuit threats from towns-people. It's not international law, not intellectual property, or economic sanctions. For chrissakes, you passed the bar at twenty-three. My father's using you, Nezam, and you're letting him."

"I make a decent living."

"Oh, please. It's not about that."

"Mitra, I don't want to talk about this now. Maybe another time, but not now." He pressed hard on the brake. "I need a pit stop. You?"

"Might as well."

He turned in to a two-pump gas station that looked like something out of *The Waltons*, with a faded Fill 'er Up! sign nailed above the door of a weatherworn garage. The bathroom was around the side. "You go first," Mitra said. He smirked but high-tailed it, and for a split second, they were eight years old on summer vacation and his mom was scolding him for not using the toilet before they left.

Back on the road, Nezam said, "Are you sure your dad never brought you up here? He's had this property since the 1960s."

"I'm pretty sure. If he did, I don't remember."

"Back then, the area was a hot summer vacation getaway for city people. He was going to build a hotel on it, but the market went bad, so he just held on to it, and now —" Nezam braked hard again. "Shit, I missed the turnoff."

160

Mitra swallowed a twinge of carsickness as he turned the SUV around and steered them through a barely visible opening in the forest marked by a small cardboard sign planted on a post in the dirt: Marvelous Lake Estates. They bumped along on a narrow, pitted track, the woods surrounding them, dapples of sunlight splashing through leaves and branches onto the hood.

"Shit," Nezam said, stopping the car. Dust kicked up by the tires clouded around them. Ahead, the muscular face of a semi truck wobbled toward them. Nezam put the car in reverse and twisted in his seat.

"What are you doing?" Mitra asked.

"Backing up to the main road. No way that guy's gonna get around me."

"Chicken."

Nezam stopped the car, looked at her. "What?"

"You heard me." She smiled and felt a tightness loosen in her chest. "What's the point of having a four-wheeler if you never go off-road?"

He smiled back and pushed his glasses up on his nose, a nervous gesture. "Are you challenging me, twerp?"

She laughed. "That old word!" She opened the door, stepped out, and gestured to her empty seat. "Climb over, dweeb. You

161

wouldn't want to get your Ferragamos dusty." She went around, opened his door, and gave him a little push.

"You get one scratch on my car, Mitra, and I'll slaughter you," he said.

She took the wheel, feeling its perforated leather, and headed straight for the lumbering semi. Warmth rushed into her fingers. She looked to her right for an opening in the trees, found one, and scanned for obstructions — a boulder, a tree limb, a stump. A berm separated the road from the forest; this, she knew, would scare the shit out of Nezam. "Hang on," she said just before turning the SUV sharply, bouncing it over the berm, and lifting them both off their seats, forcing a frightened "Fuuuuck!" from Nezam. She manipulated the vehicle to align it parallel to the road and brought it to a halt between two tree trunks in the forest mulch. Nezam exhaled.

"What a rush!" Mitra said.

After catching his breath, Nezam said in a barely controlled tremolo, "Happy to accommodate." He looked at her. "Nice to see some color in your cheeks, cousin."

Marvelous Lake Estates had her father's mark all over it. In the first place, the lake was fake, barely deep enough to hide a massive drainage pipe that the town inspector wanted extended beyond the property line to a nearby stream; Nezam was trying to assure the neighboring farmer that the runoff would be so minimal there was no need to worry about it flooding his adjacent corn crop. Mitra was dubious about that, but said nothing. She figured her father didn't give a damn about the adjacent farmer because he expected to buy that land too. In the second place, the "estates" were split-levels, larger than their forebears, but still in an outmoded style that Mitra (and Nezam) felt doomed them to be hard sells.

Blacktop already meandered through the cleared land, and Mitra couldn't help but be reminded of the cemetery. Over a hundred houses were planned. The first five were in the process of being framed; the semi had brought lumber, and the sharp scent of fresh-cut wood filled the morning air.

"You go to your meeting," she said. "I'll just wander around." Nezam was meeting with one of the subcontractors and the town inspector over the water issue.

"I'll be as quick as I can," he said. "And then we can go for lunch."

"No rush."

The high white cement curb that edged

the blacktop lanes took Mitra back thirty years or more to weekends spent with her father at one project or another. When she wasn't riding on his shoulders, reaching up to touch the I beams (*Watch out for esplinters, Mitra*) or tagging behind him past dangling electrical wires (*Never touch; you kill us both*), she would plant her small bum on a curb and rest her chin on her bony knees, waiting impatiently for him to finish with some contractor or other. He always warned her to stay away from the sewer drains that abutted the curbs; they were frightening enough with their iron grates, gaping rectangular mouths, and water-swooshing sounds, but she remembered wanting badly to know how the tunnels below connected.

As she got older, she wandered. Outside, she'd run her hands over the hard raised tread of bulldozer tires and pick at the dried mud that came off in satisfying chunks. She squatted and stirred wet mortar and cement, enjoying the purling sound as much as Anahita enjoyed mixing flour and water for muffins. She shadowed Bob, a black man who'd been the first person her father hired when he came to America; Bob had a face as creased as his old leather tool belt. He taught Mitra the name of all his tools even before she could pronounce them properly. He would test her, stand there while she craned her neck to look up at him as he took each one out for her to name — *Flips swoodwiver, pickask, hamner, stwaight scwoodwiver, pwyers, wench* — and when she got old enough, he'd let her use them if her father wasn't looking. Bob's son, Adam, three years older than Mitra, had shown her how to climb a banister-less staircase without fear: *You gotta imagine the railing's there so's you can grab it and save yourself. Worse thing is to think about it not being there. You'll fall for sure.* Adam, last she heard, had dropped out of high school and moved away. Bob had been diagnosed with cancer when Mitra was in college, but her father didn't mention it until he was near the end in the hospital. Vivian told her that her father had gotten Bob into a clinical trial at Sloan-Kettering, using his contacts and his money, but Bob had passed on anyway.

When she was too big to sit on her father's shoulders, she sometimes held his hand as they toured houses or apartment buildings, and once an office building with ten floors, but she didn't like the constraint of this. Baba's hand was always dry and twitchy, and Mitra always saw something she wanted to inspect closely: the innards of an unex-

165

pected trench, brickwork in a fireplace, pipes like petrified boa constrictors in the walls. In the site trailers were the models under glass, and her fingers itched to touch the little houses, the miniature trees, and the grass that looked more like moss. She wanted to wrap her hand around a building, a King Kong hand, and dip it in the blue watercolor of a stream and imagine rearranging it all in different configurations that she would think about at night before she fell asleep.

On the slope above the "lake" was a charred rectangular area. "The farmhouse," Nezam said, approaching Mitra, his meeting over. "We let the local fire department practice on it."

Mitra's shoulders folded in. "How old was it?"

"Late 1800s. The posts in the basement were tree trunks. The windowpanes were the original glass, wavy."

"The floors?"

"Chestnut."

Mitra sighed and shook her head. Her father had no understanding of restoration, no heart for the past. It was easy for him to destroy it. To him, this was very American. *You make things modern and you make them better.* Ironically, her father's idea of modern was now passé.

"Look here," Mitra said, pointing along the weedy ground. "There must have been an outhouse here before. You can still see the desire line."

"The what?"

"Desire line. The most convenient way to get from one point to another. People find them naturally, without consciously thinking. My father called them donkey paths, like from the old country. He hated them, especially when people made them over the grass between the concrete paths he'd already put in place."

"You mean shortcuts, right?"

She tilted her head. "Not always. Sometimes it's a more beautiful route or a quieter one or maybe what feels like a safer way. Before I renovate a property, the first thing I do is look for the desire lines so I can design the landscaping around them. People know best how they want to get from one place to another."

"That's so sweet."

"Are you mocking me, little cousin?"

"Never," he said, winking.

After cheeseburgers at a local diner, Nezam met with the architect in the site trailer while Mitra strolled the property away from the construction. The racket of crickets in the tall grasses and a light humidity made it feel less like fall and more like summer. Mitra tied her sweater around her waist and dialed Julian's mobile.

"I see you remembered to call me when you got in," he said.

"Sorry. I almost did, but you would've been asleep, and then things here got a little hectic."

"Just wondered if you were in one piece, darling."

"You sound like my mother."

"Great."

"Well, *darling,*" she said, imitating his British accent, "I conked out once I got here. The red-eye was brutal. Again, I'm sorry." If he wanted to argue, she was ready.

He yawned loudly. "No worries as long as you're all right. How's it going over there?"

It always surprised her that he needed little more than an apology to move on. Lately, she'd been wishing he'd stay mad so she could take a defensive posture: *Don't tell me what or what not to do.*

"I wouldn't call it fun," she said. "How about you?"

"Your bed feels a bit large, if you get my meaning. I might stay at my place tonight. I'm on call. Can't remember the last time I slept on that bloody futon."

"I like your futon." She remembered the night they met, both drunk and miserable, she for Ana and the children, he for an eight-month-old he couldn't save from a carbon monoxide coma. Sober, they would not have wound up on that futon staring at each other across a down pillow at 4:00 a.m. Julian didn't agree with this assessment; he thought they would have found each other eventually. He was idealistic and romantic, the kind of guy who might use the word *destiny* if he didn't know it would make Mitra cringe.

"You'll remember to feed the cat, right?"

"Of course."

"And not too many treats. You spoil her."

"Aww, she deserves them, don't you, Jezebel?"

"She slept with you?"

"She did. She spoons better than you do."

"Very funny."

"How's your mum?"

"Older."

"Huh? You're breaking up, couldn't hear."

"She looks a lot older than her years. Hello? Can you hear me?"

"Yeah, but it's not a great connection. Sounds like you're outside."

"I'm in the boonies, visiting one of my

father's housing projects."

"With your father?"

"Of course not. With my cousin."

"The one you like best, I presume. Nezam, right?"

"That's the one. What, have you been memorizing my family tree? You can hardly remember the names of the residents at the trauma center, and they mostly have three-letter Anglo names."

"What? You faded. Are you moving around?"

She sat on a slab of glacial rock and turned so the sun was at her back. "Can you hear me now?"

"Better. What were you saying?"

"Nothing important." She was glad he hadn't heard her snide remark. She worried that he was becoming attached to her family, who knew nothing of him. "Anything new in the last two days?"

"Not much. The mail is mostly junk. A little problem with the refugees, though. How on earth do you get them to stay in the dungeon? A magical Persian phrase you can teach me?"

"What are you talking about?"

"Akram and Salimeh," he said, his syllabic pronunciation all wrong, but cute. "Haven't left me alone since you took off, the mum especially."

"Shit. Like how? In what way?"

"Always sending the girl with a tray of tea in one of those little glasses and a bowl of lump sugar. Brings a fresh one every few hours. Christ, can she blush! And you know I'm not fond of tea."

"I still don't get that. What Brit prefers coffee?"

"Watch out for stereotypes, darling. I keep telling you I'm special."

"That you are. So what else are they doing?"

"When I came home last night, there was a plate of oily orange stew and a mound of rice waiting for me."

"They're cooking in my kitchen?"

"Cleaning too. The mum makes the girl scrub the floors. I found her washing out the half-bath toilet with a rag yesterday. Pretty nasty."

"Julian, you have to tell them to stop."

"You think I haven't? They don't understand me."

"Are you that challenged in mime? Shake your head. Thrust your chin up and click your tongue. Make forbidding hand gestures. Anyway, they understand the word no. Salimeh understands more than that; she's been in ESL for a month now."

"I've done all that. Trust me, they don't want to understand. Besides, they're trying to be nice."

"Julian, don't let them in."

"No can do, M. If they're at the back door, I can't ignore them."

She groaned. He was such a pushover. Part of his charm, but not in this instance. "Well," she said, "if you're not staying there tonight, they'll have the run of the house."

"I thought about that. I'm going to sneak out. I'll get my coffee at the hospital. If I don't go into the kitchen, I can't let them in."

Mitra sighed. "And Jezebel?"

"I'll come by after dark. No big deal. It's just a few days until you come back."

Mitra remembered what her mother had said the day before about the women stealing things. Luckily, she wasn't a jewelry person; Ana had fully compensated for Mitra's lack of interest in gems and precious metals. Mitra's valuables were considerably larger to manage: Persian carpets, some antique furniture and art that Akram, the "mum," would consider cheap. What mattered most was the violation of her space by strangers. Julian, of course, thought of them as her compatriots, simply because they were Iranian. It was the kind of ignorance that made American tourists laugh derisively when a foreigner asked, "Do you know so-and-so? They live in America too." But she forgave him because of what she knew — about his childhood, his family, his aloneness.

"It'll all be fine, M. Don't worry. Focus on your family. When's the party?"

She'd made the mistake of describing the One Year gathering in a way that led him to imagine it as a party, like an Irish wake, she supposed. She let it go not to embarrass him. "Tomorrow," she said. "I'm not looking forward to it."

"I know. Wish I could be there." He said this as if it might have been a possibility, as if his responsibilities had prevented him from going with her. The truth was that she hadn't asked him. She hoped he understood, or rather that he *mis*understood: the One Year wasn't the kind of event you took a date to, certainly not for the purpose of introducing him to your family. She couldn't imagine ever introducing him to her family, even in the best of times. Boyfriends had never been welcome unless they were sanctioned marriage prospects, and though norms had changed for the younger generation since the family had immigrated, she preferred her privacy. And the idea that her father might be rude to or dismissive of Julian, that others may pester him with questions about their relationship and pass judgment was not something she wanted to risk. Julian didn't deserve that.

"Listen, I've got to jump in the shower," he said.

"Okay. Thanks for taking care of Jezebel."

"Of course. Call me after the party. Love you, M."

"Me too," she said quickly, her throat constricting with guilt.

As she walked back to the site trailer, she thought back to that first morning she woke up next to him, that moment when she could have left him as she'd left others after a brief romantic encounter. In her grief and loneliness, she'd been weak about Julian, keeping him in her life for this long, taking what she needed: companionship, sex. They'd become a couple, and she was afraid that he'd begun to imagine a future with her that she couldn't give him. Oh, she'd been aboveboard to a certain extent, making sure he knew she wasn't the "marrying kind," but beyond that she'd said nothing. Yes, she'd selfishly kept Julian for way too long.

MOURNING

In the time of our history when our nations were between wars, a young man lost his life uselessly, taking in his heart a crazy flying bullet during an army training exercise. The boy's mother bore the news first with rage — when there is no war, why must there be games of war? — and then with enviable stoicism. On the first anniversary of her son's death, family and friends came to reminisce and sympathize with her in the customary manner. We have always gathered to mourn our prophets and saints and kings, our matriarchs and daughters and sisters. With each new death, we remember old deaths. At each death anniversary, we weep for all who have been lost. We have laid wreaths and balanced stones; we have keened and beaten our chests; we have swallowed tea after tea after tea, refusing all things sweet to show respect for the Heartbroken. We have acknowledged the weight of their grief while lightening the load of it with memories and jokes and gossip sprinkled with tears salty as blood. No mourner shall endure alone.

And yet, sometimes the Feast of Mourning ends in misery.

The mother who lost her soldier son so long ago hosted her guests flawlessly. But when an old friend of her son's presented her with a pencil drawing of her child's boyhood face, she slid into a catatonic sorrow from which no one could lure her back. That evening, she tried to pull out every hair on her head, and finally, in a frenzy, she set her braid on fire. What remained was her scarred head and her shriveled ears, the lobes soldered to either side of her jaw. She wore the injustice of her son's death on her skin for the world to ponder.

And now, this old story is remembered by the mother who has lost her daughter and grandchildren as she prepares for her own One Year gathering. The story slithers like a snake between her thoughts. Inexplicably. Unwelcome. Certainly not portentous. After all, this is the diaspora. We continue with our traditions, but there is wine, and there is sugar. We binge on sorrow with crystal carafes and silver spoons. Drunkenly, we gorge on grief as if it were a crater of ice cream: Chocolate Chip Anguish, Vanilla Bean Sorrow, Strawberry Despair. But the Feast of Mourning does not end so histrionically. Or so we believe.

CHAPTER 9

Mitra's gabardine slacks, faded from too many washings, looked gray against her inky blouse. The color black, she knew, had an infinite number of shades; she just didn't pay attention to that when it came to her clothes. Worse, she'd brought the wrong shoes: low-heeled pumps that Anahita would have called stewardess shoes. With trousers, they made her feet look like hooves.

"I've forgotten how to dress up," she said, scowling at herself in Libby's full-length mirror.

Libby rolled her eyes. "How can you forget something you never knew?"

"Watch it, girl."

Libby brought a black silk skirt from her closet. "Here. This won't fit around my waist for another year, if ever."

"I'll have to shave my legs if you want me to wear that."

178

"Better get started."

"How about a pair of opaque tights?"

"Don't have any," Libby said, smoothing out the bedspread.

"Liar."

"Sheers will look better."

"Fashion fascist."

"Your sister taught me everything I know. Now hurry up so we can get to your mom's before the guests do."

When Libby, Nezam, and Mitra approached the New Jersey house a half hour before the guests were due to arrive, Mitra had heartburn. It was more than the Tabasco sauce she'd eaten with her eggs; it was the prospect of coming face-to-face with her father. Her cheeks grew hot remembering how he'd hung up on her just three days before. Given the chance, he would snub her again, this time publicly. She wasn't sure she could keep her cool if that happened.

"I'm just going to avoid him," she said when Libby brought it up in the car. "Pretend he's not there."

"You're going to say hello, right?"

"If he says it first."

"Oh, Mitra, that's so childish."

"That's what I am, his child. I'm also my mother's child. The last thing she needs is a

179

confrontation between me and my father."

"Libby," Nezam interrupted. "Leave it alone. It's between them."

Libby huffed. "You Iranians are so weird."

"That we are," said Nezam, winking at her. "But you married us anyway."

She slapped his shoulder and turned back to Mitra. "Did your mom say how many people she was expecting?"

"No one's officially invited to these things. It's all word of mouth, but it's a social production like everything else." Mitra sat forward and pointed to a car parked at the front edge of the rock garden. "Hey, Nez, isn't that your dad?"

Uncle Parviz, dressed in his usual chinos and blazer, was halfway into his trunk. Auntie Golnaz was already halfway up the hill, her tight curls bouncing as she climbed the wide wooden steps carrying a covered platter. Nezam pulled up behind his parents' car and made the horn hiccup. His father straightened and turned, each arm holding a floral arrangement. When his eyes lit on Mitra, he gave her his crackling smile and bid Nezam to take the flowers so he could embrace her, which he did for a long time, petting her head and kissing her forehead, calling her *gol,* which was how he always addressed his girls — she, Anahita, and

Libby — as a flower or a rose. "Your hair is so long, Uncle," Mitra teased. Parviz had more hair than most thirtysomethings, silver and wind-blown, always in need of a trim. He pinched her cheek, then kissed Libby and relieved Nezam of one of the floral arrangements.

The house smelled like basmati, which was Mitra's hunger trigger. Shireen had no doubt prepared a feast, even though at this time of day — late afternoon — she could've gotten away with finger foods. When it came to social occasions, everyone still acted like they were living in the old Iran when there had been plenty of family members and cheap servants to help bring a party together. And it must all seem effortless. Afterward, Shireen would collapse from exhaustion and muscle ache, but pretend (even to herself) that she was fulfilled by every sacrificial moment of it.

Much to Mitra's relief, Yusef was in the garden reading the newspaper. Nezam went out to say hello. In the kitchen, Golnaz had wrapped an apron around her lanky frame and was issuing orders. Mitra knew she wouldn't get the same kind of greeting from her auntie as she had from her uncle, and she didn't mind. Sentimentality was not Golnaz's style, at least not openly. She told

Parviz where to take the flowers and set Libby to work arranging the pastry trays of baghlava and chickpea cookies and profiteroles. To Mitra, she handed a small bowl of green plums sprinkled with salt, a rare favorite snack, and a gesture that would've choked Mitra up if Golnaz hadn't immediately introduced the new maid, Maria, stationed by the sink. The woman smiled when Mitra spoke to her in Spanish. Her son Jorge was opening wine and dispensing ice with a telltale flourish. Mitra turned away and smiled. *Oh dear, Baba, a gay man is serving drinks in your house.*

Golnaz deposited a Carmen Miranda fruit bowl in front of Mitra. "Here, darling, put the finishing touches on this, won't you?" She pointed to a colander of champagne grapes. It had been Ana who'd always arranged the fruit bowl, her fingers daintily handling oranges and apricots and figs. Mitra did the task quickly and went to look for her mother.

In the living room, Shireen was lighting candles. Her forehead showed the lines of concentration that were reserved for pre-party worries. Next to the fireplace, a veiled canvas rested on an easel, like something in an art gallery. "What's that?" Mitra whispered.

Shireen shrugged. "Your father will not tell me. A surprise, he says. He brought it home this morning." She held out several burnt matches for Mitra to discard.

"He's not into surprises," Mitra said. "And art? He wouldn't know a Picasso from a Warhol." She considered lifting the veil to peek; it was one of those Persian tapestry cloths from the Tehran bazaar that her parents used to give to American friends who wouldn't know how cheap and common they were. Fingering it, Mitra said, "Aren't you curious?"

"Too busy to be curious, daughter." Shireen held out the matchbox to Mitra. "Light the pillars on the mantel, please. I must check the oven." Her eyes rested on the hidden painting. She continued in English. "I do not have a good feeling about this thing. Last time your father gave me surprise, it was a trip for African safari."

Mitra laughed. "You're kidding."

"She's not kidding," said Vivian, appearing in the entryway. "I researched and booked it, knowing full well she wouldn't go."

Mitra blew out her match and went to embrace Vivian, who pecked her cheek and quietly said, "Welcome home."

"When was this safari?" Mitra asked.

183

"Oh, years ago," said Shireen as they followed her back to the kitchen. "I made him go with Uncle Jafar. That was what he wanted anyway."

Shireen peered into the oven, looked at her watch, and announced that she was going upstairs to get ready. She would tend to the dark shadows under her eyes with makeup and reconstruct her bun. She would change out of her dark clothing into darker clothing.

When the doorbell began ringing, Mitra panicked a little. Her father, she knew, would play Master Greeter for a while. She sat at the kitchen table and ate her salted plums. Once the house filled with guests, it would be easier to mingle without getting too close to him. It was an art and a craft, this mutual evasion: diffuse to the public, concentrated between the two of them like an invisible current. Finally, she wiped her hands, stood, and took a deep breath. She pushed against the swinging door and was immediately beckoned by Golnaz from the living room. "Come, your aunties are here."

Mitra relaxed a bit. If there was anything she missed about home, it was these women she'd called aunties for as long as she could remember. Squeezed onto the long sofa, they sat stiff in their nylons and suit jackets, already quietly engaged in a collective inspection of and commentary on the guests. As Mitra bent over and kissed each one of them, they caressed parts of her body and offered opinions: *Your hair is so long; you've gained a little weight; you're skinnier than ever.* They each praised her for being a good daughter, as if none of them had phoned her to insist that she come to the gathering for Shireen's sake. At least they no longer had the audacity to raise the subject of her unmarried status — she was way too old now. In the past it had often been Anahita who came to her rescue in that subtle way she had of manipulating a subject, even if it meant causing a distraction — dropping a glass, bursting out with some strange gossip, begging for advice on a difficult personal matter. Yes, the aunties were prying and preachy, but they were also hilarious. They rarely agreed on anything and thus reveled in heated disagreements and snide remarks about everything from the cost of designer handbags to the accomplishments of their grandchildren. Nezam called them The Golden Girls after the sitcom. Mitra especially enjoyed it when they competed over the severity of their physical ailments: backaches, bunions, hot flashes, and — always — constipation. For all their faults, Mitra loved them. In times of crisis, they acted in complete solidarity and became as organized as a government, as when they took over the packing up of Anahita's house once Bijan decided he would be moving to London. Their devotion was unquestionable, and it gave her the confidence to make it through the next few hours.

She made her way from family room to living room to dining room, air-kissing relatives and friends, shaking hands with the few non-Iranians, smiling tightly at fatuous words of condolence and gazes of pity. In her peripheral vision, she was wary of her father's location and moved to avoid him. When she couldn't see him, she sensed his nearness, heard a snippet of his voice, caught a whiff of his cologne. Every once in a while, Uncle Parviz would show up with a calming hand on her shoulder or a small plate of something delicious for her to pick at. When she found herself next to an armchair where her Uncle Jafar sat holding a cane between his legs, she leaned over and said her name in his ear so he would know who she was, then kissed his stubbly cheek.

"A happy welcome," he said dryly, using the Farsi phrase for anyone who has arrived from a long trip.

He'd grown significantly older, frail and feeble. She felt sorry for him, sightless now and with that good-for-nothing son, his daughters all having moved to LA. "Are you growing a beard, Uncle?" she asked, making her voice light to contrast with his.

He thrust up his chin. "My son was too lazy to shave me."

"But, Baba," said Kareem, sneaking up from behind, "you're in fashion. The women love that look." He placed a glass of amber liquid in his father's hand, then raised his own glass to Mitra and actually winked. "Right, Mitra?"

"Sure," she said. "If you're into radical Islamists." She narrowed her eyes. "Excuse me, my mom needs me in the dining room."

She wove past Yusef's "surprise easel" to the credenza and poured herself a Merlot, which felt warm in her throat but burned in her chest. Kareem always made her feel this way. She watched him do his sickly-sweet thing with the other guests: smiling like a chimp, using a shy, childlike voice to greet people, kissing too much, hugging too long, and showering everyone with disingenuous compliments. Why didn't anyone else see how false he was? She slipped out the side door for a cigarette and inhaled deeply. All these years, Kareem had pretended that the incident of Mitra pulling him off Anahita hadn't happened. She was content to let him wonder and worry whether she'd told or would tell anyone. But on the rare occasion when she came face-to-face with him, she was struck by how small this punishment was, how little satisfaction she got from it. He seemed to think she'd never tell. And wasn't that true? No one would ever confront him; it was too "unpleasant," and of course, "it happened so long ago." She threw her cigarette down and stomped on it. At least there was some poetic justice, she thought: after years of obsessively preening his long, wavy hair, Kareem was now mostly bald, though he still pulled what was left into a dorky thin ponytail. She chuckled and picked up her butt to throw in the trash can.

When the abundant buffet dinner was served, the gathering took on the character of a hushed mob scene, the redolence of saffron and basmati spurring a barely suppressed lust for the food. A line formed, plates were loaded, small groups stood or sat while they ate, and conversation was spare until all were sated, though there were pleasurable moans and kudos to Shireen. Mitra ate in the kitchen with Nezam and Libby. Her previous hunger had been vanquished by anxiety, and her taste buds refused to react normally to her mother's food, which felt disloyal. Then she reminded herself why she was here.

Uncle Parviz and Nezam helped Jorge gather the dirty dishes for Maria in the kitchen, while Golnaz helped Shireen get the tea and coffee going. The desserts came out, and predictably, the guests rearranged themselves by gender: the men out on the patio and the women at the dining room table. This was subliminal, Mitra knew, but there were outliers. When she was a child, she got used to lazing next to her father while the men talked about business and politics; she'd squish into his chair, let his arm wrap around her, and rest her head on his chest. Absent-mindedly, she'd play with his expandable watch, sometimes catching his arm hairs and causing him to flinch and pinch her cheek in mock exasperation. But then she was older and he was suddenly asking her to *pazeerayi,* which was nothing more than performing the duties of a cocktail waitress, offering platters of snacks to each of the guests, sometimes preparing plates of fruit, even going so far as to peel small cucumbers and sprinkle them with salt. If she tried to speak in response to a topic that was being discussed, he interrupted to send her off for more ice or gestured for her to clear plates and wadded-up napkins. She dealt with this no more than a handful of times before quitting the patio altogether. Never mind, she thought. The men were poseurs, proffering opinions on everything but rarely listening to one another. It was like watching a bunch of ham actors read from different scripts. No wonder Uncle Parviz always hung out with the women.

Mitra went into the family room, where a group of twentysomethings sat watching *Friends,* volume on low. One of her Ali cousins was completely engrossed in a Game Boy. "Hey, aren't you a little old for that?" Mitra asked. He didn't look up. "I bought it for my kid — it's the new one with the color screen — but I can't separate myself from it long enough to give it to him." It was always strange and oddly comforting that Mitra could pop into a family gathering and be treated as if she'd never left, especially since so much of her identity was *about* the fact that she'd left. These cousins, the children of cousins, and the cousins of cousins — she knew very little about them. They picked at the bowls of nuts and fruit on the table, threw choice insults at one another, rested a head on a shoulder, tickled someone's neck, laughed collectively at the sitcom. The family grew bigger and bigger, Mitra thought, like an aspen grove proliferating from a single tree. Or dividing and multiplying like an amoeba. Except for the three who'd been subtracted.

She headed for the powder room and sat on the closed toilet seat. Another half hour, she figured, until the guests would begin lining up to say goodbye. In her parents' culture, saying goodbye was as important as saying hello. Words and gestures of gratitude from guest and host (for being invited/for attending) were taken seriously for their expanse and uniqueness. That meant over-the-top compliments for the food, the decor, the graciousness, the outfits, even the shine of the floor. It meant Mitra would have to stand near her father at the front door and pretend that they were still a family. Not doing so would be disrespectful and embarrassing. She couldn't do that to her mother. She ran a cloth under cold water, dabbed her face, and went back into the fray.

Jorge was circulating a tray of cardamom tea, but before Mitra could take a glass, Yusef called everyone into the living room. Mitra stepped back to allow people by. She saw Uncle Parviz give up his seat on one of the sofas to Auntie Marzieh, who had once bought Anahita and Mitra a Suzy Homemaker kitchen set for Christmas. The room wasn't large enough to hold everyone, and guests spilled into the dining room and the hallway, jockeying for a view as Yusef stepped to the easel and gestured for Shireen to come stand next to him. She looked so small, like a shy child, and Mitra felt yet another stab of guilt for telling her about Kareem and Ana. Reckless.

Shushes filtered through the crowd, and finally, Yusef began. "I will speak in English for the benefit of our good American friends who have honored us with their presence." He nodded to several people. "As you know, this is a sad day of many sad days my family has endured since the death of our precious Anahita and our beautiful grandchildren, Nikku and Nina." Not one wet flicker appeared in his eyes, nor did his voice falter. He was a good orator, Mitra thought, charming to women and inspiring to men, handsome with his white head of hair and salt-and-pepper mustache. He put his arm around Shireen's shoulder, and she stiffened. They had never been a physically demonstrative couple; in fact, Mitra had never seen them kiss or embrace or even hold hands. At the funeral, Mitra and

Auntie Golnaz had held Shireen on either side while Yusef stood alone. The look on his face was sheer fury; no one would go near him. Now he looked as if . . . as if he was gloating. Mitra was suddenly anxious, and she saw that Shireen, her fake smile on, was too. Mitra found herself backing up carefully to put more people between her and her parents.

Yusef continued. "I'm sure all of you are wondering what could be behind this veil." He turned toward the easel, taking Shireen awkwardly with him. "Even my wife does not know. It is a painting, of course, as you may have guessed. A portrait, actually, done by a master artist it took me a long time to discover. The idea to have it produced came to me in a dream, and in my culture we are taught to pay attention to our dreams because the departed come to us in them."

A dream? Mitra felt slightly nauseated. Her father didn't believe in that kind of stuff. He prided himself on being a man of reason, certainly not disposed to superstitions or ghosts. She supposed the death of a child and two grandchildren could change a person's beliefs, but she didn't trust it in his case.

"So, without further delay, I reveal" — *re-*

wheel — "a gift for my wife and a solace to me."

He whipped the cloth off like a magician. Mitra heard her own short gasp, which was thankfully drowned out by oohs and aahs and a smattering of applause. To most everyone else, what her father had unveiled was a stunning portrait of Anahita and the children. The painter had been very good. Not only had he caught their likenesses perfectly, he'd enhanced every color, including skin tone (the kids' slightly browner than Ana's) and hair color (Nina's streaked lighter from the summer sun). Ana stood behind the children, her arms falling over their shoulders, her hands over their hearts. Even those special hands, so delicate that Mitra's childhood self had crushed them easily in her own like tissue paper, were precisely rendered. Actually, Ana looked more radiant than she ever had in real life, more beautiful, even a little thinner. Her hair had no frizz to it, just soft curls framing her flushed face like a halo. And her Persian eyes — long and tilted up as if a hidden tendon tugged at each outside corner — were as sweet and giving as they had been in life. It was hard to believe that her sister hadn't been alive to pose for this painting, but Mitra knew it had been created from a photograph — an *altered* photograph, because Mitra had been expunged from it.

This was what had made her gasp, had made Shireen continue to exhibit her fake smile, and had given her father — who was looking straight at Mitra for the first time in years — his gloating demeanor. More than anything, she wanted to scream. But she wouldn't give him the satisfaction of knowing that he'd succeeded with one of his oblique punishments. No one else would know; they hadn't seen the photograph. Even if they had, they might consider Yusef's action justifiable — a form of protection, of guarding against the evil eye. Bad luck, certainly, to put the living sister side by side with the dead one. She closed her eyes briefly, opened them to look past him, as if he'd become invisible to her. Her heart thumped in her chest, pulse beat in her ears, and she willed the world of people to blur and hush. The painting, however, was crystal clear, and slowly, without realizing she had moved, Mitra was in front of it.

She remembered the day Bijan took that photograph, nearly two years ago in the driveway of his and Ana's house. One arm draped over Nina's shoulder, she'd felt the sun on the top of her head and smelled the strawberry shampoo in Nina's hair. As Bijan was about to snap the picture, he wrinkled his nose and asked if someone had farted. The kids cracked up, and their belly laughter infected Ana and Mitra. Nina had leaned back against Mitra's leg, and Mitra felt her tiny heart beating through her palm. At the last second, she stretched her other arm around Ana's waist and drew her in. Surprised, Ana turned her face to Mitra quizzically, then gratefully, and Mitra made a vow to herself that she would hug her sister more often.

It was uncanny, the expression on Anahita's face. Mitra had witnessed that bold look only twice in her sister's life: when the crazy maid named Jannat asserted that their father preferred her over their mother, and the time Nikku's teacher accused him of cheating on a test. All Anahita said in both cases was simply the word *no,* but her unyielding expression harpooned each accuser and shut them up immediately. It was an expression that came mostly from her eyes, a combination of intelligence and rare certitude that gave off an aura of prophesy, as if to argue with her would've been like arguing with a soothsayer and suffering the consequences on Judgment Day.

Mitra caught her breath. The painter had

to have known her.

She teetered slightly. A firm hand steadied her, and she was grateful until she saw that it was Kareem's. "You okay?" he smirked. She wrenched her arm away and felt the mark of his sweaty grasp. The cacophony of guests gathering their things and beginning to say their goodbyes cracked open and Mitra felt faint. She heard her name, close, and a familiar hand, Nezam's hand, wrap around her waist and lead her to the kitchen and out the side door. Mitra gulped air so she wouldn't vomit. Libby joined them, holding Mitra's handbag, tears on her cheeks. Nezam said, "We're leaving." And they lurched down the driveway to the car.

CHAPTER 10

"Who painted it, Mom?"

"Ach, Mitra-joon. I'm so sorry for what your father did. Are you all right?"

"I'm fine, though I didn't get to sleep until nearly dawn. I'm sorry I couldn't stay to help you clean up."

"It doesn't matter, my daughter."

"Who painted it, Mom?"

"Can you believe he took it to the framing gallery where you and Ana used to take art classes?"

"That old place is still there?"

"It seems so."

"But the old witch who owned it died a while ago."

"Mrs. Gold-e-blatt."

"That's right. She was awful, smelled like mothballs and turpentine, wore those ortho-pedic shoes. When she bent over, the rolled-down tops of her stockings showed."

Shireen was laughing. "Mitra, you remember silly details. Anahita loved that woman."

Of course she had. The pasty-faced German woman bestowed approval on Ana's artistic talent from the get-go. On Mitra, she'd inflicted scorn. This, after administering an evaluative task — to draw a tree. Ana's tree was surrounded by a green carpet of grass and possessed leaves of varying colors against a blue sky, with a bright yellow half orb of a sun perched in the top left corner of her paper. Mitra's tree was — in answer to Goldblatt's "Vat iz dis?" — a Winter Tree: drawn in charcoal, the trunk a totem pole of bumpy bark sprouting branches as crooked as lightning streaks, a lone crow near the top. Realistic. Goldblatt said she'd be happy to teach art to the younger fräulein, but not to the older. Ana blinked back tears of guilt for outdoing her sister, which made Mitra punch her arm. She was thrilled that Goldblatt didn't want her in her musty basement classroom. She took her drawing home and added to it a front-gabled tree house with a dangling rope ladder.

"Anyway," Shireen said, "your father told me it is a relative of Gold-e-blatt who is operating the shop, and that he met Anahita a few times when she went to have things framed. He has a good memory, I think. He painted her so well."

Mitra's stomach suddenly hurt and her chest bloomed with heat. *The painter.*

"Mitra-joon, are you still there?"

"Yes, I'm here."

"Please do not be upset about the painting. Your father is an emotional man; he cannot help himself. I apologize for him."

"Listen, Mom, I've got to go. I'll call you later, okay?"

Mitra hung up, waited a second, then called down to Libby's garage for her rental.

On the sidewalk in Devon, Mitra swallowed an anxious queasiness. She'd become soft since Ana died. She used to wake up every morning, figure out what she feared doing most, and set out to tackle it. The idea of a challenge was what kept her moving forward; it was something she'd learned in childhood from her father. But in the past year, she'd stopped working on her projects, put off phone calls and emails, quit her gym membership, and avoided her small group of neighborhood friends. Most atypical of all, she was in what would seem to anyone a committed romantic relationship, and she'd opened her home to a pair of refugees, compromising her independence and her privacy, the things she valued most.

As she approached the corner shop, she realized that she'd spent the last year lamenting the fact that she'd never know more about the shocking secret her sister revealed the weekend before she died. Now, here was the possibility that she might learn something, as if her sister wasn't entirely gone from her.

Goldblatt's Art and Frame Shop. The old peeling script etched into the storefront glass had been refreshed in gold. The narrow entrance door, set in from the façade, had the same divided-light panes, but the wood was freshly stained and the glass new. In the front window, an easel like the one her father had displayed at the One Year stood on a floor of rippling sumptuous fabric; it held a portrait, spotlit from above, of a bespectacled boy and his golden retriever.

This was not the old store with its shopworn artwork and afterschool basement classes. It was a neoquaint upscale boutique/gallery for wealthy baby boomers who had Wall Street and Silicon Alley jobs, suburbanites with urban tastes.

The bell tinkled as Mitra opened the door, bringing back the memory of coming to the shop with Shireen to drop off or pick up artwork Yusef wanted framed. The left wall had been covered (as it was now) in frame samples, vertical rows of boomerangs that Shireen took forever to contemplate and choose from. She always opted for something ornate, clearly much grander than what it was meant to hold. Mitra suddenly remembered how intense her preteen annoyance had been for every aspect of her mother's being, from Shireen's rolling *r*'s and dropped articles to the flabbiness of her late-in-the-day bun as she inclined her neck to compare the samples on the wall. And Goldblatt, her protuberant belly suspended like a shelf above skinny long legs, would always suggest something different from what Shireen had chosen. Mitra understood condescension, and it made her furious at the both of them, at Goldblatt's *Might I suggest a more appropriate style, Mrs. Jahani?* and at Shireen's capitulation to it. Her mother was a mouse with everyone, right down to the Esso owner who later proved to be adding a fee to her credit card each time he filled her tank; unbelievably, after being informed of this by a livid Yusef, she drove to the opposite end of town to get her gas rather than chance the owner seeing her across the street at the Mobil station — so as not to embarrass *him.* It never occurred to her that she didn't deserve to be taken advantage of. Even back then, Mitra had wondered how, with a mother so blatantly submissive and apologetic, she'd ended up the opposite and Ana more or less the same.

Mitra looked away from the frame sample wall. Everything else about the shop was different.

The wood floor was glossy with polyurethane, the walls faux-painted in a textured beige-gold wash. In place of the hulking butcher block island that had held Goldblatt's wooden money box, a collection of standing file folders, scissors hanging by a frayed ribbon, and rectangles of matting paper, there was a round table with a flower arrangement on it, flanked by two wing chairs upholstered in an understated off-white fabric. The remaining three walls were covered from floor to ceiling with framed portraits, mostly of children. Clearly, they'd all been painted by the same artist — beautifully done, the eyes of each child capturing a lively soul or a hidden mischief, eyes that were brilliant with secrets and desires, like the portrait of Anahita and the children.

In the old days, Goldblatt had displayed imposing oil paintings, their prices written on tiny labels Scotch-taped to the wall beneath them. The numbers were written in elaborate penmanship, the sevens with a line through the middle, the way Mitra's parents wrote their numbers. Mitra hadn't liked the paintings, dreary scapes of spired old European towns under gray skies, portraits of stiff men with red-rimmed eyes and ladies with sharp noses and thin lips, like Goldblatt herself.

"Be right with you," said a male voice from beyond the door in the back. Mitra's throat went dry. *I'm about to meet my sister's lover.* She had an urge to bolt, as if she were about to commit a sin. She heard the squeak of an office chair, and then he was walking toward her.

"Good afternoon, Madame. Can I help you with something?"

Well, this can't be him, Mitra thought, relieved. A man in his sixties, wavy silver hair combed back from a tanned face, dark eyebrows, chiseled cheekbones, attractive lines that came from experience and the outdoors. She relaxed. "I'm just browsing, thank you."

"Of course," he said, smiling. "Feel free. Take your time." His teeth were white and straight, probably implants or veneers. Mitra placed his accent. She'd developed a knack for that, hiring laborers over the years. He was an Arab.

A telephone rang. "Excuse me for a moment," he said, turning and walking to a Baroque desk in the far corner. He stood with his back to her and spoke into the receiver quietly . . . in Hebrew. Intrigued, she inspected him further: about six feet tall, wearing a black turtleneck tucked into ironed khaki trousers, a belt that showed off a flat stomach, and black thin-soled loafers. As he hung up, she caught the glint of a thick gold wedding band.

Mitra pretended to inspect the portraits on the wall, making her way toward the basement door and straining to hear for the presence of someone else. Would she have to come back to the shop over and over until the painter showed his face? Maybe he painted elsewhere. Of course, he must. She stood before a portrait depicting a young boy wearing an orange-and-black-checkered kaffiyeh.

"It is painted from the photo of a Palestinian boy," the older man said from close behind her. "That is his father's headdress." He chuckled. "See how boastful he is, wearing it?"

Indeed, the boy's chest was puffed out, his chin lifted, but his suppressed smile made him irresistibly cute.

"This was painted from a photograph?"

she asked, stepping back so they were side by side.

"Yes." He extended his arm to encompass the whole shop. "All of these portraits are painted from photographs, sometimes very poor photographs, even black and whites."

"How interesting."

"I think so."

"How difficult."

"Occasionally."

"I'd love to meet the artist."

He threw back his head and laughed, then turned to her and bowed. "At your service, Madame."

"Oh."

He peered at her, still smiling. "I am sorry. You are disappointed."

"What? No! Of course not! Just surprised. I . . . I always picture artists holed up in garrets, hunched in front of their easels."

"Yes, yes." He touched his jaw. "With unshaven faces and haunted eyes."

She forced a smile and exhaled. "Exactly."

"Well, in my case, the studio is downstairs, and I'm not fond of myself with a beard. I'm usually down there, but the saleswoman is ill today."

"Your . . . your portraits are beautiful." Her mouth was so dry she could hear her tongue unsticking from her palate.

"Thank you, Madame. Are you interested? I can ship to any location in the world."

"I . . . I . . ." she stumbled. "I'd like to look a little longer." And she managed to turn toward another portrait. Her voice sounded stiff and far away.

"By all means. Take as long as you like."

She felt him drift away and tried hard to collect herself and rearrange her thoughts. Suddenly it seemed obvious that Anahita would have been attracted to an older man — it was Mitra's own tastes that had influenced her expectations, and Ana was always her opposite. Mitra also hadn't expected him to be married, but that was her rule too. Biting the inside of her cheek, she approached the desk, where the man was leafing through some papers. He looked up. "Actually," she said, "I grew up in this town. I remember the woman who used to own this shop."

"She was my wife's aunt," he said.

"Well, it's really different from the way I remember it. My sister used to take art lessons in the basement."

His demeanor suddenly changed. He frowned, staring into Mitra's face as if to look under her skin. The silence was awkward. Finally, he said, "You are Mitra."

He pronounced it the Persian way, as if

he'd known her all her life, as if Anahita had told him everything about her. And of course she had. Tears welled up in Mitra's eyes and she fought them in vain. He came around the desk, guided her to one of the two customer chairs, and placed a box of tissues in her lap. She blinked and blinked, but the tears kept rising up. He walked to the front door, bolted it, flipped the Open sign to Closed, lowered the shade, and shut off the overhead lights. A lamp on the desk cast a warm gold tint.

He sat in the other customer chair and leaned toward Mitra, arms on his thighs. She wiped her eyes and nose. "When you first came in," he said quietly, "I felt I had met you. But it is the photograph I recognize you from."

She nodded. Thankfully, the tears had stopped. "The photograph you used to *not* paint me."

"Yes," he said with a sigh of regret. "It was your father's wish."

"I know."

"It was not right of him to do that."

Mitra raised her chin. "It doesn't matter."

"No, it doesn't. I used to tell Ana the same thing. I also had a difficult father. Some people cannot abandon their misery."

Mitra studied him. His face was drawn,

his mouth pulled down on either end. "Is that how you justify their behavior?"

"No, it is how I keep from hating them. Hate takes too much energy."

She looked away, rested an elbow on the arm of the chair. "This is too weird. I don't even know your name."

"Aden," he said.

"She wouldn't tell me anything about you."

"She didn't want you to feel complicit."

"But she told you about me," she said, hating herself for sounding jealous.

"Yes. To know her, I had to know about you."

Though no one had ever said this and Mitra didn't remember ever thinking it, she was stunned by its truth, not only for Ana, but for herself.

He stood up. "I'll get us some tea," he said. "It is a Persian blend; I brew it in the back."

Mitra was about to say that she wasn't here for a fucking social visit, but her sudden craving for a tea fix kept her silent. He came back with a tray holding two delicate glasses of dark tea and a dessert plate of Milano Mints, which Mitra loathed but Ana had loved. Mitra imagined Aden serving tea to all his best customers, certainly to her father, who would have appreciated an Old World *bazaari* touch. She shivered at the notion that she was probably sitting exactly where her father had sat to order the portrait. And then it dawned on her that Anahita had managed — from the grave — to humiliate their father in the most inconspicuous way, and this made her want to laugh. How utterly devastated her father would be if he knew he'd negotiated with his virtuous daughter's lover.

As Aden carefully placed the tea and cookies on the desk, Mitra wondered how she would cut through the false congeniality and taciturn formality that stood for good etiquette in both their cultures. *If he thinks I'm as malleable as my sister, he's in for a surprise.* If they couldn't get beyond the social veneer, Mitra would leave here with nothing, though she didn't have a clear idea of what the something she sought was. She noticed how his silver hair fell like bird feathers over the back of his shirt collar. He hiked his trouser legs up before sitting back in the chair, a thing only men from an older generation did. She admitted again that he was handsome, but what had Ana seen in him to make her risk everything?

Aden sipped his tea noisily, and so did Mitra, as if they were competing. She wrapped her hand around the hot glass, rested it in her lap, and steeled herself. "You saw my sister the day she died."

"I did." He looked away, not to avoid her gaze, it seemed, but to calm himself. "She left here to pick up the children. It was raining. Thunderstorms were in the forecast. I told her to drive carefully." His voice was choked. "I didn't know about the accident until the next day. Marjorie — my saleswoman — showed me the article in the local newspaper."

"Your saleswoman knew about your affair?" Mitra couldn't keep the disgust out of her voice.

"Of course not," he said, his eyes flaring. "She showed me the article because it was a terrible tragedy in the town. A young mother and her two children. The car so mangled. Later, I burned the paper."

That's it? You burned the fucking paper? How dramatic. Mitra bit her cheek again, hoping for the taste of salty blood. She swigged the rest of her tea and let her eyes drift to the ring on his left hand. "Did you love my sister?"

"Very much."

"Should I believe you?"

"That's your choice," he said, holding her gaze.

Olga used to say that a liar could never hold her gaze. Mitra wanted to believe him, and yet she wanted him to persuade her, tell her all the reasons he'd loved Anahita. Every detail.

He said, "I will tell you anything you want to know."

How accommodating. His words swung Mitra's mood, and she reminded herself why she was here. This man was not her friend; he was the man who'd seduced her sister into betraying her husband, her children, and yes, Mitra too. She was not here to listen to the romantic story of their relationship; she was here to find the truth. Without hesitation now, she blurted, "Do you feel any responsibility for my sister's death?"

Aden paled. "What?"

"I spoke to her while she was in the car that day. She was distraught about your relationship. It was tearing her apart."

His face turned hard as sculpture. "Perhaps that is how you read it. If she seemed distraught, I believe it was because you had learned about . . . us."

Mitra struggled to stay seated and keep from raising her voice. "Oh, so you're saying *I'm* the one who's responsible? It was because of *me* that she was upset and

212

distracted, not because she was cheating on her husband?"

He flinched, and she readied herself for his retort. His knuckles were white on the arms of the chair, but he looked away, toward the far end of the shop. He took a tight breath through his nose, then looked back at her and exhaled. "I know this game," he said softly. "I played it myself."

She was confused but dared not show it. She kept his gaze and said nothing.

"I wracked my brain for what transpired between Ana and me before she left here. Did we argue? No. Could I have said something that hurt her? On the contrary, we talked about how your reaction to our affair pained her, how she wished she'd lied to you, but then she decided she was relieved that you finally knew, and hopeful that you would eventually understand and accept. I even asked her if she wished that we not see one another for a time, and she said of course not, one thing had nothing to do with the other. She said, I know my sister, she needs time for it to sink in. She was smiling when she walked out the door."

Mitra wanted to run, but her body was frozen.

"You know," he continued, "I found the boy who was driving the van that struck

213

Ana's car. A kid, not more than twenty-two or so. He'd been working only a week for the phone company. It was terrible of me to seek him out, to lie that I was a psychologist from the state sent to check on his mental health after such a tragedy. Yes, I'd read the news reports describing the accident. I'd even seen the police report because I have a friend in the department. But it wasn't enough. You see, Mitra, I had to try to absolve myself too.

"I told the boy he should describe what he remembered of the accident. I said that telling could be a form of healing. This may or may not be true, but at the time I didn't care what pain I caused. In my eyes, he was Ana's murderer. I wanted to be certain of it.

"I knew his guilt was stronger than mine. Only a psychopath would feel otherwise. One look at his haunted face and I could see that his life was ruined, but I had no pity, not then. We sat in his parents' over-heated living room on furniture protected by plastic covers. Instant coffee and pound cake sat untouched. I'm ashamed to say that I interrogated him calmly and relentlessly. Every detail, from the moment he climbed into the van for his shift to the moment the paramedics stopped him from trying to revive Nikku in the grass on the side of the highway. When the tears rolled down his cheeks, I gave him a packet of tissues. When he couldn't catch his breath, I laid my hand on his shoulder. As if I cared. As if I could vanquish from my imagination the desire to wrap my hands around his neck."

Mitra's peripheral vision collapsed, and Aden's face seemed disembodied. His throaty voice competed with a ringing in her ears. He sighed. "In the end, I discovered nothing helpful. The van skidded or hydroplaned into Anahita. It was the rain or the oil on the road or the nearly bald tires or a bolt of lightning that momentarily blinded the boy. He tried to regain control; he did the right things. It all happened so fast that Ana had no time to react. She was a careful driver, Mitra, especially when the kids were in the car. Still, the boy would never forgive himself. He too yearned to know the why of it, but that will remain a mystery, like so many things. All we can do is grieve and survive for those who remain. It's the human story. Random. An accident, Mitra. Neither you nor I are to blame."

She felt disagreeably near to him, felt the heat of his skin radiating. She hadn't synthesized the logic of his words yet; the scene of the crash was around her and inside her head. He stood and left the room, as if to give her privacy. She hadn't felt so hot with grief since the funeral.

He returned with a bottle of brandy, took her empty tea glass, and poured an inch of the liquid into it. Her fingers trembled as she took it. She sipped and shuddered. He sat down across from her again, his face awash with pity. And that — that expression — turned her insides. *How dare he?* Did he think his heartrending little story would convince her that the two of them were on par where Anahita was concerned? Yes, he obviously had cared for her sister. Yes, she wanted very much to believe that the deaths had been a random accident, pure and simple. But to be forced into such intimacy with a man she didn't know, the man who'd seduced her sister?

Through clenched teeth, she said, "Tell me, Aden, how did you do it? How did you manage to get her to fall for you? She was crazy about her husband."

He stiffened almost imperceptibly; he was irritated. Good, Mitra thought. "I'm afraid that isn't true," he said.

"Oh, really? That's what you convinced yourself of, that she didn't love Bijan? Well, I *know* she did, I *witnessed* it."

Now he looked ready to slap her. "There

were things she didn't tell you. Things from long ago."

"I doubt it. I knew everything about my sister." Mitra paused. "If you're implying that Bijan treated her badly, I won't believe it. He was the best thing that ever happened to her."

"When she married him, yes he was. You and he saved her. But not in the way you think." Aden suddenly looked doleful, as if he regretted every word as he spoke it. "Your cousin," he said quietly. "The one who . . . wanted her."

She shivered. "What are you talking about?" she demanded in a hoarse, accusatory tone.

"I know you saved her from him. You told her no one should touch her that way. You said all the right things. But you were a child yourself then. You didn't have the power to prevent him from continuing. That one time, you stopped him. She never forgot that. But he was persistent. All molesters are. He simply found more wily and secretive ways. And Ana, well, we both know she was easily manipulated. Already he'd made her feel complicit."

Mitra couldn't speak. Her anger was gone. She didn't know what she felt. She didn't even know how to think about what she felt.

217

Aden went on. "I'm sorry to tell you. Ana never wanted you to know, but I think it's only fair now, so you can understand who she was, why she led the life she did."

"But I *don't* understand!" Mitra nearly screeched. "How long? How long . . . did he . . . did this go on?"

Aden sighed again. "Until she met Bijan."

Mitra stared at her lap, thoughts swirling, and swigged the rest of her brandy. "Wait," she said, as if to herself. "Ana didn't meet Bijan until she was seventeen. That was five years after I discovered Kareem molesting her in the basement!" She looked at Aden. "Are you saying that he molested her for five more years?" She waited, held her breath.

"Mitra, he'd been molesting her for some time before you discovered them. In total, it was eight years. Until she married Bijan. Until you made it possible for her to marry Bijan."

Rage stuck in her throat, pulsed through her hands, which suddenly felt wet. She looked into her lap. Crimson seeped through her fingers. She'd shattered the tea glass.

Aden gasped and looked around for something to catch the dripping blood. Mitra kept staring at her lap, as if watching a violent episode in a film. Then Aden was pulling his shirt over his head, bunching it up, and sliding it under her hands. He began picking out the fine shards of glass from her palms and dropping them into a wastebasket under the desk.

"Shit," Mitra said.

"Don't move," he ordered. "I'm getting the larger pieces first, but we must go to the sink downstairs. The light is better, and I have disinfectant."

She could smell his hair. Herbal Essence. The shampoo she and Ana used when they were teenagers. His bare shoulders had a smooth, olive tone, with fine dark hairs curling up from them, burnished in the light. Had Ana liked that? Bijan was hairy too. How bizarre this was. Her sister's lover, shirtless, bending over her, ministering to her like a nurse.

He shepherded her to the rickety staircase that led to the art room, holding the bloody shirt around her hand as they descended. The handwritten *School* sign that had hung from the sloped ceiling was gone, but the pungent odor of oil paint and turpentine wafted from below.

At the deep sink, Aden held her hand under a stream of warm water. He donned a pair of rimless eyeglasses and examined the skin for small slivers. "Damned Turkish tea glasses," he said. "Thin as paper."

His hands were soft, nails cut so short. Satisfied that he'd removed all the glass, he gently washed the wound with soap. "Is it stinging?" he asked.

"No, just feels numb."

He patted her skin with a white hand towel, folded it neatly into a square, and pressed it against her palm. "Bend your fingers and apply pressure for a bit until we can be sure the bleeding is stopped." He opened the cabinet beneath the sink and pulled out a metal first aid box. "Then we'll put on antiseptic ointment and a bandage. Thank God you don't need stitches."

He led her to a chair next to a drafting table. Smudges of blood adorned the thighs of her dark jeans. Aden sat in a chair next to a long table covered with a sheet of Kenized cloth. The room was nothing like it had been in Mitra's childhood. It was white and spare, with track lighting and pendants to compensate for the lack of natural light, a wooden bench easel, a wall of shelving packed neatly with supplies, and several mobile storage carts holding palettes, brushes, and tubes of paint. Against the walls rested rows of canvases, many unfinished.

Aden looked different in the bright light,

a little yellow. "Sorry about your shirt," she said as he reached under the table and pulled out a black gym bag.

"It's nothing," he said, extracting a white polo shirt and pulling it over his head. "I carry a spare." He flashed a smile that didn't reach his still-worried eyes. "Where I come from, we're always prepared to lose our shirts and begin again."

She forced a smile, then looked down. "I'm sorry, Aden . . . for my anger . . . for my . . . ignorance." She felt raw, as if she'd been loofahed head to toe, dipped in ice water, and just now thawing. Still not looking at him, she asked, "Did Ana never love Bijan?"

"Of course she did, Mitra. But not in the passionate way everyone thought. He was her husband, the father of her children, a good man. But he was traditional, not in an extreme sense, but probably not capable of understanding or accepting what had been done to her — the physical and emotional blackmail — as abuse or molestation. If she'd told him, I'm afraid he would have labeled it differently. This is not the sort of thing that's easily understood by those to whom it has not happened."

He looked away, but she saw a flash of discomfort cross his face. He had his own secrets, but it wasn't her place to ask him about them.

"The sad truth is," he continued, exhaling, "such things go on in most families. And if not in the household, then at school or in the neighborhood or the church, the synagogue, the mosque. Places where children feel safe, where adults like to believe they are safe. To imagine otherwise would be to shatter the necessary fantasy of the communal identity. For many years, even Ana didn't think of what Kareem did to her as a crime. It wasn't until we —"

He hesitated, and she finished the sentence for him. "Began the affair."

"Yes. I suspected . . . so she finally told me."

"You suspected?"

"Because of her . . . difficulties . . . with sex."

Mitra swallowed. "Difficulties?"

"It is a consequence," he said.

Mitra's head ached, and she had a sudden desire to lie down and close her eyes. She noticed the exposed water pipes along the ceiling, painted black. She remembered Kareem grinding against Ana in the boiler room, and then she imagined what she now knew must have gone on: Kareem pulling Ana into a closet or a bathroom, creeping into her bed when Mitra hung out in Olga's room, fondling her under the dinner table while all of them — always such a full house! — watched sitcoms and gossiped over tea and played backgammon and read books and slept and sunbathed. "I want to ruin him," she snarled.

"That's exactly what Ana *didn't* want. Please don't make me sorry I've told you."

"It's what he deserves, Aden! For the whole family to know what he did. For everyone to know that he was a child molester."

"Are you quite sure that's how he would be viewed? Especially now that Ana isn't alive to tell her side?"

He was right. She had no response. She gritted her teeth.

"Mitra, she didn't believe you could stop it then, and she wouldn't believe you could expose the crime now. Not justly, anyway. Even if she thought there was a chance that Kareem would get his due, she wouldn't want to face the possibility that you would fail. When a child — when a person — has been abused, their thoughts are not logical. The shame is a pit of quicksand."

"So Kareem stopped after she started seeing Bijan."

"Yes, but he became furious and more

determined. She knew that becoming some-one else's wife was the only way to shut him out completely. Sadly, your father then created the obstacle of *your* marriage. In the end, your crazy plan — your sacrifice — worked. You rescued her. And you did it for a lesser reason than you thought. You did it simply because you thought she was in love and it would make her happy."

"It wasn't such a sacrifice. I never wanted to marry, to be trapped like my mother. Denying Anahita her wish as a way to manipulate me was cruel. My father deserved payback for that, and I deserved — everyone deserves — the freedom to make their own destiny."

He nodded. "That may be true, but it doesn't nullify what you did for her."

"Fine. Whatever." The last thing she wanted to hear now was praise; she was a fool.

He leaned forward and unwound the towel over her hand. "Doesn't look too bad." He reached into the first aid box at his feet and brought out a roll of gauze and surgical tape. "Now I get to show you what I learned in the IDF."

Sometimes, Mitra thought, an unexpected event could make people intimate. Like when a child falls down on a playground and all the mothers rush to help no matter whose child it is. Or when a man faints in an airport and within seconds there's a jacket under his head, a backpack under his feet, a woolen coat tucked around him — he's no one's stranger and everyone's responsibility, all this without hesitation or judgment. Mitra wondered if it was true what the Sufis said, that we are all connected by good intentions.

Aden stood. "I want to show you something, Mitra." He grasped the corners of the cloth that covered the long table and carefully peeled it off the way a mother might uncover her sleeping child.

A scintillation of gems took Mitra's breath away. A sea of pavé and baguette diamonds, of filigreed precious metals, of intricate chains. And in every piece — earrings, bracelets, necklaces, rings — was Persian turquoise, smooth and veinless like no other turquoise in the world. Mitra slowly slid off her chair and approached the table. The creations were all unique and meticulously detailed, all linked by an avian theme. Libby had been wrong; Ana had not tired of birds, she'd only tired of painting them.

Mitra's eyes filled and the jewelry blurred. She saw Anahita's graceful, steady fingers manipulating the delicate tools. She saw the poised hunch of her shoulders, her lips pressed tightly together in concentration, her eyes squinting, dark ringlets escaping from a thick hair clip onto the milky back of her neck. She reached out to touch the vision and stumbled forward.

Aden came around the table quickly, saying her name. She hugged herself and tried to slow her breath. Ana's presence, effulgent as her jewels, felt as close as Aden's calming voice. "You see, Mitra, she is still here."

CHAPTER 11

Aden wouldn't let Mitra drive herself back to the city, and she didn't argue much against him, especially once she learned he lived on the Upper West Side not far from Nezam's. It had taken her a good while to calm down after seeing Ana's jewelry. Aden had led her, trembling, back upstairs into the glow of the desk lamp, wrapped a shawl around her, and ordered a container of sweet-and-sour soup from the Chinese place down the street. The sting of the steam against her swollen nose and eyelids warmed her some, but her mind grew steadily colder, and she let the thoughts and images Aden had conjured sink beneath a thin membrane of ice; she would skate on that surface.

So when Aden began to talk about the jewelry — several retailers were interested — she begged him to stop. It was too soon, too much; she had to digest it all.

But she did want to know where Ana had

gotten all the turquoise. Aden widened his eyes. *She traded for it, of course* — as if Mitra knew how these things worked. And actually, she did; it just wasn't something she'd ever stayed in the room for. The aunties and their daughters constantly reworked the jewels they'd purchased before the Revolution when they'd been flush with money. They spent a ridiculous amount of time exchanging information about backroom designers in the Diamond District, the prices of gold, silver, platinum. They made drawings on napkins and squabbled about the appropriate number of baguettes or the thickness of a chain or the combination of gems. Later in private, trade negotiations took place. Emeralds for rubies, sapphires for pearls, agates for turquoise. Mitra now realized that she couldn't remember the last time she'd seen Anahita wearing her diamond engagement ring or the emerald bracelet Bijan's rich uncle had given as a wedding present. It was so hard to imagine Ana negotiating and bargaining.

Before they left the shop, Mitra couldn't help asking Aden if the jewelry had been sitting under the cloth for a year. He looked down and finally managed a nod, then he spread his hands in a helpless gesture. His eyes were brimming. It was at this moment that Mitra mentally added him to her family.

Now, Aden drove her rental car slowly across the George Washington Bridge. It was late — she didn't know exactly what time — but the bridge was eerily uncongested. Alongside them were long-haul truckers and old Hondas with single drivers. She wondered what their stories were, if they had also experienced something that threw a curve into their lives. No one was speeding; they all seemed tentative about reaching their destinations. No, she was probably wrong. These were people who worked night shifts, whose worries were far more dire than hers, really. Kids and bills and sick parents. They'd probably lost much more than she had. Every day, sisters and nieces and nephews died. Every day, women found love and joy in the arms of someone not their husbands. She supposed this should make her feel better. But it didn't.

"I'm a little confused about you, Aden," Mitra said, touching a finger to begin a list. "Your wife is Mrs. Goldblatt's niece." She touched her second finger. "Mrs. Goldblatt was German, but you're definitely not German." Touched her third finger. "Your accent is definitely Arab, not Israeli." And finally, her fourth finger. "But you speak

Hebrew. What's the deal?"

He smiled and nodded. "The American stereotype of Jews is Ashkenazi — European. I'm an Iraqi Jew. I didn't learn Hebrew until our family moved to Haifa when I was fourteen. You have a good ear for accents. Your sister thought I was Latino."

Mitra laughed, and her whole body trembled like a balloon losing its air. "That's Ana," she said, feeling suddenly on the precipice of a hysterical giggle fit.

"As for my wife, her father was Felicia Goldblatt's much younger brother. After World War Two, he emigrated to Israel, but she came to America with her husband. The rest of their family did not survive."

"Oh." Mitra's hand covered her mouth briefly. "I'm sorry. I didn't know."

A terrible sadness gripped her, the kind of sadness she felt when she saw starving children on television. Sadness for Ana, for Bijan and the children, for the unfortunate Felicia Goldblatt and this good man beside her. It was a sadness deeper than grief, closer to desperation. For the moment, her rage, even for Kareem, evaporated. She was spent. For the moment.

"Felicia never had children," Aden was saying, "so she passed the shop on to my wife." He glanced at her, smiled again.

"Sometimes lucky things happen."

Mitra wanted him to keep talking. About almost anything. They were now on the West Side Highway, creeping along in the pockmarked right lane, and Mitra was glad at the slow pace. She could hardly bear the thought of lying in that tiny bed across from the crib, alone with her convoluted thoughts and questions.

"Tell me about when you met Ana," she said.

He breathed in and exhaled slowly. "Your sister came to me because of the art," he obliged. "I knew her as an occasional customer, of course, and each time she came into the shop, we would talk about art. She was still painting then. From the start, there was a rapport between us, the kind that arises between people who have a common passion. Not of the sensual kind, mind you. That did not happen for nearly a year. Our friendship was based on the art, on her desire to discover what she wanted to do, and on my desire to help her discover it. It was clear that the time she spent at my studio was what you might call a secret, but not a secret kept out of shame or wrongdoing. She wanted something for herself, something separate from family and everyday life. I understood this because I had

231

been the same way myself. My family would never have understood my affinity for painting, certainly not my desire to make a career out of it. To them, I was a civil engineer, a soldier, and a merchant."

He took the Seventy-second Street exit and when they stopped at the light, Mitra's body buzzed in anticipation. Aden kept his eyes straight ahead. Finally, he continued. "When Ana sold her first piece of jewelry, we came together without thinking, in the excitement of our . . . of her . . . accomplishment, and it nearly ended our friendship. Yes, there was guilt, but also bewilderment, and many attempts to return to a platonic relationship, but it did not seem under our control." He paused. "And I am not sorry. I loved her."

Mitra's face was wet and she turned it toward the window, brushed the tears away. They drove silently until they reached the street corner before Nezam's building. Aden pulled up alongside a parked car and they sat for a moment.

Mitra said, "Ana told me she didn't want to leave Bijan."

"That's true. And I didn't want to leave my wife." He paused. "Love and happiness, Mitra, come from many different sources, certainly not from one exclusive relationship. The strictures of tradition need not vanquish those possibilities. In fact, they can enhance them. The truth is that we were both better spouses and Ana was a better parent once we accepted that our relationship would not hurt anyone as long as it remained a secret."

"So many things she didn't tell me! I hardly knew her!"

He bowed his head and ran his fingers through his hair. "Don't blame yourself. Ana behaved in a certain way with you, Mitra."

"What does that mean?"

"With you, she was the student, the baby sister who needed your protection, but that was a role she played for you. It was not, in the end, the way she really was."

"I still don't get your meaning," Mitra said. But she did; she realized she did.

"That was also why she didn't tell you about us and about her art. She was afraid to destroy how you saw her, afraid you would be disappointed, afraid you wouldn't know how to be with her once she showed you these . . . these . . . unexpected sides of her. She was afraid she might lose your respect, lose you altogether."

"But years, Aden? She lied to me for years."

"Those were not lies. Those were forms of protection."

"For me?"

"For you, for her, for the family. It's what women do in the patriarchy."

Mitra cringed. What arrogance. What selfishness. She'd unshackled herself from tradition while perpetuating its boundaries for her sister. Mitra was not guiltless, not even close.

"Mitra, there's no point in thinking about what could have been. In the end, Ana found some peace. With her children, with you, and with me."

He leaned over and placed his hand over hers, and she, without hesitation, brought hers to cover his. They smiled at each other, the first of many smiles, she knew, that would always be tinged with sorrow, but also with love — for Anahita.

Libby and Nezam's apartment was dark, everyone asleep, which was a relief. She was so tired and numb, she crawled onto the bed fully clothed and sighed as her head sank into the pillow. But then she was uncomfortable. Her left hand throbbed under the gauze Aden had carefully applied; her eyes burned and she had a terrible headache; her neck was stiff and her stomach crampy. She sat up.

It could have been different, she thought. What if she hadn't used her college years at Barnard to stay away? If she'd come home on weekends instead of partying and soaking up the Manhattan art scene and reveling in her independence? Just thirty minutes away, Kareem had preyed on Ana. Mitra might have figured it out if she'd been around.

Or Olga. Wait. Olga knew everything that went on in the household. Nothing slipped past her. Sometimes she was so protective of them that Mitra would tell her to stop behaving like a bodyguard, that all she needed was to dress herself in leather and she could be their bouncer. Aden had assured Mitra that Olga's knowledge of Kareem's abuse, like Mitra's, hadn't gone beyond the basement incident. But what if it had? She would've done something.

But maybe she did.

Olga was the one who gave Mitra the idea to date some of the suitors her father brought around, to pretend that she was interested so he might let Ana marry Bijan. For several weekends, Mitra endured a host of boring dates with the kind of men who were old-fashioned enough to give credence to the spirit of arranged marriage. Custom-

235

ers, she called them, who picked her up in sports cars blaring Iranian pop music, took her to stuffy restaurants where three-pound menus offered Chicken Kiev and Cherries Jubilee, subjected her to verbal résumés of college degrees and athletic achievements and career paths in engineering, orthodontia, import/export — all of this amidst the miasma of Aramis cologne. Finally, and by luck, there emerged a suitor who was as reluctant as she, though not nearly as defiant of his rich mother as Mitra was of her father. Hassan was his name, though he went by Harry, a sweet and shy accountant with a secret passion for opera, and another secret that was obvious to Mitra, but not, apparently, to anyone else involved in the matchmaking game. They agreed to pretend for a few weeks until Ana and Bijan announced a date for their wedding, then they would break up and Harry could tell his crusty old mom anything he liked. *Tell her I'm not a virgin; that'll let you off the hook.*

Olga was thrilled; her persistence in trying to help Ana was paying off. But Yusef was cunning and quick. After coming to terms with Bijan's and Harry's parents, and generously offering to take care of the initial planning — *because I know my way around this American society after so long living here* —

236

he booked the country club, ordered invitations, and announced to family and friends the advent of a lavish double wedding two months hence.

Olga was despondent, finally halfheartedly suggesting that Mitra and Harry go through with it. *Then you get fast easy Reno divorce.* Mitra was not amused. In fact, she'd felt calm, almost detached. Olga's gaze grew wary; the woman could read her. *You have another plan?*

The solution had come to her like an eruption, as if it had always been there, deep and hidden. Yusef's final volley was the spark. She would stop this repugnant power struggle once and for all. She would make herself unmarriageable. Olga was horrified, took to her bed and cried for hours, but in the end, she'd been by Mitra's side when the time came.

For as long as Mitra had known her, all Olga had cared about was their welfare. Every waking moment was spent with this intention, from delighting them with favorite foods to sacrificing her job to salvage Shireen's honor. Mitra dropped her head and rubbed her temples as if to coax her brain into accepting the likely truth: that Olga had known about Kareem's relentless abuse and had promised Anahita not to tell

237

Mitra. Because yes, Mitra would've blown the whole thing open. Marrying Bijan had been *Ana's* plan to free herself. *Her* choice, just as sterilization had been Mitra's choice. And now she understood that it was Olga who was forced to weigh the final and most difficult moral choice: Anahita's abuse versus Mitra's infertility.

Mitra cradled her midsection and bent forward. She wanted to reach across the oceans and continent to hold Olga in her arms. *You made the right choice, my friend. I'm so sorry I gave all the credit to myself.* She swiped at her tears and picked up the phone.

But as soon as she heard Olga's voice, she froze. What was she thinking? This was a mistake!

" 'Allo? 'Allo? Who is there? Mitra? Madame? I can't hear you. The connection is bad. 'Allo?"

"It's me," Mitra finally said, her mouth thick with shame and pity.

"Mitra-joon, why you speaking so softly?"

Mitra swallowed and threw out a half lie. "Because I'm an idiot. I forgot I was at Nezam's and everyone's asleep."

She hadn't thought this through! What good could come of speaking to Olga about all she'd learned and figured out on this day? Olga's despair? For what? Because misery loves company? No. She would not open the wound. She would say nothing. Let the woman have some semblance of peace. "Olga-joon," she said. "I'll call you tomorrow night after I get back to San Francisco."

"Okay, but I know what has happened, joonam."

Mitra's pulse quickened.

"Your maman told me about your baba's painting. God forgive him! I so sorry."

"Yeah," she exhaled. "What a fiasco."

"What is this word you using?"

"Fiasco — I don't know the Farsi — um . . . a disaster."

"Ah, okay. Ach, Mitra-joon, I think you should say the fuck you to that stupid painting. I proud of you. Your maman said you behaved unlike yourself and did not make trouble in front of everyone."

Mitra flinched. Unearned praise was the last thing she deserved right now. Before she could stop herself, she blurted, "I think you should know. I . . . I told Maman about what Kareem did to Anahita in the basement."

There was an expected silence, then a barrage of Farsi, the gist of which involved how *unnecessary* it was to *break another piece of*

239

your maman's heart, how Mitra had *betrayed your sister's trust,* how *secrecy is necessary for the survival of the family.* Mitra was, for once, glad her Farsi vocabulary sucked, but also glad for the tongue-lashing, wanting more. When she finally found an opening to speak, she said, "At least now Maman won't be treating Kareem like he's a poor mother-less child."

"Not worth it, Mitra."

"Whatever," Mitra said, making matters worse. "She's a lot stronger than you think, Olga. She didn't crumble."

Olga's response was terse: "And how would *you* know that she didn't?"

Oof, that slap hit its mark, Mitra thought. Now, she could sleep.

PART 2

■ ■ ■ ■

JULIAN

In the time of our history when hippie love bloomed in San Francisco, when the Kurds of Iran revolted once again, and when Britain's Twiggy wore paper clothing, a young British Red Cross nurse, at the pinnacle of her beauty and the nadir of her pragmatism, was captivated by a dark and striking physician from a faraway place she knew as Persia. They married in London and he took her to live with him in Tehran, where she was soon disappointed to discover that the people of his country were not as impoverished and downtrodden as she'd anticipated. In fact, his family, which was more populated than the north country village where the nurse was raised, lived a thoroughly modern life and demanded that she do the same. A doctor's wife. What could be better? There would be no work with the Red Lion and Sun in the poor villages of Persia, no nursing of the tribal sick, only the privilege of making babies and raising them, throwing parties and swimming at the country club. So frustrating. The Third World was a bus ride away, and yet forbidden to her. And so she left the handsome doctor, who seemed much less handsome now, freeing him to marry a more culturally appropriate woman. Mistakes happen. Caught early, mistakes can be erased. That she kept the birth of their son some months later in England undisclosed was, in her mind, for the best. The boy grew up in the loving circle of his grandparents and his mother, when she was not fulfilling her pledge to minister to the sick and starving hordes of the Third World in far-flung refugee camps. She told him little about his father, and when her ex-husband was killed by one of Saddam's bombs in a military hospital during the war many years later, she was doubly glad of her decision.

When the boy grew old enough, she took him with her to experience his chosen future as a physician, but the hardships and strife of camp life were not for him, and he struck out to make a life for himself in the West of the Western World.

CHAPTER 12

Mitra tipped the cab driver and stood on the sloping sidewalk, staring up at her yellow and white Victorian house, with its bay windows, cornices, and dentil moldings. She'd yearned for its warmth — to nestle in it — since the moment she'd left Aden's studio the night before. Something about her house looked — no, *felt* — different, like the aloof vibe you get from an insulted friend. The trumpet vines climbed the lattices as usual, boxes of impatiens still bloomed under the windows. Nothing was different. Was it that the streetlamps cast a cold light on its dark windows? Or was the difference inside her?

She inhaled San Francisco's cool mist and climbed her stoop to the indigo front door and let herself in. The odor of onions fried in oil and turmeric struck her. She listened for sounds, for the presence of the mother and daughter — Akram and Salimeh — in case Julian hadn't been able to keep them out. Silent and dark. She switched on the hall light, made her way past the living and dining rooms, dropped her luggage at the foot of the staircase, and went into the kitchen.

Jezebel was in her usual spot on the chair Mitra usually sat in, protected from above by the underside of the table. Mitra bent over and slid her hand between two slats of the ladderback, murmuring low greetings and letting the cat smell her fingers, then rubbing between her ears and under her chin. No purring yet. The pinpoint pupils of her green eyes stared accusingly. *Where have you been?* "Fine," Mitra exhaled, withdrawing her hand and straightening. "Sulk, pretty kitty. I can wait."

The kitchen was not as she'd left it, at least not at second glance. The teakettle was splattered with cooking grease, and the inside of the teapot was stained a reddish brown from lack of washing between brews. She hated that. The burner wells on the stove had become havens for crumbs and crusty crud. The granite counters were dull and streaky from being wiped down with just water, like a car abandoned in the middle of a wax job. The sink was marked with the silver scratches caused by metal pots, and she had a compulsive urge to begin scrubbing away.

Why not? She'd slept through the flight home after a dose of bourbon; she needed to move and be out of her head.

She kicked off her shoes, hiked up her sleeves, and pulled her hair back in a clip. To protect and cushion her wounded hand, she pressed a folded paper towel over it and tugged on a pair of rubber dishwashing gloves. Head down, muscles working, she scoured and scrubbed and cleansed: the counters, the appliances, the floor, the tiled backsplash, and her mind — of filth and grease, of Akram's trespass, of Aden and Kareem and Shireen and her father. And when the kitchen was spotless, smelling of bleach and citrus, what was left was the ache in her arms and hands, and the ache of Anahita and the children, but that was familiar, and now so was her home.

She looked at her watch. Midnight. Almost noon in Tehran.

She reached into the freezer for a bottle of vodka, poured herself a smidgen, tossed it back, then poured another. Jezebel left her perch with a light thump, sauntered over to rub herself against Mitra's shins. "Knew you'd come around," she said, reaching down to pick the cat up, but Jezebel slinked away and darted toward the living room. "Good idea," said Mitra, grabbing the vodka bottle and the cordless. In the dark room, Mitra sat on a kilim pillow next to the stone fireplace. Jezebel crawled onto her lap and curled up. Mitra dialed Olga's number.

"It's me. I'm back in San Francisco."

"Mitra-joon?"

"No, Wonder Woman. Are you still angry with me? Should I apologize?"

Olga sighed loudly. "Not angry, no. It is passed. What can I do? Maybe not so bad your maman know what a piece of *goh* Kareem is."

Mitra laughed for the first time in days. "You can say shit, Olga."

"Shit not satisfying me. Ach, Mitra, I wish I see your smiling face, like picture phones from that Jetmans cartoon show."

"Jetsons," she corrected, taking another sip.

"You are drinking, Mitra-joon."

"Vodka." Mitra lifted her glass. *"Beh salamati,"* she toasted.

"To your own health," Olga replied in Farsi.

Her neck was beginning to loosen, and she felt a warmth traveling through her veins.

248

Olga sighed. "Okay, joonam. Sometimes is good to drink and forget."

"Thank you for the permission," Mitra teased.

"Did you say goodbye to your maman?"

"I'll call her tomorrow. She knew I probably wasn't going to see her before my flight."

"Ach, Mitra, I hope maybe you bring her back to visit with you."

"Are you kidding? That's a dream. What made you think she would agree this time?" Mitra snorted, but she'd had the same flicker of hope that Shireen's year of grief and loneliness without Anahita and the children might have eroded her loyalty to Yusef.

"So?" Olga prodded. "She okay, then?"

"No, she's terrible. But she won't leave him, even though I think he's at home less and less."

"Did you invite her?"

"What? Of course. I tell her to come all the time." Mitra put her glass down. "You know that, Olga. She always says no."

"Yes, yes, I know. Don't be angry with me now."

"I'm not. Sorry." Mitra raked her fingers through her hair. "Are you eating? You sound like you're eating."

249

"My breakfast, yes."

"Kind of late for breakfast."

"Second breakfast. What else to do? I getting fat like Mama Cass."

"Some people say she choked on a sandwich and died, you know."

"What? No! Which kind of sandwich?"

"I don't know," Mitra said, slurring slightly. "She was in London alone in her apartment."

"No one should live alone. See? You choke and die alone."

"So you and I are going to choke and die, huh?"

"Do not say it!" Olga said in Farsi. "You bring the evil eye."

"I'm sure the evil eye has had enough of me."

Olga laughed, coughed, laughed again. "You are drunk."

"Getting there, thank God." Jezebel lifted her paw as Mitra's fingers sunk into her belly fur.

"Mitra-joon, azizam, about your maman —"

"Yes? I hear a wise woman's advice coming on."

"Forgive me," Olga said. "Advice, a little, yes. Because I love you."

"Okay, I'm listening." Mitra felt buzzed

enough now to take anything in stride. Silly Olga, always spewing advice.

"Mitra-joon, perhaps you need your maman."

"Need her? For what?"

"For many things. For . . . for . . ." Olga took a deep breath.

"Yes?" Mitra singsonged, drawing the syllable out like an amused schoolteacher.

"Mitra-joon, a daughter can sometimes need her mother for comfort. I do not mean you cannot get along without her, you always have, but I mean even for little things like making you barley soup or washing your clothes or amusing you with a story from your childhood. Of course, some mothers are terrible, trying to control and whining all the time about the decay of their bodies, but your maman is not like this. Just to have her in the rooms of your house, saying nothing, just being there, could give you great comfort now. You are alone. It is not bad to need her a little. Perhaps you do need her, Mitra-joon, just a tiny bit. Hahn? Mitra? 'Allo? Are you there still?"

Mitra's mind had wandered. "I'm here," she said, attempting to hoist herself up from her supine position. Jezebel hopped off her lap and padded away.

"You are silent. I have made you angry."

251

"Huh? No, no. I'm listening." Mitra felt as if she'd drunk the whole bottle of vodka. Had she? She glanced over. No, but a fair amount, and she'd hardly slept in the last twenty-four hours.

"I'm so glad you are listening," Olga said, and Mitra heard a smile of relief in her voice. She tried to concentrate. "I have wanted to say these things to you for a long time, but I know how you feel about your independence."

"Right," Mitra managed, trying to recover from her clouded memory exactly what Olga had been talking about.

"Of course you have always been stronger than your maman, but I think you need her very much now. It is true that perhaps she needs you more. Yes, she needs you more, but you must be together now. If you do not tell your mother that you need her, Mitra-joon, she will not come to you. Even if you do not believe this — that you need her — you must say it. You must."

Mitra lifted the bottle and swigged. "Mmm, okay, whatever. But I better . . . go now. I'm . . . really tired."

"Ah, okay. But, azizam," said Olga, continuing in Farsi. "Remember: there is a reason why women like your maman are called saints, and it is not only because they are good-hearted. They sacrifice and they suffer. It is their identity. An ox is born and bred to carry our burdens. A saint is like an ox."

As Mitra hung up, she wondered hazily why Olga was talking about cows . . . no, not cows . . . another animal. Ugh, one of those old Persian sayings, probably. In the silence she hobbled upstairs to her bedroom, stripped her clothes into a puddle, and slid into bed. She cupped her wounded left hand with her other palm and placed it against her cheek.

Julian sneezed twice upon entering the house. Bleach made his nose itch. Mitra had been cleaning. She did that a lot, usually when she was trying to ignore something that was bothering her. He'd once pointed it out, said it was a bit uncharacteristic that a domestic chore would calm her. The observation hadn't gone over well: *Cleaning is not necessarily domestic.* And she'd relocated to the garden with her leaf blower.

The lights were all off, but he felt his way easily up the stairs to the bedroom. He blew into his hands to warm them, but the anticipation of touching her skin was already taking the night chill out of him faster than a hot shower. She would be asleep, he knew, and he would dissolve her sleep with his fingers and the gentle pressure of his naked body. She would reach for him with a sigh.

Carefully, he turned the doorknob to the left (to the right, it squeaked), let himself in. Dark. She usually left the vanity lamp on, or a candle glowed. He knew she was there; he smelled her perfume mixed with her minty scent. He slipped his shoes off, tiptoed to the foot of the bed, let his eyes adjust. She was there, breathing deeply. He exhaled and inhaled to her rhythm, and it felt like the first full breath he'd taken since she left.

He went to the bathroom, brushed his teeth quietly, removed his clothing, lit a candle, and reentered the bedroom. It wasn't until he set the candle down and slid under the ivory duvet that he saw the glint of the near-empty Stoli bottle on her bedside table. Like a slap in the face. He smelled the alcohol now, rising from her pores, mixed into the heat of her heavy breath. He laid on his back, hands under his head, erection wilting, and watched the flickering shadows on the vaulted ceiling beams. He told himself not to be upset, that she'd been through a difficult week, that she had a right to medicate her sorrow, to seek unconsciousness. Forgiveness was what a good man would do. He blew out the candle, closed his eyes, and eventually dozed off.

Some hours later, he woke with a start, bathed in sweat. It was the first time he'd had the nightmare in Mitra's bed, maybe the only time he'd had it since they met. The smells of the refugee camp: propane, pus, and sandalwood (his mother's scent, a cheap oil she'd found in India as a young backpacker). The surgery's vivid reds — the scarlet of hemorrhage, the burgundy of bulging organs. And finally, Desta's scream, her thrush-infested tongue, and the ashy blue veneer of her stillborn, and then the cavernous silence of all the dead infants, piled like skeins on gurneys from one end of the hospital tent to the other.

Julian shivered. Mitra had asked him once why he came to America twelve years ago, and he dodged the question, didn't tell her about the death of Desta in childbirth — brave, proud Desta, an orphan like so many, pregnant from a rape like so many — didn't tell her that he was trying to escape the searing memories of the refugee camp he'd worked in with his mother until he got so sick that she sent him home. Mitra had kept the nightmare away. Watching her now as she slept, he had an idea that there were things she hadn't told him too.

She wasn't like any woman he'd known, certainly not like the other Persian women he'd sought out in hopes of making a connection with his lost heritage. He didn't know why he cared; he'd never met his father. True, when he was about eleven, he'd developed a fascination for the few letters his father had written during his parents' courtship, but his mum had shut that down with her usual indifference toward her brief marriage. He thought when he came to America he'd forget about all that. Still, he'd met Persian women all the time — at university, in med school, during his residency — and he was drawn to them. They were distinct. To him, anyway. It wasn't only the dark features, peanut-butter skin, or high arch and long tail of carefully tweezed eyebrows. Nor was it solely the waxed arms, smooth as tumbled marble, or the delicate, expressive hand gestures that accompanied every phrase, or the omnipresent scent of perfume. It was more than that. Silly, but he thought (to himself only) that there was some genetic connection between them, a primitive ancestral thing that his science-mind could never explain.

The night almost a year ago when he met Mitra at the Gay Goose on Twenty-fourth

Street, he knew at first glance that she was Persian. This, even though he'd seen only her profile at first. Maybe it was her hair, jet and glossy, thick and smooth as raven's feathers. Or the nose. Strong, but not Semitic — the subtle difference between Middle Eastern and Asian, an Indo-European mixture. Persian.

After they'd staggered back to his loft apartment, made love in that uninhibited frenzied way that inebriation allows, she told him of the accident that had killed her sister, niece, and nephew, her eyes red-rimmed and large with tears. He'd brought out a joint then, and they'd dissolved into a mellow silliness, he donning his well-worn Aussie outback hat and squinting at her like Eastwood himself, she choking out a laugh while slurping a glass of orange juice, dribbling the sticky liquid onto her chin. They shared a package of Hostess cupcakes, scooping out the cream filling with their tongues.

Their lovemaking, that second time, was less frenzied. She was demanding but generous. It was no impediment to their conversation or the playful banter they'd established without thinking. So different from the silent concentration or raving enthusiasm of his previous experiences. Maybe it

257

was her age. She had a few years on him — ten or so, they'd discovered. Well, if that was the reason, he was glad of it. She didn't hesitate to lift her head during a particularly passionate act to ask him if he liked dark chocolate or had ever been to China. And when he discovered the faint surgical scar in her pelvic triangle, it felt perfectly natural to say, matter-of-factly, "Nice work." She snickered and told him he had no business admiring the result of what had been, to her, a painful ovarian cyst rupture in her twenties.

Now he felt her stir in the bed beside him, a languorous movement accompanied by the sibilance of a whisper. He sensed her moving toward him, and shivered as she pressed the length of her body against his back and curled into him. Her arm went around him and moved like silk up his chest to rest there. He felt her nipples against his back, her thighs and pelvis against his ass. Wasn't this perfect? He could tell her he loved her, wanted her forever, but she wouldn't hear, wouldn't remember. The yearning to tell her burned in his chest like a gas flame, unflagging. If he'd learned one thing over the past week that she'd been gone, it was that he couldn't pretend non-chalance anymore. It disgusted him that he suffered in silence because he was afraid of losing her altogether. Pathetic, he thought. He needed to tell her, lay it out honestly, settle it once and for all. Risk it. He felt the muscles in his neck relax, his jaw unclench. His body was telling him it was the right decision. He could sleep now. Later — today — he would force the conversation.

CHAPTER 13

As the sun rose over the East Bay hills, Mitra was still a bit drunk, which gave her a sense of being unmoored by thought. Standing on the deck outside her bedroom, she savored a kind of disconnect between thinking and feeling, a pleasurable psychic numbness. The cloudless periwinkle sky looked close enough to kiss, and her bare feet tingled against the morning coolness of the wood deck. She inhaled the bouquet of jasmine vines she'd planted down in the garden some five years ago. She closed her eyes and her body tilted and hummed, her silk kimono feeling like butterfly wings against her legs.

It was good to be home.

Home. Here. Not back east, where Ana and the children no longer were. She'd been thinking for all these years that east was home and west was simply "away." Now San Francisco was home, or some semblance of home that she couldn't yet define. When had that happened? Over the past year? Or had it taken less than one New Jersey week to make her feel like she belonged here and not there? And yet she knew it had been years since she felt like she fully belonged in the east, if ever she had felt that way. Even though she'd visited often, she'd been removed from the character of the place, like an immigrant who visited the old country, like her parents visiting Iran before the Revolution, complaining about the pollution, the traffic, the drivers, the marketplace haggling, the dust, the excessive heat. As if they were foreigners. Imperious Americans. And now, she harbored the same disapproval about the East Coast, thinking often about how California had better weather, fewer potholes, kinder strangers, healthier people, and a more convenient lifestyle. She said nothing to Ana or Shireen about these opinions, but once when she and Ana took the kids shopping and Mitra was unreasonably incensed by the length of the drive to the closest mall and then by the sweltering humidity they had to endure while walking through the vast parking lot, Ana elbowed her and playfully chided, *Excuse us for being so backward!*

Ana and the kids had visited her in San

Francisco twice. Once when Nina was still crawling, another time just months before the accident, when they'd driven to Tahoe and gone white-water rafting on the tame Truckee River, getting stuck in the reeds midway, Ana taking a dangling tree branch in the forehead and flipping back-first into the cold water, the kids squealing with delight at the rare klutzy performance by their mother. But having them in California had felt cumbersome to Mitra; she had wanted so badly to have them fall in love with it, and in some ways Nikku did, promising that he imagined going to college here (astonishing to Mitra that kids were already thinking about college in primary school). All these years, Mitra had secretly harbored the desire that her family move to the West Coast, knowing full well that Bijan's job with the bank required him to be in Manhattan, knowing full well that her father thought New York was the center of the universe — not that she wanted *him* to move — and that her mother would never leave him. Besides an occasional *I wish you lived here* to Ana, Mitra hid her hope; the idea would have seemed silly out loud, like asking a camel to move to the jungle. Ana got her sense of security from familiarity; adventure freaked her out.

Or so Mitra had thought. Because of Aden, Ana was now a mystery to her.

But no, she wouldn't think about that right now, not on this beautiful California morning, this chosen home of hers, the frontier feeling of it even now, the fact that so many people were, like her, recent transplants. Sometimes (she'd never mentioned this foolishness), she felt like a pioneer woman, a trailblazer — when her work was slow, she would read novels by Steinbeck and McMurtry in order to inhale this feeling of kinship with those who had left everything behind to start fresh. Part of her longed for the Gold Rush days when life was filled with dire obstacles: disease, extreme elements (Donner Party frostbite), bandits, angry Indians or Mexicans, cane-wielding preachers, brothels. Facing it all alone and surviving it was an accomplishment.

Still, she had hoped to be followed.

Inhaling deeply, she opened her eyes. Amazing how the dawn passed so quickly while the midday sun could seem like it lasted for hours. The sky had lightened to a milky blue, and the undulating brown hills across San Francisco Bay were beginning to smudge with a haze that portended a blisteringly hot September day. She smelled a hint of brushfire instead of jasmine, and her mouth suddenly tasted like dental fillings. She picked a handful of mint leaves from a corner planter, blew on them, scrunched one into her mouth like a true Iranian at table, and pocketed the rest for her tea, to be taken with three Advil to stave off the headache lurking behind her eyes.

She tiptoed into the bedroom because Julian could be a light sleeper. There he was, sprawled facedown and naked on the mattress, his taut, round ass marked with a stripe of sun from the skylight. His breathing was steady and strong, like the breathing of the young and guiltless. She turned her gaze from his honey-colored skin, soccer-muscled thighs, and unruly curls. *He is my Mistake,* came the unbidden thought. She cringed, then spotted his small suitcase in the corner. She'd forgotten about the medical conference. Was it in Vegas? Seattle? How many days? He would have left yesterday but had stayed so he could be here when she got back — *in case you're down in the dumps.* Ever solicitous Julian, unmistakable son of a Red Cross nurse. And Mitra: oblivious. A week back east — a week filled with uncovered secrets — had snapped her back to reality. This relationship was wrong.

She closed the bedroom door softly and

marveled at the way one torment could so quickly be replaced by another. She'd forced her painful thoughts of Ana to the back of her mind, but now it would be her relationship with Julian that tormented her.

It amazed her that they'd been practically living together for almost a year. That night they'd met at the bar, she hadn't thought twice about going to his place; one-nighters were a pleasant escape for her, and as she got older, the men got younger. There were several she'd seen more than once, one she'd dated for almost three months — Michael, a software engineer who had the crazy idea of starting a dot-com site where people could auction off collectibles. Men like this had proliferated in the city, and they made for perfect occasional partners as long as a woman was willing to listen (or pretend to listen) to their hyperbole about changing the world. She recognized them by their spindly bodies, bobbing Adam's apples, wire-rimmed eyeglasses, and eager brows, curled in that expression so often seen on dogs who welcome their owners at the end of a lonely, housebound day. They were the new Gold Rush men, panning for venture capital, electrically charged with dreams of wealth and power. The last thing they wanted was a relationship.

She'd mistaken Julian for one of them that first night. When he told her he was a physician, she balked. She didn't date physicians. Her father had always wanted her to marry a doctor. *Best kind of husband for you is doctor, Mitra. Doctor is stable, calm, practical. Good person for taming you.* She'd suppressed a shiver but hadn't made an excuse to leave the bar. She'd been too buzzed or too lazy or too sad; she'd wanted sex. And the sex was good, so good, she realized now, that she'd ignored the most important warning sign: Julian was kind, kind and caring and devoted — the type of man sought by most women, the type she avoided precisely because she craved autonomy and emotional simplicity.

She knew she could justify what she'd done. She'd been vulnerable in her grief. And lonely. She'd allowed herself to care for him despite the warning signs. She'd luxuriated in his British accent, even though she'd fallen for that before; it was an accent that could hide a great many faults. Years ago, she'd gone to see Alaska and had met a photographer from Leeds on a hike outside Nome. All he had to say was "Mornin', luv," and Mitra was smitten. The curly long hair helped, and the Oxford education (which turned out to be a lie). They made love under the midnight sun and fed each other fresh sautéed salmon. Lucky for her, she had a bit of a stomach flu their last night, so she didn't drink. What things one sees when one is sober: the dirt under his toe-nails and embedded in the skin around his neck, the beeswax yellowness of his crooked teeth, and the moist lint he picked out of his navel, the way he called her "babe" and his compulsion to check the UK football scores by phone every hour (whooping and chugging a beer when his team was ahead), and finally the really shitty pictures he developed to show her — he'd managed to turn the strikingly beautiful glacial forma-tions they'd visited into vanilla Swiss al-mond. Mitra didn't even remember his name, only that he gave her crabs.

As she descended to the first floor, the stairs creaking and squeaking, she thought about termites. Old Victorians were prone to them, but it wasn't the tenting or spray-ing that worried Mitra (although it would be a royal pain), it was simply the wormy idea of them. She had a twitchiness about insects, and it reminded her of Carlos, her longtime contractor, who knew part of his job was to visit crawl spaces and attics when necessary because Mitra couldn't stomach them. "It's quite an ironic phobia for a building renovator to have," Julian once teased, knowing full well that Mitra loathed having any weakness. He'd begun teasing her that very first night, after they'd made love in his loft apartment, which looked more like an artist's place than a doctor's (she'd expected sterile and organized). She was pleased by the several framed charcoals of nude Rubens-like women, one on the wall above the futon. Their lovemaking was frenzied and sloppy. Bodies coming together for the first time, discovery and newness fueling desire. But he hadn't tried to remain serious like so many others; she couldn't count the times her partners had prided themselves on the quick one-handed un-hooking of her bra, as if such a feat was enough to bring her to orgasm. But Julian, fumbling unsuccessfully, chuckled hotly against her ear at their awkwardness. "Let's make a deal; you get the brassiere and I'll get my zipper." She'd loved that. When it was over, they flopped back panting, the usual post-sex sleep sure to descend on them. But it hadn't. "I'm starving," he said. "You?" That had been her first mistake: sitting across from him at what he called his dining table — an old picnic table painted crimson — Mitra wrapped in a terrycloth robe that had obviously been washed with something royal blue, each of them scooping from a bowl of Cheerios. What else would a situation like that prompt but the first step toward familiarity and intimacy and attachment? She should've left.

After he'd told her that his mother was a nurse, she asked him the usual follow-up question: if his father was a doctor. "He was, but I never met him. They split up before I was born. He was a foreigner who resettled back in his country."

"I'm sorry."

He waved his spoon dismissively. "No need. My grandfather stood in pretty well."

She liked the matter-of-fact way he revealed the facts of his life. Unpretentious and unaffected. Not like what she was used to: men who demanded, even in their tone, to be thought of as unique, as having "been through stuff," as if being benched through half a Little League season or missing the junior prom were deep psychological wounds.

"He never tried to contact you?" Mitra asked.

"We think he died." Julian was slicing a banana into their cereal. "There was a war in his country," he added, lifting his gaze. "The Iran–Iraq War in the eighties. He probably fought in it. He was from Iran."

Words like a gale of wind throwing Mitra back against the wall.

"Sorry," he said at her stunned reaction. "I don't mean to play with you. I know you're Persian."

She pulled the robe tight around her neck, as if he hadn't already seen her naked. "How do you know?"

He shrugged, but in a bashful way, which relaxed her a bit. "I just know; I can tell. It's hard to explain. Looks, gestures, something . . ."

She knew the "something" he was talking about. She looked for some telltale Persian feature in him — almond-shaped eyes, high cheekbones, eyebrows that threatened to connect in the middle. They were all there. It was the light hair and skin, the freckles and thin nose, that had thrown her off, and the complete lack of Iranian gesture. She'd fought an urge to flee. "I need a drink," she said, but he offered her something better, and after a few tokes on a joint, she was calm enough to think more reasonably: *He isn't Iranian. He's as British as I am American. He's never been to Iran, never met his father, grew up without all the cultural bullshit.* On technical grounds, her father would disagree: paternal genes were the ones that counted. And this made the situation rather amusing. Her father's hackneyed words came back to her: *There is a doctor. Thirty-two years old. He noticed you at the Yazdi wedding.* And when she ignored him: *What kind of a girl are you? Irreverent, unfeminine, frightening men away like a growling dog. If your sister marries before you, people will assume something is wrong with you, and you will never find a husband!* Oh, if her father could see her now. Finally with an Iranian doctor — half better than nothing, but horrifically immoral. Even now, the memory made her smirk.

She entered her kitchen and turned on the flame under her stovetop samovar kettle. She filled a small teapot with loose cardamom-laced tea leaves she bought at the Persian grocery store on Polk Street, and emptied the dishwasher while the water heated to a boil, careful not to clang the plates and silverware together because the noise would travel like waves up to the bedroom. She poured boiling water over the tea leaves and fitted the pot into a round basin on top of the kettle, where she would let it steep for a while. She leaned against the counter and crossed her arms, still remembering: Julian reaching for her hand across the table, his touch gentle and warm, not proprietary or insistent. He'd turned her hand over and casually inspected her palm and fingers.

Mitra said, "You are *not* going to pretend to read my palm, are you?"

He met her mocking eyes with his own. "Sorry, no. I don't believe in that shite, not even as a pickup strategy." She laughed. He reached for her other hand and brought them side by side, examined them lightly with his thumbs. "Your hands are a mess, luv," he said.

She tried to snatch them away, but he held firmly. "Wait, all these scars. Fascinating. Are you a sculptor?"

She snorted. "Nothing as lofty as that."

"When I was a kid, my mum had a friend, a sculptor. Aunt Rina. Her hands were covered in scars and scabs, sometimes fresh wounds, blisters and bruises and calluses. I'd sit next to her and she'd let me inspect them, tell me what tool had caused this or that, and then what piece of art she'd been working on. I just thought it was incredibly cool."

She chuckled. "Well, most of my scars are from rusty nails or broken glass or wood splinters. I restore old houses."

"I wasn't that far off, then," he said, entwining his fingers with hers. "Aunt Rina used to say, 'I shape things, Boyo, not the

272

other way around.' "

"I love that," Mitra said.

"Yeah, most kids — hell, most people — avoided her. She was intimidating." He'd kissed her palm then. "Their loss," he added, eyes sparkling.

She shivered at the memory and closed her eyes, realizing that she was going to have to shove those unbidden chemicals of attraction into a box in her mind if she was going to follow through with her decision. And it *was* the right decision. She thought about Ana and Bijan, the inevitable consequences that came from an uneven union. Already she had let things go too far; Julian would be hurt. He was young; he would find someone else. But she would miss him terribly.

Water rushed through the pipes; Julian was up. No doubt he had an early flight. Her stomach twisted with nerves. Of course she wasn't going to talk to him about their relationship now, but just knowing her decision made her feel self-conscious about greeting him. She'd been gone a week, but it felt like a year. She reached for the moka pot to make Julian's espresso.

When she took it up to him, he was in front of the mirror combing his wet hair back.

"Hey," she said, placing the cup on the counter.

"Just what the doctor ordered," he said. It was not something she did often, bring him his coffee.

"You being the doctor, yes," she said as she turned and kissed him, pulling back before coming in contact with his shirtless torso. "Sorry I was asleep when you got home," she said. "I was exhausted."

"More than exhausted," he said, and she heard the admonition in his voice. He was using the comb rather aggressively to futilely flatten the curls at his nape.

"I needed to relax," she said, then thought twice. "Okay, I needed to pass out. The trip was more difficult emotionally than I expected." She couldn't help feeling defensive. Her elbow knocked against the towel rack, and the clang dramatized her irritation.

He dropped his arms. "I'm sorry," he said. Now he was contrite, and she hadn't wanted that. He tossed the comb onto the counter and she let him put his arms around her. "Welcome home," he whispered in her ear. His lips found her neck, his hands slid down her back, her hips, he pressed her into the wall, and she felt . . . she felt . . . nothing. He could've been her brother, if she'd had one, or Nezam.

"What is it?" Julian asked, pulling back and looking at her.

Had she tensed up? No, but her palms were on his chest, lightly, not pressing, not saying no, but not saying yes either. "Nothing," she said, tears suddenly stinging behind her eyes. He spied the bandage on her hand, took her wrist to get a better look. "What's this?"

"Oh," she exhaled. "Stupid me, I was a bit rough with one of my mom's paper-thin tea glasses."

"Let me take a look at it."

"Don't be silly. It's nothing. The bandage is just so I won't irritate it." She gently withdrew her wrist and he placed his hands on either side of her face, rubbing his thumbs against her cheeks. "Everything all right with your family?"

She forced a smile. "Yes, everyone's all right. It was just stressful. I need some downtime, that's all."

He straightened. "Sorry about this conference. I'd rather stay and pamper you, but I have to —"

"No worries, Jules. I think I'm just gonna sleep until you get back."

CHAPTER 14

Mitra did spend much of the next five days in her home office, curled up on an over-stuffed love seat, Jezebel next to her. She screened her calls, ignored the doorbell, and avoided the family room during the day, when Akram tended to show herself at the back door.

Her office was the room she loved best — the smallest in the house, tucked away behind the kitchen, a maid's room in earlier times. Mitra had designed it to be dark. Julian called it the Womb, much to her disgust. The walls were sponged a deep red over brown, bamboo window shades blocked out the daylight, and low-slung velvet drapes puddled onto the Tabrizi carpet Shireen had shipped to Mitra without Yusef's knowledge (he thought it was in storage). Two walls were outfitted with floor-to-ceiling cherry-wood bookcases lined with art and architecture books. It looked more like a writer's office than an artist's, but from the beginning, this was her vision for the room and she hadn't questioned it. It had something to do with blocking out stimuli and provoking imagination. When she needed natural light, she raised the shades or set up her drafting table at the picture window in her family room.

Work had always been Mitra's joy and escape. But since the accident, a crushing fatigue gripped her when she came into her office. Across the room, her desktop was so neat it made her angry. When she worked for real, it was a mess. Over the last year, her weekly housekeeper had managed to make it look staged, like a photograph in a home decor magazine. All of its items — laptop, black mesh pen/pencil holder, sleek cordless phone with headset lying at the ready, mini-printer, halogen lamp with movable arm, square wooden tray with compartments for paperclips, rubber bands, stapler, and stamps; black coil file holder with two manila folders standing upright, one labeled Kitchen Remodel, the other Landscaping — seemed to be waiting for someone other than Mitra.

On the love seat, which she'd found at a garage sale and had reupholstered by an old Chinese man whose fingers were as small and lithe as those of the little girls in Iran who wove carpets, she slept in fits and starts, her face against a scratchy pillow. Waking was difficult, a kind of mind assault: about what words she would use to break up with Julian; about calling Olga to offer a real apology, not a drunk one; about writing to Aden about Ana's jewelry. Each issue came at her muddled and filled her chest with anxiety. She would get up briefly for a glass of juice or a handful of almonds or to splash water on her face.

Finally, it was Friday evening and she sat in her family room waiting for Julian to arrive from the airport. She'd showered and put on a fresh pair of jeans and a sweatshirt, made a salad and cut up a watermelon for a light dinner. She was nervous, still unsure of the words she would use. She'd set the kitchen table, all the while wondering if the evening would end sadly or angrily. She'd thought hard about whether to have the conversation tonight or wait until the morning. It seemed cruel to drop such a bombshell when he was sure to be tired and clueless, but wasn't it more cruel to share her bed with a man she no longer desired? Not that she intended to spell it out; not that she could, but she would try.

She looked at her watch — *he should be*

here by now — and grabbed the phone to check for delays. Sure enough, the fog at SFO was thick and Julian's plane was still on the tarmac in Vegas. ETA: midnight. At least tomorrow was Saturday; he could sleep in. She put the salad and fruit into the fridge and sat to watch TV, determined to stay alert.

Using the remote, she stopped at the first movie she found. The sound was too low to hear, but it took her only a few seconds to figure out the genre — square-jawed actor in military uniform before a blip-lighted map of the world, speaking seriously to a dew-faced actor in a politician's suit. So many shows about war. Propaganda in the form of entertainment, Julian would say.

She turned to HGTV and raised the volume. House-hunting. Stupid show: never revealed the price of the homes. The Learning Channel panned a condo packed to the ceilings with the junk of hoarders who would soon be persuaded to part with it all so that a team of designers could organize and redecorate tastefully, though Mitra knew all bets would be off once the cameras were gone. CNN had a turbaned guy defending the Islamic world's indignation over a Danish newspaper's "blasphemous" cartoons depicting the Prophet Mohammad wearing a bomb on his head. The anchor-woman was trying desperately to be empathetic — almost apologetic — about her guest's point of view. She had no idea that the depiction of the prophet was a debate that had been going on between Muslims for centuries. And when had it officially become Muslims instead of Moslems? She could hear her father's disapproval at this Arab-centric articulation.

No. She didn't want to think about her father. She turned the TV off, but the afterimage of the turbaned man lingered. Her father was just like that man, despite his secularism. Extremists, both. Righteous manipulators whose beliefs were simply a way of enhancing their own power. Heaping ignominy on others to draw praise for themselves.

She got up and opened the cabinet to search for a music CD, something that wouldn't stir memory or emotion. She settled on a classical piano mix. On the shelf above the stereo was the usual bank of family photos. She straightened Anahita's black-and-white senior yearbook photo — the very one that the *Bulletin* had used — enlarged to an eight-by-ten and set in a simple silver frame. Two smaller frames sat on either side, one of Shireen next to a yellow rosebush, the other of Olga with hair teased up and eyelashes curled. She wondered: Was it time to bring out the kids' photos she'd placed in the drawer below? Could she bear it now? Shouldn't she try? But she turned around and on her way back to the sofa picked up the new John Grisham novel Julian was reading. A distraction, she hoped.

When she opened her eyes, it was morning. She leapt up in a panic. Bleary-eyed, she walked through the family room as she checked the phone for messages. None. On her way out of the kitchen, she nearly tripped over Julian's suitcase at the bottom of the stairs. She'd slept through his arrival? She felt terrible. And relieved. She looked up the staircase. The door to her bedroom was closed. Asleep or not, he would be expecting her. She turned away and used the powder room, then grabbed her cigarettes — *this will be my last pack* — and headed out onto the deck.

The temperature outside had already risen, and Mitra reminded herself to water the container plants, especially the impatiens, later in the day. She sat in one of two folding camp chairs she'd bought a little over a year ago as temporary outdoor furniture; the sun had faded their canvases from a hunter green to a dirty pastel. It was the perfect time of year to shop for some good outdoor furniture; past Labor Day, anything that was left would be marked down by more than half. But she didn't have the energy. Or the interest, really. She couldn't remember the last time she'd gone shopping just for the pleasure of it.

A burnt smell that wasn't from her cigarette caught her attention. Akram had charred her toast again. Even the temperature gauge on a small appliance addled the woman. She didn't trust it, turned it up to "dark" (which she couldn't read) when the bread didn't pop up in due time. She reminded Mitra of a young maid her uncle Jafar had sent over from Iran in the seventies who told Olga that she thought there was a little man inside the washing machine who did the work. She smelled like those maids, too — of onions eaten raw and bodies washed only with water. Mitra had bought shower gel and shampoo and synthetic loofahs. Salimeh, the daughter, used them. Akram washed five times daily, in preparation for prayer — ritual ablutions that amounted to wet swipes on forehead, forearms, and tops of the feet. If she took a bath once a week, Mitra would have been surprised. She used dishwashing detergent, as if her body was an inanimate object. Her teeth were rotting. Her hair was so thin and damaged at the ends that it looked burnt. The calluses on her heels were like peanut brittle, her hands as rough as a scouring pad, cuticles like old grout.

Ugh, she thought, stubbing out her cigarette, *I'm being so uncharitable.* Mitra hoped Akram hadn't heard her on the deck. Quietly, she returned to the kitchen and put on the tea. She jumped when the doorbell rang. Padding through the front hall, she glanced at her watch: nearly 9:30. Out of habit, she squinted through the peephole and was not surprised to see only the distorted view of a poplar tree and parked cars on the street. She opened the door wide, leaned against the jamb, looked down. "Two orphans begging for their breakfast, huh?"

Jacob, the little one, squinted up at her, unsure of her mood because she wasn't smiling. He was wearing a baseball cap backward, and his fine blond hair stuck up from the cap hole in wisps. His cheeks were pink and shiny, his bottom lip red and wet from habitually grabbing it with his upper teeth. Scotty, the older one — all of seven and still wearing his plaid pajama bottoms — had no use for Mitra and tried to peer around her into the house. "Is Julian here?" he asked.

"He's asleep. How about a 'good morning, Mitra'?"

Scotty let his head droop a little and mumbled the words. "Good morning, Mitra."

Jacob whispered the phrase, eyeing her through nearly white lashes, watching intently, carefully. This shyness in him was new, and she didn't doubt it had something to do with her not seeing him as frequently as she used to. She hadn't realized it until a few weeks ago when she and Karen found themselves putting the recycling out at the same time. "Hey, stranger," Karen had called from across the street. Mitra felt immediately guilty; she hadn't talked to her neighbor friends in weeks, it seemed, as she'd been too preoccupied by worries over her upcoming trip for the One Year. And now Jacob was stepping backward down one step. Scotty was turning, his head drooping lower.

Mitra said, "Julian's pretty lazy today. He's hard to wake up, you know." Scotty looked up, swiped at his too-long bangs. "But I bet you guys could get him up," she continued. "Like, jump on him maybe. He's very ticklish, you know." She was still trying to look serious, let them figure out her intentions from the language. Scotty was already getting it. He grinned and said, "Yeah! Let's go, Jake!"

Jacob didn't really get it, but from his brother's excited voice and because of his natural propensity to follow him without question, he bounced his knee thrice and took a step up. Mitra turned her body sideways to allow Scotty into the house, and he took off toward the stairs. Before Jacob could follow, she squatted directly in front of him. "Pay the toll," she said. "One hug." He was reluctant and antsy. She smiled and poked his belly; he laughed and twisted away. Finally, she grabbed him. His arms went around her neck and he squeezed briefly. She resisted pressing her lips into his cheek; the shampoo and sour sleep smell of his nape made her dizzy with longing. She let him go, remembering why she visited them less now. It was just too hard. After the accident, she'd tried to return to the pre-auntie Mitra who barely noticed children, sidestepping them as if they were ill-placed ottomans or a family pet, but it was impossible. From the moment Nikku was born, and then even more intensely after Nina came along, Mitra's heart had expanded in a way she never could've imagined. For the first time in her life, she'd understood infatuation.

Back in the kitchen, the sounds from upstairs — the thumping, the child laughter, and the mock imitation of a growling bear — reminded Mitra of when relatives visited from Tehran before the Revolution, filling her parents' house with uncles and aunts and cousins for weeks on end, every corner of the guest rooms piled with Bloomingdale's shopping bags and kids' bedrolls. The din of human beings — present and living — had transformed her life. If they couldn't live in a city, that was the next best thing — a house transformed into a city. There was a lot of wrestling. Not only was professional wrestling an Iranian obsession (having roots in the mythology of the Zoroastrian strongmen), it was a family sport that fathers used as an excuse to hold and kiss and tickle their small children. Even Mitra's father had once in a while played a weekend pajama game of catch and release with her and Ana on the king-size bed in her parents' bedroom. She could still summon a memory of the tangy scent of his cologne and the near-tears laughter from Ana, who often couldn't take the characteristic roughness of it all. One common trait of Iranian men was the physical attention they paid to their small children. A father who didn't smother his child — kissing, sniffing, petting, nuzzling — was weird. It struck her suddenly that Kareem had wrestled with the little ones more than any of them. Of course he had. Did he still? And of course it had been easy for him to do what he'd done. This was what a taboo did; it created a dangerous ignorance, a vacuum of vocabulary, an inability to discern between a right or a wrong feeling — all because of a priggish anxiety to talk about sex.

Mitra poured two inches of ruby tea into her glass mug, then topped it off with boiling water from the kettle; it was just the right amber color. She blew on the hot liquid and heard her breath tremble. She popped a few golden raisins into her mouth as a sweetener and sipped, burned her tongue. She heard the kids and Julian bounding down the stairs, and then the room flooded with giggles.

Mitra put her glass on the counter and prepared to greet Julian, but before she could, he positioned himself behind her, slid one arm around her waist, and held the other out in front as if to set up a force field that Jacob and Scotty couldn't penetrate. The boys' faces were blotchy red, their hair sticking to their brows, as they breathed like demons and reached around Mitra for Julian, who jerkily moved the two of them as a unit to evade little grabbing fingers. In a high voice, Julian exclaimed, "Save me! Save me, Mitra!"

No wonder he was a pediatrician.

"Hey, guys, stop," she managed to say, wanting desperately to be free of Julian's warm chest against her back and the soft brush of his genitals against her buttocks. Sensing her irritation, Julian let go and used his serious voice to say, "Time out, guys. Time out." That voice — what Mitra suspected was his quiet-now-I-have-to-take-your-pulse voice — could stop a kid in his tracks. "Take a deep breath . . . deep breath," he said, doing it himself, the boys following as if this was Simon Says, their shoulders rising up to their ears and dropping abruptly. Mitra stifled a smile. Julian leaned over and pointed his finger at Scotty's chest, only to catch his nose when he looked down to inspect the spot. Julian said, "Okay, good. Now quick to the table, in chairs, for . . . blueberry pancakes." They did it in a flash, and Julian turned to open the cabinet, but first, to shoot Mitra a line. "Sleep well?" He clearly wasn't looking for an answer.

Mitra leaned against the counter and found herself chewing on her cuticles, like

288

when she was a kid; Shireen had polished them with a foul-tasting solution from the pharmacy that made her stop. She got busy setting the table, pouring two tall glasses of milk, microwaving the maple syrup, and returning unconsciously to her cuticles.

"Ready, kids?" Julian said, swooping two plates toward the table. "Here they come."

The boys bounced up and down as he then dolloped each stack with whipped cream, poured the syrup, and gave them permission to dig in.

Acting in his own fatherhood skit. Mitra tasted blood as she tore through a cuticle. *You selfish, stupid woman.* She moved to wash the skillet.

The steam from the faucet curled her eyelashes and she realized she was practically scrubbing the shine off the pan. She rinsed and jerked her hand back from the scalding water. She and Julian had stopped using condoms long ago. He thought she was on the pill. It had been a natural segue from the fib she'd told him that first night when he noticed her pelvic scar and she'd taken on Ana's ovarian cyst rupture as her own. After Ana's surgery, her doctor had advocated she take the pill for several years to prevent ovulation until her ovary healed. Mitra's throat swelled and her hand trembled as she reached for a bowl to rinse. Until now, she hadn't felt a twinge of regret about the lie. She'd guarded her reproductive privacy the way she always had in her short and shallow past relationships. But she'd known it was wrong. She'd nearly said as much when Olga had asked her if Julian was in love with her — that it was unfair that he didn't know she couldn't have children. And yet this was the first time she'd allowed herself to admit the guilt. There's a time, she thought, when a secret becomes a lie, when it has the power to harm.

The slam of the front door made Mitra jump, and she nearly dropped the plate she was rinsing. She'd been so in her head, she hadn't registered that breakfast was over, the kids now off to soccer practice. The shuffle of Julian's feet along the hallway sounded to her like a countdown. They were alone now. If she could compose herself and focus, it could all be over in a matter of minutes.

"I told Karen you'd gone up to take a shower," Julian said. "She wants us to come for a barbecue later on; the boys want burgers."

Mitra kept her back to him, loaded the breakfast plates into the dishwasher. "Okay," she said, thinking he could go by himself if he wanted to; Karen would comfort him, and the kids too. Then again, Karen would probably be as upset about their breakup as Julian. Despite her situation — a husband who was so obsessed by his merchant banking career that he spent more time on planes and in hotels than at home — Karen was a ferocious advocate of marriage, of couplehood. She wouldn't understand what Mitra had done at all. If only she, Mitra, were more like Karen, if only Julian had met Karen before she married Dave. Lives crossed at the most inopportune time, Mitra thought. She imagined Julian and Karen sitting across from each other at Karen's kitchen table, their hands entwined in morning marital joy. She waited for a rush of jealousy to wash over her, but it didn't come, and she realized that she did truly care about him — enough to let him go.

Finally, there were no more dirty dishes, cutlery, glasses, or pans, and she had to shut the tap, admit the silence, and say something. Without turning around, busying herself with wiping down the counter, she said, "We have to talk, Julian."

"I should think so, luv, among other things." She glanced up. He'd splayed the newspaper before him. Suddenly, he leaned left to peek into the family room and the glass door to the deck. "Um, Akram's here."

"Shit," Mitra said. "Don't let on that you saw her. She'll go away."

"You know she won't. She's sitting, waiting."

Mitra didn't have to look to know that Akram was squatting by the door. A flat-footed village squat that people who sat in chairs all their lives had trouble doing without toppling backward. A yoga pose. Elbows resting on her knees, butt hovering inches above the ground. Despite the heat, her body would be sealed with fabric: scarf, tunic, trousers, socks. Fortressed against Julian, who thought her ways were culturally interesting — respectfully, of course. All Mitra saw was the trick of organized oppression. She sighed. "Okay, let her in, would you?"

"You do it. She gets all flustered with me."

"She needs to stop that," Mitra said, reaching into the cabinet for tea glasses.

"She can't help it," he said. "I'm a man."

"She's been in America for eight months, Jules. She should get over that."

Julian reached for the soccer cleats he'd tossed under a kitchen chair when he came downstairs — on weekends, he played with a league in the park — and went to let

Akram in while Mitra prepared two glasses of strong tea.

Akram followed Julian into the kitchen, having insisted that he walk ahead of her, not only because she couldn't fathom the notion of equality of station, but because it was easier for her to shield her face from his eyes. He didn't even glance at her face; Mitra had taught him this: woman's duty was to cover up, man's duty was to avert eyes. Still, Akram pulled the scarf below her eyebrows and stretched it to cover half her mouth. Mitra wondered if the woman could sense the strain between her and Julian, if she cared that she was trespassing on their intimacy, as she'd done over the past week by "playing house" in Mitra's domain.

"Salaam Alaykom," Akram said in her sibilant way, bowing slightly. "Welcome back, Khanoom."

"Salaam," Mitra replied. "Thank you. Sit, Khanoom. I'm bringing tea." One could still use the polite honorific, Mitra thought; it was the tone that mattered.

"Please don't bother yourself, Khanoom," said Akram, still standing. "I have had my morning tea. I came up only to ask Julian Agha to give my regards to Kourosh Agha."

Julian was pulling on his cleats. Kourosh was Julian's teammate in the league; he was also Akram's relative, the dermatologist who'd begged them to house the mother and daughter temporarily.

Akram smiled thinly. "And also to please tell Kourosh Agha that Salimeh and I would like to visit very soon."

Mitra translated, but there was no need; Akram said the same thing every week. And Kourosh responded to Julian every week with a promise that he would arrange to come and get them one Sunday soon; he would talk to his wife and work out the logistics. But in three months, he'd collected them only once and had returned them just three hours later. Julian thought the problem must be with Kourosh's wife, an American woman raised in Iowa, who liked to seem charitable but really just wanted the company of her nuclear family. Though Mitra had seen Caitlin only that one time when they'd gone to the house in Fremont, Mitra felt sorry for her. She was overweight and haggard, with dark roots and premature gray, desperately trying to make a cozy home out of a flimsy forties ranch with aluminum windows, self-sewn needlepoint pillows, and a saltwater fish tank that gave the house a perpetual seaweed smell. Kourosh had tacked a wall-to-wall carpet in the garage and turned it into an extra room for the ten unexpected relatives that his mother, once she arrived, begged him to vouch for as "mere visitors" to the immigration officials. No question Kourosh was experiencing the downside of becoming the first doctor in his family: perpetual relative encroachment.

Walking into that damp garage, Mitra had been transported. There was no furniture, just neatly bundled bedrolls against the walls. Women and children sat cross-legged around a rectangular tablecloth, eating from platters of lavash bread, goat cheese, and fresh herbs. An electric samovar sat in a corner. The women rose as she entered the room, and Kourosh's mother, whose eyes bulged with what Julian later called "a definite thyroid condition," led Mitra into the circle and began immediately complimenting her on her altruism, as if she'd already offered to take some of them in. And Mitra had been seduced — by the aroma of mint and basil, by the droopy eyes of a jet-lagged toddler, by the mingling of advice, superstition, and magical tales, by the language of her parents and Olga. But mostly by the wide-open face of Salimeh, a village girl who reminded her of Ana at that young age. Too bad she hadn't taken a harder look at Akram that day in Fremont;

she might have seen the ignorance in those raisin eyes, the intolerance in the fissured marionette lines. When Caitlin and Kourosh begged her to take the women "until we can get a handle on the situation," which to Mitra and Julian meant until they could find permanent housing, it was Salimeh's eager smile, smooth caramel skin, slightly sunken cheeks, and bony wrists that stirred Mitra to say yes.

Julian finished lacing up his cleats and looked at his watch. "I'm off," he said, standing and pocketing his car keys. He gave Akram a quick smile. He glanced at Mitra. "See you later," he said, before heading for the hallway.

"Have fun!" she called, hating herself.

Chapter 15

"Mitra-joon, I am Olga."

"Really? Not Mary Poppins?"

"Hah. I was happy to hear the sound of you on my machine, joonam."

"Oli-joon, I'm sorry about the other night. Was I mean? I don't remember."

"No, azizam, not mean. Funny. Like always when you drink wodka."

"Yeah, well, I wasn't funny after I woke up the next morning. I slept for most of the last three days."

"*Afareen!* You deserve this. Sleeping is good for sorrow. And sleeping with someone else is *very* good."

"He was on a business trip, so there was none of that."

"Ah."

"Where were you when I called?"

"I went to doctor for checkup."

"Everything okay?"

"Doctor says five polyp in my colon now.

297

Don't worry; not cancer. He want to take them out, but I do not want operation again. It is all right; not really pain, just aching."

"Don't have any operations over there, Olga."

"But doctors are good here. We have everything. You should see how many women are having the face-lifts, making the boobies bigger too. The noses, of course, made smaller. And Botox very in fashion."

"Of course it is."

"Hah, you being smart-alex."

"Alec. Yes. Anyway, thanks for calling me back."

"Why you thank me? I am not stranger."

"I didn't mean it that way, Oli. It's just that I've been calling you too much lately and getting all emotional."

"So what? If I be living in America, I be living next to you, and you be talking to me all the times. This make me happy. I mean, not *happy* to hear you unhappy, but happy to listen. For what am I on this earth? But, Mitra-joon, maybe you go see doctor."

"I'm not sick, Olga."

"You 'pressed, joonam. I hear this in your voice."

"I'm not depressed. I'm sad. There's a difference."

"You sad. You nervous. You angry. Go see psych-aye-trist. Ask for the blue pill. You know it saved me."

"Not this again, Olga. I'm not taking Prozac. It gives me the shakes."

"Mitra, you are a stubborn child. There are other medicines for suffering besides the Prozac. My doctor told me. So many people here now take this, even the young ones."

"No. I just have to get back to work. That's my Prozac."

"*Basheh,* but you not working. Too much happening in your house. Those village women, they keep you from taking care of yourself."

"Olga, I hardly see them."

"Doesn't matter. You thinking about them. They in your life. And now One Year is passed, it is time to wake up."

Mitra's jaw ached from grinding her teeth. As if to stress Olga's point, Akram appeared on the deck and tapped on the door, returning to her iteration of the village well not two hours since she'd left. "Oli-joon, you're right."

"What?"

"I said, you're right; I have to do something about this situation, but let's talk later. Someone's at my door."

Mitra motioned for Akram to come in and went to put a load of laundry on. She realized that she'd resigned herself to Akram's social visits and while she didn't treat her as she would a friend or neighbor — with undivided attention — she had let the woman make it a habit. Mitra was polite, but went about her business. She hadn't realized what an imposition it was until now.

Mitra plunked Akram's tea in front of her, letting it slosh. Whatever Mitra's feelings, not to serve tea was outside the boundary of etiquette.

"May your hands not ache," Akram said, as always.

"It is nothing," Mitra replied, as always. Rote Persian pleasantries.

Mitra uncovered the lid of the lump sugar bowl and sat down to busy herself with a pile of accumulated mail. This was the moment to bring up the issue of Akram's use of the house while Mitra was gone, but Mitra was at a loss for how to voice her displeasure without sounding petulantly displeased. Akram would apologize in an obsequious and hurt tone, and it would sound to the both of them like an exchange between spoiled princess and bullied servant. This was the dynamic, false though it was on its face. Mitra tried to see Akram the way Julian did. "She's just confused, Mitra. Wouldn't you be? She's never known anything different. We have to teach her." Mitra hated those lines; they sounded like something from a Kipling story about the civilized enlightening the natives. As if the Western world was devoid of poor, uneducated, and bitter people.

Mitra sorted through her mail, opened a handwritten bill from the gardener for her property in Woodside, discarded a pretentious local magazine called *Gentry,* and slurped her tea. She felt like her father at the breakfast table, reading the newspaper as if no one else was there, no one worth his attention anyway. The thought shamed her, and she lifted her face and forced a smile.

Akram tugged back her scarf since Julian wasn't around. "Your family was well, Mitra Khanoom?"

"Yes, thank you."

"My condolences again for your loss." She sighed heavily with feigned grief. "May your sister and her children rest in God's hands!"

"Yes, thank you very much." Mitra bit the inside of her cheek. How she hated this fakery. "Is Salimeh coming up?" she asked as she wrote a check for the gardener.

Akram tsked. "She went early for a study

group." She sighed heavily again. "She left without saying her namaz, lazy girl."

"I'm sure God won't mind if she says it later."

"She stays up late with her books and then cannot wake at dawn to honor Allah. Only a bad girl sleeps through her prayers and later says them fast and sloppily."

Mitra had made Salimeh's ESL classes a condition of the women's residence in her house, but Akram couldn't let go of the idea that such independence could only lead to an immoral end. In Fremont she had forbidden her teenage daughter from venturing without an adult beyond the cul-de-sac where they squatted. Mitra guessed that no mother would feel comfortable with new rules set by an outsider, but instead of taking it up with Mitra or making an effort to try alternative ways to keep an eye on her daughter, Akram upped her expectations for obedience and berated the girl, yelling often and loudly enough for Mitra to hear, and using debasing words that Mitra recognized from the village maids her uncle Jafar used to send over before Auntie Golnaz found Olga: unlady-like, unworthy, sloppy, and "pickled," which was what spinsters were called — a fate all of the girls dreaded, no matter how young they were. Mitra had also noticed the bruises along Salimeh's arms, and she suspected Akram — pinching, she surmised — but Julian said that malnourishment often caused people to bruise easily, and that they shouldn't assume the worst until Salimeh was healthier; he'd bought a basketful of supplements for her to take. And maybe he was right, Mitra thought. She was being too judgmental.

"Don't worry about Salimeh," Mitra said. "She's a very good girl." These words, said so many times, rarely put an end to Akram's complaints about Salimeh. Mitra had begun to feel like a worn-out husband who longed for some peace after a hard day's work. And Akram's constant appeal for Mitra to validate her grievances, as if they were co-mothers, tested Mitra's patience. Perhaps they were, in a way, like co-mothers. After all, they were only two years apart in age, but Akram, at forty-two, looked as lined and liver-spotted as a granny.

All the more reason to pity her, Mitra told herself. "Akram-joon," she said, trying for a compassionate tone. "Your daughter is smart, sweet, helpful, and pretty. Have faith that everything will turn out all right."

Faith was a word that triggered Akram's religiosity, causing a pause for the usual "Inshallah"s and a few moments of silent

303

respect. Mitra tried not to think about how, for this woman, "everything" and "all right" meant that her daughter would find a man to marry her and take care of them both. It was for this reason that Akram wanted so badly to visit Kourosh's house more often: she hoped to find a husband for her daughter through her associations with the other Iranian women, and through Kourosh. She hadn't realized that moving in with Mitra would cut her off from this network, that Mitra didn't mingle with Iranians. Marriage for Salimeh was the only favorable option Akram could imagine. Mitra, of course, was not an example of another possibility; Mitra was an alien, an aberrant female, certainly not a role model. Case in point: one day early on, Akram announced that she was praying to God for Mitra's motherhood, that surely God would reward Mitra for taking a pair of poor women into her care. When Mitra explained that she and Julian were not married and that she didn't want children, Akram willfully misinterpreted the situation and vowed to make a *nazr* — a covenant with God — that if He led Julian to marry Mitra and caused her to conceive, Akram would make a pilgrimage to the Shrine of Imam Hossein in the holy city of Mashhad. Yeah, Mitra thought, and who

304

was going to make that happen? Hadn't the woman come to America to escape the poverty of widowhood and to end the cycle of dependence for her daughter? Or was she really "just visiting"? More likely, she was allowing the world to take her along, like a bobbing piece of debris in a canal.

"I have finished the ironing," Akram said. "Perhaps you have more for me to do?"

The ironing. It was what Akram did. That and mending clothes. She darned socks, took in seams, adjusted hems. She touted herself as a fine seamstress, and in the beginning Mitra imagined that she might help Akram develop a little alterations business. She bought her a sewing machine from Costco and collected clothes from neighbor friends — Karen and Mrs. Tokuda, who was looking for someone to sew pillowcases for her. Akram ruined everything. Worst of all, she destroyed Mrs. Tokuda's Japanese silk fabric, sewing it into uneven squares, forgetting to leave one side open for inserting the pillow, then rending the fabric as she removed the stitches. Socks were darned so tightly that they puckered at the toes, creating a lump in one's shoe. Trousers were hemmed too short, and skirts too long. When confronted, Akram would bridle with insult and insist that Mitra was mistaken, as if Mitra didn't know any better. And so Akram's "work" had devolved mostly into ironing, which she did well. But how much ironing could there be? Even Mitra's sheets were ironed now, not that ironed sheets weren't a lovely thing.

"I'll have some ironing for you after I do the laundry today," Mitra said. "And I'll ask Karen if she would like you to do some of the boys' things."

"All right. Perhaps you could buy some more handkerchiefs as well; I have finished decorating the last batch."

"Okay," Mitra said, unable to meet Akram's eyes. The handkerchiefs were a boondoggle. Akram stitched little geometric designs into them, sometimes created an uneven pastel border. She'd presented these handkerchiefs to Julian, who at first didn't have a clue what they were for. "Blowing your nose," Mitra had said, then, under her breath, "wiping your ass." Julian had thanked Akram profusely, smiling as if someone were pulling strings attached to the corners of his mouth. Later, he'd said to Mitra, "Hankies are awfully unsanitary."

"Duh," she'd replied. "I'm sure Akram imagines you wearing them in the breast pocket of your white coat, displaying the design to the envious eyes of your coworkers." In the end, he doled out the hankies to the little girls in the pediatric ward to use as diapers for their dolls.

Mitra felt the vibration of footfalls on the deck stairs, and soon enough Salimeh appeared at the back door. Mitra smiled and waved her in. Salimeh bounced through the sitting room in a pair of Mitra's old running shoes that she'd stuffed with cotton. She let her backpack fall to the floor and sat across from her mother, who eyed her suspiciously and said nothing.

"How was your study group?" Mitra asked.

Salimeh nodded. "Great," she said in English.

"What?" snapped Akram.

"I just said that my study group was good, Maman," her voice soft and fearful.

"Then say it so I can understand."

"Forgive me."

Salimeh looked down at her hands, and Akram was pleased. Mitra's father used to try to make her do this with her elders. Anahita had it down pat as a child; she rarely looked straight into anyone's eyes, not even people her own age. But Mitra had made a point of never looking away, rudely holding someone's gaze for too long when she was introduced to elderly guests in her parents' house, just to irk her father. She'd told Salimeh several times to "look at me when I'm talking to you," explaining that Americans think you're hiding something or you're untrustworthy if you can't look them in the eye.

"Have you made any friends, Salimeh?" Mitra asked, setting a glass of tea in front of her.

Salimeh half rose in distress. "I can get a tea for myself, Khanoom. Please, you embarrass me."

Akram shook her head in exaggerated disappointment. Mitra put her hand on Salimeh's shoulder and pressed her gently down. "I was next to the tea, so I got you a glass. It's my house and my tea. You're not a servant here. So, any friends?"

"There's a girl from Africa. She shared her apple with me during the break."

"A black?" Akram snapped.

"Yes. She wants to start college when her English gets better. She's very kind."

"Is she Moslem?"

"I don't know. She wants to become a doctor."

"Does she wear hejab?"

"No, Maman." Turning to Mitra, Salimeh continued. "Then she wants to go back to her country and work in a hospital."

"That sounds great," Mitra said. "Does she live nearby?"

"I don't know. I'll ask her next time."

"Good. Maybe you can do something together. A walk or an ice cream."

Salimeh blushed, eyed her mother. "Maybe."

Akram said, "You have no business making friends with a black infidel who thinks she can become a doctor."

"Want some cookies?" Mitra asked Salimeh.

She shook her head, sipped the tea. "No, thank you. I'm not hungry."

Mitra filled a plate with mini palmiers and placed it in front of her. "You don't have to be hungry for cookies."

"You spoil my daughter, Khanoom."

"Nonsense," Mitra said. "She's finally putting on some weight. She looks good."

"Yes, maybe she will find a husband after all."

Salimeh nibbled at a palmier, eyes fixed on the plate as if she might read her fortune in the crumbs. Mitra was reminded of Ana when she was that age, not because Salimeh looked at all like Ana, though she had filled out quite a bit in the last months — no more bony wrists, cheeks now pillowy and pinkish despite her olive skin color, no longer swimming in the gray sweat suit Mitra had given her. It was her demeanor that reminded Mitra of Ana, her anxiety about pleasing her mother and Mitra at the same time, despite their opposing positions. A strenuous task. Mitra suddenly remembered what Aden said about how Ana had not presented her complete self to Mitra, how she behaved in certain ways with certain people. Maybe what had really tormented her sister was her desire to be *both* traditional and modern. Instead, she did what Salimeh was doing: not just switching between languages with Mitra and Akram, but trying to accommodate the wishes of each one. For Mitra, her identity was either one or the other, a choice. Obviously, Ana hadn't wanted to make that choice, and maybe Salimeh didn't either. No, Mitra thought. Maybe they simply couldn't figure out how.

The doorbell rang and the knocker sounded in quick succession. Only Mrs. Tokuda did that, demanding as she was. Mitra went quickly to answer it, surprised at how eager she was to see her neighbor from two doors down. And there she was, all four feet ten of her, silver pageboy haircut, silk pantsuit with a Nehru collar, black ballet slippers, arms cradling an iron teapot

310

covered with a fawn-colored cozy. She always brought over her own tea.

"Ah, today you answer door."

"Sorry, Tokuda-san. I was really tired from my trip."

She waved Mitra's words away. "Glad you home," she said, stepping in and glancing down the hall to the kitchen. "That silly woman here?"

"Of course," Mitra said, rolling her eyes.

Mrs. Tokuda peered up at Mitra's face. "You looking bad," she said. "You drink some Japanese tea. Feel better."

"You know I hate that stuff."

Mrs. Tokuda headed down the hallway. "I hate your stuff too. Like drinking hot juice." Mitra smiled and followed.

Akram and Salimeh rose when Mrs. Tokuda entered the kitchen. "Good afternoon," she said loudly, bowing curtly. Akram and Salimeh mirrored her, though Mitra was sure Mrs. Tokuda would have preferred a deep Japanese bow to indicate the distinction in class. And age, of course. Mrs. Tokuda was an amazing eighty-seven years old and she never let anyone forget it. She was a Judo Master, a sensei, a one-of-a-kind woman. A recent article in *More* magazine had dubbed her "The Ageless Athlete," and she now had an arm's-length waiting list for the self-defense class she held in her studio living room, a space that Mitra had remodeled with skylights and state-of-the-art matted flooring. Once in a while, Mrs. Tokuda would try to lure Mitra to the class, but Mitra always replied, "Never again." The bruises on her arms and back had lasted weeks.

Mrs. Tokuda set her teapot on the table and went directly to grab a cup from the cupboard. Mitra poured herself another glass of tea from the samovar and placed a bowl of dates on the table. Akram's expression was sour; the level of disgust between the old woman and her was equal.

Now they were all sitting at the table, Mrs. Tokuda chasing bites of a date with slurps of her green tea, a habit she'd picked up from Mitra — "a Persian thing not too bad." Salimeh plucked another palmier from the dish. "You have good appetite," Mrs. Tokuda said. Salimeh gave a puzzled frown. Mitra translated. Salimeh smiled with crumbs stuck to her lips and nodded her head. Akram said to Mitra, "Is the tight-eye making fun of my daughter?"

"Not at all," Mitra said.

Mrs. Tokuda flashed a fake smile at Akram. "Is the barbarian complaining?" she asked Mitra.

"Not at all," Mitra said, watching as Akram smiled falsely back.

"She is stinkier than usual today," Mrs. Tokuda said.

Mitra chuckled quietly. "You're so bad, Tokuda-san."

"I only speak truth."

"Be careful. The girl is learning English pretty quickly."

"My English is not normal English; she no understand. Anyway, better she know her mother is idiot."

"Stop. You're making me laugh."

Salimeh opened her ESL workbook. "Good you study," Mrs. Tokuda said, pointing to the book and enunciating her words.

Salimeh looked up. "Yes," she said.

"Most important thing is education."

Mitra translated.

Akram snorted, looked away. Mrs. Tokuda crinkled her face into a severe sneer. She'd put two daughters through college and one through law school; the other was a therapist. Neither were married, and that was just fine with Mrs. Tokuda. "Husbands are like heavy rocks in pockets, pulling women down and down." She'd been widowed after the war, after the internment camps. Her mother had been a geisha in Kyoto, which was how Mitra thought she got her independent streak, as well as a distinctive bias toward the rare male who showed modesty and humility. She liked Julian.

Salimeh undid her scarf and let it fall to her shoulders. Her hair was stick-straight and shiny. Mrs. Tokuda said, "She walks in the neighborhood without that scarf on, you know."

"I know," said Mitra.

"Soon maybe she show the belly too. And the barbarian mother have heart attack. We be rid of her."

Mitra sputtered, coughed up half a raisin. "What? What belly?"

Chapter 16

When Julian got back from soccer, Mitra was dressed and pacing the living room. "We need to go for a walk," she said.

He dropped his gym bag and picked at his damp T-shirt: a British flag with the word GREECE under it. "Gotta jump in the shower first."

She stopped pacing, stood with her hands in her jeans pockets, shoulders tense. "You can shower when we get back."

"What's wrong?"

"I'll tell you when we're out of here." Her voice sounded at once pleading and angry.

She was silent as they climbed the hill away from the Sunday bustle of Twenty-fourth Street. Usually they took their weekend walks past neighborhood shops or at farmers' markets or craft fairs; sometimes they hiked in the Headlands across the Golden Gate, but they rarely walked the quiet residential streets; Mitra did this often enough on her own in order to stay familiar with home sales and renovations. She led him toward a bank of eucalyptus trees along the ridge, and they sat down on a weathered wooden bench. The peeling bark of the massive trees reminded Mitra of shedding skin.

"Salimeh's pregnant," she blurted.

"What? Shit. You're joking, right?" Stupid words, all of them.

"Take a good look. One thing a Moslem girl knows is how to make her body invisible and her face unreadable."

Julian put his elbows on his knees, held his head with both hands. "Did she tell you this?"

"No, Mrs. Tokuda noticed it."

"She's been looking so much healthier, filling out."

"Exactly."

"And she's happier, even a little carefree. You think she's in denial?"

"Either that or she's adept at hiding and playacting like most Persian girls." Like Ana, Mitra thought.

"How far along is she?"

"Mrs. Tokuda surmised seven months."

"Jesus, that far?" He sat up, looked at her. "You think the mother knows?"

"Of course she doesn't know."

"How could she not?"

"She's a mother whose worst nightmare is this. I mean, you're a doctor, and you didn't even notice."

"That's not fair. I don't live in the same room with her. We barely communicate — just good morning, how are you, good night. I doubt she knows the English word for pregnant."

"Still."

"You're blaming me? Come on, Mitra."

She stood up, walked a few paces away, then turned. "It was your idea to bring them here. Your idealistic sense of chivalry, and all these exoticized notions you have about Iranians. Tell me, if they were British or American, would you've considered taking them in? A couple of homeless strangers?"

"I see I should be more like you, eh? Cold and insular."

Touché, she thought. His face was red with anger, a muscle next to his eye twitching. Her words had cut him, and she immediately regretted her callousness. He was right; this wasn't his fault. "I'm sorry," she said. "I'm just freaking out." She tried to remain calm, but she couldn't tamp her fury. "How did this *happen*?" she said, flinging her arms up.

"She's a teenager," he huffed. "Evolutionary imperative."

"You're making jokes?"

"Not really. It's true. I just can't imagine her having a boyfriend. She's so shy."

Mitra sat up straight. "Do you think she was raped?"

"Jeez, Mitra. By whom?"

"By anyone! By Kourosh!"

"Mitra!"

"It happens and you know it. All those girls in the refugee camps where your mother works? Raped and pregnant, you told me. Men prey on women everywhere. I mean, I'm not saying it *was* Kourosh, but it had to have been someone who had access to her in that house of his."

Julian was silent, staring, thinking.

"You have to talk to Kourosh, Julian. He's going to have to deal with this — her care, an adoption, whatever. They're his family members."

"Agreed," he said with a sharp nod. "I'll call him and set up a time to talk tomorrow at the hospital." He looked up at her. "Now stop pacing and sit down. We have the first step of a plan."

She sat, and they both stared down the hill at a boy playing fetch with his dog. The breeze fluttered through her hair. It was cool; the fog was coming in. "It's amazing how we don't see things that are right in front of us." She was trying not to think of Ana and Kareem. "Those little pimples around Sali's mouth, the slight pregnancy mask on her cheeks, her wider neck, swollen fingers. I saw it all as soon as Tokuda mentioned it."

He took her hand, and she didn't resist. "Those are some fancy medical details you seem to know."

"When Ana was pregnant, I went back east every few months, made sure I was there for the births. Nina came early; I almost didn't make it. Bijan didn't have the stomach for labor or delivery — one of those people who has to use the toilet whenever someone is in pain or bleeding."

Julian chuckled. "I've known interns like that."

She smirked. "How comforting."

"Come on, let's get some Chinese takeaway and watch a movie. Until I meet with Kourosh, there's nothing we can do."

"I have no appetite, Jules. I just need to think."

"All right. So we'll think." He stood up. "I need that shower. My sweat has turned to ice." He turned and Mitra rose to follow.

"Jules," she said. "I think I need to think about this alone."

He stopped, turned back. "What's going

on, Mitra?"

It was the perfect opening, but she side-stepped it. "*This* is what's going on. I need some time to absorb it. I know you like to talk things through — and I love that about you — but I'm different."

Julian rubbed his eyes. "It's more than that, Mitra. I can feel it. Something happened back east. Why won't you tell me?"

She shook her head. "What happened was the death anniversary of my sister and her kids. Isn't that enough? A year has passed, a whole year, and I lost myself."

He sucked in his breath. She reached up quickly and put her hands on either side of his face. The ends of his curls gleamed red in the misty sunset. "Please, Jules, give me a little space?" She paused. "A few days?"

It was a temporary lie, she told herself, a lie born out of love and affection. And necessity. The situation with Sali had to be resolved before anything else.

Julian loathed the hospital cafeteria, but on short notice, it was the most convenient place to meet Kourosh after morning rounds. Fluorescent lights and worried faces staring into space, tissues balled up and dropped into empty paper cups and trays, lips moving in prayer, legs bouncing under tables. Anxiety like a mist in the air.

Julian grabbed a coffee and sat at a corner table to wait. Kourosh was always late — for soccer, for his patients, for staff meetings — and this put Julian in a fouler mood than he already was. He hadn't slept well the last two nights. Among other things, he wasn't used to his own bed with its lumpy pillows. He'd forgotten how noisy his fridge was and that he'd canceled his cable TV subscription, which meant the distraction of a decent football match was out of the question. Distraction was the path he'd decided to walk after Mitra told him she wanted "space," that ridiculous word that could mean nothing important or something essential. He wasn't stupid; he could tell when a woman wasn't into him, but he felt confident it was temporary. It was tough not to ruminate over what was going on in that willful head of hers. He was trying to be patient, but he was pissed, mostly at himself. He should never have brought those women into their lives. Sure, he felt sorry for the girl, but the situation was complex now. Kourosh needed to take them back so he and Mitra could move on with their lives.

Julian was almost down to the last drop of his lousy coffee, ready to take the lift back up to his department, when Kourosh came sauntering in, white coat flapping behind him like a cape.

"Hey, man, sorry I'm late. Had a patient with a rash that stumped me."

"No problem," said Julian, not meaning it. "Figure it out?"

"Nope. Story of my life. Rashes and zits. I should close my office to teens, start doing Botox exclusively. Hold on, I'll get myself a coffee."

Kourosh's cologne was overpowering. His hair, gelled and neatly combed away from his forehead, gleamed like a new black car, like his shoes. Julian heard him joking with the cashier, a flirty laugh. Who would guess this guy had a frazzled wife, three young children, and a houseful of dependents? On his best day, Julian couldn't be bothered to put on a tie.

"So, what's up?" Kourosh asked, sliding into the chair opposite.

Julian cleared his throat. "It's about Akram and Salimeh." He heard his own poor pronunciation of the names and suddenly felt self-conscious, as if Kourosh might not take him seriously.

"You know I can't thank you enough for helping me out with them." He said this every time they saw each other, as if the words were an installment on a debt. "I'm getting close to figuring it all out. Been talking to a friend of mine who has an apartment in Fresno — he bought it as an investment — just waiting until the lease is up with the current tenants." A few weeks ago, it was a different friend with an apartment in Santa Rosa. But Julian hadn't cared so much then. Was Mitra right? That he liked the chivalry of it? It was true that he saw promise in Sali: she was curious and eager with a character that could be sculpted, the moldy traditions chiseled away. Was this an imperialist attitude?

"So I think in a couple of months," Kourosh was saying, "I'll be able to take them off your hands."

"The girl is pregnant."

For an instant, Kourosh's smile disappeared. Then he reconstituted it and snorted. "Hah! Impossible!"

Julian remained silent, expressionless. Let it sink in.

The smile disappeared again, and Julian could have sworn he heard the guy gulp. Kourosh fiddled with his cup, his spoon, his empty sugar packets. "This . . . this . . . it . . . can't be. I mean, how?"

"You tell me. She was living at your place."

Kourosh wriggled in his chair, frowning, eyes darting with rapid thought. Julian relaxed a little; in this stunned behavior, he saw what he'd hoped to see: that Kourosh was blameless. The guy wasn't a lech. Almost as bad, however: he was an oblivious buffoon who hadn't protected Sali.

Finally, Kourosh managed to say, "This is just terrible!" His voice was a strained whisper; Julian had never seen him so emotional. And then, with balled fists, trembling lips, and set jaw, he said, "That slut!"

The words were so unexpected, Julian sat stunned, and before he knew it, Kourosh was on his feet, suddenly in a rush, saying how he needed to digest it all, but he had to get home, he was exhausted, could they talk about this tomorrow when his head was clear? And he was gone.

I'm a colossal moron, Julian thought. He was so embarrassed by his naïveté that he related the gist of the meeting to Mitra that evening in the simplest of terms, saying that Kourosh was horrified by the news and needed some time to figure out what and how to deal with it. He clasped his phone and braced for words of angry judgment, but all he got was a quiet almost dispassionate voice — "Huh. Okay." — and he wished he could see her face to figure out whether she was in shock, as he was, or if she was shutting down the way she often did when she grieved.

He asked her what she'd learned from Sali about who had done this to her; they needed more ammunition to force Kourosh's engagement. Again, that remote quiet voice: "I haven't told her yet that I know she's pregnant." He couldn't believe it. It wasn't like her. "Well," he said, wishing he could rush over there to shake her loose. "Now that Kourosh knows, you better do it or we could lose control entirely." With Mitra, it was all about control. He knew her well enough to use that like a rocket booster.

Mitra knew she had to do more than just watch Sali, but she felt paralyzed, unable to say or do a thing. Watching Salimeh made her fingers itch. From behind a window or on the deck, she tracked the girl as she left the house or returned, walking her own desire line through the struggling succulents in the backyard, to and from the apartment door and the gate into the alley. Mitra imagined Sali's flesh beneath her clothing, swollen with the hormonal fluids of pregnancy, faintly giving off the fragrance of warm milk. She felt wistful for Ana's pregnancies, a yearning to touch her sister's living skin once more. Ana's joints and muscles had ached both times, so when Mitra visited, she armed herself with a jar of Nivea cream and gave her sister massages, an act she found tedious and uncomfortable with anyone else, but now gave her a sense of redemption for those years of childhood malevolence.

Watching Salimeh, Mitra felt Ana's muscles slowly relaxing under her fingers, heard Ana's sighs and moans of pleasure and relief. Her brain was thick with emotion. Any benefit she might have gotten from the few days of rest after returning from the East Coast was gone. She knew this was stress and grief and shock. Too much at once. Her thoughts were disjointed and incomplete, though she had to admit a relief in being able to shift her focus away from Anahita and Aden and Kareem. At night, she dreamed of Nikku and Nina in a mini-series of their lives, as they said their first words (*kiki* for cookie, *fava* for flower), as they giggled with their first teetering steps, as their dimpled hands found security in her own, looking up at her with trusting eyes: *why this, why that, why, why, why* — Mitra's favorite question. Ana saying, *Of course you don't mind answering the whys; you don't have them twenty-four/seven.* And she dreamed of babies, faceless babies. It made her not want to sleep.

After Julian related his encounter with Kourosh, she felt numb and then resigned. She realized that she hadn't put much faith in Kourosh coming to the rescue, but Julian had and still was. He would have to find out for himself how rarely people stuck their necks out. She, on the other hand, would swallow her pride and call Olga for advice.

It was early morning in Tehran, almost a full twelve hours difference.

"Yes, hello, yes," Olga answered, startled from sleep, pretending alertness.

Mitra laughed. "Put your teeth in, Olga-joon. You sound like Sylvester." She imagined the yellowy enamel nuggets attached to metal wires immersed in a glass of water, Olga's two fingers dipping in to retrieve them, shake the water off, and click them into her mouth.

"Sylwester? Who is Sylwester? Forgive me, I have gotten old; I do not remember the names of your friends anymore. I have even forgotten some of your younger family members, which is very impolite of me. Please remind me."

"The cat, Olga. Sylvester the Cat."

"Aah," she said, chuckling a morning rasp she called her Old Goat's Voice. "Cartoon cat," she said in English.

"If I don't remind you of America, you'll forget everything. You won't even know it's me on the phone."

"Don't be ridiculous."

Mitra laughed. "Say that again, please."

"Ridiculous." *Redickoolas.*

Mitra took a deep breath. "I'm sorry to wake you up, Olga-joon, but I have a problem. With the village women."

"Oh, God," moaned Olga. "What I tell you? Village people always make problem. More bad than Afghanis coming here with no money, no home, no future, like Mexiki in America. Anyway, Afghanis not bad people, just ole-fashioned and poor, like Mexiki looking for hope. But Irooni village people, they try to take over you life. Very stupid and big-headed, like American hillbilly Jed Clampett. They have nothing, know nothing, want everything. Want to pull you down like donkey with too much hay on you back. I tole you best to find other donkeys to carry them, but you tell me I am es-snob."

"Do you want to know the problem, Olga, or do you just want to give me a lecture?"

"Okay. I stop talking."

"Good." Mitra swallowed. "The girl is going to have a baby."

Silence from Olga was the profoundest of

328

reactions. Finally, "How did this happen? Is she bad girl? Going off with boys?"

"I don't think so. It happened before she came to live with us. I haven't talked to her yet. I don't know *how* to talk to her. Or to the mother, who doesn't know."

Olga sighed. "Mother is bigger problem than girl."

"That's what I was thinking too. But I want to help the girl. She's sweet, Oli; I want to make sure she'll be all right."

"Best thing is 'bortion. Mother never know."

"It's too late for an abortion."

"*Vai.* This disaster problem."

Mitra gritted her teeth. "I know. So what do I do about it?"

The next evening, Mitra found Salimeh in the yard gazing up at the stars and the roiling fog. Mitra's steps on the gravel path were loud enough for Salimeh to hear, but the girl didn't move until Mitra sat down beside her on the stone bench. She made to get up in polite greeting, but Mitra touched her shoulder to keep her seated.

"The nights are often cold in San Francisco," Mitra said, glad she'd given Sali one of her old ski jackets. "But with the fog so low in the sky like a blanket, it sometimes makes me feel cozy to be outside."

Salimeh nodded in agreement, continuing to look at the sky or shyly into her lap. Her scarf was so tight she had a double chin. Mitra had needed only a glance to see her swollen nose and tear-brimming eyes. So, Mitra thought, she *was* upset, perhaps despairing, but she'd been hiding it well from everyone.

"I miss the stars," said Salimeh. "Back home in my village, they're very close."

"I remember them being close in Tehran."

"You miss Iran too, Mitra Khanoom?"

"No, I only visited twice. I was a little older than you the last time. My father sent me because he thought I was too wild and that a summer with my uncle Jafar, who was traditional, would teach me manners and respect for my elders." She shook her head, remembering the grand house with its heavy dark furniture and whispering servants, its one black-and-white television, before which her perpetually depressed aunt sat. Her children were summering in America, and Mitra was clearly not a good stand-in for Kareem and his sisters, not that she'd tried to be. She had a sudden image of Kareem and a ten-year-old Ana in the Devon house together, but she pushed it away. To Sali, she said, "I looked at the stars from my uncle's rooftop. His house was in Shemran, which was still a suburb in the foothills back then. I bet I saw them as clearly as you did in your mountaintop village." Sali nodded and sighed.

The rooftop had been one of two bright spots for Mitra that summer; she could sneak up there at night and pretend the house was hers, imagine how she would change it to suit her. The other was her uncle's garden — acres and acres of it thick as a forest with wells and pools and a small stream, rosebushes as ancient as Cyrus the Great probably, fruit trees at every turn. The only way you could tell you were in the middle of the high desert was to look up at the brown mountains with their glaciers on top, like puddles of cream. She remembered in a flash the secluded corner hidden by honeysuckle vines, the rough texture of the kilim on her buttocks, the initial pleasure, and the disappointing diminution of it. A boy her age, his first time, the relief when she learned he was leaving for boarding school in England before the week was out. If not for luck, she could've found herself in Sali's situation. Who could she have leaned on? Certainly not her parents, whose sympathy would have been compromised by their own shame and sense of victimhood. And suddenly she knew: she would have had Olga. Even if only to stand by her side without judgment, she'd always had — and still had — Olga's presence to give her courage.

She put her arm around Sali's shoulder. "Anyway, I didn't have a very good time. I felt out of place."

Salimeh nodded. "I know how that feels."

Mitra pulled the girl against her. "Let's go inside," she said. "You don't want to greet your baby with a sneeze and a cough, do you?"

Registering Mitra's words, Salimeh snapped to her feet and clamped a hand over her mouth; even in profile, Mitra saw the horror in her wide eyes. She wrapped her fingers around Salimeh's wrist. "Don't be afraid." The girl wrenched herself free, stumbled toward the bushes, and vomited. Mitra contained the urge to go to her, hold her head the way she'd done with Nina and Nikku when they were sick. Salimeh wiped her mouth on the tail of her scarf. She turned slightly, eyes downcast, weeping. "Khanoom, I don't know . . . I can't remember . . . I never would . . . I'm not a bad girl. . . ."

Mitra stood. "Come on, we'll go inside and talk. We'll find a solution. You're not

332

the first girl in the world to have a baby without a husband."

Olga had told Mitra to meet with Akram alone, without Salimeh. And when Mitra tried to say that Olga was perhaps overreacting, Olga made her promise on the soul of Anahita that she would follow this advice. After a quick call to Julian to tell him what Sali had said, Mitra descended the deck stairs and knocked on the apartment door. Already she was mentally exhausted and bleary-eyed, as she used to be after standardized tests. She looked at her watch. It was nearly 10:00 p.m. Julian had called an hour ago and she'd told him she would call him back, but if it got too late, so be it.

"It's open," she heard Akram say in a gruff voice, her tone changing when she saw Mitra. "Khanoom," she said meekly, standing up from her bedroll.

"Salaam," Mitra said solemnly. She hadn't been down here but once since they'd moved in. Nothing was changed. Still no furniture but Mitra's old oak kitchen table and chairs and two twin mattresses. She'd told them to look through the adjacent garage for anything they might want to use — bookcases, a trunk, wall hangings, some old curtains, cheap tchotchkes — but they

hadn't brought in a thing. It occurred to her that she should have urged them several more times to do this, or simply fetched items and put them in the apartment for them to pick through. Iranians can't receive a gift without sustained persuasion, but Mitra hadn't bothered. She nearly blushed.

"Can we sit?" she asked, gesturing toward the table.

Recovering from the shock of Mitra's presence, Akram uttered a quick yes-yes and scurried into the kitchenette to light the kettle for tea. She was bare-headed, and her hennaed hair fell in a messy thin braid down her back. She brushed crumbs off a chair, and Mitra sat.

"Salimeh is in the garden," Akram said. "I will call her." She made to dash for the door.

"She's upstairs," Mitra said, stopping her. "I saw her. It was cold. She's watching television."

"I am sorry. It is not right. She should come down."

"It doesn't matter. I want to talk to you alone."

Akram frowned, wrung her hands. The kettle whistled, and she poured two very dark teas and brought them to the table. She sat and slid a cracked bowl of lump sugar between them. The table was sticky with splatters of old food. Akram stared hard at Mitra, waiting.

Mitra inhaled. "Akram Khanoom." She paused. "Akram-jaan," she said, using a more formal endearment that felt distasteful on her tongue. "Your daughter was raped." It was the first time she'd ever said this word in Farsi; she hadn't known it until Olga told her on the phone.

"What? What are you saying?"

"She is pregnant, Khanoom." Mitra looked down at her tea.

Akram was mute. Then she began to shake and sputter. Finally, she was able to choke out "no" several times. Her beady eyes darted in an effort to figure out, Mitra supposed, exactly how such a thing could happen. Mitra tried to help by explaining in as soothing a voice as she could muster. "It was a boy from Kourosh's street, someone visiting a neighbor. She does not know his name, and she never saw him again. It happened when she went to borrow some flour. He offered her a soda. I think he drugged her. She remembers nothing. It was not her fault."

Akram looked at Mitra wild-eyed. "A boy cannot help himself when a girl draws attention to herself. My daughter is a whore."

"She is a child," Mitra said. "Boys are not

335

animals; they can control themselves."

Akram's body seemed locked in a prolonged shiver. "Please, Khanoom, take us to the doctor who can end the pregnancy. I will find a way to pay you back."

Mitra shook her head. "The baby is already stirring," she said. "No doctor would do it."

Akram slouched and hugged her abdomen, keening and rocking. She raised her arms and began striking herself on the head, cursing herself, asking God to kill her. Shit. Mitra hated this melodrama. The maids used to act this way when they broke something and wanted Shireen to forgive them; they would launch into self-flagellation and wailing. All for pity, which they usually got. If Julian were here, he would have urged Mitra to comfort and soothe the woman, perhaps wrap her arms around Akram until she calmed down, the way one might do with a toddler having a tantrum. Mitra didn't move; the melodrama was working the opposite magic on her. When Akram began striking her chest, Mitra snapped, "Stop it! Calm yourself!"

Akram sucked in her breath as if Mitra had punched her stomach. The deep indentations beneath her cheekbones turned blotchy with anger. Despite the wailing, no tears streaked her face. *What an actress,* Mitra thought.

"Don't you have any feelings for your daughter? She was attacked, and she's been suffering for months."

Akram's expression turned sour. "God kill her," she said.

CHAPTER 17

Mitra put Salimeh in the guest bedroom across from her own. Trying to hide her trembling rage and shock, she told Sali that her mother was upset, but that was to be expected. She needed time alone to adjust to the news. But she would, of course she would! "She's your mother; she loves you." And Mitra believed this. She believed it, but she didn't sleep a wink that night.

In the morning, she called Julian to ask him to get Sali an appointment with an obstetrician. He was thrilled, but that was because he assumed too much. When she told him it would be just her and Sali going to the appointment, that Akram was sulking in the apartment, his tone dropped and Mitra pictured him slumping with disappointment. *Yeah, well, join the club.* All they could do now was wait for Akram and Kourosh to come to their senses. Of course he offered to come over, bring dinner, cheer Sali up, tell her a little about the doctor he was recommending, answer any medical questions, but Mitra managed to dissuade him. "Let's wait for Kourosh to get back to you."

Julian agreed, but he wasn't sure Kourosh would ever get back to him. He'd left multiple voice messages, each one more edgy than the last. Finally, he went to Kourosh's office, only to find out that he'd taken a last-minute vacation to Tahoe with his wife and would be back after the weekend. Julian had a mind to drive out to Fremont and blow the story open, demand action. He wouldn't, of course. That would be like throwing Sali to the wolves. And Mitra would never forgive him. So he left a note and a stern message with Kourosh's receptionist saying that Dr. Julian Stevenson would be waiting for him in the pediatric clinic Monday evening to discuss a case they were working on together.

When Kourosh finally appeared after patient hours while Julian was finishing off his notes, he stood sheepishly at the exam room door and admitted that he hadn't yet broken the news of Salimeh's "trouble" to his mother or his wife. Julian lost his usual cool and found himself spouting a line he never thought he'd hear himself say: "What is *wrong* with you people?"

Kourosh sat down on the exam room stool, rolled himself close to Julian, and clasped his shoulder in distress. "Listen, man. You don't know what these Persian women are capable of. They'll skin that girl alive, man. It'll be all her fault. And my wife, she'll freak. She'll probably want to adopt the baby, and my mother will want to crucify her. I've got enough problems with these women in my house, every one of whom has some imagined ailment and wants to visit a doctor or be prescribed some ridiculous snake oil medication; I've used all my professional courtesy points. You've got to give me some time, man."

Julian resisted the urge to lift his foot and shove Kourosh across the room. Instead, he yanked free of the sweaty palms, onion breath, and seventies man-language by getting up and crossing the room to the window, which looked out across an alley onto another window, this one dark. Julian saw a blurry aura-laden reflection of himself, white lab coat and angry eyes. He shoved his hands into his trouser pockets and sighed. "You're a coward . . . man," he said.

"Yes," Kourosh said. "Yes, I am. But you don't know Persian mothers. I'm telling you, the girl is better off with you and Mitra. I promise I'll figure out something soon."

"How about finding the fucker who raped her? That might help."

Kourosh's reflection lifted its hands in a helpless gesture. "Aw, come on, buddy," he said. "We don't know for sure that she was raped. I can't start questioning my neighbors. There must be ten boys between the ages of fifteen and twenty on my block. What am I going to do? Knock on everybody's door and ask them if some guy in the house could be the father of my mother's cousin's daughter's child? I mean, they're my neighbors; I don't want to antagonize them."

Julian whipped around. "She's a child! Someone has to take responsibility."

Kourosh bridled and rose stiffly. "She's fourteen. My mother was already married at that age. Americans coddle their children. They think writing a law that says a person isn't an adult until they're eighteen makes it so. But that's not the reality. You and I both know girls are just as horny as boys, and I don't have any evidence that she wasn't happy to accommodate. She didn't even tell anyone that it happened, for God's sake!" He held up his hand to forestall Julian's interjection. "Anyway, what does it matter?

It's her word against whomever, and she won't tell us who it is. Even if she did remember and we confronted that person and/or his parents, we'd be throwing ourselves into the middle of a legal battle with paternity tests and restraining orders and custody issues."

"What are you, a *Judge Judy* fanatic?"

Kourosh chuckled. "My wife can't get enough of that show," he said, as if Julian had made a joke. Kourosh looked at his watch. "Shit, man, I'm late. Look, I promise I'll figure this mess out. I just need more time." He grabbed the doorknob, turned back, and actually winked. "Thanks, man. I owe you one." His finely tuned American accent slipped on the last word: *I owe you von.* Julian winced with the force of his own fury.

He went home and got stoned. He couldn't bring himself to call Mitra just yet.

Mitra forced herself to smile as she and Sali drove back from the obstetrician's office. "Looks like your due date is in the month of Yalda," Mitra said, trying to sound upbeat. "The longest night of the year is good luck, I think. The Zoroastrians believed that the next day's sunrise had special healing powers."

Salimeh nodded, looking out her window as if she found the sights interesting. The examination had been rough on her. Mitra stayed in the room, translated everything the woman doctor said, and added a few explanations of her own — "She's not harming you, but I know it feels like she's opening a tunnel big enough for a truck to go through" — while she held Salimeh's hand and patted her hair. Salimeh cried silently. Mitra was at a loss as to how to persuade her that what was happening to her wasn't a humiliation. Thankfully, the ensuing ultrasound had done the trick: a grainy image of the fetus with its pattering heart made it clear that Salimeh was going to have a baby boy.

"Do you celebrate Yalda?" Salimeh asked.

"I do. Besides Norooz, it's the only Iranian holiday I celebrate. They both make sense to me. The Islamic ones don't. Like Ashura; I don't observe Ashura." She recalled a conversation with Julian about this most fervent of Shiite holy days, the seventh-century Death Day of Imam Hossein, Prophet Mohammad's grandson, he and his family killed by Sunnis. Julian was trying to understand — and maybe find a justification for — the armies of boys and men in the streets carrying black banners, beating

343

their chests, bloodying their backs and foreheads with chains and razor blades. She told him to combine what he knew of two extremist factions of Christianity — Opus Dei and Pentecostal, the cilice and hysteria. She also told him not to be fooled that it was solely a religious commemoration; for centuries, regimes had used it as a political tool to rally the masses.

"But my mother says you are a Moslem, Mitra Khanoom."

"I was raised a Moslem, but I am not anymore. I don't like any religion."

"So you don't believe in God?" Salimeh asked, head down, clearly afraid to hear the answer.

Mitra chose not to say that indeed she didn't believe in God or heaven or hell, that the world alone was large enough to hold all such concepts if you looked closely enough. After Ana's death, she'd wavered, but not for long. It was less cruel to believe that death was nothingness, that only in life could you feel the pain of separation and loss, that once death came, one could truly rest.

"I believe we all belong to a larger thing. If you wish, you can call it God, but God is different from religion."

Salimeh nodded again. "It has lots of

rules, and the mullahs change them all the time. People don't like them, the prayer-singers; they're big-headed and mean. I'm glad there aren't any in America."

Mitra chuckled. "Mullahs are everywhere, Sali. Some of them are good and don't bother anyone; they help and comfort people. The priests and ministers and lamas and gurus and rabbis —" Sali was concentrating on the English words. "I'll teach you about these mullahs of other religions. Some of them are bad and mean, like you said, just like some ordinary people are. They think they know what's best for everyone, or they only care about what's best for themselves, and if you give them power over you, they will use it."

Mitra turned the car off and unbuckled her seat belt, but Salimeh didn't move. "So we have to fight the prayer-singers, right, Mitra Khanoom? Everyone says just ignore them, find a way around them, but don't fight. People are tired of fighting, first in the Revolution and then in the war."

Mitra wished her father could hear these words; he and his friends thought Iranians needed just a little nudge and some American military support to rise up and make another revolution. She smiled at Salimeh. "Fighting is good, but little by little maybe,

345

so not too many people get hurt."

"Back in my village, I have a friend whose parents sent her to school in Shiraz, and she wears her scarf way back on her head so her hair falls over her forehead. I think this is a little-by-little fight, Mitra Khanoom, don't you?"

"Yes, I do." Mitra reached over and lightly grabbed Salimeh's ponytail. "And maybe one day all your friends and all the girls your age will take their scarves off like you have and wear their hair like you do, and if every girl does it, the police won't be able to stop them all at once. Little by little."

For a week, and then two weeks, Akram didn't show herself. Mitra wondered if she was running out of food, and would have wondered if she was still alive but for the smell of burnt toast and the sound of water running through the pipes. Every time Salimeh made to enter the kitchen, she peeked at the back door and quietly sighed in relief that her mother wasn't there. She also asked after "Doctor Julian," but Mitra told her it was a busy time for him.

Mitra said nothing to Sali about Julian's encounters with Kourosh. When Julian finally told her about their last discussion at the clinic, she found herself unsurprised. It was typical; she realized she'd expected it. Even Kourosh's reluctance to search for the father of Sali's baby didn't faze her much. Anyway, the guy was a rapist; why should he have any rights? Julian was stunned by her reaction, and for a moment, she wondered if she had become numb or perhaps callous. But no. She simply understood more clearly how such things worked. Justice was never assured, rarely attained, and often not worthy of pursuit. All Julian's intentions — finding the guy, thrashing the guy, calling the police, demanding compensation or child support — they could do more harm than simply letting things be, at least for the moment. Julian was baffled, but Mitra's hope that the solution would present itself to her was solid. She simply had to give her thoughts time to coalesce, and sometimes that simply meant not thinking too hard.

Mitra taught Salimeh how to use the washing machine, what products to use in cleaning her room, how to vacuum and scour the toilet bowl with a brush instead of a rag. They made brownies from a supermarket box, and Sali learned how to read measurements — a cup, a tablespoon, oven temperatures. They bought maternity jeans and flowery baby-doll tops, a pair of pink flip-flops. Mitra warned that the weather would soon turn colder during the day and the rains would come, but neither of them could imagine it. The periwinkle sky of San Francisco in autumn, the abundance of sails in the Bay — like seagulls bobbing on their wingtips — kept their spirits high. Sali's caramel arms turned darker, and Mitra found herself happy just to watch the girl taste cookie dough ice cream for the first time. On Pier 39, Mitra imitated the honking sound of the sea lions the way she'd done for Nina and Nikku, and Sali doubled over in laughter. For Mitra, it was a bittersweet respite that she knew wouldn't last but was eager to accept just for a little while.

There was one ironclad rule: Sali must never miss her afternoon ESL class. While she was there, Mitra tried again to tend to the affairs of her business, if she could still call it that. She owned three properties that needed renovation, an Edwardian in the city, a bungalow in Sausalito, and a property down on the Peninsula. When she opened the files pertaining to these properties, her gut clenched with distaste. Her mail was piled high, fax machine out of paper, email box overflowing. When she sat down to work, she wound up attending only to the junk: fliers and coupons into the recycle bin, penis enlargement offers and chain letters deleted. The rest — essential stuff — she found herself leaving for "later." The phone would ring and she let voice mail answer. She called Carlos and again rescheduled a meeting to discuss lifting the work stoppage she'd put on the properties, but he knew her too well to believe that she was ready. Inevitably he would say, "The rental market is very hot, Señora. It is a shame to be missing it." Carlos was too polite to state his true concern: that without the rent from the downstairs apartment or the sale of at least one property, her income was dwindling. There was just so long she could go on with her self-imposed sabbatical. Carlos was on salary; he made sure the properties were maintained, that they were not vandalized, and if a pipe broke or a wall seemed about to collapse, as in the Sausalito house, which had survived the 1906 earthquake and a long-term renter with ten cats, he would fix the problem as economically as possible. Mitra resisted renting her properties; it reminded her of her father. She preferred to buy, restore, and sell to someone who would appreciate her work and take care of it.

When Sali was at class, Mitra often sat at her desk doing nothing, acutely aware of the ticking clock, the orange-streaked morning sunlight at the southern-facing window, the nearly invisible wisps of cobwebs strung like suspension bridges between the arms of the iron chandelier. She could hardly conjure up the woman she used to be — hunched over her drafting table (folded now against the wall) or pacing with the telephone headset clamped to her head or creating timelines and punch lists for her projects. Instead, she kept an ear to the door for the sound of Sali returning, then sitting at the kitchen table to do her homework — an occasional flip of a page, the tinkle of a teacup meeting the saucer, the *tap-tap* of a pencil against the table, a stifled yawn. Sometimes the girl would pad into the office to ask Mitra the meaning of a word that could not be found in her English-Persian dictionary.

Once Sali was home, Mitra felt right about being in her office. The chair felt downier, her neck less stiff, her life less cluttered. Not that she suddenly became productive; she was simply not bothered by her lack of productivity. She would flutter her fingers along the spines of her tall books until she found one of her favorites, one that contained photographs of Iranian gardens with arched arbors and blue mosaic pools. She'd memorized these photos over the years, but now, each time she studied them while aware of Sali's hushed presence, she climbed into them — built herself into them — and she rested. Sometimes she brought Nikku and Nina with her, sat with them on a kilim in a shady corner of an inner courtyard, one on each side, while she read to them from *The Book of Persian Fairytales.* She couldn't bear, however, to imagine Anahita by her side. When she thought of her sister now, she thought of what she would say to her about Kareem, about Aden, about how Mitra had failed her, about never having the chance to hold her and tell her how sorry she was.

October weather in San Francisco always took Julian by surprise. The night temperature plunged into the forties and people put out their Halloween pumpkins, then the fog parked itself offshore and the air became crackling hot. Fire weather. Rotting pumpkin weather. He found himself kicking the bedclothes off during the night, angry not only to be awakened by the heat, but to realize once again that he was in his own apartment alone.

When Mitra finally phoned and invited him for dinner — *Sali misses, um, Sali and I miss you* — he pretended to check his calendar, then said *Sure* in a measured tone. After he hung up, he went to the gym and lifted weights to stave off any hopeful imaginings. It was just dinner.

He arrived at Mitra's as Carlos, her contractor, was on his way out. "Ms. Mitra is more herself these days," he confirmed. Carlos's boy, the little one with the lazy eye, held on to his father's belt loop as if he might otherwise lose his balance in the world; Mitra had charged Sali with babysitting him while Carlos and she discussed business matters. And for the first time, Julian learned from Carlos how Mitra always arranged informal daycare for the children of her workers, many of whom had wives who were housekeepers or nannies. When Julian peeked into Mitra's office and told her how great he thought it was, she dismissed it as nothing special, smiled, and told him to open a bottle of wine and she'd be done in a minute.

He felt different in her house, not exactly like an interloper, but also not like someone who lived there, as he'd come to feel. He no longer felt the heaviness of sorrow and paralysis in the air. In fact, he hadn't realized how present those had been before. Over the last year, he'd done what he could to unleash Mitra from her grief. Often, he'd stop by in the middle of the day and find her stationed in a chair on the deck next to a half-empty bottle of wine or napping on the sofa, tangled in a chenille throw as if she'd been fighting snakes in a dream, the television tuned to an inane celebrity game show. Sometimes he succeeded in lifting her mood, catching glimpses of her fiery spirit, her biting dry humor and forthright grace. Tonight, he couldn't read her. It didn't help when she came into the kitchen and greeted him with a kiss on the cheek.

"Where's Sali?" he asked, pouring the wine.

"Washing up. She got back from class late." Mitra pointed to a small, lidless cardboard box on the counter. "Oh, Jules. Can you do me a favor before Sali comes down and take this box to Akram? You can just leave it outside her door."

Julian peered inside: teabags, sugar, toilet paper, eggs, soap, a small electric fan. Staples, because as far as he knew, the mother had never ventured outside Mitra's property alone. "Sure," he said.

As he descended the deck stairs to the ground floor, he couldn't help thinking how long this collective sulk had gone on. Akram was going into the third week of being holed up downstairs and still, neither mother nor daughter had made an effort to see each other. Julian could understand the girl's fear of a confrontation, but the mum's behavior was a mystery to him. And Mitra's too. She wasn't talking to the woman, but she was feeding the woman. The woman wasn't talking to Mitra, but she was taking Mitra's charity. Bizarre. Why not just hash it out until a solution was found? *It's not what Iranians do, at least not until and unless it's absolutely necessary.* Apparently, this was the common way Iranians conveyed hurt and anger, the way they disciplined their children, the way they instilled guilt. It even had its own single word in Farsi, which Julian made a point of not memorizing. *My father and I have been doing this for the past seventeen years.*

He decided he wouldn't leave the box outside the door, knocked on it instead. When it opened, he wasn't surprised to see Akram's swollen eyes and red nose, and he could smell that she hadn't bathed in some time. He moved to take the box inside, but she didn't retreat or open the door wider, just took it from him. As usual, what passed between them in place of words were mostly self-conscious bowing gestures. He asked her in several ways if she needed anything, hoping she would understand a word or two. Finally, she thrust her chin up in that way that meant no, then closed the door quickly. He was reminded of the way the elderly women in Africa had behaved toward him when he was a young health worker — gregarious, then reserved; trusting, then suspicious. He wanted to believe she was capable of forgiving her daughter and coming to terms with the situation, but until this sulking charade ended, they were all in limbo. Frustrated, he shook his head and went back upstairs.

Sali had put a cloth on the long kitchen table, set out plates and glasses Julian had never seen, and was lighting candles. She wasn't wearing a scarf, and for the first time he saw that her hair was wavy and to her shoulders. She wore a maternity tunic that Mitra must've bought her. It still shocked him that she'd been able to hide that swollen belly. When she saw him, she smiled widely. Well, he thought, someone's happy to see me.

Mitra placed several steaming dishes on the table, then sat down at the head and waited for Julian and Sali to sit on either side of her. This sit-down meal was noteworthy; the only formal dinners he and Mitra had ever had were in a restaurant. She'd once let it slip that she didn't have good memories from her childhood dinners; her father used it as a time of interrogation and pontification. Clearly, however, she cared enough about Sali to tolerate it.

It took a few minutes before Julian realized that the dinner was takeout, dished nicely into serving bowls. At least this was in keeping with the Mitra he knew. Soon, he became aware that the dishes were his favorites — moo shoo this and kung pao that — circled on a menu that was stuck to the front of the refrigerator with a Greenpeace magnet. He found himself saying, "You shouldn't have," and "You're spoiling me." He reached over to give Mitra's arm a quick caress. She smiled and said, "Our pleasure," then reached for her glass so his hand was displaced, intimacy vaporized. The gesture made him think of his mother, which was weird, not only because sons rarely want to compare their girlfriends to their mothers, but because he wondered how he hadn't thought of this before. Mitra *was* like his mother, especially in the restrained way she managed a crisis: calm, almost dispassionate, until a solution came to her. He relaxed a bit. Maybe he'd been wrong to assume that her trip back east had reopened her wounds. That One Year mourning event had sounded like another funeral, though he'd encouraged her to go because the idea of a family coming together so resolutely, bound by tradition, felt right to him. But what did he know about family?

As they ate, Sali was the center of attention. Julian didn't mind. The girl was sweet; he felt sorry for her. And it was interesting to see her adjusting to Mitra's more liberal way of thinking. He was sure she could barely fathom a future in which her life might not be a horrifying mess of being ostracized, ridiculed, dependent, and helpless. But Mitra did her best to disabuse her of these notions. *Of course you'll go back to school. Of course your mother will love the baby. Of course you'll eventually get married.* Julian nodded and smiled and interjected appropriate words, but it all sounded a bit fantastical. Maybe, he surmised, this was a way for Mitra to feel in control of her life, by pretending to be unfazed by the confusion and unpredictability Sali's situation had wrought. A controlled state of limbo. Had the mere proximity of Sali's pregnancy been a catalyst? He'd seen it in the camps, how the birth of a child, the urgency of taking care of a new life, could knock the grief out of a person.

Sali began talking about her ESL teacher,

but Julian couldn't concentrate. He realized his plate was empty and went in for seconds. The kitchen was pleasantly warm from heating food and from their bodies. The candlelight gave everything an intimate glow. He hadn't had this — a family sitting around a table — since his adolescence, before his grandmother died and his mother began going on assignment more often, leaving him and his grandfather lost without their women. There were things women were better at than men; home was one of them. They carried it with them like an ancestral perfume. He and his grandfather could build cozy fires in the hearth and arrange tulips in vases and keep the house as neat as a pin, but none of this could replace the virtual embrace their hearts felt when his mother was home. And Mitra was no exception, though he knew he would never be able to tell her this, just as he would never tell his mum. They both loved him — he couldn't question that — but the *way* they loved, was that enough for him?

He tried to imagine a future right here, in this room, at this table. Sali faded, and in her place was a smaller child; next to her, another child; Mitra dishing out portions to each of them. Mitra as Mommy, wearing an apron. He almost laughed out loud. Is that what he wanted? Some version of *Little House on the Prairie* or *The Waltons*? Sure, he could imagine Mitra doing all of the proper motherhood things without complaint, but also without relish. Three a.m. feedings or first days of school would be tasks, and she would do them out of love, but they would not be the things that made her feel loved. She didn't need that. She knew her own worth.

He was thinking too much; he had to stop. This limbo was temporary. Mitra would come around. Couples went through things; this was just a bump in the road. Once this mess with Akram and Salimeh was over, they would have space and time to talk. There had always been more between them than romance. He just had to have patience.

Sali was asking him what kind of ice cream he wanted. Apparently, she'd given him a few choices. "A little bit of each," he said, making her laugh and pull an armful of pints out of the freezer. Mitra had stacked their empty plates and put them in the sink. Julian started to get up. "Sit. We'll do them later. Let's enjoy." He let her face come into focus. She was beautiful to him, despite the dark circles around her eyes and an insouciant expression that made him feel unseen.

CHAPTER 18

The following week Julian was sweating as he walked the sloping sidewalk to Mitra's from the grocery store, cradling his paper bags and breathing in the aroma of fresh basil for the pesto sauce he planned to make. As he passed the low brick wall that surrounded Mrs. Tokuda's flower bed, he noticed Kourosh's BMW double-parked in front of Mitra's house, its passenger door and trunk wide open. From the alley came Kourosh, a bulging brown shopping bag hanging from each hand. "Hey, man," he said, smiling crookedly, sprinting to throw the bags into the trunk as if they were contraband, then coming back onto the sidewalk. "How you doin'?"

"What's up?" Julian asked. So, he thought, the guy is finally redeeming himself, here to collect Akram and Sali. The groceries suddenly felt lighter in his arms. He and Mitra, just the two of them, were going to have a feast tonight. Life on track.

He noticed Kourosh's mother sitting in the passenger seat, a scarf — one of those slippery French makes painted with gold chains — covering her poofy hairdo; she made no motion to wave or smile at him, but turned her eyes away. Kourosh saw Julian looking. "My mother's not in such a good mood. I apologize."

"No problem," Julian said, shrugging. "I understand." But he didn't. "Need any help?" he asked, glancing into the alley.

"Uh, no. There isn't much stuff, just one more bag, I think." Kourosh edged toward the alley. Akram stepped out from the gate leading into the garden, her legs clad in thick, flesh-colored stockings, her feet in plastic slippers. She balanced a large bundle against her hip, one of Mitra's old sheets tied neatly into a makeshift carryall; it reminded Julian of cartoons depicting a runaway child, stick and hanging bundle slung over his shoulder. Kourosh stepped forward and relieved Akram of the heavy thing. Her eyes met Julian's. He smiled, but she'd already looked away, raised her chin, and pulled her scarf over her cheek. Julian felt a heat in his chest. Fucking ingrate. He adjusted his grocery bags to get a better grip. "Well then," he said to Kourosh. "I've

361

got to get these things inside." But he hesitated. He didn't want Sali to leave without saying goodbye. He decided then and there that when she came out, he'd give her a hug — damn the mum, he'd give her a nice big hug.

Kourosh closed the trunk, moved to help Akram into the back seat. Shit, it couldn't be. They weren't taking the girl with them? Julian bounded up the stoop and was relieved to find the front door unlocked. Sliding the bags onto the kitchen counter, he called to Mitra, who responded from her office. As he turned, he saw Sali sitting on the window seat in the family room, a book in her hands, chewing on a pencil.

Mitra was sitting behind her desk. "Kourosh is here," Julian said. "He's loading the car with their stuff."

She frowned, rose slowly. "What?" Then her face revealed a sudden look of comprehension. "Shit!" she spat, coming quickly around the desk, her hip brushing against a sheaf of blueprints that knocked over a cup of mechanical pencils. She flew past him. Sali appeared next to him, her hands against her cheeks, wide-eyed, shoulders grazing her earlobes. "Stay here," he told her.

Out on the stoop, Julian watched the confrontation unfold. Kourosh had started the car. Mitra pulled open the rear passenger door just as he was inching away. He stopped short and the engine stalled. Julian heard him curse and pull up the hand brake. An edge of Akram's coat spilled onto the running board. Mitra beckoned to the woman to get out of the car, spitting words in quick Farsi. Kourosh's mother twisted her fat neck and threw a sentence toward the back, and Mitra yelled at her: *"Khafeh sho!"* He knew that phrase: Shut up! Mitra had told him that she made up for being illiterate in Farsi by memorizing every nasty idiom she could cajole Olga into teaching her. "And it's not just street curses," she'd said. "In Farsi, a clever insult is as revered as love poetry."

Julian felt a thrill watching Mitra down on the sidewalk, hands on her hips now, a string of raspy words tumbling from her mouth, her mane of wavy hair swinging with her hand motions. Kourosh got out of the car but didn't come around. Over the roof, he spoke quietly, but Julian could hear a tremor in his voice. Clearly, he was begging Mitra to calm down. In English, Mitra said, "You stay out of this." She went immediately back to her diatribe against Akram, who had now stepped out of the car and was looking up at Mitra in a defiant stance that was new to Julian. She'd removed her coat in the car and stood there in an inky shapeless shift and scarf. And then Kourosh's mother was out of the car too, screaming like a banshee, stabbing the air with her hands, spittle bubbling onto her chin. Whoa, Julian thought, catfight. He held in a smile.

Mrs. Tokuda emerged from her house, followed by a gaggle of sweaty women in yoga pants, one of whom sported a baseball-size purple bruise on her arm. Mrs. Tokuda looked ready to practice some of her judo on Mitra's behalf. Julian closed his eyes briefly, willing the woman not to interfere, knowing that if he said anything, she would throw him that look of disdain and probably jump in just because he asked her not to.

Mitra stood her ground, but Julian couldn't help sensing that she was losing the battle. Mrs. Tokuda said, "You need me, girl?" Mitra glanced back and shook her head, put her hand up in a halt sign. Akram was yelling now, in a squeaky voice like nails against a blackboard. She bared her teeth, and Julian thought about the appointment he'd made at the dental school to have the women's teeth looked at; Akram's were rotting, and Sali clearly needed braces. Mitra had grown quiet. Kourosh's mother crossed her thick arms beneath her shelf of a bosom and nodded at Akram's spate of words. *Is she looking at me?* Julian suddenly thought. *Why is she looking at me?* And then he felt the lightweight presence behind him: Sali in the doorway, hands still covering her cheeks, staring down at her mother with tear-filled eyes. Mitra turned and saw the girl too. It was useless, but Julian tried to pick out words that he might understand. *Dokhtar,* he heard several times. Didn't that mean "daughter"? Well, that didn't help much. Kourosh slid back into the driver's seat, not before Julian noticed an embarrassed blush on his face. His mother kept nodding and saying, *"Baleh, baleh"* — yes, yes — to Akram's words. She threw dagger looks up at Sali. Mitra rested her brow in her palm, shoulders hunched, and shook her head. Defeated? He heard Sali sobbing quietly but kept himself from turning to comfort her as he would any crying child; he didn't want to make things worse.

Finally, Mitra stood up straight, flicked her wrist dismissively at Akram, and said something Julian wouldn't have caught even if she'd spoken in English. When this failed to halt Akram's harangue, Mitra said, *"Boro,"* which he knew meant "Go," followed by a string of tired-sounding words, and again,

"Boro." She turned her back on Akram and walked slowly toward the stoop, looking up at Sali as if he didn't exist, her gaze filled with pity. He saw Mrs. Tokuda herding her students back into her house. "Show over, ladies." She nodded at Julian. "I come over later. You take care of her," she ordered, gesturing her head at Mitra. He had a mind to salute the bossy old woman.

Akram had gone silent. Kourosh gunned his engine, and she folded herself into the car, yanking in the hem of her shift before closing the door. And then they were gone.

Mitra's arm circled Sali's waist as they walked slowly down the hallway toward the back of the house. Julian shut the front door and followed. "What happened?" he asked. Mitra was murmuring to the girl. "Will you tell me what's going on?" He sounded like an orphan begging for a morsel, and he felt his anger rise. "Mitra!" he shouted.

"Hold on!" she snapped back. She deposited a stunned Sali on the sofa in the family room, draped her in the chenille throw despite the heat, and came into the kitchen. Julian watched her take a glass from the cabinet and reach into the refrigerator for the carafe of cold water. Finally, he said, "Well? You told her to shut up and go; that's about all I understood. And the word *dokhtar* several times." His pronunciation, he knew, was awful; he'd put way too much emphasis on the *kh* sound, hawking it like spit instead of lightly eliding it into a throat whisper. "It means 'daughter,' right?"

She raised her eyes to his face, exhausted and sad. "Yes, it means 'daughter.' In the vernacular, it also means 'girl' and 'virgin.' It means all three, depending on the context." Her gaze moved to the window behind him, sunlight speckling her brown eyes. "I never realized that before. Girl, daughter, virgin. One word for all." Her attention came back to him as a bitter curl formed on her lips. "Interesting, huh?"

"I'm in here," Mitra said, hearing Julian pass the living room.

"In the dark?"

"Sun went down while I was sitting here. Sorry about dinner."

He leaned against the doorway, a glass of wine in each hand. "No worries. Making the pesto calmed me down. It's in the fridge if you get hungry later, or we can have it tomorrow. How's Sali?"

"A mess, though not as bad as when I first went up. She's soaking in a warm bath now. It took me forever to convince her she didn't have to leave. She'd packed all her stuff in a garbage bag and was sitting on the bed rocking back and forth."

"Jeez. Where and how was she planning to go?"

Mitra shrugged.

He stepped through the dim room and placed the glasses on the coffee table. He found the lamp switch next to her. "You look like you could use some wine," he said.

She squinted at the light and avoided his eyes. With the first sip, she felt her neck muscles begin to loosen. "I don't know why I'm so tense. I've had worse shouting matches with plumbers."

He chuckled. "Your least favorite subcontractor." He sat in the armchair across from her.

"Akram's words keep echoing in my ears." He didn't ask her to translate them, for which she was grateful, but she heard them just the same: *Whore of a daughter, nothing girl, filthy, shameful, dishonored, throwaway girl, dead to me.* "I keep trying to resurrect my anger, but I'm just really sad for Sali."

"Well, I'm pissed enough for both of us. Pretty harsh punishment, walking out on your kid. I mean, it's not like Sali can say she's sorry and un-pregnant herself."

"That wasn't a punishment today, Jules. It was a banishment."

He shook his head. "I knew it was a bad idea to keep them separate after you told the mum about the pregnancy. They should've begun the healing process right away."

"The healing process?" she scoffed. "You sound like a pastor."

"She needs her mother, and her mother's forgiveness."

Mitra sat forward, both pitying him and admiring him for clinging to his faith in unconditional love. "Julian, the mother will never forgive her."

"I don't think it's that easy to predict. In Bosnia, many of the women who'd been raped by soldiers found a way beyond the stigma; my mother helped them."

"You don't know that. You didn't go back to their villages with them. And even if that was true for some of them — that they freed themselves of shame and their families forgave them — they still had to live among people who'd been raised for generations with certain implacable ideas. I mean, look at our own society. We're just beginning to accept the concept of date rape. You can't tell me that the majority of people don't still think that if a girl dresses provocatively, whatever that means, she's asking for it."

"I don't care what other people think. We

369

could have a debate about this, M, but the issue is about what's happening in this house, with these two people we've taken under our wing."

Our wing? she thought.

"The longer those two don't talk," he continued, "the more difficult it's going to be for them to fix their relationship."

Our wing? She gritted her teeth. "It's not an option, Julian. I won't subject Sali to that again. Even if Akram were to come to me and say she'd made a mistake, I wouldn't trust Sali's well-being to her."

He ran his fingers through his hair. "Well then, what do you propose we do?"

"Take care of her."

He frowned. "Keep her here?"

"Why not?" She took a gulp of wine.

He rubbed his forehead in frustration. "First of all, she's a minor. Second, she's going to have a baby. Third, we don't even know her legal status. She's probably here on a visitor's visa that will expire at some point. Be realistic, Mitra."

"Excuse me?"

"I think we should drive her over to Fremont tomorrow for an intervention."

"Talk about unrealistic. They wouldn't let us over the threshold. Akram and Kourosh's mother made that clear."

"They actually said that to you?"

"Are you implying that I'm lying?"

"No." He exhaled and looked away in distaste. "I just don't get it."

"What is it that you don't get, Julian? That Akram would abandon Sali or that I won't?"

"You're not Sali's mother, Mitra."

She snorted. "No, and I don't want to be."

He looked up and squinted. "You could've fooled me."

She didn't speak or move, though the urge to do both was strong. *Not a word more, Julian. There will be no going back. Please.*

"If you want to be a mother so badly," he challenged, "go off those birth control pills."

She winced, then felt a burning behind her eyes. It was over. Their paths had diverged. "Jules," she said quietly. "This isn't about my biological clock, but about yours." He paled. She leaned forward and reached to touch his hand. "I'm sorry," she said. "I can't give you what you want."

He pulled back. "Correction," he said. "You won't give me what I want."

She held her tongue. She'd made her decision, it seemed: she wasn't going to tell him about the lie. And yes, it was indeed a lie, not a matter of personal privacy. She'd deceived him and would have to live with the guilt and shame of that. To reveal the lie in order to make the breakup easier on her would be unforgivable. It was enough that she was breaking his heart. Whatever he said to her now, she'd earned every word.

"Jules —"

"We've been together a year," he interrupted. "Tell me honestly, Mitra, do you love me?"

"Yes, I love you." She held his gaze; it was easy when you told the truth.

He fell back against the cushion and sighed. "But not enough, apparently. You'd rather have a patchwork family than commit to one with me."

"Families aren't always about blood ties," she heard herself murmur. *Is that true?*

"Tell me," he said. "What happened back east that changed you?"

"Changed me? Nothing changed me."

"Bollocks. Don't gaslight me, Mitra."

She sighed and stood up, walked to the window so she didn't have to look at him. "All right. What happened is I woke up. You know those five stages of grief? I think I got stuck in the fog stage for a year."

Julian snorted. "Not in the mood for a joke, Mitra."

She faced him. "I don't know how else to describe it, Jules. Maybe it's true what they say about the One Year anniversary; it shook me up, yanked me out . . . something like that. I don't think I changed, necessarily; I think I'm just more like myself."

His frown was deep, eyes unfocused. She wasn't sure he'd heard her words, or understood the implication in them. She didn't want to spell it out for him: that she never wanted commitment with any man, that it felt to her like a trap, that she couldn't bear the idea of growing to resent someone she loved. And for all these reasons and more, she no longer desired him.

She came back to her chair and leaned toward him. "Julian, this is not about love — how much or how little — it's about the shape we each want our lives to take. There's nothing wrong with what you want."

"It's my own fault," he said in a bitter tone. "I never should've brought those two into our lives. It was naïve."

"It wouldn't have made my choice about us any different," she said, her mouth dry.

Julian shook his head. "It's our age difference, isn't it?"

"What? No." She raked her fingers through her hair. "If Sali had walked into my life ten years ago, I would have felt exactly as I do now."

She closed her eyes, willing him to stop

trying to make sense of something that would never make sense to him. Every cruel sentence that came out of her mouth stung like acid on her tongue. She wanted to say more. Kind words about their year-long romance and friendship, about her hopes for his future and for his continued relationship with Sali. But it was too soon for that. With time, maybe . . .

Julian stood up and walked to the living room entry. Hands in his pockets, he gestured with his chin toward the stairway. "I think she's crying," he said. "You should go up."

Mitra was on her feet and moving past him. Halfway up the stairs, she realized he wasn't following. She turned. He nodded tiredly and looked at his watch. "My shift starts in an hour."

"Okay," she said. "Um, maybe you could prescribe something for Sali, a sleeping pill or a tranquilizer."

"She's pregnant, Mitra. You'll have to take that up with her obstetrician." He donned his jacket. "I'll call tomorrow to check on her." He was already moving toward the door, his back to her. Without another word, he let himself out.

Sali was not crying, though a wad of crumpled tissues lay next to her on the bed where she sat cross-legged with Jezebel curled against her belly. The cat hadn't spent much time upstairs since Mitra began dating Julian. Now she was getting more attention than Mitra had given her in a year. Sali stroked and cuddled her in a way that Jezebel had never allowed Mitra to do, speaking to her in a high, singsong voice, her lips only centimeters from the animal's fur.

"She loves you," Mitra said, startling the girl, who moved to leap up. "No, no! Stay where you are. I'll be right back."

Mitra went downstairs and warmed two glasses of milk, put them on a tray next to a plate of rice cookies, and returned to the room. Sali thanked her meekly, unable to look her in the eye. Jezebel sniffed, eyed the milk, inched close, then backed away when Mitra said no. Sali's long dark hair was loose, some of the strands wet and stringy. Her eyes and nose were swollen and rosy from weeping, but she was calm and seemed comfortable. That was all Mitra wanted.

When they finished their milk and cookies, Mitra said she would leave her bedroom door open so Sali could come to her if she needed anything. As she was leaving, Sali said, "Mitra Khanoom, I want to thank you . . ." Her voice trailed off as she pulled a small worn jewelry pouch from her robe pocket and held it out for Mitra to take. "It is what I have of value," Sali said to Mitra's puzzled look. "They are real gold, given to me by a friend I knew when I was little." Mitra opened the pouch and shook four gold bangles out onto her palm. She felt dizzy and had to sit back on the bed. Persian bangles from the bazaar — Ana had worn them, too; never took them off, and you always knew where she was from the sound of them tinkling against one another. "Please do not tell my mother. She does not know about them. She hated my friend and made her go away from our village." Suddenly Sali wrapped her arms around Mitra's waist and pressed her face to Mitra's chest. "I am unworthy," she whispered through tears. "God kill me."

Mitra felt such a rush of anger that she grabbed Sali's arms and jerked her away. "Don't ever say that again." Even as she saw Sali's eyes grow wide with shame and fear, she couldn't tamp down her fury enough to say more, to say the compassionate sentences that might buoy her self-esteem. What was the use? Such words hadn't helped Ana.

"Dokhtar-joon," she finally said, tucking the bangles back into the pouch and putting

376

them into the girl's palm. "You owe me nothing but your well-being. Do you understand?" She pulled Sali back to her and felt the nod of her head against her shoulder. "Now let's get you to sleep. I'll stay with you for a bit."

Mitra woke in a way she hadn't since adolescence: like the girl in the fairy tale with everything just right, nestled as if on a cloud of eiderdown, her mind serene as it floated between dream and reality. She slid her hand lazily toward Ana's warmth.

Her eyes flew open. It was dark. Sali breathed evenly, her back turned. Mitra bit the inside of her cheek to stop from sobbing. Slowly, she sat up. The clock said 2:00 a.m. She wiped her cheeks and crept out of the room.

Downstairs, in the living room, the cushions still bore her indentation next to Julian's. In the kitchen, the aroma of basil hung in the air. In the den, Julian's gym bag was gone from the corner, and a stack of U2 CDs had disappeared from a bookshelf. Had he come back while she and Sali slept?

Up in her bedroom, she had her answer. Only remnants of Julian's life remained: his toothbrush on the shower ledge, a cardboard 49ers coaster on the dresser, and one

T-shirt in the closet, her favorite, the one that said: DEPARTMENT OF REDUNDANCY DEPARTMENT. Everything else — toiletries, shaver, clothing, his pile of books and magazines from the bedside table, even the glass beer mug half-filled with coins — was gone.

She shivered. Pulling a mohair shawl around her shoulders, she padded to the thermostat and turned it up to seventy. The forecast said rain and Mitra hoped for it. The first rain of the season, perhaps snow in the mountains, the storm door bursting open to let in week after week of water to quench the parched hills and flood the ravines and cleanse the dust off the leaves and the stucco. All she wanted was the sound of it on the roof, trickling through the gutters, slashing in short gusts against the second-floor windows. The house was too quiet.

Yes, she missed him. She hated that she'd hurt him. She didn't blame him for being angry; she had treated him badly. She'd been weak in her grief and she'd used him. "I suck," she said aloud. Would she never see him again? Would they meet by chance, on the street or at a restaurant, and pretend they hadn't noticed each other? Or exchange awkward words? She imagined him alone in his apartment and her throat swelled. She cared about him, she did. Deeply. She didn't want him completely out of her life, but how selfish was that?

She crawled under the duvet, nestled into her pillow, and left the bedside light on. She wondered if she'd sleep at all. The silent dark was a breeding ground for a hundred disparate thoughts that wired her tight against sleep. She cringed slightly at the silence, but she was determined to make it not matter. She'd lived for years without Julian and hadn't been lonely.

ZOYA

In the time of our history after the people voted in droves to elect a reformist president and the regime lifted the death fatwa against Salman Rushdie for writing something bad about the Prophet (though the people who took this fatwa seriously were mostly illiterate), a young girl of nineteen came home to find her house ransacked and her father, who was also a writer, missing. Unlike that famous Hindi, he and his colleagues did not write about the Prophet, but about politicians who thought of themselves as prophets. Of late, their stories and opinions and poetry were printed in periodicals that bloomed like hyacinths in spring. The people read as if starved.

The girl, frantic and blinded by fear and grief, fled her home and roamed the city, unmindful of the need for food or sleep or washing. From the northern hills, she walked south, along wide avenues shaded by sequoia trees and through meandering alleyways marked by graffiti: "Khomeini the Pimp!" "Faith No More!" The rush of people — lady shoppers, hawkers, artisans, schoolchildren, businessmen — paid her no mind, but as she walked farther south, the Sisters of Zaynab scrutinized her for dress code violations, gangs of poor boys stilled their soiled footballs to stare at her, addicts lolling in corners focused their watery eyes for a moment, and when the darkness came, teen prostitutes in frayed chadors followed her with their made-up eyes even as they remained alert to the morality patrols. The wretched know the wretched by sight, while the well-off blind themselves.

She wandered toward the university, where now she knew the spies and informants of the shadow theocracy lurked and blended and set traps for the Thinkers. She stood hidden on the periphery. Silently, she bade farewell to the professor who loved Kundera and COBOL, the light-eyed poet who came from Tabriz, and the sisters who swooned over Metallica in the hallways. She turned her back on the place where she had once belonged, where her poetry lived in pixels poised to fly on the wings of Code, and remembered what all the children of writers begin to sense from the moment their eyes see the light of the world: that in all of our histories — in the East and the

West, in the North and the South — the Writers have been hunted and silenced by the cowards who seek power.

Near dawn, she found herself — sneakers dusty, ears buzzing with exhaustion, headscarf rank with sweat — back in the city's familiar north at the base of a modern apartment building. Looking up, there on the fourth-floor balcony, she saw the old woman she sought, peering down at her as if a *jenn* had foretold her arrival. In that loving gaze, the girl felt ten years old again. And safe.

CHAPTER 19

WABC News blared and rumbled from the Jaguar's six speakers as Yusef rolled down his window to spit a mouthful of sunflower seed shells out onto a slick Route 9W. He wondered what the world was coming to when the former leader of a country could be arrested like a common criminal. Not that he knew much about the history of Chile's Pinochet, only that the Americans had rightly been behind the assassination of the dirty communist Allende back in the 1970s. No one understood how difficult it was to be an effective dictator, and he was certain this ignorance had led to the arrest of Pinochet. In London, no less. The British had truly forgotten their legacy of clever colonialism, which was to civilize and then utilize the natives to carry out their agenda. The British had turned soft. Not that he had ever liked the British. What Iranian who knew his history did? He remembered their greed and sense of entitlement over oil. Not to mention the sharp racist divide they created between Iranians and their own in oil cities like Abadan, where they had treated the Iranians as if they were lowly Hindis or filthy Arabs. And where was their loyalty to old friends? Even that silly Jimmy Carter had known a little bit about that. Imagine if he had allowed the arrest of the Shah when he came to New York for the cancer treatment in 1979? Of course, the Hostage Crisis might never have happened, but Carter did the right thing, especially since he had already betrayed the Shah by making such a big deal over human rights — that ridiculously impractical concept that had paved the road to Revolution. That's what the world got when Americans elected a peanut farmer. Now, Eisenhower — *he'd* been an icon. If not for his people — the Dulles brothers and Kermit Roosevelt masterminding that coup against the communist Mossadegh in 1953 — Iran would have been eaten alive and digested by the Soviets. If only that wishy-washy, spineless Carter had been clever enough to do what his predecessors had done: keep the Shah in power. If Reagan had been president, Khomeini would have withered away in exile on French soil.

Yusef swung into a lucky parking space directly in front of The Cigar Shoppe in Devon. The mullions of the new store window had been stained a deep brown. He smiled; cigars had made a comeback. The popularity of tobacco, like port, always measured the success or failure of a society's economy. It was one of his theories.

He wasn't low on his stash of tobacco for his pipes, but the aroma in the shop of the processed leaves relaxed him, reminding him of his father's study. It had been a place where he wasn't often welcomed, but to him it was the heart of that big house, where business was planned and politics was discussed and vulgar jokes were told.

Entering the shop, Yusef sank into one of the new leather armchairs. The owner, a Palestinian named Omar whose English was as stiff as his joints, ambled out from behind the glass counter with a wide smile.

"Mr. Jahani! I had a feeling you would be in today. May I take your coat? A glass of tea?"

"No, thank you, Omar. I cannot stay long." He was already late for dinner, but it was the vision of him and Shireen sitting in near silence at the table that had inspired him to take this detour. Her dispirited moods were becoming tedious.

"Allow me to make a special pipe for you, a new blend that arrived from South America just today," Omar said, and went back behind the counter.

The door opened as another customer came in, and Yusef felt that the chill of autumn had finally set in during the last week. He closed his eyes for a moment. "Sir," said Omar too loudly, standing over him with a pipe. "Smell first," he said, waving the bowl under Yusef's nose.

"Very nice," said Yusef, taking the pipe and allowing Omar to light it while he puffed. "Mmm. Yes." He exhaled a stream of smoke above his head. "A bit of coconut, eh?"

Omar bowed slightly. "Exactly."

"Mmm, yes," Yusef said again.

"Please enjoy. I will help my other customer. Excuse me a moment."

Yusef leaned back and closed his eyes again. Immediately he pictured Lubyana, her milky breasts with their tumescent nipples, her white-blond hair touching the curve of her back, her lips smeared with pink and the gloss of his ejaculation. He snapped his eyes open; this was not the time. He was acting like a dreamy adolescent. All week he'd been beset and distracted by such images. His extracurricular women belonged within certain parameters he'd drawn long ago, but Lubyana haunted him.

"This is very good, Omar. I'm enjoying it."

"Shall I ring up a tin for you?"

"Maybe next time. I'll just take my usual." Yusef continued to sit and smoke, and felt a sadness as the tobacco quickly turned to ash. He rested the cold pipe in an enormous butterscotch-colored glass ashtray and approached the counter to pay for his goods. "More peace talks coming, eh, Omar? Pennsylvania this time."

Omar sneered. "Not peace talks, my friend. With those two, Netanyahu and Arafat, more like fake talks or war talks."

"Have faith, Omar. One day you will go home."

"And you as well, my friend."

Yusef was taken aback. How dare this polyester-clad Arab, this thick-accented new immigrant, this *refugee,* put himself on a par with Yusef? Even if by some miracle the Shah's son was reinstalled on the throne and all the Jahani family properties were returned, Yusef would *never* go back to live in Iran. He realized suddenly that this was the very thing that was weakening the Western powers: all these foreigners with ties to the old country swarming into Europe and America with their own agenda, their outside allegiances. The Cold War was over and the world had turned inside out. The ants were colonizing the earth!

He paid Omar and offered him a stiff goodbye. At this point, Shireen's sullen company was preferable.

Yusef swung into the driveway and felt the steering wheel loosen slightly as his tires came in contact with a layer of wet maple leaves. He'd told Manuel specifically to keep the pavement free of them, but gardeners didn't sweep or rake in the rain anymore. Insolent workers. The slippery leaves reminded him of the accident that had killed his precious daughter.

He heard the oven door closing as he came in from the garage. "You are late," Shireen said. "The food has gone dry."

He ignored her and went up to change into his loungewear. Recently, she'd stopped offering him a greeting when he arrived. He found it extremely rude. At first, he'd greeted her nonetheless, stressing his words in an attempt to remind her that she was remiss. *And good evening to you, lady.* She hadn't responded to this demand for respect, and he decided it wasn't worth it to tackle the issue. After more than forty years, he didn't feel like greeting her at the end of a long, hard day either.

He took his seat at the round kitchen table, noticed that something was missing. He took an inventory; two place settings in mirror images — dinner and salad plates, napkins clutched by silver rings, stemware, forks on the left, knives on the right, dessert spoons horizontal above the plates. Water pitcher. Two iron trivets, serving fork and spoon. Salad bowl with sliced tomatoes, cucumbers, and carrots in perfect symmetry on top of the lettuce mix. He pulled his chair in and spread the napkin on his lap, still wondering what was missing. Shireen brought the meal to the table in two serving dishes, set them on the trivets.

"What's this?" Yusef asked, sniffing suspiciously.

Shireen pointed. "Schnitzel." Pointed again. "Baby potatoes and asparagus."

"I am able to be at home twice this week for dinner and you serve me German food?" he scolded. "I ate a mere yogurt lunch in anticipation of *ghormeh sabzi,* Khanoom."

"I am sorry," Shireen said, not looking at him, taking her seat and unfolding her napkin. "I did not have time. Iranian food takes time."

No flowers! That's what was missing. He couldn't remember an evening when Shireen had set the table without, at the very least, a single rose in a vase. Even in the dead of winter, a snowstorm blowing outside, she managed to have flowers to accompany them at the table.

"You had no time to make me a decent meal?" he said, allowing his incredulity to show. "What *important* deed kept you so busy, may I ask?"

She served him portions of the breaded veal, potatoes, and asparagus. "I had my Meals on Wheels today." She plopped a lemon half on his plate, then began to serve herself.

"Wheels and Meals? What is that? It sounds like a gambling game."

"Meals on Wheels," she enunciated, though replacing the *w* with a *v* sound. "I've told you, Yusef, several times. Have you really forgotten, or are you trying to annoy me?"

He squeezed lemon over his meat, purposely letting the spray fall on the table, a pet peeve of Shireen's. "I remember," he said reluctantly. He cut into the meat, added a golden potato to the fork, and poured a glass of water for himself.

"Actually," she said, "it was quite extraordinary what happened to me today. Poor Mr. Higgins with emphysema, who is the second person on my route, lives in the Colony Apartments, where I also have another client, a wonderful Mrs. Manning, who is a writer, though she can't use her arthritic hands anymore and speaks into a tape recorder. Anyway, when I arrived at Mr. Higgins's apartment, he wasn't like his usual self. Even though he has the oxygen, he is normally very talkative, telling me about his grandchildren who live in Arizona and offering me a cup of coffee, which I always decline because I have two more people to go and the food can get cold if I take my time, and believe me, it is not the kind of food you want to eat unless it is hot, as that helps it to taste like a home-cooked meal instead of processed cafeteria food . . ."

What was she going on about? Yusef was half-finished with his veal and Shireen had not taken her first bite, though she was cutting it up. She liked to cut her meat entirely before beginning, like a child. He forbade her to do this when they ate out.

". . . and Mr. Higgins was slumped in his easy chair, with the television remote fallen to the floor. And he is a very fast channel surfer . . ." She interjected the English phrase here. Where had she learned that?

391

Soap operas, no doubt. That's where she learned everything. ". . . white as a ghost and I pinched the skin on the top of his hand — I learned that from *ER* — and realized he was completely dehydrated." Yusef drank his glass of water and poured another. ". . . and the nurse at the hospital told me to stay there until the ambulance came. Poor man! He was near *death*! If I hadn't been there, he surely would have lapsed into a coma. I don't think anyone visits him, poor soul. The nurse said that not every volunteer would have understood that the situation was serious; others would have assumed he was asleep and left the food without a backward glance." Finally, Shireen took a piece of meat into her mouth, chewed, and swallowed. "Yes, it was a most extraordinary day."

Yusef said nothing. The sound of her chewing and swallowing irritated him. He glanced at her face. For the first time since the One Year, her expression was not hangdog. In fact, she looked proud of herself. He leaned back in his chair.

"So this is why you did not have time to make me a decent meal? Next thing you will be serving me hot dogs or hamburgers for dinner."

Shireen put down her fork and leaned

forward. "Well, we are Americans. Why wouldn't we want hot dogs and hamburgers?"

"*Baleh?* Excuse me?"

"I think you heard me, husband."

He felt his lip curl. "This volunteering has made you very bigheaded, lady. You go to other people's houses to feed them like a servant when you should be feeding your own family. You think carrying around trays of food in your trunk like a delivery boy makes you special? And for free, no less!"

Her cheeks flushed, but she did not lower her eyes. "It is good work that I do, Yusef. I saved a man's life today."

He chuckled. "And if the man had not lived? Or if you had arrived there and he was already dead? You could get sued. Do you think people will not try to take advantage of our wealth? Do you wish to be responsible for our poverty? For the squandering of our life savings for the mere satisfaction of having an 'extraordinary day'? This is not Iran, where a well-placed wad of money can erase unpleasant circumstances. Your stupidity amazes me, Shireen. I thought I had taught you better than this. You think like a simpleton."

Finally, she lowered her gaze. He resumed eating. She pushed her plate away. Tears

393

welled up in her eyes. She blinked rapidly. *Just like Anahita,* he thought, *no control over the tears.*

He continued. "Instead of this silly volunteering, give your energies to the family and our friends. We have not had a dinner party since the One Year. Almost two months!" He gestured with his fork. "And I know you have not been getting together with the women — I ran into that Gisu and her sister; they said you never join them for shopping or playing bridge. And what about your looks, lady? I have never seen so much gray in your hair. It is an embarrassment."

"Parties are not easy," she said quietly. "It is not like the old days when Olga was here."

He shook his head. "Olga, Olga . . . I'm tired of hearing this excuse. That donkey hardly did anything but cause trouble in this household. I have told you to hire maids. There are Hispanic girls everywhere. They cost nothing! Hire two or three of them."

She gave him a sidelong glance, and yes, he knew exactly what she was thinking. Apparently, she *had* learned of his girl. He shouldn't have taken Lubyana to that restaurant on Sixty-first Street; it was too popular. But it had been a Monday night late, after nine, and yet he'd come face-to-face with Nezam and Libby as they were ending one of those farcical date nights young couples talked about. It had been awkward, of course. He'd had to make introductions, and perhaps he could have come up with a reasonable lie about Lubyana — that she was an architect or a decorator or even a property owner — but she looked like none of those things in her backless dress and stilettos. He didn't worry about Nezam; Nezam would say nothing, though he'd refused to make eye contact. But Libby must have told Golnaz, and that was as good as a megaphone put to Shireen's ear. So what? He would never be sorry about Lubyana or his dalliances with the servant girls. A man took care of his needs; it was the natural way of the world. His only responsibility was to be discreet, and he always was. He would never be sorry. What was he supposed to do? Ask his wife to tend to him the way he liked? Wives were not meant for that. He shuddered with repugnance at the thought of it.

"The problem, Shireen, is that you have become antisocial," he said.

She threw her napkin on the table. "I cannot go on with my life as if nothing has happened. This is the way I grieve. I have nothing to talk about with our so-called friends. It is difficult to listen to people talk about their grandchildren, and to tell the truth, other subjects seem absurd. I have been thinking that I should perhaps take a class at the community college, make my English better or learn accounting. If I like it, I could go back to school."

"Don't be ridiculous, Shireen." He was using his knife to shove the last bits of his meal onto his fork. "You want to become like these American women who wear Gypsy clothes and display their cellulite-covered arms and work in nonprofit organizations that waste taxpayers' money? Like that Betty down the street, Jim's wife, as soon as the children went to college, she stopped taking care of the house and now joins demonstrations led by that repulsive hat-wearing Bella Abzug. That Jim used to be a smart man until Betty began acting like she knew as much as he did about politics and economics. Everyone thinks he is a nitwit now." He placed his silverware on his empty plate, leaned back. "No, Shireen. School is not for a woman like you."

She rose and collected their plates, hers barely touched, and took them to the sink. She came back to the table with a bowl of strawberries. "I'll have salad first," he said, and she used the utensils to break through her tomato, cucumber, and carrot design and dish out a portion for him. Her expression was impassive, with the usual tinge of sadness, so when she spoke, he wasn't expecting her to say anything of significance.

"Perhaps, then, I should visit our other daughter for a while."

He had no words for her, just a look of utter disbelief.

Sprinkling oil and lemon juice onto his salad, she said, "What?" As if she didn't know.

"You. Will. Not," he said in English.

She lifted the plate and practically dropped it in front of him. "And why not?" she asked. "She is my only daughter now. Why should I suffer because of your differences with her? I have been more loyal to you in these past seventeen years than I have been to her."

"As well you should be, lady!" He rose from his chair.

She looked up at him, made no move to back away. They were so close he could see the blood vessels in the whites of her eyes. Quietly, tiredly, she said, "This time it is your fault, Yusef. That painting you displayed to everyone in which you erased Mitra, it was cruel. You dashed all my hopes of a reconciliation between the two of you." She turned and began walking away.

"Again, this!" He kicked the chair away, threw his hands up. "It has become an obsession with you, that painting. I should have *forbidden* you from allowing Mitra to come to the One Year; her influence over you is diabolical. And now you want to visit her. Hah!" He turned to leave the room, glancing back to throw her his final words. "And what makes you think she would want you?"

"Madame Shireen, good evening. I am Olga."

"Olga-joon, good morning. How are you?"

"I am living, Madame. And you?"

"I am living also. These days are difficult."

"Is something wrong, Madame?"

"Oh, you know. Some people are not easy."

"Mitra?"

"Yusef."

"I am sorry, Madame. Perhaps I called at a bad time."

"No, Olga-joon. It is a good time. You know I cannot mention these things to anyone else."

"Yes, I understand. Is it the usual problem?"

"In part. He cannot control himself. This one, however, seems to have him very tight

398

in her grip. She is very young."

"They are all young, Madame."

"This one is demanding; she is a Russian girl."

"Ach, Madame, Russian girls have no scruples. Communism made them this way. Love is cheap. Money is everything."

"You should not disparage your people, Olga. Think what your mother would say."

"Yes, but that was long ago. My father was Irooni; I lived my whole life in Iran; I am Irooni. My mother, she was from another time when people were different."

"Are people different now, Olga? I am not sure. The landscapes are different, but the people? I think we are the same. Everyone living their small lives, worried about their children and their health and their hunger for simple things, like sweets and nice clothes. We think we are different from our ancestors, with our cars instead of horses, our medicines that make us live long, our computers and airplanes and wrinkle treatments."

"Ach, Madame. I am truly sorry to hear about your troubles with the Agha. Just do not think about it. What can you do? You have always kept your dignity."

"Yes, well, there were many distractions in the past. Now, life is empty. At times, I am envious of our President Clinton's wife; she has my same problem, yet she is busy and counseled by so many."

"But, Madame, the world is talking about her husband's *dool.* At least you have your privacy."

"This is true, Olga. So, how is the weather there, joonam?"

"Ey, not so hot anymore, Madame. But the air is bad again. The mountains are invisible."

"Ach, this is hard to imagine."

"Even on good days, I see only their outline from my balcony. And the city has grown so much that there are high-rises in the foothills where villages used to be."

"I have heard this. Unbelievable. Still, I hope to one day visit you. When things are . . . different."

"Inshallah. Perhaps instead you should visit Mitra in California."

"I have thought about it, but I don't wish to be an intrusion. You know how she is, Olga. Like Yusef, she prizes her independence."

"Yes, but this past year has changed her. I think she is lonely, as you are. And she could use a mother's advice about those peasants in her house."

"Ach, Olga-joon, my daughter does not

value my advice. She ignores me. When she was here, I told her about a new procedure for reversing her infertility. She ignored me; she thinks I don't know the difference between science and a fable."

"Madame, please listen to me. We must stop thinking of what Mitra did as a mutilation. There are girls who commit suicide to avoid marriage, sew up their hymens to hide their promiscuity, cut the skin on their arms or inside their thighs in hidden parts to relieve the pain of their married lives. And what of my own eleven operations? Were they not mutilations simply because I was trying to reconstruct my fertility? Mitra did not commit a sin; she made a choice and followed through. This is fearlessness."

"Ach, Olga-joon . . ."

"Madame, do not cry."

"Forgive me for bringing up this subject. It was insensitive of me."

"Do not be concerned, Madame. I no longer care about that part of my destiny; it was Allah's wish. I have had other children to mother — your children, and sometimes my cousin Oranoos's children, and . . . and a new child."

"A new child, Olga?"

"An orphan, Madame."

"Ach, very sad, Olga-joon."

401

"Ey, Madame, there are childless women, and there are orphans. Sometimes they exist for one another. In fact, I am hoping for your advice about her circumstances. She needs assistance that is only available in America."

"A sick child?"

"Not sick . . . yet, but . . . in a dangerous situation . . . which could lead to sickness. It is not easy to explain, Madame."

"All right."

"She is a great surprise of a girl. She reminds me of Mitra when she was a teenager."

"I am not sure that is a compliment, Olga."

"You make me laugh, Madame, but in these times, over here, a girl like that is refreshing. I do not think she will survive . . . here. I am hoping you can help."

"It is not the old days, Olga-joon."

"Yes, Madame, I know, but this is a special case."

"I will see what I can do, aziz, but I cannot promise anything."

"I do not have expectations, Madame. I can only thank you for being the most generous of women. And if you please, not a word of this to Mitra. Forgive me, but your daughter can be reckless in her conver-

402

sations."

"This is true, Olga-joon. She is an American girl after all."

CHAPTER 20

In the mornings following her breakup with Julian, Mitra woke later than usual, and with an overwhelming desire to stay in bed all day. This, she knew, was dangerous, so she decided to pack her days with tasks. In the light of morning, she scolded herself: *You made your choices; now get on with it.* The memories came unwanted at times — of Julian, yes, but always of Ana, tousling her wet hair after a shower, leaning over to kiss the top of Nina's head, humming from *Swan Lake* as she stirred a pot of soup.

Sometimes Mitra talked to herself, a trick she'd learned from Mrs. Tokuda, who'd learned it from her therapist daughter. "You change bad thought into good thought, just by telling good thought to yourself," Mrs. Tokuda had said. It seemed so simple Mitra almost hadn't paid attention, ticked it off as another one of Mrs. Tokuda's wacky pieces of advice, but then she'd tried it and it seemed to help.

She finally called Aden and was surprised to find that the sound of his throaty voice didn't spur the return of the turbulent emotions she'd experienced with him in New Jersey. They had an ordinary back-and-forth conversation that could've been one with a close friend, someone she talked to often, no need to catch up on things, just the usual glad-your-life-is-proceeding-as-usual. They were touching base, but not going deep. No need to go deep; they already had. Now it was just about connection, and it felt strangely natural. Until he mentioned Anahita's jewelry.

He'd inventoried and boxed it all, offered to send it by special courier whenever Mitra wished. She covered her mouth so he wouldn't hear her gasp. The idea that the pieces were no longer right where Ana had left them cut deep, but she said nothing; Aden was only doing what he thought was right.

He also wanted her know that, before Ana died, several retailers had shown interest in consigning the pieces, particularly Bendel's. That Ana had received validation for her work filled Mitra's heart. She visualized her sister's reaction: hands to her mouth in surprise, wide, watery eyes, cheeks flushed

— a combination of joy and bashfulness. Before Mitra knew it, her face was wet and she was unable to speak more than a few words without choking up. It was too much at once; she needed to postpone any decisions. Aden said she could have all the time in the world.

Often, she picked up the phone to dial Olga, then put it down. And when the phone rang, she hoped it might be Olga, then found herself relieved that it wasn't. What would Olga say about this new development in the saga of "the peasant women"? Mitra knew. *Take the girl to the mother and leave.* This, after much cursing directed at the mother. Olga would be more opposed to Mitra's decision to keep Sali than Julian was. And Mitra didn't want to hear it or argue about it. Oh, she knew Olga's intentions were out of love, and part of her understood that if the shoe were on the other foot, she would probably give the same advice. But to imagine dropping Sali off at Kourosh's house was too much to bear.

She'd always been able to put her emotions in a compartment when they threatened to stand in the way of moving forward rationally, but not now. She didn't want to fall into the depression she'd been in after

406

she returned home. Sali needed her, and yes, she needed Sali. Mitra may not have been a deep thinker, but she understood that life — that *living* — required a purpose. She had to find a way to restore her equilibrium, though she couldn't remember when she last felt as if her life was balanced.

Finally, she planted herself in the living room and placed the cordless in her lap. *Stop being a wuss. You need Olga's advice.* She dialed. "Why are you out of breath?"

"Mitra?"

"No, um . . ." For the first time, she didn't have an amusing comeback.

"I am old, Mitra. This is old people breathing."

"Okay." Something wasn't right. "Are you angry with me?"

"No, why? Never angry with you, joonam."

"Well, *that's* bullshit."

"Hah. Yes, you right. Is bullshit. Sometimes angry."

Usually Mitra would laugh when Olga used an English curse word, but it didn't sound funny this time. She realized Olga had always *made* it sound funny for Mitra's pleasure; now it just sounded like *bullshit* with a mild accent. "Are you okay, Oli? You're not sick, are you?"

"No, I am a little busy."

"Okay, well, I just wanted to update you on the situation with the village women."

"Ah, yes."

"The mother left." Mitra felt her pulse quicken as she prepared for a freak-out, but Olga was silent. "She left, but didn't take the daughter. Oli, she *abandoned* the daughter." Her voice had cracked, and she cleared her throat. This was not the time to become emotional; she had to remain as composed and practical as she had with Julian.

Olga sighed, then spoke in Farsi. "What did you expect?" The disappointment in her tone nearly took Mitra's breath away. "If you had listened to me, you wouldn't have reached this point. But now you are here, and you have grown attached to the girl. Am I right?"

"Yes," Mitra rasped.

"Now you must decide what you will do."

"Do you think the mother will come back?"

"Do you?"

Mitra swallowed. "No."

There was silence between them. Mitra had never felt so alone. She whispered, "I wish you were here."

"Mitra, listen to me," still speaking in Farsi. "When I came to you almost thirty years ago, I was an aging, childless woman. In my time, such a woman was seen as a failed woman, a throwaway woman, forever searching for self-worth, steeped in loneliness and brewed into a bitter tea. You and your sister were not my blood, but I came to love you as my own children in a very short time. I don't know why or how, but you filled my heart and gave me value."

Mitra couldn't speak, felt the taste of salty tears at the back of her throat.

"I want you to know your own nature," Olga continued, and Mitra had to focus to understand the Farsi. "Do you remember the night of a big storm when the tree crashed onto the house? Your parents were at a party. The maids ran outside like frightened rats and I cowered on the staircase with Ana in my arms. But you, you got the flashlight, inspected the branches that had broken through the roof onto the living room floor, then called the police."

"I remember," Mitra whispered.

"Good. Do you remember the dog from the next-door neighbor Shapiro? The one that stood almost one meter tall."

Mitra chuckled softly. "The Saint Bernard; Bernie."

"You taught me how not to be afraid of this animal, how the tail wagging was a good

409

sign, how I should extend my hand to his snout, how the tone of my voice and the stance of my body could be understood by him. This was a gift for a person who had been brainwashed to believe a dog is as impure as urine or feces or blood."

Mitra wasn't sure why Olga was bringing these old stories up, but she knew not to ask. "Okay," she said softly.

"And remember that religious woman down the street in the white-columned house who put the Jesus Cross on her lawn at Halloween and told trick-or-treaters that they would go to hell? She frightened Anahita and Libby, made them cry. You marched over there and told her off, told her *she* was the trickster for turning on her outside lights so she could bully children."

"Actually," Mitra said, "I think what I told her was —"

"I am not finished, my girl," Olga interrupted. "I am reminding you of your nature. You are a protector, Mitra. You cannot alter this about yourself. It is a good trait. The pregnant girl is yours now to care for; you made this choice. You will figure out how to protect her until she can protect herself. But do not do it alone. Find the support of others. Do not make of yourself an island, but rather an oasis. Now, azizam and light

410

of my eyes, I must go. I am leaving tomorrow to visit my people in Mazandaran."

"What? Why? You hate the provinces."

"Hate," Olga repeated, now in English. "It is a strong word."

"Okay, you hate the boonies."

Olga chuckled. "Yes, the boomeez. It is boring there, but maybe I am old, boring lady now. Anyway, I am going to a wedding, which will make my time there maybe only half-boring."

Several days later, Mrs. Tokuda crept up on Mitra sitting in the garden, talking to herself; she'd been thinking about Nina and Nikku, conjuring them up the way she sometimes found herself doing, knowing it was going to hurt like hell, but wanting to remember how their necks once smelled like baby powder and later like sweat and peanut butter. Mrs. Tokuda saw the expression on Mitra's face before Mitra could snap out of it. She sat down beside Mitra, stretched out her slight legs, and shoved her hands into the pockets of her white windbreaker. "During the war," she said, "more people were lost than saved. Whole families of many sons and uncles and grandmothers were suddenly just two people — a daughter and a mother perhaps, or a boy and a grandfather.

411

It was senseless." She shivered at a sudden cool gust of wind, and it seemed as if she was shrugging at the same time. "But this is life," she said. "People who want answers go to the church. People like us, Mitra, we accept the not knowing."

Had Mrs. Tokuda said something like this to her before? Had anyone? Julian? No — Julian was always reverent of her grief, as if he had no right to analyze it or expect her to take responsibility for it. Surely someone had reminded her of this fact: that few people escaped the tragedy of senseless death, that suffering had no purpose, no meaning, no justification. But she hadn't heard, hadn't listened. Until now. Why now? She didn't know. It didn't matter. She got it.

Mrs. Tokuda got up and leaned over to pull a weed from between the oleander bushes. There were times when the woman wouldn't shut up. This wasn't one of them. She left the remainder of her advice unsaid: *Time to move on. What has happened to you — such loss — is not the exception to the rule; it is the norm.* Mitra looked at Mrs. Tokuda's petit features — date-colored eyes, smooth plump lips, walnut skin — and her own eyes filled with tears. She let them fall, didn't look away. "Thank you," she said quietly. A frown lifted off the old woman's forehead. Still, she stared, cautious as the seasoned teacher who has known the error of a too-quick conclusion: Has her pupil understood the lesson?

Mitra stood, arched her back in a stretch, and leaned over to pull a clump of errant ivy from beneath a bush. She held the deep green wad in her fist, the root hanging like a yo-yo between the two women.

"That nasty stuff take over yard if you don't pay attention," Mrs. Tokuda said.

When the phone rang, Mitra's muscles jumped.

"Mitti?" said Shireen in an urgent whisper.

"Mom?" Her chest filled with anxiety. "What's wrong? It's still dark here." Was it? No, it looked like dawn. "What's happened, Mom?" Her father was dying. What else could it be? Buried memories rushed in: her frozen fingers tucked against his warm neck on a bitter cold day, the smell of Elmer's glue and pipe tobacco as they sat side by side silently building a model, the sound of his slippers skimming across the hallway floor and onto her bedroom carpet as he came in to kiss her good night. She held her breath, waiting for her mother's words; he was her father after all.

"Nothing, darling. I thought you would be awake. I'm sorry."

Mitra exhaled and sat up. "It's okay. It's almost time to wake up. You okay?"

"Mitti, listen." Shireen's whisper was still urgent, but excited. "I cut my hair yesterday."

"What?" Mitra's mouth was dry, her pulse still pounding in her ears. She rubbed her neck. "You're kidding me," she said, infusing her voice with interest. They had talked about this hundreds of times. Shireen's gamut of misgivings — *it will make my head look too small, too round, too lumpy; it will look like I am trying to be young; it will draw attention; it will be inelegant* — were all really related to how Yusef would react. Mitra had once complained to Ana that the issue was as tough as the Palestinian problem.

"Your father is very angry," Shireen said, words rushing out like she was a child with a new toy. "I cut it very short. To my ears. When he saw me, I was afraid he would have a heart attack."

"Mom, you're giggling."

"Mitti, he called me lesbian," Shireen said, using the English word.

Mitra burst out laughing. "Oh, Mom. Your timing is perfect. I need a good laugh."

"Yes, it is funny. I do not know what has

414

come over me, but my heart feels happy."

"You did something for yourself."

"Yes, but it is more. I-I am happy to make your father angry. In the name of God, do not repeat this to anyone, but it is how I feel."

"Who am I going to tell? Anyway, it's about time. But you know he's going to make your life miserable."

"Mitra-joon, do you know what Eleanor Roosevelt said once?"

"Since when do you know anything about Eleanor Roosevelt?"

"I have been reading some things. The Internet is wonderful, Mitra. You were right. So many things in Farsi, and pages where only women talk to one another anonymously. So, Eleanor Roosevelt said, 'No one can make you feel inferior without your consent.' Is this not brilliant? I am going to be like Eleanor Roosevelt with your father."

"That's great, Mom, but it's going to be hard. You know how stubborn he is, how cruel he can be. I mean, Eleanor Roosevelt wasn't talking about her husband when she said that; she was talking about the male political establishment, and she didn't have to live with them twenty-four/seven."

"Are you trying to discourage me, my daughter?"

"No! Not at all."

"You have been after me to be like this since the day you could make words."

"I know, I know. Look, why don't you come and visit me now that you're an independent-minded woman?"

"You know how I feel about that, Mitra. Thank you, but you have your own life. I do not want to become your burden. I did not call you to tell you about what is going on in my life so you would feel responsible."

"I don't. I would really like you to visit me, Mom. Really." Mitra felt tears suddenly pool in her eyes.

"What is wrong? Has something happened, my daughter?"

"No. I mean, yes."

"Tell me."

So she did. About Sali's pregnancy, Akram's reaction, and her decision to take care of the girl. She steeled herself for Shireen's gasp or expletive after each revelation, but her mother was uncharacteristically quiet until Mitra was finished. And then, in a level voice, Shireen said, "You remember that Jannat girl who worked for us before Olga came? I tried to help her be a good girl, but in the end I had to give up. Of course, it was your father who stood in my way, but even if he hadn't, I do not think

I could have changed the girl. Sometimes there is no fixing people."

"I never thought I'd see the day when you mentioned Jannat."

"Well, as I told you, something has happened to me lately. I am tired of feeling humiliated by your father's sins. They belong to him. I do not want to be responsible for them anymore. . . . Are you still there, my daughter?"

"Yes."

"Mitti, my darling daughter, you must not feel responsible for these people."

"But, Mom, I want to help the girl. I know I shouldn't have brought them into my life, but it seemed like a simple thing when I did it. Actually, sometimes I don't really know why I did it. Maybe it's because I miss Ana. But that's a terrible reason, a selfish one. And now I'm not sure what I should do. All I know is that I don't want to abandon the girl the way her mother has. She's a good girl, Mom; you'd really like her. She's sweet and smart and she's suffered needlessly. I know she could have a better life if I can just help her the right way."

Shireen was atypically silent again.

"I'm sorry to burden you with this, Mom."

"Don't be foolish, Mitra-joon. I am your mother. It is my purpose to be burdened; it

417

is my reason. Although it breaks my heart, I am glad that you are crying. You never did cry enough."

Mitra hadn't realized, but yes, her cheeks were wet.

Shireen continued. "You are a good person, Mitti. You always took on the task of champion to those of us who were not so strong. What you did for Ana with Kareem that time? I have no words for my gratitude —"

"Maman, don't you cry now," Mitra said, fighting back more tears herself, thinking about how little she had actually done to help Ana.

Shireen sniffed and cleared her throat. "Mitra, light of my eyes, I want to help you with this girl. I know you think I do not know the world very well, but I have had some experiences, especially with girls. My advice is sometimes good. Tell me what I can do."

Mitra braced herself against the wall and turned away from the receiver so Shireen wouldn't hear her sob.

"Mitti? Tell me."

Mitra inhaled and swallowed, managed to say, "Maman, can you" — she breathed in again — "can you come? I . . . I need you, Maman."

CHAPTER 21

Vivian heard them yelling through the wall between her office and Mr. J's. It was the third time in a month that her boss and Nezam had fought. She didn't think Nezam had it in him to shout so loud. He was a mild-mannered fellow, her favorite among the Jahani clan, always polite and as modest as the others were arrogant. Vivian didn't understand why he continued to work for his uncle; he could earn a lot more as counsel for a large company. Oh, she knew it had to do with loyalty to the family, but she wished Nezam would let go of that notion, at least where Mr. J was concerned. The loyalty, she knew, didn't go both ways, though Mr. J, enamored of his own benevolence, believed it did.

Lately, Mr. J was getting on Vivian's nerves more than usual. She chalked it up to hormones — her own; menopause was no better than puberty — but maybe she was wrong. Obviously, she wasn't the only person having problems with the boss. She scooted her chair closer to the wall in hopes of making out a word or two of the argument, though her hearing wasn't as keen as it used to be. She easily distinguished their voices by the inflection. Nezam had no accent when he spoke English; in fact, she rarely heard him speak Farsi. The words she heard — *not right, lien on the property, underpaid, INS* — were enough to tell her what the subject of contention was. Well, she thought, who didn't hire illegals these days? Her Nicaraguan cleaning lady, Rosa. Her brother-in-law's Guatemalan delivery boys. If the illegals didn't exist, no one could afford to hire anyone at all, so what was the difference? Oh, she understood Nezam's beef about the issue; he'd been through quite enough with the INS over the years, dealing with endless red tape and bigoted officials who thought every Iranian was a hostage-taker holding a burning American flag in his fist. He'd made all his clients, even family members, follow the rules, and now they were all safely citizens. Nezam wasn't a risk-taker; he didn't want to be responsible for anyone's deportation.

It had been hugely helpful to Mr. J that Vivian's brother had been an employee of the INS. Mr. J thought Peter was retired, but that was a lie she created five years ago to put a halt to the favors for which Mr. J constantly badgered her. In truth, Peter had been transferred to a different office. She hadn't been able to hide this fact from Nezam, but the boy, bless his soul, was sharp. He realized what she was trying to do and went along with the charade, never again trying to contact Peter. Not that he'd ever asked Peter to perform anything illegal. He simply "expedited" things in that convoluted bureaucracy. Peter still complained that the agency was more capable of losing aliens than finding them, and that included the legal ones.

Vivian started and pushed quickly away from the wall as she heard Mr. J's office door open, then close with the force of a strong hand. Her intercom sounded with Mr. J's gruff voice, summoning her. She picked up her pad and pencil, scolding herself for nosing at the wall and foregoing a trip to the ladies' room. As she walked calmly around the corner, she remembered how quick her step used to be when Mr. J beckoned. It was a long time ago.

After two soft raps on the door, she glided into his office and cringed slightly at the portrait he'd recently hung behind his desk.

She didn't think she'd ever get used to its ethereal presence, the radiance of colors and tones; an incarnation, she felt, of Anahita and her children's souls. It belonged somewhere else — a shrine, a temple, a church — not in a mundane place, and certainly not as a monument for the purpose of making a vengeful statement.

Because that's what the portrait was. It was the absence of Mitra from it that meant the most to Mr. J. Even more, it was the absence of Mitra that had further elevated Anahita to a level of perfection no child could sustain even in death.

When Mr. J first brought the portrait to the office, Vivian was caught completely off guard. She prided herself on never being surprised by anything her boss did anymore. She knew him as well as his wife knew him, and while she and Mrs. J had never mentioned this aloud to each other, Vivian felt it was understood between them. For the past thirty years, she and Mrs. J had spoken on the phone at least five times a week (and often as many times in one day) — short conversations about schedules, travel arrangements, doctor's appointments, or catering issues, and of course the ceaseless details involving the smooth settlement of foreigners of all ages. Between such particulars, there was always a bit of gossip, opinion, and commiseration for the quotidian difficulties of life. And plenty of tacit empathy. Vivian didn't have to be told that the portrait of Ana and the children was in the office because Mrs. J wouldn't have it at home. She'd seen the look on the poor woman's face when Mr. J unveiled the painting at the memorial gathering. For the first time in all these years, Vivian thought with the kind of thrill she got at ball games when the underdog team pulled ahead, Mrs. J had put her foot down without slipping on a banana peel.

Vivian sat quietly in her chair as Mr. J studied a sheaf of papers. Sometimes she waited ten minutes before he acknowledged her presence. He leaned forward and tapped at his adding machine, looked at the printout, and muttered numbers in Farsi like he always did. He knew she was there, but it was her job to be there. That, she felt, was not a fault of his cultural difference, but one of class. People who'd been wealthy all their lives couldn't imagine that their underlings might have anything more important to do than wait for instructions. Erroneously, they assumed the common man couldn't make a move without their guidance. Vivian had a load of work on her desk, work that would have a negative impact on Mr. J's life if left undone, but he couldn't comprehend that because he'd never been in her shoes. There were, she admitted, some wealthy people who had a natural empathy, but they were rare, and always women. You could change a man's thinking only by thrusting him into a situation. She couldn't help a small smile from breaking through her stoic exterior. Recently, she'd developed an allergy to laundry detergent (angry hives on her hands and around her eyes), and Tom had had to do the washing — oh, such mistakes he made, turning his athletic socks and briefs pink and shrinking his golf shirts; he'd taken to displaying a puppy-dog expression in her presence, as if for the first time in all their decades together he understood the trials of domesticity. She'd been a fool not to realize he had this capacity for empathy sooner, but her example had been her own mother (wasn't that the case for all of them?), and without question she'd assigned Tom and herself roles that could only breed resentment.

"Something funny, Vivian?"

Oh, he was a keen one, Mr. J was. "Not at all," she said. "Why do you ask?"

She didn't expect him to answer. He tapped again at the adding machine, his reading glasses perched just beneath the bump on his nose. The shadows under his eyes were darker than usual, and his color was off. He was an excessively healthy boss who hardly ever gave his workers a much-needed break by taking a sick day. Vivian was uncomfortable with any form of change, as are all fastidious people, and there had been a little too much of that lately. The possibility that her boss might be unhealthy caused a flutter of anxiety in her chest. After all, he wasn't a terrible man; he'd grown on her. And he'd helped her cope with several crises — Tom's operation, her own gall bladder issues, and a generous leave when her boy was struck with pleurisy. All illnesses. She knew he couldn't bear their existence, avoiding them where possible, showering money over them for cures. Whenever Anahita's children had their colds and other childhood diseases, he wouldn't see them until they recovered, and if he contracted anything himself, he carried a sack full of vitamins and pharmaceuticals, had her book doctor's appointments (never trusting one diagnostic opinion), and ran the office as if it were a military base. Mr. J was all about control. But there was more, she'd learned once from Mitra. It had to do with his mother, a woman who had been committed to an insane asylum for nothing more than the misfortune of having epilepsy. Vivian wasn't as shocked by this as Mitra, who, like so many kids these days, had a skewed view that ignorance was principally a feature of the old countries. Vivian remembered the ignominy of epilepsy, how it was as misunderstood, feared, and reviled as leprosy or retardation.

Yes, Mr. J looked peaked, looked his age, which had never been the case. Vivian softened. Not for the first time, she thought about how difficult it must be to pretend strength when you didn't feel it. She'd tried to raise her sons not to be like this, but they'd followed their father's example. They weren't as bad as Mr. J, but they weren't like Nezam or her sister Lucy's son, who had no qualms about asking for directions or weeping over a touching film or changing a poopy diaper. Well, she'd order a nice lunch for Mr. J from the Persian restaurant in Englewood; a bit of kebab and rice would cheer him up.

"Vivian," he suddenly said, leaning back in his chair and clamping a stem of his reading glasses between his teeth. "I have let Nezam go." A bubble of acid caught in her throat. "Give him two weeks' severance and make sure to collect all of his keys: to the filing cabinets, safe room, front door, et cetera. And inspect his boxes; I don't want him leaving with any documents." He put his glasses back on and leaned forward, shuffled through some papers. She wanted to see his eyes. If she could just see his eyes, she might find a trace of regret there. She'd seen it before, fleetingly, like a spark. After that last argument with Mitra and when he fired Olga. Men like this — like her own father and brothers, like all of her bosses — they swallow their regret for the sake of their egos. The veneer remains while the interior rots.

He swiveled the chair to reach into a lower cabinet behind him. "Is there a problem, Vivian? Did you hear me?"

"No, Mr. J, no problem," she managed to say, and got up and made her way back to her office. Why did she feel like they'd suddenly hit an iceberg?

Yusef stuffed his pipe and leaned back in his chair. Now that everyone had gone home, he could smoke and think. It had been nearly two weeks since he and Shireen had argued, and still she hadn't apologized. An entire weekend without a word to each other. He'd visited Marvelous Lake on Saturday and spent Sunday lounging at the country club. Just his luck that Lubyana was visiting her parents in Fort Lauderdale.

He blew a steady stream of smoke into the air and watched it curl like ghostly claws around the swing arm lamp on his desk. *She wouldn't dare go to Mitra,* he reminded himself. If she went to San Francisco, he would divorce her. A woman did not choose a daughter over her husband. But this was the problem with women: no foresight. They let their emotions dictate their actions. How could he blame her entirely? She was a mother, a vessel of procreation, and therefore inherently illogical where it concerned her children. It was partially his own fault. He had allowed her and Anahita to carry on a relationship with Mitra over the years. He should have forbidden it. When Mitra came to town, he said nothing. He took the high road. Everyone knew it. But everyone was careful never to mention her name in front of him and to prevent the two of them from running into each other. An effective patriarch instilled a little bit of healthy fear in his family. On two occasions, when Anahita wanted to visit Mitra in San Francisco, she came and asked his permission first, assuring him that she meant no disrespect and that she understood it was her sisterly weakness that compelled her to go.

She pleaded with him to allow it. And he had been benevolent (it was difficult not to be with Anahita), knowing that her loyalty to him would always be stronger than her love for Mitra. Anahita, that perfect girl-child, did not have it in her blood to go against tradition.

But Anahita was gone, and now Shireen was under Mitra's influence alone. Mitra: a formidable opponent. When he saw her at the One Year, his heart had pounded in his ears. His flesh and blood. Memories of her childhood flooded his eyes, crisp as the snap of a dead branch.

How talented she'd been! Her comprehension, her creativity, and her focus: sharp as a sniper's eye. He had indulged her from the moment she asked the question, "Baba, what is that shape?" It was an arch, specifically an ogee on the cover of a book about Persian architecture. That she had noticed it and was interested in it at such a young age astonished him. Oh, how she'd followed him around! Dipping her silky head under his arm to peer at blueprints; sitting on the floor with tracing paper over a page of one of his volumes, the tip of her pink tongue protruding like the nub of an eraser as she penciled meticulous lines to create whole structures: "Build this, Baba." And eventually her eagerness — her demand — that he take her with him to inspect the building projects each weekend. And he had taken her, amused by the smudges of dried mortar on her bean-pole legs, sawdust in her hair, filthy ridges of calluses on her palm from hammering and screwdriving.

He'd been beside himself with pride in her, even imagined that this amazing child — who built a cardboard model of Versailles when she was eight years old and drew a complex aqueduct system for northern New Jersey when she was eleven — had the prospect of becoming a brilliant architect. How shortsighted he'd been! He'd refused to let himself peer into the future, to see that she would grow into an oddball woman, an aberration, because of his lack of foresight.

His face crinkled into a sour expression, one that had often prompted Shireen to comment facetiously, "Don't bother your father, he has a mouthful of tamarind." He couldn't help it; he was remembering the day he noticed that Mitra was no longer a child; it struck him like a thunderbolt. In the garden, there she was, lying on a towel in a bathing suit, taking the sun. On a Saturday afternoon, from the window in this very study, he'd squinted to peer through the hydrangea bushes for a better look at the nymph who stirred his loins — one of Shireen's young friends or perhaps the daughter of a visiting cousin. He didn't know it was his own daughter until he'd heard Olga call her name from the patio, and when she'd raised her head to answer, he'd heard himself gasp. He'd closed his eyes to swallow his self-disgust, then had felt the fury rise into his chest. How had he not *seen* that his daughter was no longer a little girl? He'd glanced out at her again but had to look away. What a stupid, stupid man he was. A fool!

From that moment — a wake-up call — he pledged to set Mitra right, to repair the damage he'd done, to expunge the rebelliousness, bad manners, back talk, and boy interest. He was determined to bring out the woman in Mitra, even with the smallest tricks. He coaxed her in the direction of interior design or even painting, something appropriate for a girl. She scoffed at him, assumed he was joking. When a button fell off one of his dress shirts, he gave it to Mitra instead of having the Chinese laundry take care of it, reminding her that sewing was a very important aspect of wifehood; of course, she passed the job on to Anahita, who never revealed the subterfuge. Finally, he arranged a month's summer trip to Iran, expressly for the purpose of exposing her to a lifestyle and traditions that would straighten her out. He'd thought he was so clever! As if it were enough merely to remove her from the liberal American ideas of hippies and middle-class weirdos who allowed their children — and themselves! — a promiscuity he never thought he would see in his adopted country: the swingers, the antiwar factions, the marijuana smokers. As if Iran could influence Mitra in the way her frequent exposure to their household of Iranian visitors and to the elegant dinner parties he held for his equally elegant American business acquaintances had not done. As if. Mitra had a mind of her own, whether generated by his indulgent fatherly attention in childhood or simply an inherent abnormality. A trip to the old country did not sway that stubborn girl in the least. She came back unchanged, except for an uncanny ability to speak and understand a vernacular Farsi, and an even more pronounced insouciant expression.

Shireen had once said to him back then, "Can't you see that Mitra is like you?" Hah! Mitra was not a man. It disconcerted him that several relatives told him Mitra reminded them of his mother. All those years of his childhood and his mother was mentioned only in whispers, and now when he didn't want to think of her, people felt they could bring her name into conversation as if there had never been a disgrace attached to it. What resemblance did they see in Mitra? She certainly didn't look anything like his mother, who had been squat and bug-eyed. "Her spirit," one of his aunts had said. Had everyone forgotten that his mother was insane?

In any case, he'd refused to give up. Mitra's talent and genius had become her weaknesses. She simply refused to be female. As a father, his paramount duty was to care for his daughters until he passed them on to suitable husbands. He'd vowed to be patient and relentless in this task.

He'd been a fool.

Relighting his pipe, he remembered his last argument with Mitra as if it were yesterday — no, as if were just a moment ago that she stomped out of this very office, hair flying like the mane of a galloping horse. That was his eldest daughter for sure: the horse in the stable that no one wanted to ride, the one who would as soon kick you as nuzzle your sugar-filled fist. But also the one you wanted for a dangerous journey, even at just twenty-four years old. Competent, she was. Like a man. Yusef rubbed a spot beneath his sternum and reached for his antacid pills.

"I've changed my mind, Baba," Mitra had said to him that day. He knew exactly what she was referring to: the marriage to Ahmadi's son Hassan, to whom she was engaged, to whom she'd *agreed* to become engaged. She sat where Vivian usually sat, across the desk from him.

He swiveled in his chair, his elbow grazing the tea saucer. They both watched the tea glass as if their eyes could will the sloshing liquid not to spill over. Looking up, Yusef spat, "What are you talking about?"

Mitra shrugged. "I don't want to marry Hassan."

It was Yusef's own fault that she dared come to him to discuss personal issues at the office. He'd given her free rein there as a child. He'd been naïve, a new father, a man whose own father's disregard still rankled, and so had allowed his paternal feelings to flow freely. And now she had grown into this uncontrollable, insolent woman-child.

"This is not a game, Mitra. You cannot change your mind."

"Why not? He's got problems."

"Everyone has problems. You think you're

434

perfect? Anyway, this is neither the time nor the place for debate. We will talk at home tonight."

She didn't move. "Baba, Hassan is an idiot."

He slapped his palm on the desk. "Hassan is a successful accountant! An Iranian boy! And everything has already been arranged. Do you not understand that such fickleness will embarrass the whole family?"

Well, of course she did! She was manipulating him as if they were playing poker, but he would not fold. "I am not stupid, Mitra. I call your bluff. If you do not marry, neither will Anahita. The whole wedding will be off! You hear me? Off!"

She fixed him with an unwavering stare, her irises nearly black. "No, Baba. You *are* going to let Ana marry, not only because you won't be able to bear the embarrassment of canceling two weddings instead of one, but because I'm no longer on the market. The goods are spoiled." And with that, she pulled an envelope from her purse, unfolded a document with trembling hands, and held it out to him.

"What is that?" he asked, not moving to take it.

"Read it yourself," she said.

Steely eyes met. Two generations, five

thousand miles of culture apart. Righteousness hard as stone on both sides.

He snatched the paper, read, puzzled. A paid invoice from a medical outfit for a procedure called a tubal ligation. Such an idiot he was; he had no idea what the words meant. Which only added to his anger — she was further tricking him into exposing an ignorance. Of course she saw his confusion. Leaning forward slightly, in a venomous voice — his daughter speaking to him like the Serpent itself — she said, "Now try finding a husband for a sterile daughter."

She hadn't waited to see his reaction; no doubt she knew what the look on his face would be like. Yes, he'd felt his face turn red with fury, but just as quickly he'd felt the blood drain. He'd dropped the medical document as if it were contaminated. Indeed, he thought now, that one document had poisoned all of their lives. How had he raised a daughter who would do such a thing? Now she had nothing. No husband, no children, no family. His own foolish creation, a barren and estranged daughter. He'd committed the ultimate sin: he'd raised a bankrupt child who would die alone. And now, as further punishment, he too was left alone.

He reached for the newspaper on his desk,

knocking over a cup of sharpened pencils. He was a childless man. Where was the justice in life? He snorted at such a naïve thought. Justice was a vapor; he knew that better than anyone. If justice existed, it would have been Mitra who died in that mangled car. And with this unbidden thought, bile rose in Yusef's throat. Bile and self-disgust.

CHAPTER 22

Vivian and Shireen had never been out together. Certainly not to a restaurant, just the two of them, sitting across a white linen tablecloth from each other. There had, of course, been office-related weddings and funerals and parties they'd both attended, but this tête-à-tête felt as strange as wearing their shoes on the wrong feet. They were each aware of how they must look to others, olive-skinned Shireen dressed fastidiously in her dark suit and pink-skinned Vivian in a floral dress with a Peter Pan collar. One thing they had in common: the short haircut, because of course Shireen had gone to Vivian's stylist.

The waitress placed a fried calamari appetizer between them. "I am glad, Wivian," said Shireen, "that you agreed to share the es-quid. I do not know if I will like it. It will be difficult to ignore the antennas. We Iranians are not used to this kind of ugly fish, you know."

"You mean the tentacles, Mrs. J. That's what they're called. Ten-ta-cles. And I don't mind at all."

"Tentacles. Yes, thank you." Shireen went to stroke her hair back, caught herself and daintily scratched the point of her nose. "Anahita used to love the es-quid, but I would never try."

Vivian smiled. "I'm sure she's pleased."

"Yes," said Shireen, nodding gratefully. It was so nice to be with someone who did not question the afterlife.

"I must say that your new hairstyle looks very cute on you."

Shireen curled her fingers around her ear and blushed. "Thank you. My husband is very angry about it."

I bet he is, thought Vivian with satisfaction. She still hadn't gotten over Mr. J's firing Nezam two days ago and was in no mood to empathize with him. The truth was, she was sad to see Mrs. J in the severe cut; what beautiful hair the woman had had! With it twisted elegantly on the back of her head, she'd looked quite regal.

"Lemon?" asked Vivian, grasping the fruit in her palm.

Shireen nodded. "Thank you."

Squeezing the juice out with her strong,

slender fingers, Vivian gestured to the plate. "The white sauce here is tasty, better than the cocktail sauce, or you can mix the two." Shireen was trying not to gag at the look of the stiff batter-encrusted tentacles. Not being a shellfish, squid was not technically against Islamic law, but such slender appendages reminded Shireen of lobster, an animal that most Iranians of her generation had been conditioned to think of as vomitous. She persevered, however, remembering her recent resolution to try new things, especially things that disturbed her.

"Eat the round pieces," Vivian said, and Shireen took her advice. Indeed, the squid was tasty, familiarly fish, yet delightfully chewy.

Shireen nodded. "I like," she said.

Vivian smiled. Mrs. J was a strange mixture of pluck and passivity. A woman who could organize a party down to the finest detail, ordering a staff of non-English speakers to perform uncommon tasks such as flipping a pot of Persian rice to look like a crusty cake on a platter or paring radishes and tomatoes to resemble flowers in a salad bowl. A woman who could coordinate all the necessary particulars relating to a foreign student's arrival in the US — school documents, transportation, living quarters, wardrobe — and then handle frantic bouts of homesickness, cultural confusions, academic meltdowns, and near-scandals involving alcohol, drugs, sex, and plain old foolhardy antics. Vivian didn't know how Shireen handled these issues in her weak English, but she did. She would've made a great manager. And yet, she was also a woman who capitulated to her husband's every edict. Vivian had seen her transform — in body language, facial expression, and tone of voice — in the space of seconds after Mr. J walked into a room. From self-possession to self-surrender. But maybe Mrs. J was leaning more in the direction of courage these days. Vivian never thought she'd see it.

Shireen drank from her ice water, blotted her lips, and said, "Wivian, I know you think it is strange I ask you to lunch. I will be honest with you. I want to ask a favor. Please excuse me."

It was endearing the way Mrs. J always pre-apologized. There were some leftover customs from the old countries that were worth spreading around. "I'm happy to do anything I can, Mrs. J," Vivian said.

"First, I want tell you how much I appreciate you all these years working for our family."

"It's been my pleasure, Mrs. J."

"Well, I know my husband is a difficult person."

Vivian dismissed the notion with a slight wave of her hand, but it was hard not to show her astonishment at this first-ever acknowledgment. Mrs. J had had many opportunities to recognize her husband's transgressions openly — specifically the way he tauntingly criticized others publicly, often moving people to tears and then calling them sissies for not being able to take a ribbing. Vivian would not have tolerated that kind of behavior from Tom, but Mrs. J would simply cast her eyes downward or find a way to leave the vicinity.

Shireen continued. "I want to tell you that I am leaving my husband."

Their eyes met, the brown pair casting a tinge of appeal — *please do not disapprove* — and the blue pair clearly stunned. At that moment, the waitress delivered their entrées and asked if they would like fresh pepper, which elicited no response from either woman. She backed away, and Vivian croaked, "Divorce?"

"Oh!" Shireen jumped. "No, no. I am going to Mitra for a while."

Vivian swallowed, somewhat relieved. "I think that's a fine idea, Mrs. J."

"But of course you know he will think of me as traitor wife."

"Yes."

"He will try hurt me."

"Yes."

"Wivian?"

"Yes?"

"Do I have money under my own name?"

Vivian closed her eyes briefly. "Well," she said, her pulse quickening, "you have your joint checking account, the one you use for household expenses. I make a check out to you for that every month." Mr. J made her write "salary" on the memo line.

"Nothing more than that?" Shireen asked in a small voice.

Vivian's mouth went dry. "There are several large life insurance policies."

"What does this mean?"

Vivian cleared her throat. "It means that when Mr. J dies, you'll be a very rich woman."

Shireen placed her palm on her chest. "God forbids!" Guilt and fear infused her face and darting eyes. "This is not what I mean, Wivian," she whispered. "He has been a difficult man to live with, but I do not want him to die."

"I know." She took a sip of water, tried to keep from showing the tremble in her hand as she replaced the glass on the table. "Of course, you can use your credit cards."

"He will cancel them, I'm sure."

"Probably."

Shireen rested her chin on her knuckles and gazed out the window into the parking lot. The afternoon sun picked up gold flecks in her irises. This was a good woman, Vivian thought. Almost too good. A prisoner to her goodness. "Eat your pasta, Mrs. J. It's getting cold. We'll figure something out."

Did she mean that? She was being asked to make a choice here: between her employer and his wife — soon-to-be-estranged wife. Loyalty was very important to Vivian. In that, she and her boss were alike. She couldn't tolerate disloyalty. Could she help Mrs. J and still look Mr. J in the eye? She was surprised to realize that she didn't know the answer to this question. It was simple enough. Or perhaps it wasn't.

Each woman picked at her food in an attempt to assure the other that the meal was being enjoyed. Finally, Shireen placed her knife and fork side by side on her still-full plate and dabbed at her lips. "I apologize. I am not hungry, Wivian. It is not your fault, but I am upset. I do not know what to do now. Maybe I will stay after all. It was estupid idea. I am not smart enough to think of all obstacles."

Vivian felt struck. No one she cared about dared call themselves stupid in her presence. It infuriated her. If she hadn't believed in her own intelligence, and in cultivating it on her own, she wouldn't have been able to surpass her wealthier or younger counterparts with their college educations and vocational training. She'd watched her own mother — to Vivian's mind a mathematical genius — wither away as a homemaker because she accepted her husband's proclamation that she wasn't smart enough to survive in the working world. She dropped her utensils and leaned forward over the table, looked straight into Shireen's eyes. "Nothing stupid about you, Mrs. J. Nothing. You go on and pack your bags. I'll see what I can do. And I know Mitra won't think twice about taking care of you financially. It's one of the things good children do for their parents. That doesn't mean you're not entitled to half of what your husband has. I can't promise that, but I can try my best to help. Then, later, if you want to pursue a divorce, Mitra will get you a good lawyer."

"I don't want to think about divorce. So embarrassing."

"Well, I understand what you're saying,

but in some cases, *not* divorcing is the embarrassment."

Shireen's eyes were full now. She dabbed at the corners with her maroon-polished fingertips. "I don't know how to thank you, Wivian."

"No thanks necessary." Vivian gestured to the waitress and directed her to remove their entrées and bring them the dessert menu. "Now, Mrs. J, let's talk about something else, shall we? What have you heard from Olga?"

Shireen smiled. "She's very good. I spoke with her yesterday. This remind me that I promised her to seek some advice from your brother."

Vivian frowned. "Mrs. J, you know there's nothing Peter or anyone at the INS can do about Olga's expired green card. Believe me, if anything had changed in the rules, Peter would've told me. He was very fond of Olga."

Mrs. J shook her head, rested her hand on Vivian's forearm. "No, no. I understand that is not possible. This about another person, a young girl of Olga, a friend who needs to get out. Olga would not ask such a thing unless there was much danger for this person. I think it is the asylum that she wants to know about. I just . . . if it's okay

446

with you . . . I would like to talk to Peter. Just talk . . . for information."

Vivian readied herself to remind Mrs. J that Peter was retired, that he couldn't do any favors — the usual lie — but she hesitated. Here was a good woman trying to assert herself for the first time in her life. The least Vivian could do was respect her enough to set her apart from her privilege-seeking husband. She leaned back in her chair and said, "I don't see why not."

"Golnaz-joon, I've come to tell you that I'm going to visit Mitra for a while."

Golnaz hesitated, suppressed her surprise, and smiled broadly. "I'm glad for you, my sister." She rubbed Shireen's hand with her own.

"I don't know how long I'll stay. I don't have a return ticket yet."

Golnaz's pulse quickened. Was this the change she'd sensed in her sister earlier as she walked down the hallway from the elevator, almost a stranger with her short hair, and without the deep frown between her brows that she'd had since Yusef unveiled that cursed painting? Making her voice light, she said, "You should stay for as long as you feel like it, azizam. Have fun! You deserve it."

447

"I'm sorry. I'll miss you."

"Crazy girl! Since when do we see one another more than once a week anyway? You rarely come to the city, and I can't bear to visit that village you live in."

Shireen laughed.

"We'll talk by phone, as usual. It will be as if you're still here. Will Yusef join you at all?"

Shireen looked at her lap. Golnaz squeezed her arm. "What is it, my sister?"

"Goli-joon, I once believed that it was a woman's natural disposition to be the strength of the men in her life, that it was a woman's pride to give this strength without revealing that it was a gift." She paused, but Golnaz remained silent. "Olga tried to live without a man, and she succeeded for some years. But then she failed. I felt sorry for her. I thought, well, a woman gets older and needs a husband to share her life with, to have a home with, to be protected by. Olga seemed so lonely. But then she had us. If not for Yusef, she would still have us. And Goli, if not for Yusef, I would still have Olga. And more important, Mitra."

Golnaz still didn't reply; she could see that her sister was figuring things out as she spoke.

"How is a woman successful, Goli? Is she

448

successful when she spends a lifetime allowing her husband to subjugate her? This is what we were taught."

"Yes, Shireen-joon, it's what we were taught, but I gave it up a long time ago. Long before the Revolution."

"I know this, but how? We were raised in the same household. There are not five years between us. Yes, you have always been more outgoing than me, but you were not rebellious."

"No. That's true. I think you moving to America was a disadvantage in this regard."

"A *disadvantage*? America was the modern place, Goli-joon. It was Iran that was trying so hard to *become* modern."

"Exactly, Shireen. Remember when you and Yusef visited Iran that summer when the girls were small? I think Anahita and Nezam were about eight and five."

Shireen nodded. "It was a strange trip. So much had changed. I felt out of place in my own country."

"This is what I'm explaining, Shireen. You came to America, and while you were here, Iran moved forward. After the Kennedys invited the Shah and Farah to visit America, the rush to reform was on. Not only did the landscape change — the buildings and roads and modern conveniences — but also the

449

people, the culture. Even the traditional families couldn't ignore the excitement of it — the opportunities for prosperity, for technology, for resistance against Soviet influence. How else would I have been allowed to go to university, to meet Parviz there, to actually marry someone our parents hadn't chosen for me?" Golnaz regretted this example as soon as it left her mouth; the last thing she wanted was Shireen's envy. Quickly, she added, "And of course, once The Beatles' music arrived, there was no going back."

Shireen smiled. "Yes, I was shocked that you already had the new records I'd packed in my suitcase."

"Forgive me, joonam, but I remember thinking that you seemed behind the times. I don't mean this in a bad way. I think Yusef influenced you, of course. He was so much older and conservative. And he left Iran long before as well."

"It's true. He was very irritable during our trip, complaining about how people were imitating European-style promiscuity in the way they dressed and spent the nights in cabarets and discotheques drinking and dancing. Oh! And I remember being shocked at the TV programs. I thought they were wonderful, but surprising in their bawdiness and the loud, American-like music. I think I would've gotten used to it, but Yusef was upset. He kept shaking his head and wondering what had happened to the quiet, pious lifestyle of our people."

Golnaz threw her head back and laughed. "I think Yusef is selective in his memory. Our people have always been as corrupt or pious as any other people. This is a problem that happens with immigrants, Shireen-joon. I have studied it since I became an immigrant myself. I am sure when I visit Iran now, I will be as behind as you were when you visited."

"Oh, but Goli-joon, Iran has gone back to the Stone Age!"

Golnaz poked her sister gently. "I don't think so. That's what we believe as outsiders. Sure, the government has gone backwards in their philosophy, but we both know from friends that life behind closed doors is keeping pace with life in the West. Bah! Iranians are less religious now than ever; this is what a theocracy will do. Anyway, soon you will know for sure because I will tell you."

It took Shireen a moment to digest what her sister had just said. "What?"

"Parviz and I are going. Just for a couple of months."

"Are you crazy?"

"Calm down, my sister. Things are better with this new president Khatami. Lots of people are visiting. Some are even managing to get some of their property back from the government thieves."

"What if you get stuck there? Golnaz, this is a terrible idea! Please don't. So many people have been forbidden from leaving once they go."

"We aren't on any blacklist, Shireen. Parviz has checked into everything. All we have to do is show immigration that we have US green cards and they allow us to enter and leave. We are older people; they don't care about us. We were never involved with any political groups." She took Shireen's hand in hers. "You mustn't have such anxiety. This is why I didn't tell you sooner. I am very excited, my sister, and eager to reclaim my house. Please be excited for me too."

"When are you going?"

"Next week. We'll return for the Christmas holidays. You'll be back from San Francisco by then, I'm sure."

Shireen looked down, said nothing.

Golnaz said, "What is it?"

Shireen looked up, her eyes glistening. "I haven't purchased my return ticket."

"Yes, you said that, but —"

"And I don't know if I will at all." She allowed this to sink in and continued when Golnaz's brow furrowed. "I am . . . I have . . ." She cleared her throat. "Yusef and I had a very bad argument. I can't . . . I —"

"What are you saying?" Golnaz's voice turned raspy. "He is *making* you leave?"

"No! No! It is my choice, sister. But I am not leaving with his blessing. I am leaving with his disdain. Which means I may be leaving him for good." She looked away, then quickly spoke before Golnaz could respond. "I'm sorry if my action embarrasses you. Of course, I will keep up appearances; no one outside of us will know that my marriage is anything but normal." Golnaz seemed speechless, her eyes wide and searching Shireen's face. "My sister, if you prefer that I not go to San —"

Suddenly, Golnaz grabbed Shireen's arms and pulled her into an embrace. In English, she said, "I don't give a shit." And she kissed her cheek. "People can think or say what they want. I don't care about people."

For a moment, they allowed themselves to laugh and cry at the same time. Then Shireen said, "You will be able to see Olga! Ach, Golnaz, will you visit her for me? Or she will come to you; I'm sure she would love that. You won't mind, please?"

"Shireen, sssh. I had already thought of it. We'll be staying in Marjan's house in Shemran; I was planning on asking Olga to visit us."

"Oh! So good of you! Thank you."

"I'm not doing it just for you, dear sister. You forget that I hired Olga myself."

They tittered at the long-ago memory. Golnaz said, "I'm glad I finally got it right with Olga. And Ensi, of course — such a doll. After that married couple I sent you, I thought Yusef would never give me another chance. But you convinced him, Shireenjoon, with your sweetness."

The married couple had been a disaster, though Golnaz had been certain a married couple was the perfect answer to the problem of the pretty and useless maids that Jafar was sending. Yes, it meant that they had to use one of the guest rooms, but Golnaz was sure they'd work out so well that the young maids would all be sent back and then the couple would occupy the basement room. The woman would do the housework, and the manservant would take care of the cooking (he was a trained cook, according to his papers) and the gardening, which would please Yusef. But the couple had lasted only two months because one evening Yusef had found the thick end of a toenail in his soup. Golnaz had lost face completely. Yusef still found a way to bring up the toenail whenever they were together, even if it was to make a joke about it.

Golnaz said, "Olga and I still occasionally exchange holiday cards, you know."

"Really? I didn't know. What does she say? We only speak on the phone, and I feel as if there is a great deal that I don't know about her life."

"Letters are even more difficult than the phone. Not much a person can say when you know the officials can open and read anything they wish. At least by phone you can sense certain things, and sometimes you can use a combination of uninteresting words to suggest something complicated. That's how we found out that the government had confiscated Parviz's brother's business. And also that his niece was moving to Dubai — well, we didn't know it was Dubai until she called us from there, but we knew she was leaving Iran for good just in the way my brother-in-law's voice sounded when he said she was going on vacation to the Caspian; she hated the beach. You don't realize how often you use a kind of code with family and close friends until you can't speak freely, and then it becomes natural."

"Yes," Shireen said with a preoccupied look. "This is true."

"What are you thinking, my sister?"

Shireen's gaze sharpened. "Goli-joon, this is exactly what happened when I last spoke with Olga. She asked for my help about a young girl she knows, an orphan. Not the usual request for me to send clothing or medicine, but a big request to help the girl come to America. I was so involved in my problems with Yusef that I did not think deeply about it; I simply asked Wivian if I could speak to her brother about the possibilities."

"And what did Peter say?"

"He explained the asylum rules to me. The girl can apply once she is out of Iran. Before that, he can do nothing."

"Did you tell Olga?"

Shireen shook her head ruefully. "I've been putting it off. Olga would not have burdened me with such an appeal unless she was desperate, unless this girl is extra important to her or in true danger. I guess I hoped an idea would come to me . . . ." Shireen leaned forward, eyes suddenly wide. "And it has, Goli-joon." Golnaz lifted one eyebrow. "Perhaps, little sister, it is fate that

you are going to Iran. If anyone can help
Olga with this girl, it is you."

CHAPTER 23

Mitra squinted at the tube of the jetway and spotted her mother between the hulking arms of two businessmen, their suit bags hanging off their shoulders like slaughtered game. Shireen's haircut was indeed a bit butch, but it suited her petite form. She might have been less attractive from a male point of view, but she looked more serious, which could only be good. Of course she had freshened up before disembarking; Mitra imagined her during the descent, holding a compact mirror to apply her rouge and lipstick, a cover-up stick to hide the darkness under her eyes, eyes that now darted with concern, searching for Mitra. Eyes that finally spotted her daughter and filled, it seemed, with an inner light. Relief.

She waddled with the weight of a stuffed handbag and a carry-on. They kissed on both cheeks, and Mitra took the bags. "Too heavy," Shireen said, reaching for the handbag. "I carry one."

"No, Mom. I'm fine." Mitra gestured with her head. "Let's move out of the way, let the other passengers by."

Shireen looked behind her sharply. "Oh, excuse me," she said to no one and everyone. She switched her heavy mink coat from one arm to the other. Mitra stopped herself from mentioning that the fur would not go over well in San Francisco. There would be plenty of time for her mother to learn the rules of the West.

On the freeway into the city, Shireen was frightened by the force of the rain. "Coming down like dogs and cats," she said, leaning stiffly forward in the passenger seat, peering into the blurry darkness. "Can you see the road? I cannot see it."

"Relax, Mom. I'm used to it. This is how it rains here in the winter, and I know the road. Are you warm enough? Should I turn the heat up?"

"I am good. Not so cold here. Snowing in New York."

"It doesn't snow here."

Shireen looked at her doubtfully. "Huh," she puffed, absorbing this odd fact.

Mitra laughed. "And from April until October, the sun shines every day."

Shireen's eyes widened. "Like summer in

Tehran."

"Sort of. In the city, though, it's cold and foggy in the summer. The city weather is different than in the suburbs. We have something called microclimates."

Shireen nodded her head slowly. "I feel I am in a different country."

Mitra glanced at her, found herself reaching over and laying her hand on Shireen's. "You are," she said. Shireen hid her surprise at Mitra's touch and quickly skimmed her thumb across the top of her daughter's hand before Mitra drew it away. Shireen blinked back a surge of tears.

When Mitra downshifted to climb the steep hill to her house, Shireen gripped the safety strap. "Oof," she said.

"This is nothing, Mom. I'll take you on a tour of the city tomorrow. The hills are amazing." Mitra hadn't thought about this part of her mother's visit: the sightseeing part. It would be a thrill to show her mother around, take her over the Golden Gate, up into the Headlands, down to Big Sur, to Alcatraz, and eventually up into the Sierra to the beauty of Lake Tahoe. And her mother would appreciate all of it in that winsome way she and Anahita shared — faces unabashedly showing wonder and approval, not a prideful bone in their bodies. As Mitra pulled into her driveway, she glanced up at her house and realized more than ever before that this was her home.

Sali stood waiting in the center of the kitchen, wringing her hands. Mitra recognized the trepidation on her face. Of course the girl would be frightened. What if Mitra's mother was as coarsely judgmental as her own? Mitra scolded herself for not thinking to reassure her earlier, but was pleased Sali hadn't retreated to hide in her room; she was prepared to face the music.

Mitra introduced them, and Sali bowed from the waist. "*Salaam,* Khanoom," she said in a strong voice. Shireen bowed less deeply and *salaamed* in return, but it was her earnest smile that put Sali at ease. Gesturing toward the spotless stove and its steaming samovar pot, she said, "I have made tea." On the counter was a plate of butter biscuits.

Shireen looked at her watch. "*Vai,* what a good girl, but it is too late for tea. I will not sleep."

"Of course, Khanoom," said Sali, her eyes downcast.

Shireen was struck by how much this girl reminded her of Ensi, the young maid with the cleft palate who'd come to them so long ago by way of Golnaz, and had gone back to Iran and thankfully married, and then faded like so many once-knowns into the miasma of the theocracy.

"But a glass of simple hot water will be perfect. And, of course, a biscuit," Shireen said.

Sali smiled broadly and moved to the stove. Suddenly, Shireen understood how useful the maids from Iran had made her feel as she taught them how to keep house and watched them marvel at America's curiosities: washing machines and *American Bandstand* and department stores; frozen dinners, garbage disposals, and housewives in short-shorts. How long had it been since she'd felt she knew more than someone else?

Mitra took Shireen's mink and stowed it in the coat closet. "Sit, Mom, I'll take the bags upstairs."

Shireen sat down at the kitchen table, thought twice, and called out to Mitra. "Azizam, bring me my slippers when you come back; they are on top of the clothes in the suitcase."

Mitra smiled as she struggled up the stairs with the carry-on and the big blue American Tourister suitcase they'd collected at baggage claim; her mother couldn't bear to wear street shoes at home. At home. Was this Shireen's home now? The reality was, she was probably here to stay. Yusef's pride would prevent him from taking Shireen back without a list of harsh concessions, if at all. The question was whether Mitra could help her mother be happier here than she was back in the hollow nest of her New Jersey life. Should Mitra dare hope that, after all these years, *someone* might consider following her across the country? Did her mother's arrival feel like an intrusion into the life she'd created for herself in San Francisco? Well, yes — a welcome and wonderful intrusion. After all, she hadn't left the east because of a desire to *be* alone, but because of the need to be *left* alone in her desires.

Unlatching the suitcase, she breathed in a mixture of Shireen's flowery perfume and the faint shoe polish odor she associated with her parents' closet. Shireen was a master packer, organizing items according to drawer and closet placement — shoes and belts at the bottom, underwear in the left quadrant, socks and hose in the right, shirts in the lower left, grooming articles next to those, then a layer each of trousers, blouses, dresses, jackets. On top: robe, nightgown, and slippers in a plastic bag. Such obsessive organization would have irritated Mitra once, but it only amused her now. Hadn't she inherited a strand of this trait from her mother? It wasn't something she would have admitted to twenty years ago, but those had been the uncertain days when she hadn't settled into who she was. A time when she might've worried that her mother's presence in California would stifle her or burden her. And what did she feel now? Excitement, for certain. Hope, maybe. Hope for what, she didn't know. She removed the slippers from the plastic bag. Soft black leather, thick crisscross straps, a slight heel. Like holding a worn book of fairy tales.

Mitra had given Shireen the room where Sali had been staying; it was the largest of the guest rooms. She'd moved Sali down the hall to the small third bedroom. Looking around, Mitra noticed that Sali had folded down the bedcovers in a diagonal on one side, spread a white bathmat over the carpet next to the bed, and placed a fresh bottle of Evian next to a water glass on the nightstand. On the other nightstand sat a vase of holly berries from the garden. In the bathroom Shireen and Sali would share, next to the toilet was a small tin watering can (rubbed as clean as when Mitra had first bought it a year ago) that Shireen could use as a manual bidet. Mitra smiled. She wouldn't have remembered to provide this;

Iranians didn't trust mere toilet paper for big jobs.

She closed the window she'd cracked earlier to give the room a fresh smell, headed back down to the kitchen, and set Shireen's slippers at her feet.

"Ah! Thank you, my daughter," she said, removing her pumps and sliding her small feet into the mules.

Sali poured Mitra a glass of tea. Mitra sat and wrapped her hand around the warm glass. "You must be tired, Mom. It's after midnight for you."

Sali slid into the chair next to Mitra, across from Shireen.

"Yes, I am tired, but now I am also relaxed. The airplane splintered my nerves."

Sali kept her eyes on her folded hands, which rested on the table. "I like the airplane. Taking off is like a ride at Luna Park." She had brought her chair as close as possible to the table in an attempt to hide her pregnant belly, which had grown to watermelon proportions now that she'd entered her eighth month.

"Luna Park!" Shireen exclaimed. "I have not thought of that place in years!" She addressed Mitra in English. "It was amusement park, like a — what do you say? — caravel."

"Carnival," Mitra corrected.

"Yes. I have good memories of it. Tell me, Salimeh-joon," she said, switching back to Farsi, "do they still sell Akbar Mashti ice cream there?"

Sali smiled. "Oh, yes, Khanoom." Her eyes were still appropriately downcast, but the smile broadened and her cheeks took on a shiny blush. *Bless you, Mom,* Mitra thought. Not that she had ever seen her mother show anyone open disapproval — and she knew Shireen was scandalized by Sali's situation — but she hadn't dared hope that her mother would make such an immediate effort to establish a sweet relationship with the girl. Respected auntie and obedient niece, benevolent queen and revered lady-in-waiting — in the space of five minutes, these two had found their roles.

Mitra screwed up her face. "You mean that ice cream with pistachio and rose water in it? Yuck."

Shireen shook her head and gestured with an open palm at Mitra, saying to Sali, "See what America has done to my daughter? Who can think Akbar Mashti ice cream is yuck?" She winked at Sali, who giggled. "Yuck," she pronounced again. "This is an essential American word, my girl."

■ ■ ■ ■

Mitra woke with anxiety the next morning. Her mother was here! What the hell was she going to do with her? In the glow of her arrival last night, Mitra had foolishly forgotten about the rest of her life, namely, the flurry of work she'd taken on since she and Julian parted.

While the winter rains prevented her from demolishing and reframing part of the house in Sausalito, the interior renovation of the Victorian on Dolores Street was in full swing. She'd reached a point where in the early morning, as she placed her tea on the desk in her office and lifted the blinds to see either the sunlight or the fog on the Bay in the distance, she felt a flood of self-possession, a grip on her life that could only come from having a full day of achievable tasks ahead of her. But *this* morning — her mother's first morning in San Francisco — Mitra felt compromised. She had a guest in her house. She couldn't remember the last time she'd had someone over for dinner, let alone spending the night. She hadn't even shopped for her mother's favorite foods: nine-grain bread, unsalted butter, blueberry yogurt, raw spinach, sunflower seeds. She

467

looked at the clock. It was almost 8:00 a.m.! She was meeting the flooring guy at nine. Shit. How had she managed to consider taking her mother sightseeing last night? She was thinking like a Persian woman, she knew, but it couldn't be fought; the rules of hospitality were etched in her psyche. She jumped out of bed, pulling on her jeans as she hopped to the bathroom, and brushing her teeth so quickly that the toothpaste came out in clumps when she spat. She took the stairs at an uneven clip while buttoning her flannel shirt and stopped dead in the kitchen.

"Good morning, my daughter," said Shireen in Farsi with a broad smile.

"Good morning," Sali echoed.

But for the fact that Shireen was wearing her muumuu, the two women could've been sitting at the table all night long.

"I overslept," Mitra blurted. It was an apology.

"Good!" said Shireen. "I'm sure you needed it."

Sali began to get up. "Your chai—"

"Sit. I'll get it."

The samovar kettle bubbled on the stove, and the windows were slightly steamed up. Mitra couldn't remember when the kitchen floor had been so warm against her bare soles. The butter smell of fried eggs came to her, and she glanced over at the drain-board, where a clean frying pan had been placed to air-dry. She put her tea on the table and took a quick inventory while tuck-ing her shirt into her jeans: half a piece of toast sitting in a bread basket she hadn't used in months, strawberry jam, cream cheese, two plates with the sticky yellow smear of yolks, and her cloth napkins. "I've been looking all over for those napkins," she said. "Where did you find them?"

Shireen pointed to the cabinet above the oven. "There. Same place I put my own."

"Oh." Mitra sat down, brought the tea up to sip, and instead managed to dunk a loose strand of hair into the liquid. Shireen leaned forward and gently drew it away, blotting at it with her napkin. For a second, two decades melted away and Mitra chuckled at herself. "I'm such a klutz," she said.

"Some things do not change," said Shireen. "I know you will say no, but shall I make you some eggs?"

Mitra shook her head. "Listen, Mom, I'm sorry, but I have a meeting at one of my projects." She glanced at her watch. "I'll try to make it quick."

Shireen bridled. "Quick for what? Are you

469

not working? Don't you stay in the office all day?"

"What? Uh, yeah, yes, usually. But you're here. We'll go —"

"Salimeh-joon is going to show me the neighborhood." Sali nodded eagerly. "The market, the pharmacy, then maybe the Persian store. I am so excited to *walk;* so many years of driving everywhere."

"Well, Mom, San Francisco isn't like Manhattan, where you're better off without a car. The hills can make a person who's not used to it very tired, and we have terrible mass transit, so don't even try —"

"Don't worry, my daughter. I am not a frail old lady. And I know how to get a taxi if I need one. I have lived in this country for over forty years. Do not treat me like a foreigner. I want to explore. Salimeh is with me. You do your work and we will see you for dinner."

With this, Shireen stood up. "I will shower and dress now." She planted a kiss on the top of Mitra's head and disappeared up the stairs. Mitra met Sali's cautious gaze, then allowed herself to expel a laugh. Sali's jaw loosened and she giggled. "I like your mother."

Mitra cocked her head. "Yeah, I'd forgotten how likable she can be." And Mitra

470

recalled the sometime-Shireen of her child-hood: when the house was filled with visitors who needed three square meals, snacks, toiletries, reading material, beds made, laundry washed, jokes laughed at, troubles aired, spats mediated, children entertained, soap operas translated, doctor checkups scheduled. This was a Shireen she'd forgotten, her mother in the absence of her father.

In the space of a week, Shireen learned everything she needed to know in order to run Mitra's household. Consequently, every evening, they ate a full-blown Iranian meal — basmati rice, stews made with eggplant or split peas or kidney beans, kebabs, yogurt and cucumber soup. Shireen insisted on dinner guests: Mrs. Tokuda, of course, but also the small group of neighborhood friends Mitra had managed to put at a distance over the past year with unanswered doorbells, unreturned telephone calls, and the impenetrable posture that turned a grieving person into a narcissist. Karen and the kids, Andy and his partner Misha ("They are fruities, no?" "Gay, Mom — we say gay."), with whom Mitra had had a running backgammon match for three years.

Within that week, Shireen had diagnosed Carlos with a reflux problem and bought

471

him a supply of antacid pills that she placed by the now-decaffeinated morning mug of coffee he took into Mitra's office. She bonded with his wife, Carmen, who owned a cleaning service, over ammonia, detergent, and lemon oil, and introduced their boy, Juan, to animal crackers and rock candy. Jezebel, as befit her feline disloyalty, took a liking to — no, a preference for — Shireen's lap as the three women watched television in the evenings. And Mitra, in her bed at night, found herself feeling a certain relief at the presence of her mother in the house, just across the hall. Relief? Or was it — dare she admit? — a sense of security? She'd never felt such a thing in her parents' house, unless she counted the times she slept in Olga's bedroom. Not that Olga would've saved her from some kind of danger, just that she and Olga, in their nearness, were braver in their individuality. Having her mother near rather than far was like the difference between getting lost when you were driving with someone as opposed to when you were alone; even if the passenger couldn't read a map, you somehow didn't feel as panicky. It was a confidence, a strength that came merely from the presence of someone else, from another person's need for you to act competently. And wasn't this, in fact, reciprocal? Both of them — the mother and the daughter — were feeding off the need of the other. And why not?

Shireen, for her part, had never slept so well. At least not since childhood when she woke to larks chirping in the plane trees outside her window, the aroma of brick-oven-baked bread wafting through the house, the delicate splash of water sounding from the courtyard as the servants performed their ablutions. Shireen woke in the morning in nearly the same curled position in which she fell asleep, the night having passed as smoothly as a silk thread through the eye of a needle. What had she so often proclaimed to her friends at dinner parties when they complained about their husbands' snoring? That she'd become inured to Yusef's rattle, to his jerky movements, even to the cacophony of his frequent urine stream in their toilet. It had been a lie! A lie that even she had believed. For decades, she now realized, she'd slept as episodically as a cat, in fitful fragments. She'd denied any problem. And now, such joy she got from being a woman with a bed of her own!

As the weeks went by, she occasionally wondered how Yusef was handling life without her. She'd expected to think of him more often, to miss him. Part of her wanted to miss him, if only to make worthy their years together. Several times during dinner, the phone rang and the party hung up after Mitra answered. Shireen found herself holding her breath, heart thumping, but she realized this reaction was more to do with an anxiety about Mitra being subjected to Yusef's abuse than anything else. When she thought about the east, it was the graves she pictured. Vivian had agreed to hire someone to care for the plots, and Shireen trusted Vivian, but she still worried about bird droppings soiling the tombstones, fallen leaves obscuring the engravings, and the lack of fresh flowers. Well, she thought, if that was all she missed . . .

Salimeh was Shireen's surprise. She was a good girl. Smiling often, eager in the way of curious children, helpful to a fault, and well-mannered. She was *pak* — pure — despite her condition. Shireen, who had always defined herself as a conservative woman, marveled at her lack of disapproval — even of sorrow — for Salimeh's circumstances. Had America changed her? Perhaps she'd seen too many TV talk shows where women displayed their mistakes and misfortunes as if they were wares on a blanket at the bazaar. Or perhaps she knew now that so few outcomes in life could be controlled.

474

Unless, of course, one was a woman like her eldest daughter, a woman who bound herself to no man. And yet, her Mitra was lonely, unfulfilled somehow — something a mother sensed despite confident words and frequent laughter. That boy — the one Salimeh called Mitra Khanoom's Mister-Doctor, her voice fading for a moment as if remembering a martyr — he still filled the shadows that crossed her daughter's face. But Shireen said nothing.

She also asked Salimeh nothing about how she had come to be pregnant or about the mother who had disowned her. Some things, Shireen believed, were not mitigated by talk; only kind words and actions over time could bleach bad memories and build trust. Anyway, these things were not Shireen's business. She was a guest, perhaps indefinitely, but a guest just the same, and she had always prided herself on resisting gossip and nosiness. It was one of the reasons that her friendships with other transplants from her country were pleasant, but superficial. It was something she and Mitra had in common.

When Shireen found herself thinking about what would happen to Salimeh and the coming baby, she told herself that Mitra had a plan. Mitra always had a plan. And

knowing her daughter's penchant for pragmatism, she speculated that it involved giving the baby up for adoption. Mitra would
believe, and rightly so, that a girl Salimeh's
age should not sacrifice her future to the
burdens of a child. It would be best for the
child as well. Still, Shireen could not erase
her feelings about adoption, about orphans.
In Iran, they called them side-of-the-road
children. That was where the poor left the
extra mouth they could not feed or, for
whatever reason, did not want. The children
died there, or were taken by the authorities
to an orphanage, from which they rarely
emerged until they were grown. The mere
fact of their abandonment was a stigma, a
curse almost, that prevented them from being wanted by anyone. They came from bad
stock, from people in such dire straits or
lacking such humanity and sense of goodness that they could abandon their own
offspring. For in normal families, orphans
were always adopted by relatives; children
were not only of the parents, but of the family. What was a person without a family?
Shireen knew she had to shed this bias, that
in America an adopted child was deemed a
precious gift, that bloodline was often
dismissed as unimportant. And she thought
this was correct and fair. But some things

were ingrained, and when she allowed herself to contemplate Salimeh's growing belly, she was sad.

For her part, Salimeh never mentioned her pregnancy. She would've liked to forget it, and sometimes, since Shireen Khanoom had come, she did. It was only when she lay in her bed in the quiet dark that she became aware of the movements in her belly and a shivery fear ran through her body. Like that frightening movie she saw on the TV of the lizard-like monster eating its way out of a man's stomach. That confusing word *alien,* used for imagined monsters from other planets and at the same time for people like her who took ESL classes. She would have given her eyes to move back in time and erase what she had let happen to her. If she had only refused the glass of soda from the handsome boy when she went to borrow the flour. If she had only been able to keep her eyes open.

But such thoughts came only at night now. Shireen Khanoom kept her too busy, and made her laugh. Unlike her own mother, Shireen Khanoom was never still. She was like a train that never stopped. Not a fast or noisy train, but a smooth and gentle mono-rail, like Salimeh had seen when Kourosh Khan took them all to Disneyland.

Already Shireen Khanoom had developed a routine for them. After breakfast, they visited the neighborhood shops: the florist to admire and smell the flowers, the hardware store that sold everything for the house but that Khanoom complained was overpriced, the women's shoe store where the shoes looked like they were made for men, the gift shop that sold tiny statues of rosy-cheeked little boys and girls kissing, where Khanoom liked to read the greeting cards and giggle. The market, of course, where Khanoom and the Chinese man behind the counter talked like they were old friends, understanding each other even though their accents made it difficult for Salimeh to follow the conversation. As they passed the dry cleaner, Khanoom would wave at the Hindi lady in her sari, and then at the fat Spanish man working with his hands in the cobbler shop. There was one shop they had visited only once. It had a very strong smell and glass cases filled with small items that reminded Salimeh of the hookah her grandfather used to smoke as he sat in his corner, his crooked legs folded beneath him. The blond man behind the counter wore an *amameh* on his head, and this looked very strange to her; the last time she'd seen an *amameh* was on the head of a mullah back in Iran. Khanoom had suddenly said, "Oh!" and pulled at the sleeve of Salimeh's jacket until they were back on the sidewalk.

Sometimes Khanoom bought Salimeh a little something — a bag of the round chocolate candies with the letter *M* on them or a vial of flowery perfume. Salimeh was embarrassed by this and quietly asked Khanoom not to buy her things, but Khanoom told her, "It's nothing." And yesterday, Khanoom took her into the secondhand clothing shop and bought her a pair of jeans made with a stretching material in the waist to fit over her belly. "Now you won't have to wear those messy-looking sweatpants to your class," Khanoom said, and Salimeh had to look away to hide the tears in her eyes.

When they were finished visiting the shops, they went to the ice cream parlor. Khanoom loved ice cream; she liked it soft, almost drinkable, and while Salimeh scooped spoonfuls into her mouth, Khanoom sat patiently waiting for her vanilla to soften, telling stories of when Mitra Khanoom and her poor sister were children.

Khanoom was so different from Salimeh's maman — from any maman Sali had ever known — that she sometimes thought she was dreaming. Such kindness, and never a disappointed look. And Khanoom loved to cook, which was Sali's favorite task. Her maman had believed her cooking superior, and she'd made Sali stand behind her and watch everything she did over her shoulder, to prepare for her life as a wife. But in the afternoons, when Sali came back from her class and Shireen Khanoom was done with her siesta, they would begin cooking the evening meal, and Khanoom was not content with Salimeh merely watching over her shoulder; she showed her how to chop, to sauté, to stir ingredients, and then bade her copy, gently correcting or praising. Such variety of food Salimeh had never known. Her maman had used onions, turmeric, and tomato sauce in everything, mixing in lamb or chickpeas or potatoes, sometimes fava beans. But Khanoom grabbed every kind of vegetable at the market, marinated meats in spices that smelled as pungent as the farms at home, and baked her rice to perfection, each grain separate, plump, and elongated. As they cooked, they watched cooking shows on the small TV that sat on a shelf in the wall made especially for it, and Khanoom particularly liked an old lady with a cluck-cluck chicken voice who Khanoom said was famous for teaching American women how to make food like the French, and who made a big mess when she poured ingredients into her bowls, and who once dropped a whole hen onto the floor, picked it up, and put it back in the pan. Khanoom had clamped her hand over her mouth, then said, "Well, never mind. It is a TV show. They probably throw it out."

The only thing that was not wonderful was Dr. Julian's absence.

CHAPTER 24

Shireen brought Mitra a mug of tea in her office; when working, Mitra drank like the British, with sugar and cream. Shireen gauged her daughter's state of mind. She wanted to talk to her alone but didn't want to interrupt at the wrong time. If Mitra was staring into space, it was best to stay silent; she wouldn't even notice Shireen's entry or exit. If Mitra was working with papers or the computer, she would not mind a distraction. Yes, this was the opposite of most people, but Mitra said her best work was hidden behind her eyes.

"Thanks, Mom," she said, as Shireen placed the fresh tea on the leather coaster. Looking up from her computer, she asked, "Do you like side-by-side refrigerator-freezers or up-down?"

"Up-down in kitchen. Side by side in garage."

Mitra laughed. "And if you could only

have one? Like most people?"

"Up-down. As long as the down part is a drawer, not a door. It is better for knees."

Mitra typed at her keyboard. "Okay, thanks," she said.

"My daughter, do you have a moment to speak?" Shireen said in Farsi.

Mitra leaned back. "Sure. What's up?"

Shireen closed the door to the office and sat in the wing chair across from the desk. "Sali's due date is not so far away, I think. I have tried to talk to her about the delivery, but she changes the subject. I do not want to push. She is shy. Has her doctor not said anything about the birthing classes? Did she refuse them?"

"Yikes, Mom. I totally forgot about birthing classes. Jeez, I feel terrible. I'll call the doctor's office and find out when and where I have to take her."

"I would like to go with her. If you don't mind, my daughter."

"Not at all."

"I am asking because your sister preferred you to do it with her rather than me. Perhaps Sali prefers that too."

"Well, *I* would prefer not. Ana was the only person I could've done it with. And, Mom, I hope it didn't hurt your feelings that Ana asked me. It didn't occur to me."

"Of course not. When Bijan said he could not manage it, I told Ana that I thought you would be a better choice than me. It was a joy to know my daughters were doing such a thing together. And, of course, it was a reason for you to travel home."

Mitra was stunned. Her mother had influenced that decision?

"Now," Shireen continued. "Can we talk about the adoption? How is it arranged? I think it is good if we prepare Sali."

"Um . . . I haven't looked into it yet."

"Mitti!"

"I know, I know." Mitra rubbed her eyes. "I've just been so busy . . .."

Shireen frowned. "This, I think, would not be the reason."

Mitra saw that her mother was staring at her. "What?"

"Such an organized person does not put off important things unless she is uncertain."

"What could I possibly be uncertain about?"

"Perhaps you are thinking to send Sali back to her mother?"

"Never," Mitra said, readying herself for an argument. "If you think Sali should leave my house, you're wrong, Maman."

Shireen bridled. "I did not think this."

"Because I don't care that she's not blood family or from a different class or doesn't have papers. And her being here isn't going to prevent me from finding a husband and having children of my own. I never wanted that and I never will."

Shireen leaned forward and held out her hands, palms up. "Mitra, I have thought a great deal about this recently."

"I know. I wasn't asleep in Devon when you told me about your friend's daughter who had her tubal ligation reversed."

"*Vai,* Mitti, I am sorry about that. I was my old self. Please, listen to me."

Mitra held her tongue, but she wasn't hopeful.

"I was horrified when you had the surgery those years ago. I blamed myself. It was a terrible thing to force you to choose a husband so that your sister could have happiness. I was too weak to fight your father. I was so weak! It is a mother's *duty* to be strong for her children. It took the death of my own child for me to find the courage to stand up to my husband. The death of one child and the strength of another. It should not be this way."

"Mom, there is no 'should' about how we choose to do things. It's what *you* decide is best for you. It may seem strange to others;

485

people may say you're weird or selfish or bad or crazy. It doesn't matter as long as you don't hurt people needlessly."

Shireen held her hand up. "Please, Mitra, I have more to say."

Mitra sighed. "Okay."

"You see, Mitra, forgive me, but I was not raised in a world where this kind of life for a woman was possible. And I did not have the imagination to see it. It is my fault. I lived in America, but I did not see its benefits beyond the shop windows. I thought it was my fault that you did not want to marry. That I had not raised you properly. That you were not romantic."

"Well," Mitra interjected. "If you mean did your example as a wife and mother influence me, I'd say yes. Sorry, Mom, but I didn't want to end up like you, kowtowing to my husband's every wish and whim."

"Yes, yes, I understand this. I do not mind. You were right. But I had to come to this knowledge by myself. It was a journey."

Mitra nodded.

"I understand why you do not want a husband and children. I have seen your life — it is full — and it would have to change if you became a mother. I cannot tell you that I am not sad that you will not know the feeling of being a mother, but I see that you achieved contentment. I worried that you would be alone, like Olga, poor thing."

"Olga's alone because Baba made her go back to Iran. If she'd stayed here, she would've been with me. With us."

"Yes, this is true. I realized that even if a person is a mother, the guarantee of being lucky enough to have children who will want to take care of you in old age does not exist. There are many ways a parent can lose a child."

They were silent for a moment, then Mitra said, "You haven't lost me, Mom."

Shireen tried to respond, but tears blocked her voice and she tapped at her lips. Mitra looked away to give her time to collect herself, then slid a tissue box toward her. After Shireen wiped her eyes and cleared her throat a few times, Mitra said, "Just because I don't want children, Mom, doesn't mean I can't love them or love taking care of them."

"I know this, azizam. I think about how I feel about Nezam. He has always had a special place in my heart. I love to be with him, and I worry about him no less than I worry about you. If this is how you felt for Nina and Nikku — and I know it is — then that is as good as motherhood."

"I think I'm better at being an aunt than

487

being a mother."

"Yes, it is possible. It requires other abilities. And I remember my relationships with my aunties, one in particular who was so important to me that I do not think I would be the person I am without her guidance and love." Shireen noticed that Mitra seemed to be calmer now. Her face was smoother, the frown in her brow gone, and Shireen felt suddenly lighter, but also more solid, like a tree that has been transplanted into better soil.

They remained silent for a while, each with her own thoughts, until Shireen spoke in a subdued voice. "Mitti, perhaps Sali keeps the baby. With our help . . ." She braced herself for Mitra's astonished disapproval, but her daughter didn't move. Shireen inched forward. "You have thought of it too?"

Some days later, a miffed Carlos apologized for interrupting Ms. Mitra, but a delivery boy was refusing to hand over some items without Mitra herself signing for them *and* showing her license. His boss didn't seem surprised, except for a slight lift of her eyebrow. The courier handed her a manila envelope, which she didn't open, and brought two large items in to fill the foyer: a square box and a tall rectangle, both professionally wrapped and taped with padding. Carlos took out his box cutter, but Ms. Mitra put her hand up. "No need," she said. "I know what's inside, and I won't be using them for a while." This was not odd; plenty of items ordered for the restorations came in before they were ready to be installed and had to be stored in the garage. What *was* odd, though Carlos didn't comment, was that Ms. Mitra wanted the items stowed in her bedroom closet. Luckily, they weren't heavy, just wieldy enough to require that they carry each up the stairs together. Yes, he wondered what was in the boxes, but he knew his boss well enough not to ask: those stiff shoulders, that hard expression, eyes averted. Anyway, being in her bedroom was revealing in itself. The last time had been just a few weeks before the sister's tragedy, when he'd given the room a fresh coat of paint. The artworks that had covered the walls remained leaning in a corner where he'd set them over a year ago. Two of the lightbulbs in the vaulted ceiling had blown, the bed was unmade, and one of the side tables was cluttered with coins and pencils and tissues. Carmen had mentioned that Ms. Mitra often told her to skip cleaning the bedroom. They both figured it was because of the young doctor; he was not so *inmaculado.* But this was more than unclean and cluttered; it was *sombrío.* For Ms. Mitra, it was *muy sombrío.* Carlos was glad to leave it.

Mitra, on the other hand, was glad her mother and Sali weren't home. Even so, she closed her office door before shaking out the contents of a manila envelope the courier had given her. She pushed aside a typed inventory of Anahita's jewelry — fifty-one pieces — and picked up a smaller envelope on which her name was written in an Old World flourish. She drew out a single page. The paper was rich and thick, Aden's unbroken letters clearly formed by the nib of a fountain pen. First, he apologized for sending the jewelry before she'd given him the go-ahead; he simply couldn't bear seeing the box every day. Until he'd shown Mitra the pieces, their presence was a comfort, *a kind of illusion that Ana was still alive.* Now, it felt to him as if he'd put all that was left of Ana into darkness. *This part of her must be in the light, Mitra, and it must be you who does that.* She sighed. He went on to stress that he wasn't signaling her to do anything, not even open the box, until she was ready. *You will know when it is time.*

Great, Mitra thought, looking up from the

letter, trying not to be mad at Aden for such a burden. After all, he was trying to be loyal and responsible. The only way he knew how to do that was to keep his promise of discretion. Neither of them could divert from that promise. If the jewelry was ever to be made public, it would have to be done carefully and craftily by Mitra. *It must be you.*

Clutching the letter, she went back up to her bedroom and stood before the closet. It was not lost on her that the parcels sat in the naked area where Julian had kept his clothing. Loss and more loss. She knew without unwrapping the rectangular parcel that it was a painting, had to be of the original photograph that her father had given Aden, this time without Mitra removed. *A gift that gave me great joy and comfort to paint.* She had no interest in looking at it; she knew the photo by heart and by heartache. The box of jewelry, she decided, would also remain unopened. *When you are ready.* Well, she wasn't ready, not even close. "Shit, Aden," she muttered, as if he were standing next to her. "Just call me Pandora." And she slid the door shut.

CHAPTER 25

As the winter holidays approached, a heaviness descended on Mitra and Shireen. Each of them saw reflected in the other's eyes memories of past Thanksgivings when the Jahani house was filled with cousins attending boarding school or college in the States, and with their shy and homesick friends, because Shireen couldn't bear the idea of a foreign student spending such a family holiday in an emptied-out dorm. Over the years, the number of guests and food and board games had grown to become the highlight of their year; even Mitra looked forward to it. Yusef might have objected to the throng of young people with their duffels and sleeping bags, but the kids were so deferential in their gratitude that he'd grown fond of having them around. When they gathered to watch football games or play charades, which they did until the wee hours, he simply retired to his study, where he preferred to be anyway. Having spent his childhood in a large household, he quite liked the sound of it all.

If not for Sali's inquiries about their plans, Mitra and Shireen might have pretended that Thanksgiving didn't exist. As far as Mitra was concerned, they were better off expunging family holidays from now on. Last year, Julian had taken her to an overpriced resort hotel in Tahoe, where they spent the holiday in bed, drunk on mulled wine, sex, and science fiction movies. But this year, the extreme El Niño weather made travel risky, especially since Sali's due date was less than three weeks away. Mitra was about to ask Karen if Sali might tag along (and help look after Scotty and Jacob) for the holiday meal at her in-laws in Menlo Park when Shireen and Sali came back from the grocery store with a small turkey and numerous bags containing all the fixings. Shireen had relented, and Sali's face glowed with anticipation. Though Shireen smiled and busied herself in the kitchen over the next day with Sali at her elbow, Mitra couldn't put on this false front, and she couldn't stand to be so near to the nostalgic aromas of poultry and cornbread and pecan pie. She stayed in her office or bedroom until her mother called her for the meal, and when she got to the table, she immediately saw what was missing: the sweet potatoes — Ana and Nina's favorite, and the biscuits Nikku hoarded the minute they came out of the oven — and she was relieved. Still, there was enough food to last a week, and Sali had her *Tanx-geeving.* By Sunday, of course, she was asking about Christmas, but Mitra shut that down abruptly. "You need to be planning for something else before that," she said.

Sali went into labor on a Tuesday afternoon when Mitra was looking at granite slabs at a wholesale house in Monterey. By the time Mitra reached the hospital back in the city, Sali's contractions were minutes apart. She peeked into the birthing room to see the girl's twisted face as Shireen led her competently through the pain in Farsi, and then she took a nap in the waiting room until Shireen shook her awake.

"I'm going to name him Jack," said Sali, cradling her new son.

"Jack?" Mitra said.

Shireen softly elbowed her and whispered, *"Titanic."*

Oh, no, thought Mitra, struggling to maintain the smile on her face. She hadn't anticipated that the perils of teenage motherhood would show themselves so immediately. "Are you sure?" she ventured. "It's an old-fashioned name."

They were sitting by Sali's bed in the hospital room, and she couldn't seem to look away from her baby. "I am sure," she said. "Look, he even has the blue eyes of Jack. And his hair is not very black."

"He is beautiful," said Shireen. "And so calm."

"You can give him a Persian middle name."

Shireen elbowed Mitra again, this time more firmly. "Later," she whispered.

Sali ignored the suggestion anyway. She was infatuated. Mitra had seen it before. It was lovely. The infant's eyes rolled groggily from side to side, and his fingers stretched and folded lazily. Bundled in a blue-and-pink-striped blanket — maternity ward unisex — he reminded Mitra of a Thumbelina doll Ana once had. And then she winced, remembering how she'd punctured Thumbelina's arm with a safety pin: *She needs her rubella shot.* She'd just learned that word — *rubella* — and she liked saying it. Ana was distraught. Mitra imitated a baby howling, then handed the doll to Ana. *There. You can calm her down now. If she stops crying, she can have a lollipop.*

As if reading her imagination, Julian appeared at the foot of the bed. She hadn't seen him since their breakup nearly two months ago, and her pulse quickened. She didn't know how it would be between them. He was smiling at Sali.

"You did a great job," he said. "I see you're getting acquainted."

Sali looked at Mitra. "Getting acquainted means getting to know someone," Mitra said, translating English to English.

Sali beamed at Julian. "Jack is perfect," she said.

"Jack?"

Mitra had to pretend to look for something in her purse so as not to burst out laughing. Shireen was again helpful. "*Titanic* movie," she said.

"Ah," Mitra heard, focusing harder on rummaging through her purse, but then she couldn't help herself, glanced up and saw Julian struggling hard to suppress his dismay and hilarity. Their eyes met, and it was surprisingly natural: close friends trading thoughts. Not for the first time, she pushed away the thought of an amicable break-up in which Julian continued to be a part of her life; she knew how rare such a thing was.

Julian cleared his throat. "So, Sali, have you decided whether you want to do the circumcision?"

Sali looked up sharply from the baby. "I don't know," she said, looking at Mitra and Shireen, who both looked at Julian.

Shireen said, "The teacher in the birthing class, she was very against it. She said it was barba . . . barbie . . . for savages."

Julian shoved his hands into his lab coat. "I wouldn't go that far. It's very quick. Medically, there are pros and cons to each choice. I'm sure your teacher went over them with you. As a pediatrician, I recommend whatever the Dad —"

"Oops," Mitra said, narrowing her eyes at him. "Wrong speech." He blushed and scratched his forehead, and Mitra turned to Sali. "I think he should be circumcised, Sali; it's the Moslem way."

"Yes, okay," she said, but she held the infant tighter to her body.

Julian came around the bed and leaned over to take him from her. "I promise to be gentle. It takes literally a second. I'll have him back to you in a few minutes." And he lifted the baby like a pro, held him in the crook of his arm, and whispered, "Hey there, kiddo. Hey there, Jackie boy. Shall we go for a little stroll?"

They all watched as he left the room, and they remained tensely silent waiting for his return. But it was a nurse who brought the baby back, and a nurse who told them visiting hours were over and that Sali was in good hands for the night, that (pointing at Shireen) "grandma" needed to go home and get some sleep. They kissed Sali good night, and Mitra linked her arm around Shireen's as they worked their way around medicine carts and helium balloons toward the elevator. Julian was nowhere to be seen. Mitra had scanned every room and hallway along the way.

The next morning, after receiving a call from the doctor that Sali would be discharged by late afternoon, Mitra dropped Shireen off at the hospital entrance before parking her car in the lot. When she walked into the lobby, Julian was waiting for her, sitting at the end of a bank of chairs, brows furrowed and eyes a stony navy blue. It was one of those rare moments when she saw the Persian in him, the dark and chiseled.

He stood. "Can we talk?"

He led her to an elevator and down several corridors, greeting people curtly as his sneakers squeaked and her boots clacked on the linoleum. They entered a small, windowless office where he gestured for her to sit in one of two chairs across from a dark wooden desk. He sat down behind it, and she realized how odd it was that she'd never been to his office, which she knew he shared with another junior doctor. Had it hurt his feelings? Probably. She'd shown almost no interest in his career.

"Would you like a coffee?" He gestured toward an electric kettle and a jar of Folgers.

He knew she didn't drink the stuff, but she said, "No thanks. I'm fine." If he wanted to wound her with small slights, she would let him.

He leaned back and crossed his legs, did not look at her. Behind him was a massive bookcase containing rows of fat medical books. The shelves must've had a centimeter of dust on them. Finally, he exhaled and spoke. "I've a few things to say to you, M. I hope you'll hear me out until I'm done."

"Okay."

His belt buckle sagged; he'd lost weight. He took a deep breath, fixed his eyes in a thousand-yard stare, and said, "I know it's best for the both of us if we let time pass until we build new routines and our feelings fade, but when I ran into Sali at the Women's Care Center, going for classes with your mum —" He noticed her head tilt. "They didn't tell you?"

499

"Not a peep," she said. So Shireen knew about Julian and had said nothing. Mitra was relieved. She didn't want to explain, to go back over the last year and possibly have to deal with her mother's attempts at rekindling the relationship. Then again, maybe this was an indication that the "new" Shireen understood what had happened or just accepted that her daughter knew what was best for herself. Finally.

"I like your mum. She's not what I expected after hearing you talk about her. Not brooding or passive. I mean, she's definitely traditional, but nothing like Akram."

"Yikes! Of course not," Mitra exclaimed. It came out as a put-down of Julian's judgment. "I guess I misrepresented her," she added quickly.

He grabbed a rubber stress ball imprinted with the Pfizer logo and held it in his lap, squeezing gently. "You know by now that Sali wants me to be her pediatrician. I want to be in Sali's life, and in the life of that little one." He put his hand up to forestall her from saying anything. "I'm not talking about us, M. I understand that we're over. I still believe her mum needs to play a role in her life, or at least given a chance to redeem herself."

"Jules —" She'd moved to the edge of her seat.

"I don't want to discuss it, Mitra."

She scooted back and tried to will her mouth shut.

"Look," he continued, his voice lower. "I'd like nothing more than to sod off and get back to my life as it was before we met, but I can't. No: I don't want to. Don't worry, I'm not making a case for us to get back together. I realize that I fell for this idea of us — a fantasy. When we met, I think we recognized something similar in one another, a melancholia, a yearning to shape a family of our own. Maybe we mistook it for romance, or maybe that was the only way we knew how to express it. At any rate, it happened. You're a part of my life I can't erase. We may not have a future together as a couple, but I don't want us to have no contact at all. You and Sali, even your mum, I don't want to lose the connection. I'm not saying it'll be easy, but I'd like to try." He smiled bashfully. "Besides, I miss Jezebel."

She managed to smile and resist a sudden urge to cry. Ugh, all these tears . . . of heartache and also of joy. "I'm glad," she managed to say.

What had he called it? A melancholia that they'd recognized in each other. It was true.

501

He from his fatherlessness and his mother's absences, and she from her family estrangements. In a phrase, loneliness had drawn them together. And hadn't he been a good companion to her? She hadn't grown bored with his conversation, his smart and yet vulnerable way of expressing himself, nor had she become irritated by his peccadilloes — the nervous sniffing, the brown ring his shaving lotion container left in the shower, his penchant for potato chips in bed, the holey T-shirts he wouldn't get rid of. Most of all, he'd fit into every part of her quotidian life, which she was very proprietary about. It was his lack of intrusion — his acceptance — that had made her forget to attend to the boundary that separated their intentions for the future.

"Well," she said, wiping damp palms on her jeans and rising from the chair. "I should get back to my mom, take her home. She probably needs a nap after all that birthing stuff."

"She was a trouper," Julian said, rising too and coming around the desk.

They hugged awkwardly. Then Mitra smiled and said, "You'll come for dinner once Sali and the baby settle in?"

"I'll come and make dinner," he said.

"Good luck with that. My mom's here now."

And they laughed.

Walking the hallways back to Sali's room, Mitra realized how much Julian had given her, more than he knew. Not all men were like those she'd known and battled and run away from. Some had humility instead of outsized pride, were gentle and thoughtful and kind. It was harder to be like that. It took practice, experience, self-respect, and love. Julian was going to make a wonderful father when the time came. Unlike his own father, who'd disappeared. Unlike her own father, who'd been spared having to face and cope with the horrific truths that came with raising children. She stopped moving and leaned against the wall. Yes, her father had been spared the knowledge of Kareem's sins, but did he deserve that protection? Perhaps the only person who deserved it was Ana, and that was only because she'd felt such shame about it. And that shame was concocted and preserved by those who stuck fast to the old traditions or those who benefited from the silence of their victims.

She pushed away from the wall and walked to the elevator. Her legs felt rubbery and her hands and neck hot. She managed to hide her agitation from Sali and her mother.

After a bit, Shireen said there was no need for Mitra to stay, that she should go on and tend to her work until the late afternoon when Sali would be discharged. Relieved, she went home and stood, edgy and indecisive, in the foyer. She climbed the stairs. There was a vanity in her bedroom that she never used. She'd found it in an antique shop, sanded it, painted it white. It reminded her of old Hollywood movies, its vintage mirror scratched and smudged. On it was a crystal lamp with a fringed cream-colored shade, a thin glass vase that she used to put fresh flowers in every week, and a pad of off-white stationery with a pen on top. It was for show, for ambience: when night fell, it was this lamp she turned on; it cast a warm glow throughout the room. The low chair that matched the vanity was a repository for clothes she'd been too lazy to put away. She removed these and put them on the bed. She sat down and picked up the pen. Her pulse quickened. She realized she'd never sat here. Her face in the mirror looked flushed. She pressed the nib of the pen to the paper and wrote, *Dear Baba.* She hesitated, looked at her reflection, closed her eyes. What did she want? Perhaps solace; simply to share the burden and pain of knowing. No, she wasn't that benevolent or forgiving. She wanted revenge and — this stung — she wanted him to know that she'd fulfilled, at least partially, a duty he'd shirked. He hadn't been the exceptional father he believed. He'd clung so dearly to his authoritative image that he'd failed to protect and nurture his own children. She opened her eyes, moved the pen to the next line, and began.

The story of Ana and Kareem in the basement. Every detail. It wasn't easy. She'd never spoken to her father about sex. Seeing certain words in ink made her cringe. *Grinding. Erection.* Several times, she moved her hand onto the page to crumple it and throw it in the garbage. But she resisted. If *she* could feel the shame of telling, imagine the depth of Ana's shame. It had been ingrained in them to carry this burden of the family's honor, an honor that was constantly threatened by the very gender that created its self-serving rules of oppression and possession. She tightened her lips and soldiered on.

She would not spare him, as she had spared Shireen and Olga. He would know how long his sweet daughter had suffered at his nephew's hands. But Mitra wouldn't betray Aden. That was none of her father's business. If, without evidence of how she'd learned the facts, he didn't believe Mitra, she didn't care. She knew it was likely. Too painful. Underneath it all, he was too weak to face the truth. This, Mitra realized, was why abusers rarely admitted the crime, and why their victims continued to feel shame and guilt — no one believed. The scars lasted for life, showing themselves in myriad ways — anxiety, depression, indecision, confusion, self-loathing. All of this she wrote to her father. Let him learn. Let him know. Let it hurt.

When the writing was done, she felt no emotional relief. Her anger and sadness were not alleviated. After all, she wasn't the victim. But the telling of Ana's story had given her a sense of justice done, and for what other use was the act of breaking silence?

PART 3

■ ■ ■ ■

BROTHERS

In the time of our history when the dust storms drove the American farmers west, when the Russians died of the typhus, and the Chinese of the swollen Yellow River, and when Iran was swindled by the oil-obsessed British, two boys, born of different mothers, bonded in their common patriarch's sprawling compound at the base of the Alborz Mountains. Shunned and neglected by the household, teased and whipped by the spoiled and arrogant sons of their father's primary wife, the boys played together in the dust, in the mud, in the soft pine needle mounds, and they came to know the tempo of each other's breath, so many years did they sleep side by side.

The bond was out of necessity, not commonality, for they were very different. In age, four years separated them, but the older sniveled and whined, the younger was stoic and fastidious. When the younger brother's mother fell ill and was taken away, the older brother's mother cared for him with kindness. After some years, she took him in secret to visit his mother. In a bleak sanitarium a far bus ride away, he witnessed the dust-misted shafts of light, the whispers and occasional staccato shouts of hidden sufferers, the freakish-looking electrical machines that rolled through the hallways bristling with knobs and dials, the fatalistic expressions on the doctors' faces — expressions that belonged to bad-news fortune catchers. His mother's room: bare as a public bath. Her form: thin and crooked as a dead branch. Her voice: choked and raspy with rage. She'd gripped his arm: "Grow up, my son! Free me from this place!"

All this time, he had imagined her sick and suffering — febrile with typhoid, bilious with cholera, suffocating with tuberculosis, wasting with cancer. But no. He would no longer envision her helpless and needing his help. It was a relief. He understood that in all but a few earthly societies, rebellion in women is the same as insanity.

When the half brothers grew old enough to strike out from the family compound, the older, who had become slovenly and jealous, chose to remain at the edges of the clan, marrying and procreating to fill his insecurity. The younger, dapper and ambitious, set out for the unpredictable West, free. Or so he thought.

When they reached middle age, the Revolution came and the mullahs twisted religion to control the politics, twisted politics to control the people, and twisted people to plunder for them. The brother in the West stretched his hand across the continents and brought his half sibling and his family to safety. This, not for love or pity, for duty or righteousness, but in memory of his now-dead foster mother.

CHAPTER 26

As always, the corridor leading to Jafar's apartment smelled of turmeric and saffron from the Persian meals he reheated in his microwave. Yusef slid his key into the lock and heard the cat meow. He hated the cat, its white fur that clung to his suit jacket and trousers, but the pet was his half brother's necessary companion, sprawling insouciantly as it did on Jafar's lap as he reclined in his plush La-Z-Boy, listening nonstop to Farsi satellite radio, sniffling at histrionic love songs and cursing at commentators.

At least the apartment was warm; the weather had turned suddenly cold. He removed his cashmere coat and hung it on a hook. He didn't have to announce himself; Jafar knew the sound of his movements, the scent of his body. This had been true even before the glaucoma had taken Jafar's sight.

Yusef veered into the kitchen, a window-less square room with unevenly hung white

511

melamine cabinets. He emptied the teapot of its bloated day-old leaves and scooped fresh ones in, turned on the kettle to boil, and extricated a box of butter biscuits from one of the cabinets. He went into the living room and sat heavily on the sofa. A ballad had just finished, and Jafar was dabbing his cheeks with a tissue.

"Is it sunny outside?" Jafar asked.

"No," Yusef said, though it was.

Jafar smiled, causing his thick chapped lips to crack. "Good, then I am not missing anything."

Yusef reached for the ChapStick among the collection of prescription bottles on the side table and leaned over to place the tube in Jafar's hand. He used it.

"They sent a different nurse this morning. I think she's prettier than the other one. Her voice is soft, in the way of pretty girls, and her fingers slender. She is not fat and angry."

"Hmm," said Yusef. "Most American girls have become fat and angry. This country is not the way it used to be."

The radio announcer was reciting a Hafez poem about the beauty of spring. It made Yusef wish for that season — a rush forward or a rush backward to any year, a wish that he could be transported out of this deadly

512

winter. The kettle began to whistle, and he went to pour the boiling water into the teapot and set it to steep in the mouth of the simmering kettle with a potholder balanced on top. As he returned to the living room, Jafar said, "What is wrong, brother? You walk like a condemned man. You smell unhappy."

"Nothing," Yusef said, sitting down again, putting a biscuit between his teeth, leaning back.

"Tell me," prodded Jafar, reaching his crooked fingers to the radio dial, turning the volume down. "I also smell cheap perfume." A leer reconfigured his old face, displaying his yellowed teeth. "You did not spend last night alone."

"I'm sleepy," Yusef said. "Let me nap for ten minutes while the tea steeps." He leaned his head against the back of the sofa and closed his eyes for all of thirty seconds, then opened them, stared at Jafar's feet, clad in black socks that wrinkled at the ankles and puffed out beyond the toes like pom-poms. His trousers and sweater seemed borrowed from a larger person, and his face — why, he looked like a man on the cusp of a century! Unlike Yusef, he had not inherited their father's longevity. Still, even the frailest could live long these days while the healthiest and most youthful-looking dropped dead. Yusef had made financial arrangements for Jafar in the unlikely event that such a thing happened.

"I can sense when your eyes are open, brother," said Jafar, a slight smile on his lips. "You just do not want to talk to me."

Yusef stood up. "I'll bring the tea."

Jafar raised his voice so Yusef could hear him as he walked toward the kitchen. "Has your traitor wife asked you to take her back, then?"

No answer.

Yusef overfilled the tea glasses and bent to sip at each one before carrying them to the living room. He poured half of Jafar's tea into the glass saucer so it would cool.

"Well?" Jafar prodded. "Did she?"

"Did she what, Agha?"

"Oho, calling me Agha. I've made you angry with me. Shall we arm-wrestle? I will beat you like last time."

"Last time must have been forty years ago, brother."

"It is like yesterday for me. When there is nothing to see but what is on the inside of one's head, time is bent."

"Lucky you," said Yusef, sucking on a sugar cube.

"All right. Tell me about the gathering

yesterday. For Pirooz's new child — a son — is that right?"

"It is. The gathering was fine. The eggplant *khoresh* was too salty, the children too noisy."

"Was your sister-in-law there? They are back from Iran. What's the news?"

"The trip was unsuccessful, as I predicted. They didn't reclaim their house."

"Hah, too bad," said Jafar, his smile broader.

Yes, Yusef thought, there was a certain satisfaction in Golnaz and Parviz's failure. He'd seen their house on his last trip before the Revolution. A pristine white marble contemporary with a mix of clean lines and elegant Persian arches, banks of windows facing gardens filled with roses and jasmine and quiet fountains. A house far too sophisticated for a physics professor, no matter how respected he was in his field.

"Was it destroyed?" asked Jafar. "A highrise in its place? A country club? A mall?"

"Better than that," said Yusef, allowing himself a grin. "Taken over by filthy squatters with forged deeds. Golnaz said it wasn't worth the trouble of plodding through the stupid and corrupt bureaucracy to prove her ownership. Said it was just a house, not a home. She'd been gone too long."

"She lies," sneered Jafar. "It is her pride speaking. She is big-headed."

This was true. His sister-in-law had always been arrogant. More so in recent years since she'd been lucky with her day trading. Sometimes he wished he hadn't rejected her when she offered her services as an accountant after the Revolution; she would have been beholden to him. Yesterday at the gathering, he itched to slap her when she approached him with her usual line — *And how's the construction business these days?* As if he were a laborer with a pickup truck. *Real estate,* he'd corrected her, loathing the sound of his voice.

Yusef grimaced. "Golnaz brought back a girl with her."

"A maidservant? What trick did she pull? American visas are not given away like glasses of water these days."

"Don't be stupid, Jafar. The girl is the daughter of a friend. Apparently."

Jafar leered. "Is she a peach?"

"No, she is plain. Hardly like an Iranian woman. No makeup, hair limp, ugly clothing. Probably the daughter of one of Parviz's university colleagues. She follows him around like a disciple."

Jafar tsked and shook his head. "The young ones are somehow duped by him."

"Because he views the world like a child." Yusef poured the tea from the saucer back into the glass, leaned forward, wrapped Jafar's hand around it, and placed two sugar lumps in his free palm.

Jafar slurped. "What did Parviz say about the situation in Iran?"

"What else? It is a mess."

Yusef and Parviz never discussed politics — their relationship had always been strained — but Yusef had made certain to sit near enough to his brother-in-law so he could listen to his blather. As usual, he spoke of the university where he used to teach, about the students' thirst for freedoms they saw on satellite TV and the promise of this new thing, the Internet. And then about the Islamist militia sneakily squelching activism, and finally, about his fear that blood would be spilled, as if anything could be achieved without spilling blood. Such melodrama. Parviz had been one of the anti-Shah idealists who believed Iran could be a democracy. Ridiculous, Yusef thought; the masses were, like children, unequipped to comprehend self-rule. Yusef said to Jafar, "Even Parviz isn't hopeful about this reformist president. The hardliners are eroding his reforms from the shadows."

Jafar drank the rest of his tea in one gulp. "It is like everywhere, brother. The theocrats do what they think God has chosen them to do. Like the bombing of that abortion clinic in Texas." He extended his empty glass for Yusef to take; it was the kind of hubristic gesture that Jafar was known for, a swagger that rankled everyone: the idiot who thought he was a wise man. Only Yusef could tolerate him. Jafar leaned back in his chair and pulled a plaid throw across his legs. "Now, when is your wife returning? People are gossiping. And I had the last of her eggplant *khoresh* weeks ago."

Yusef exhaled irritably. "Stop asking me about my wife, brother. When she returns, I'll let you know."

"It is Mitra's fault. Shireen would not be in California if our angel Anahita was still here. Poor us!" Tears bloomed from his unseeing eyes. "Dirt on Mitra's head!"

"She is my daughter," Yusef said. "Do not curse her to my face."

Jafar leaned forward. "Did I not tell you, Yusef, to put Mitra away like Agha Bozorg did to your mother? After Mitra made herself unmarriageable in that lunatic way, she should have been punished."

"I have told you, Jafar, that America does not work that way. I expelled her from my

518

life. That was as far as I could go." Yusef stood up, shoved his hands into his pockets. "I don't want your advice in this matter, Agha. Can I help you use the bathroom before I leave?"

"Already you are leaving? My only visitor gives me less than an hour of his time." Jafar opened his palms to the heavens. "What have I done, Allah, to deserve such thoughtless treatment from my most valued relative. It is time, O God, for me to die."

Yusef was losing his patience. "Stop this, Jafar. I have enough on my mind." He turned to leave.

"What will you do now, my brother? Will you go out into the day and treat yourself to a steak, to an ice cream? Will you visit your mistress again? Is it still the woman with the shaved mound you described? You are a lucky man, my brother. You have always been a lucky man."

Shireen's ear was sore from holding the receiver. Since her sister had returned to New York, they'd spoken many hours over the phone, beginning early in the mornings and then several times over each day. Even so, they'd only scratched the surface of all that had happened to her and Parviz in Iran. Shireen got up, made her bed, then opened

519

the blinds to yet another sunny day.

Golnaz was not her usual self, not calm and matter-of-fact or distracted by work. She jumped from subject to subject, one moment talking about how Tehran had grown to unrecognizable proportions and the next about Olga being the same solid and trusty Cossack she'd hired for Shireen all those years ago. All of Golnaz's news was riveting, and with each piece of it, Shireen felt at once dizzier and more eager. She hadn't watched *All My Children* in days.

Most enthralling was the story of the orphan girl. Zoya was her name. Not really a girl, but a young woman of twenty years. And not really an orphan, at least not in her own mind. She believed her father, a journalist, had been taken to Evin Prison, the political section, where he had been before, even under the Shah. But this had not been confirmed. Olga had known the girl's mother, though Shireen wasn't yet clear how.

She rubbed her eyes and went to brush her teeth, and as often happened these days as she tended to common tasks, her thoughts continued to digest and contemplate all that Golnaz told her. So much had happened in Olga's life over the last ten years! And Shireen knew none of it. This was what ayatollahs and presidents did to ordinary people; cut them off from one another while saying it was for everyone's own good. Like what fathers and husbands did. Well, most fathers and husbands. Not all. Not Parviz, for example. And not Nezam. Shireen wondered what a son of hers would have been like. Not good, she thought. With Yusef as a husband and with so little exposure to varying examples, even in America, she would have raised a son as if he were a prince, giving him every reason to think of himself as extraordinary. Humility would not have been in his character. She would have done what all the women of her time had done: held up the honor of her men no matter how stupid they were.

But why? Was it, as Golnaz said, a false belief that this was the only way to have power — in the shadows, the *andaruni*? Yes, she thought, they — *she* — had shared in building the walls of her own prison. She sighed and went to dress in the casual clothing her life in California allowed — one of many small changes that fulfilled her.

Downstairs, Sali was nursing the baby in the family room while watching the *Today* show, where she could raptly examine New York City. Katie Couric was trembling in the cold on a crowded sidewalk, and Shireen quietly thanked God that she wasn't there. She took the baby to burp him so Sali could go to the bathroom. Such a bittersweet feeling to have the warm, milky-scented bundle in her arms. She had to consciously push away the bitter thoughts of her missing grandchildren — the memories that cut her heart — and focus on this one, the one she'd helped bring into the world, the one she secretly called Reza because that was the name she'd once chosen for a son. She patted his back and rested her lips against his fuzzy scalp. He burped.

"Khanoom-joon," said Sali from the kitchen. "I'm jealous; he burps so easily for you."

Shireen laughed. "I'm glad he so wants to please me!"

Sali brought a glass of tea and placed it in front of Shireen. "Will you be walking with Khanoom Tokuda today?"

"Yes," said Shireen, letting Sali take the baby. "Is Mitra here?"

"No, Khanoom. She left early, I think to Sausalito?" Shireen loved the way Sali's brows curled when she wasn't sure of something. "She said she would be back for dinner."

"And you? Your class is at the usual time this afternoon?"

"Yes, Khanoom, but I can skip it if you have something else. . . ."

Shireen thrust her chin up. "Child, you know it is my joy to mind the baby."

Sali smiled and bowed her head in delight and gratitude.

Mrs. Tokuda answered the door wearing a surgical mask. "I have sore throat, my friend. No walking today for me, but you must go."

Shireen laughed. She'd never gone alone. Of course she wouldn't go alone. She didn't even know how to get to the beautiful trail above the ocean.

"Helen!" Tokuda called over her shoulder. Her younger daughter, the plump-lipped one who was a therapist, came down the hall and greeted Shireen. "Helen is going near there, to pick up herbs for me from a friend. She will drop you." Tokuda turned and snatched something from the small table, put it in Shireen's hand. "Timer," she said in her teacher's voice. "Set for twenty minutes. Walk until bell rings, do deep breathing, walk back. Helen will be waiting."

Shireen felt a flutter in her chest. "Tokuda-san, I don't think . . . When you're better, we'll go together."

523

Tokuda dismissed Shireen's words with a wave of her tiny hand, turned to Helen. "You ready?"

"Yes, Ma." Helen's expression was of amusement and tolerance. She smiled at Shireen and opened the front door.

No, Shireen thought. Suddenly, the thing she liked so much about Mrs. Tokuda — her pluck — was the thing she liked least.

"Go, go," ushered Tokuda, her mask puffing out with each syllable. "Oh, and, Helen, do me favor and explain belly fat science to Shireen."

Helen raised her eyebrows and grinned. "Sure, Ma."

Shireen felt a blush rise into her face as they walked to the car. The belly fat discussion seemed so long ago, the first time they met for tea at Mitra's kitchen table. At that point, Shireen only knew that this slight Japanese woman who was old enough to be her mother was an exercise instructor. Her personality reminded Shireen of a childhood nanny her parents had employed for a short time. Not physically, for the nanny had been round and slow and hunched, but in disposition, for she had been at once gruff and kind, harsh and caring, blunt and loving. Shireen wondered aloud if she might take one of Mrs. Tokuda's classes (Mitra had choked on her coffee when she said this), explaining that she wished to shrink her waist, to fit into clothing more easily, like she used to. She pointed out that Tokuda was so lean and fit. Tokuda bridled. "You must have my ancestors to be like this," she said with a serious face. "You have strong ancestors, survival body." She'd pointed at Shireen's belly. "This around your middle save you in times of no food. Mine turn me to dust. This scientific truth. Anyway, judo not for you. Walking is best. We walk together."

Now, as Helen drove toward Lands End, she said, "My mom is always asking me to explain the belly fat thing. I learned about it from my colleague who's an endocrinologist." This did make Shireen feel less embarrassed about the topic, as if it were more clinical, less personal.

"I know," sighed Shireen. "It is from too much chocolate. And rice."

Helen glanced over and smiled sweetly. "Actually, no. It's a unique kind of fat that almost all middle-aged women get. It's totally different from other body fat. It can't even be dissolved in the laboratory like other human fat."

"But why?" asked Shireen, surprised now.

"We're not sure, but it seems to be evolutionary. You know, like a survival mechanism."

"Okay," nodded Shireen, slowly understanding.

"In ancient communities," Helen continued, "this abdominal fat saved older women from starvation in times of famine. Not grandfathers, mind you. Men don't have this kind of fat. Anthropologists — historical scientists — think this may show that while grandmothers were essential to the tribe, grandfathers were, well" — she tilted her head at Shireen — "unnecessary."

Shireen's brow slowly unfurled. "Unnecessary?"

Helen tittered. "Uh-huh. They were probably kicked out, sent off to fend for themselves." Shireen's eyes widened and Helen nodded. "Now my mom tells all of her students to be 'proud of the belly.' " Helen said the phrase in a perfect imitation of Tokuda's accent, the way Mitra often did to tease Shireen. It was cute, but Shireen felt slightly paralyzed. That word: *unnecessary.*

Helen pulled over and stopped at the trailhead above Seal Rock. She turned slightly in her seat so she was facing Shireen. "It's a beautiful day. My mom used to take us on the ridge trail every weekend when we were growing up."

Shireen suddenly realized it was time for her to lift the door handle and get herself out. "So sorry you had to drive me here," she managed.

"Oh, it's no problem. My mom's friend is just around the corner. I'll have tea with her and come back for you."

Shireen lifted her left hand, which still held Tokuda's timer, and she managed a smile. "Thank you, Helen."

Despite the sunshine, it was cold, but Shireen was bundled up and comfortable. The onshore wind was diminished by fir and cypress trees. This kind of cold didn't bother her; in fact, the idea that a cozy winter could be enjoyed without the prospect of snow delighted her. She'd never imagined such an option might exist for her. So many options. In her life with Yusef, she'd thought of herself as free, but now she understood that only small decisions had been hers to make. Indeed, it was she who had been deemed *unnecessary*.

When she first married, she'd hoped to fall in love with Yusef. What new bride didn't? He was handsome and successful, polite and educated. That he chose her over many other eligible girls made her feel as if there was a spark between them. She'd been

527

exposed to Hollywood and the books of Jane Austen and the star-crossed love tales of Layla and Majnoon, Romeo and Juliet. But she was also a child of her culture. Their first night together was neither as horrific nor as rapturous as she'd heard it could be. He was respectful, fairly gentle, and swift. If he glanced to see her blood proof, he did so surreptitiously. She felt lucky and knew it would take time for them to become more intimate physically and emotionally. But this didn't happen. His dispassion, and not just in the way he touched her, but in the lack of conversation he had with her, made her lonely. She learned early on that he had other women. She assumed it was for a different kind of sex, more in tune with the appetites she'd heard men had, and though she was jealous at first, she soon came to believe that this behavior was a sign of respect for her dignity; he did not see her as a sex object, but as a partner with whom to build a family. Once she was pregnant, the dye had been cast: this was her family, her job, her purpose; this was love, and it was enough. Yusef was a decent husband and father until Mitra became a teenager. He blamed Shireen for Mitra's rebelliousness; men must always find blame. After the family began arriving from the ruin of the

Revolution, fawning over him and filling the holes of his childhood insecurities, his contemptuous behavior toward her spiked. But marriage is not easy, Shireen thought; plenty of marriages become stale after so many years. She could tolerate it; she had her own life outside of it. But when Ana and the children were taken, that life became a fairy tale.

As she came around a bend in the trail, the trees parted and a view of the Pacific appeared, blue as the mosaics of a Persian mosque. A young couple stood at the edge of the trail, peering down at the roiling water against the jagged rocks, but Shireen looked ahead; she wanted to be the kind of person who could set her eyes on the horizon and never look back. Today she would think hard. Today she would make her decision about staying here or going back.

She had fears.

Mitra, for one. Was it right for Shireen to burden her daughter for years to come? Would it erode the new relationship they'd found with each other?

And money. While Yusef had not denied her access to their cash or credit cards, she couldn't know when that would change. Clearly, he expected her to return, but when would he lose his patience and threaten divorce? She understood now that, by law, she was entitled to half of what Yusef owned, but she also knew that crafty husbands protected their assets and she would need to hire a lawyer. She sat on a bench. *Divorce.* It would always sound shameful to her.

Goli had told her not to ponder these things yet, that she should focus only on which place — east or west — she wanted to live. Goli was good at taking things step by step, at seeing things plainly. For Shireen, it was so hard to figure out what she wanted without considering everyone else! She couldn't seem to separate her desires from what was best for the others. She didn't know her own mind. She had been raised to accept the duty of self-sacrifice. Just by watching, she understood that a woman's life belonged to others. Even among the housewives of America who thought themselves so free, this was true. In their hearts, they belonged to others. And perhaps it was not such a terrible thing; perhaps it was simply the natural way of humans, and perhaps it was unfair to expect to change this about herself so late in life.

She got up from the bench and headed along the trail, its fine gravel golden as the wheat fields in the northern province where

Olga came from. A red-faced jogger nodded hello as they passed each other. San Francisco was a city, she thought, but not like Manhattan or Chicago, where there seemed no place to hide or think or scratch your behind without someone seeing. Was Devon somewhere in between? Olga thought it was like a prison if a person didn't have a car; she'd stayed because of her love of Shireen and her girls. Shireen had grown used to it, enjoyed it, made a beautiful home and accumulated precious things. But after the accident, only the memories were important. And those she carried with her. Now, Devon was Yusef and his bad moods and demeaning criticisms and endless lists of things for her to do. Her mouth filled with bitterness. *Unnecessary.*

Just yesterday, Goli had said, "A person has to give herself permission to let go." She'd given herself as an example, admitting in a sad voice that she wished she'd never gone on the trip to Iran. Her memories were ruined. Even the streets had been unfamiliar; she'd gotten lost a few times. The language had changed — in just twenty years, words and phrases had been erased and replaced with new ones, slang she'd never heard. And her mannerisms and gestures were outdated. People easily knew she was one of those who had fled. She'd felt like a foreigner in her own country. She'd had to let go. Shireen reminded her that they were already foreigners in the United States. "Sister, we are Americans — all of us from an elsewhere that only exists in memory."

Shireen stood still and looked again at the horizon, the spit of far-off land where Mitra had taken her and Sali to see the big redwood trees. This place, this California — it could give her what she wanted. A simple life, some peace. A slight smile tugged the corners of her mouth, even as tears welled in her eyes. She could belong here. She *would* belong here, to Mitra.

CHAPTER 27

The letter came to the office, addressed in handwriting he vaguely recognized but couldn't place. He sucked in his breath when he saw the return address on one of those stickers that charities give in exchange for donations: Mitra Jahani living on a street called Liberty in the city of San Francisco. His daughter.

He let the envelope drop. In his chest, he was angry, but his fingers were anxious. Well, that would not do. Nothing to be anxious about. No doubt Mitra had had enough of her mother and was petitioning him to take Shireen back, or perhaps to woo her back. Hah. Never. *She* would have to do the wooing. The pleading. The apologizing.

And yet he hesitated to open the envelope. He propped it against an old souvenir figurine of the Chrysler Building and marveled at the fact that he had never corresponded with his children in written form. Yes, Anahita would give him store-bought cards for his birthday and Father's Day every year, bless her soul. She would always sign them *Love you so much, Baba!* Mitra was not so sentimental. No. If Mitra had written to him, it would be a practical matter. Like him, she was a person who used words for the purpose of accomplishing an outcome.

He decided to wait. Open it at home. Something to distract from that hollow, gloomy house and its freezer stocked with Lean Cuisine. He slipped the envelope into his briefcase and returned to his *Wall Street Journal.* It was annoying to read about Iran's economic progress. Even under this fascist theocracy, the economy was thriving. His people were devoted, first and foremost, to growth and prosperity. Golnaz had said there was a black market for everything, that the sanctions didn't stop people from buying their satellite dishes or gadgets or rationed foodstuffs, and there was a video pirate for every new film, a supplier for the best liquor, and a whirlwind of illegal house parties at which to enjoy such things. It made Yusef proud to know about such rebellions. And then Parviz had interjected one of his stupid professorial conclusions.

"Ah, the heartbeat of capitalism; no wonder our two governments swing from utter devotion to utter enmity; our people are so alike."

Yusef would later realize how fortuitous it was that he hadn't read the letter at the office. He saw his alternate self — a crazed alternate self, certainly more youthful and stronger — walking from his office to Kareem's desk, where the boy languished on the days when he wasn't pretending to be "working in the field," and right then and there running him through with his ivory-handled letter opener, straight into his gut. He could feel his nephew's warm blood seeping onto his hand, the boy's stunned face turning gray, and the sound of his own rasping voice calling him a pig. This was the word — in English — that came to him readily. He could think of no Farsi word more harsh than this to express his disgust.

Instead, at home in his study, he threw his whiskey tumbler at a framed photo of Jafar's family, shattering the glass and scratching the lacquer on his credenza, where all the family photos sat like offerings on an altar. Jafar's other children — the three useless daughters — were all in Los Angeles, none of them successful or capable enough to care for him, all of them mediocre and jealous of the others who had better jobs, none of them visiting their blind father more than once in a while, hardly calling, allowing Kareem to care for him when Kareem barely lifted a finger. It was Yusef who took care of Jafar. And now it occurred to him: Did Jafar know what Kareem had done to his sweet Anahita? When they had come to ask for her hand — the sour-faced mother still alive then — did they know what their son had been doing to his daughter? What were Mitra's words? *Sexual violation. Emotional blackmail.* He couldn't get the basement scene Mitra had described out of his head, and the fact that *even* after Mitra thrashed Kareem, he had continued. An animal!

His chest tightened and he leaned against his desk. He hoped for a quick death. Heart attack, stroke. For the first time in his life, he was glad to be an old man. And yet, in his mind's eye he suddenly became the boy who stood at the bedside of his withering and manacled mother as she begged him to free her from that horrible hospital. He fell toward the waste basket and vomited into it, heaving like an animal.

The phone rang and he left it to the machine, then heard Lubyana's purr —

Where are you, Joey? — and he cringed at the absurd nickname he'd allowed her to use, at the absurdity of his choices. Repulsive. He lurched from the room as if fleeing an armed intruder.

When finally he made his way into the shower, turned the temperature ever hotter almost as a punishment, he heard his own sobs only after they came out of his mouth, only after he was on all fours, pounding his fist on the porcelain.

Vivian looked at her watch and was shocked to see that it was 11:11. She grabbed her office calendar from the desk again and peered at today's date — December 23rd — but Mr. J had no morning appointments. Not surprising since most offices had given the week off. Again, as she'd done several times since 9:00 when her boss hadn't shown up, she riffled back and forth through the weeks and months in hopes that she'd mistakenly entered an appointment with the dentist or the architect or the banker on some other Tuesday. She had a bad feeling.

She rang Mr. J at home and on his car phone for the fifth time. No answer.

She'd imagined this from time to time: a heart attack, a stroke, a fall; calamitous visions that came unbidden as the people in her life grew old. Now that Mrs. J was gone, Vivian couldn't help but feel a certain responsibility for her boss. Her husband had told her to stop it, that she worried too much about everyone. Sadly, it was her natural inclination, being the eldest child in her family and having lost her mother at a young age. Also, she couldn't forget that she'd had a hand in helping Mrs. J leave, and though she believed rationally and on principle that she'd done the right thing, she knew Mr. J would consider even her lunch with his wife a betrayal.

She used her key to go into his office, which she'd rarely seen without the lights on and the blinds closed. Her eyes were drawn immediately to the portrait of Ana and her children; it looked especially large against the deep green wall. And the shadows — or maybe Vivian's imagination or the painter's deftness — created contours and depths to the figures so that it looked less like a portrait and more like a bas-relief. It was creepy.

Vivian made her way around Mr. J's desk to find his small leather datebook, in which he wrote all entries in pencil to avoid the clutter of cross-outs. She flipped through it and peered, then huffed in frustration and switched on the desk lamp. There it was, today's date: two afternoon meetings with subcontractors in the conference room, nothing in the morning. The same as her own datebook. She exhaled and dialed Mr. J's numbers again from the phone on his desk, which smelled like his cologne. As each ring came and went, she absent-mindedly cracked another one of her knuckles. What should she do? Whom should she alert? If she broadcast her concern around the office, she'd have the whole family in a tizzy. She imagined Mr. J's annoyance at this.

As far as she knew, he'd gone straight home yesterday. In fact, she'd brought him a helping of her pot roast and mashed potatoes to warm up for dinner. He'd been grumpy — his usual state since Mrs. J left — but otherwise normal. In all her years at the company, he'd only missed work a handful of times due to illness, and he'd *never* not called in to check on things, even if it meant he hacked and coughed through the conversation. There were trips he took, of course, for business and pleasure, but still he called, no later than 10:00 a.m.

She had a dreadful thought: Had he made a late rendezvous with his mistress? Had he suffered a heart attack or stroke with her? And would she, whoever she was, know how to reach Vivian? No. She imagined Shireen or Mitra receiving a call from a trashy young woman — oh, stop with your imagination, she scolded herself. She wished Nezam were here, and she thought about calling him, but that would be a last resort; she wouldn't drag him back into his uncle's life while he was trying so gallantly to find a new path.

She shut off the lights and left Mr. J's office. Back at her desk, she closed her office door and began dialing local hospitals, but she was disappointed, then relieved, at the end of each conversation. By lunchtime, she'd decided to do something she'd never done: go to her boss's house uninvited.

It was cold, but sunny and windless. More like October than December. As Vivian rang the doorbell for the third time, she wanted to take her wool coat off; mounting anxiety was making her sweat. Her husband's voice in the back of her head admonished her to give it up, stop fretting, it wasn't her responsibility. She took the slate steps down and around to the garage, but the door was windowless. She hesitated at the head of the gravel path leading to the backyard. What was she doing? An image flashed through her mind: a naked Mr. J doing the nasty with a Loni Anderson type on his silk Persian carpet. She turned to leave, but couldn't ignore the wash of anxiety that she truly believed was a dire premonition. She had many limitations, but intuition was not one of them.

She removed her coat and walked up the path, the gravel crunching under her shoes like dry breakfast cereal. As she wound around a row of evergreen shrubs, she saw him. Yes, she would remember later, she'd believed he was dead, sitting there on the patio with eyes open, skin ashen, stiff in the chair as if he'd been struck by a bolt of frost from an Olympian god.

Vivian was no stranger to dead bodies. Her sister had worked in a morgue years ago, and Vivian had been curious. Her husband often told her she should have become a nurse or a paramedic, so unperturbed was she by injuries and physical trauma. "Most people look away," he said. "You try to get a better look." One Christmas, her sons had given her a police scanner.

But this was someone she knew, someone she . . . well, she *cared* about. She steeled herself and approached him. He should have noticed her by now. She wasn't more than fifty yards from him. She'd call 911 from inside, wait until the paramedics came, then call Mrs. J. Poor woman, she was going to feel responsible for the rest of her life. For a brief moment, Vivian wished this had happened when he was with his mistress, to save Mrs. J the guilt. She suddenly realized how well she knew these people, this family. It was foolish of her to think of herself as an outsider.

As she reached the edge of the patio, the two steps up to where he was sitting, his gaze — just his eyes, not any other part of his body — shifted to her. She drew in her breath. "Mr. J?" She saw a slight and fleeting frown cross his brow, and then his gaze shifted again, inward or far away — the way babies sometimes stare into space, as if their souls have left their bodies. Indeed, her grandmother used to say, "Don't disturb, they're communing with the angels."

But he was alive! Oh, thank the Lord. Clearly, he'd experienced a shock of some sort, but she wouldn't have to call 911 or Shireen or Mitra or any of the overemotional cousins and half brothers and nieces. But now what? Well, Vivian, she told herself, you've known this man long enough and intimately enough to handle this. Forget that he's responsible for your paycheck. Forget that he can be a bear much of the time. Forget that you have nothing in common with him. You do. He's just like you and everybody else.

He was wrapped in a thick navy-blue robe. Flannel pajamas underneath, visible at the collar and below the knee to the top of his leather slippers. She took a tentative step up. A shadow of white stubble covered his chin and jaw, and she realized that he dyed his hair and mustache to give it that salt-and-pepper look. Of course she'd known that, but it had never occurred to her to think about it; you saw a person every day and you stopped really seeing them. They were who they were.

"Mr. J?" she said again. No change. The slight breeze set his hair fluttering.

She slowly stepped forward and reached out to touch his hand, which was resting on the arm of the wicker chair. So cold, the skin.

"Mr. J, you're going to catch your death out here. Let's go inside and I'll make you some tea." Her voice sounded strange to her, small and trembling. She stood up straight — gave him room — though she wanted to take his pulse or feel his forehead, as if he were a child. Most important, she told herself, was to bring him back from wherever he'd gone.

Finally, his eyes saw her again, recognized her, she felt. She remained still. And then something remarkable happened: those eyes that could be steely so often, that could dart and squint and glare and yes, dance and shine with humor sometimes, they filled with tears and overflowed. Vivian couldn't move, not until the tears fell onto his cheeks and dropped from his chin. Then she took his arm and gently urged him up.

CHAPTER 28

Nezam and Libby spent the Christmas holiday at her parents' house in Greenwich. It was more formal and scheduled than they liked, but Nezam didn't want to have anything to do with the Jahani clan — their questions and puzzled whispers about him leaving the company — and since his parents were in Iran and his auntie in San Francisco with Mitra, he didn't see the point.

When his parents called to wish everyone a Happy Christmas, and to talk to the twins about their presents, he was shocked to learn that they'd flown back early and were in New York. "Don't worry, we're both fine," said Golnaz. "I'll explain when you get back to the city." She sounded oddly excited. He and Libby spent the next two days in miserable anticipation and quiet speculation. His parents had stayed in Iran little more than a month, foregoing their ski

545

trip, which was the excursion they'd been looking forward to most. When Libby had asked Golnaz about reclaiming the house in Tehran, which was the very reason they'd gone back, she'd groaned and said, "Stupid bureaucrats. It was like going from one DMV office to another. All day long. A bloody waste of time." And that was that.

When they got back to the city, Golnaz was waiting for them in their apartment. The aroma of Persian soup filled the air, piano music played softly from the speakers, and a load of baby clothes left in the dryer had been neatly folded. Golnaz oohed and aahed as the twins clamored to tell her about tobogganing and caroling and going to the church where the baby Jesus was a plastic doll. She then took sleeping Katy from Libby's arms, and to Nezam's worried face said, "Your father is fine. He's home because we have a guest."

While Libby gave the boys their bath, Golnaz and Nezam went into the living room, where Golnaz sat next to the gas fireplace to keep Katy warm. Nezam didn't sit. He ran his fingers through his thick straight hair, which had gotten long since he'd stopped working. "Relax, my son," said Golnaz, not taking her eyes from the child in her arms. He snorted with frustration.

His mother wasn't a good storyteller, but she enjoyed the buildup. He knew he was going to get only the facts; the details would come later from his own observations or from his father. Finally, she said, "Your father and I, we saved a girl — an orphan — and brought her back with us."

Nezam had the cabbie drop him in front of the UN so he could walk the few blocks to his parents' building. He hoped the cold wind off the river would calm him down. It didn't. The irony of his situation wasn't lost on him. He'd finally freed himself of the Jahani business only to have his parents — the people who had interfered least in his life — ask for the same kind of assistance that Yusef had done ten years ago. That an "orphan" was involved was simply an issue of semantics. He'd been here before; he knew the words people used to prick his heart and suck him in. But his mother?

He felt like a stranger entering the lobby of the building that had been his home in high school, through college and law school, until he married Libby. In the elevator, he breathed deeply — some asshole kid had pressed all the buttons — to stave off his queasiness and his agitation. On his parents' floor, the hallway soothed him with the aroma of his mother's saffron-laced salmon lunch. The door to the apartment was ajar.

The "orphan" could've been one of his father's students in her red Che Guevara T-shirt and jeans. He looked around the living room for a shy teenager with watery eyes and baggy clothing. The Che girl stuck her hand out and said, "*Salaam.* I'm Zoya." Her shake was firm and dry, her gaze steady. She wasn't wearing a speck of makeup, which also threw him. She looked, well, like a slightly nerdy American kid. His father approached with an enormous smile, kissed his son's cheeks, and said, "Finally, you meet!"

So, thought Nezam, this girl was as much his father's project as his mother's. Sure enough, the old Persian poetry books were out on the coffee table. Nezam had never taken a shine to learning how to recite Persian poetry, which was, for Iranians, as common and emotional as sing-alongs were for Americans. It was almost like learning another language, and Nezam had seen no purpose in it once the Revolution happened.

He peeled off his coat and Parviz took it from him to hang in the hall closet. Golnaz appeared from the kitchen carrying serving dishes, and he and Zoya each took one and placed them on the dining table, as if they'd shared the chore before. Parviz handed them each a glass of wine. "A toast," he said, and they raised their glasses. "To the United States of America!" Nezam looked at Golnaz, expecting a smirk or an eye roll — Golnaz was not one for patriotic sentimentality — but she clinked his father's glass without a trace of irony, and they all followed suit. *Who are you and what have you done with my parents?* Zoya drank as if she hadn't just come from a country where the substance was illegal. Nezam took a large swig.

They sat down to eat. As usual, Brahms and then Chopin played in the background. He tried to focus on the topics of conversation — the Clinton impeachment, Madonna, the Iraq disarmament crisis, the space shuttle, the iMac — anything but this girl and what she was doing here. It was surreal. Golnaz had told Nezam: *No questions. She's fragile. We just want you to meet her.* But nothing about this Zoya seemed vulnerable. She was serious and rarely smiled, but she was not broken. He listened and didn't listen, barely tasted his food. He remembered what it had felt like to be this girl's age — late teens? early twenties? — sitting at this table with his parents day in and day out, but the memory felt like a dream he'd had; something that had never really happened. A feeling of disassociation. Finally and thankfully, he found himself responding to Parviz's inquiries about the twins and Christmas. It was a relief to talk about the ridiculous number of Legos and miniature army men they'd gotten, about the strange warm weather and sudden first winter snow on Christmas Day, about pretending to enjoy watching *It's a Wonderful Life* with his father-in-law. He'd slipped into English without realizing it and apologized. Zoya flashed him a smile, and said, "No problem. I am fluent. I understand everything. Jimmy Stewart is one of my favorites."

Floo-nt. Every-ting. StyoowART.

Her accent was so thick he had to pretend a coughing fit to stanch his laughter. As he drank from his water glass, their eyes met, and he saw some warmth and a slight crinkling of the skin around them. "I know," she said in Farsi. "My pronunciation is terrible." She shook her head and shrugged. "My father was not a very good Henry Higgins." And they all laughed openly.

Golnaz slid a plate of Mazafati dates toward Nezam. "So tell me, my son, what did you think?"

It was just the two of them now. Zoya had gone with Parviz to fetch his mail from his office at the university. She was eager to see the campus. Apparently, she'd been studying political science in Tehran.

"What did I think about what? The girl? Or the fact that you and Dad brought a complete stranger back from Iran?"

"She is not a stranger. She is the daughter of Olga's friends. They were writers, as is she. Her clandestine poetry has a small following among young people."

"Olga has something to do with this?" The Olga he knew was a warm and funny woman in a housedress who'd cooked for Mitra's family and got him hooked on *General Hospital*.

"Yes," his mother said. "What? You don't trust Olga? After everything she did for all of us over the years, her tolerance of that big-headed Yusef because she was devoted to my sister and Mitra and Anahita. And then to be expelled by him, forced to go back to a country that everyone was fleeing. She rebuilt her life there. She is a special woman. When she told Shireen about a girl in peril who needed to leave Iran, we jumped at the chance to help."

"Auntie is involved too?"

She nodded. "We were happy to help. We

thought it would simply be a question of giving advice. You know how everyone wants to come to the States. But the situation turned out to be more complicated: keeping her safe, making a plan to get her out, finding the right person to forge identity papers —"

"What?" Nezam was half out of his chair. "You *smuggled* her out?"

"Not smuggling, Nezam. *Saving.* The girl is the daughter of a dissident journalist who disappeared two months ago. The regime's thugs often go after the children of their enemies. Besides that, she is part of this new fearless generation that puts their activism on the Internet. Her mentor at the university is an old colleague of your father's; she's his top computer science student. The regime is scrambling to understand and silence this new threat. She *had* to leave the country."

Nezam put his elbows on the table and rubbed his forehead, trying to absorb the fact that his parents had done something so dangerous. And illegal. He must've said the word aloud. "Everything in that country is illegal," Golnaz said with a wave of her hand. "Once we got to Dubai, she immediately applied for political asylum."

Nezam exhaled. At least his parents had stayed on the right side of US law. They were silent for a while. Finally, Nezam said, "I don't understand all the secrecy. Why didn't you call me?"

Golnaz huffed. "It would've been too dangerous to talk to you about it over the phone. The country is a police state. They listen."

"Does Mitra know?"

"Don't be ridiculous. Of course not." Nezam raised his eyebrows. "You kids," Golnaz continued. "You don't understand these things."

There it was, he thought. *You don't understand these things* was code for *We didn't want to deal with your objections.* And now, they needed a lawyer. Obviously. All right, then. He would give her the old spiel he'd repeated so often to Iranians who'd insisted on applying for political asylum after the Revolution. Maybe it made them feel important, but what they really wanted was to have a better life than what they could get in a totalitarian theocracy that was fighting a bloody war. Nezam's task was to find a legal way for them to stay — work visas, visitor visas, medical visas — but he made it clear that he wasn't willing to lie for them.

"First thing is, can she prove that going back would be perilous for her? And by perilous, I mean physically dangerous.

Poverty, for example, isn't a valid reason. Being an orphan isn't valid either, even if she was underage. Being miserable because she wouldn't be able to speak her mind or get a good job or go to school are not valid. Going to prison for a crime that would be a crime anywhere — like stealing or shooting someone — *those* are not valid. She has to prove that her life or her freedom would be in danger *because* of her beliefs or associations. Her claim can't be about you and Dad; the fact that you want to help her is the least valid excuse of all."

Golnaz slammed her palms onto the table. "Enough!" She stood up. "I want to show you something. Stay there." She went to her home office and came back with a manila folder that she dropped in front of him. Inside was a collection of newspaper clippings in various languages. The top page displayed a series of grainy black-and-white photos of mostly men, names printed in Farsi below each one. Standing over his shoulder, Golnaz brought her finger down onto the first photo. "Poet," she said. "Poisoned." She flicked her red-painted nail at the next photo, making a snapping sound on the paper. "Translator. Strangled." And the next. "Historian: suffocated." And on. "Philosopher: heart failure in prison.

Painter: bludgeoned. Journalist, writer, novelist: fatal car crashes, all. That one, a student of your father's once." Nezam had begun to sweat, wanted her to stop, couldn't dare ask. Finally, she reached the last photo, of an elderly mustachioed man and a gray-haired woman, smiling. "These two, husband and wife activists, stabbed over twenty times in their own home just last month." She slapped the folder shut and swung around to face him across the table. "This is not fakery, my son." Her voice was scratchy with outrage. "We are not frivolous. We are not Yusef. When I say 'saved,' that is exactly what I mean. Saved from prison, torture, execution, assassination."

Nezam put his hand up. "Okay," he croaked. "Okay."

Parviz favored an Irish pub near Washington Square Park, an easy walk from his office. Nights and weekends, it was a raucous place, but on weekdays it was quiet and dim and comfortable, perfect for a man of his disposition. Today, the bartender was on a step stool hanging streamers for New Year's Eve. The only other customers were two women at a table drinking Irish coffee and speaking in German. Parviz sat in one of the few booths, nursing a scotch and soda and going over his lesson plan for the new term. He missed the classroom and his colleagues. Iran had not felt like home.

When Nezam stepped in from the cold, Parviz raised his hand. His son looked pale and thin, and Parviz's heart hurt as he watched him approach. How had it not occurred to him that their decision to rescue Zoya would so distress his son? And how was it possible that he still didn't understand the source of it? When he and Golnaz had left for Iran, all seemed bright for Nezam. Finally, he'd quit his job. They'd toasted him: *Here's to your next adventure!* Parviz expected to return to the happy news that Nezam had found his way back into international law. Instead, his son seemed lost.

Nezam kissed his father's cheeks, sat, and ordered a Guinness. "Are you hungry? The clam chowder is excellent." Wriggling out of his parka, Nezam said no, just the beer. He tapped his thumbs on the tabletop and avoided Parviz's gaze. When had the wisps of gray appeared in his son's sideburns? Wasn't it too early? He was only thirty-five. Sitting there, Parviz could conjure him at any stage of his life, not only the look of him, but the feel and smell of him, from the silky skin of his jiggling toddler cheeks to the sour odor of his teenaged scalp after a triumphant soccer game.

"Your mom gave you a hard time yesterday. I'm sorry I wasn't there."

"It's fine," he said. "It was my fault. I made the wrong assumptions." Golnaz had said, *It was my fault. I got too emotional.*

Parviz leaned in. "There is no fault here. There is only miscommunication. Ask me anything."

Nezam ran his fingers through his hair, looked at his father with bloodshot eyes. "What's Section 209?"

Parviz wasn't expecting this; Golnaz had been so distraught when she finally told him about her heated exchange with Nezam that they hadn't gotten into the details. All that mattered to her was that he mend what she had torn. Clearly, she'd revealed just enough about Zoya's situation that getting to the bottom of Nezam's angst would be delayed. He sighed. "Section 209 is the ward in Evin reserved for political prisoners."

"Zoya thinks her father is there, but you don't?"

Parviz nodded. "Olga felt we should let Zoya believe her father was alive until she was emotionally stronger. She lost her mother suddenly to an aneurysm five years ago; her father was all she had. Personally, I think she's smart enough to see the truth

557

but has chosen not to."

"But are you sure he's dead? There was no photograph of him."

Parviz looked at his hands. "We can't be sure until the body has been found. But the intellectuals are a tight group with connections; they know who's being held, even in solitary. It's more likely that he's the seventh victim in these recent murders."

"The Chain Murders."

"That is what some people are calling them. The police have suggested a serial killer, but no one believes that. The victims were all reformist intellectuals."

"But the new president is a reformist, right?"

"Yes. Khatami. It's his rivals, the fundamentalists, who are suspected of the murders." Parviz watched as Nezam tried to synthesize this information. Not for the first time, he wondered if it had been wise to allow his son to drift away from understanding Iran's political landscape after the Revolution and the humiliation of the Hostage Crisis. All of them had turned away from a place that revered such a man as Khomeini. Parviz combed his mind for an analogy to help Nezam understand: "Think of it this way: Khatami is Clinton, Parliament is Congress, the reformists are liberals, the fundamentalists are conservatives."

Nezam's eyes widened. "You're comparing a theocracy to a democracy? Who're the victims? Woodward and Bernstein? Warhol and Philip Roth?"

"Exactly!"

But Nezam had not lost his frown. In fact, Parviz detected a slight, but familiar, sneer. Most Americans could not abide such analogies. His son had assimilated more extensively than he'd thought. This made him both proud and disappointed. "Nezamjoon, I am only comparing them systemically. They are both republics, both capitalist, both run by men and organizations on the right and the left that vie for power. Of course one is a dictatorship and the other has avoided that fate for an impressive amount of time, but considering the similarities can keep us on our toes."

Nezam said nothing, but Parviz noticed a softening of his demeanor. He had given his son something to contemplate, and that was enough for now.

"But let's not get into a philosophical discussion. I just want to make sure you know that we never expected you to help us with Zoya's case. It was not our intention to hide anything from you. We simply didn't want to burden you while you were transitioning in your career. Peter has already given us the names of immigration lawyers he trusts."

Nezam rubbed his eyes. "Makes sense. Zoya's case is legitimate. I've never worked on anything like that."

"Your mom, she —"

"I'm not mad at her. We were both hot-headed."

Parviz leaned back, relieved. "Spend New Year's Day with us."

"Sure," he said with a slight smile. "But you come to our place; it's easier with the kids."

Parviz felt his shoulders relax. "With pleasure, my son." He reached over and covered Nezam's hand with his. "Now, tell me about your job search."

Nezam shrugged. "Not much to tell. Word got around that I was a free agent and I've had a few offers from construction and real estate firms, but . . ." He reached for a handful of peanuts. Parviz willed himself to stay silent. Nezam knew what he wanted to know. Finally: "The city is bursting at the seams with lawyers, Dad," his tone slightly defensive. "I've been away from international law for too many years." He signaled to the bartender for another beer, and in the tense movement of his son's jaw, Parviz recognized a certain fear.

"My son, I know that your generation is afraid to take risks because of how things fell apart for your parents after the Revolution. How your futures seemed to burn as you watched. But this open wound must now be turned into a scar. When we moved to the States, I had to take many steps back in order to reach the level I had at the university in Tehran. The tenure process took years."

This was not working. Nezam was popping nuts into his mouth, avoiding his father's gaze. Parviz didn't blame him; the advice was rote, the implication condescending. A child didn't want to hear that their parent had handled life better at their age. "Have you inquired at your old law firm?" he ventured.

Nezam looked down, shook his head slowly. "I was there barely two years. Entry level. They've doubled in size since then. I'm too old to qualify for a low-level position and too inexperienced for something else there. Dad, you don't get second chances in my line of work."

Parviz felt a growing irritation. His son had become cynical, squeezing his idealism into a ball for the trash can, thinking that only realists survived. But they didn't. They simply settled for less. Was this what too many years with Yusef had done? And could it be undone? Perhaps. But that was up to Nezam. All Parviz could do was hand his son a thread and hope that he grabbed it and pulled it through the fabric of his thoughts.

"I'll use the men's room," Parviz said, sliding out of the booth.

Nezam watched his father go. He'd lost weight in Iran, was trimmer. Nezam vaguely recalled him talking yesterday about hiking in the mountains above Tehran, the new outdoor teahouses where people lounged on carpeted wooden beds, smoking from the *ghelyoon,* and listening to *santoor* music — away from the city's crowds and pollution and prying government eyes. By comparison, Nezam's childhood memories of hiking in the mountains with his father seemed like a dream or an old movie. More real to him were his memories of coming to America: the suburban summer camp he attended where Mitra was a counselor, the chorus he sang in with Anahita, a stint as a lifeguard, the fraternity he joined for a month, Libby's family beach house brimming with generations of mementos. Was his father right to imply that Nezam had become too American, whatever that meant?

Oh, he knew there was no such thing as a "typical" American; the country was vast. But there were common attitudes and mannerisms that made it easy to spot Americans in a foreign country, and wouldn't he and his wife and kids display them all? The realization shook his perspective. He'd forgotten that when you lived in America, the rest of the world somehow receded. It was a stealthy mind-set that he'd once criticized: how the country saw itself as above and apart. It put the whole idea of America as a place of refuge and promise at risk of disappearing.

Parviz came out of the men's room still drying his hands on a paper towel. Nezam felt his face turn red with embarrassment as he slid back into the booth. "You're right, Dad," he said. "I stopped paying attention to what was happening in Iran, or anywhere else for that matter. I don't know what happened. I used to love history and politics."

"I suspect you still do." Parviz had grown a beard in Iran, cut close to his face. It made him look distinguished and, at the moment, especially serious. He was holding back, of course, as he always did, ever wary of interfering in or judging Nezam's choices. Sometimes, Nezam wished his father was less enlightened, that he would come out and say how disappointed he was that his son had wasted the last ten years of his life kowtowing to Yusef. At least Nezam could then mount a defense. He had, after all, done what his conscience had told him to do; he could claim that he'd accomplished some honorable things.

"Tell me, my son, now that some time has passed, what exactly inspired you to suddenly quit your job?"

Nezam hesitated, then took a deep breath. "It was that vile portrait of Anahita and the children. Auntie must have refused to have it in the house, so Uncle had it hung behind his office desk. When I saw it, I don't know, something came loose in my chest." He could feel it now, a skip in his pulse, a hot hole, a crucible. He ground his teeth and looked at Parviz. "He had no *right* to twist his grief into a piece of petty revenge against Mitra. And I told him so. Then I walked out."

Parviz smiled. "How did it feel?"

"Like justice."

Parviz raised his glass, tipped it toward Nezam, and drank. Something had shifted. The light in the room seemed dimmer, but the carvings in the wood tabletop — *NYC, Red Sox, Danny+Sheila* — seemed sharper. The booth cushion against Nezam's back seemed softer, the lines around his father's eyes deeper. "Mom said you visited the university."

"Of course." His tone was somber. "The atmosphere was tense, like the smell of sulfur before an eruption. Like before the clashes under the Shah."

"Those people in the photographs," Nezam said. "Anyone you knew?"

"Some," said Parviz. "None of them were close colleagues or friends," he added.

"How many in total?"

"Over the last ten years, maybe as many as one hundred killed like that, as if by random circumstance — natural and unnatural. Plenty more died in prison or are still held there. It's Khamenei's doing. Dictators don't stay in power without disappearing their critics."

"So . . . what's being done about it?"

Parviz snorted. "Plenty, but not enough." Nezam thought he saw a flash of irritation cross Parviz's face. "Maybe, my son, you should look into that. Give Peter a call. He asked after you."

"Are you telling me that our moms and Olga were involved in a cloak-and-dagger operation?"

Nezam snorted. "I guess you could call it

that, Mitra."

"So now you're going to do immigration stuff again?" Mitra dumped a pile of paper into the recycle bin; she was cleaning out her desk. She kicked the bin.

"This is entirely different from what I did for your dad. Why are you so pissed?"

"I can't believe they kept us out of the loop, especially now that my mom is actually living with me. Right under my nose!"

"They were worried we'd slip and say something to Olga."

Mitra hadn't had a proper conversation with Olga since late October when they'd talked about Akram leaving Sali behind. She hadn't forgotten the disapproval in Olga's tone, nor the humorless advice she'd given her in Farsi. She hadn't wanted to hear any of that again, and since Shireen spoke to Olga regularly, Mitra didn't worry about whether or not she was well. Now she knew that there had been more than disapproval in Olga's voice; there had been evasion.

"Oh, right," spat Mitra. "All that *danger* and *government spies.* Ooooh. *Mission Impossible.* My mom and Olga worry disproportionately about almost anything. You know that."

"Mitra . . ."

"And another thing: Do you know how

much grief they gave me about taking in Akram and Sali? All that and they go and get their *own* refugee?"

"Stop!" Oof, she hadn't heard that tone in Nezam's voice since, well, since before the accident. "She's not that kind of refugee. You need to sit down — because I know you're pacing — and stay quiet while I explain. Okay?"

Mitra exhaled into the receiver. "Fine," she finally said. "I'm sitting. Go."

For an hour, she mostly listened. Halfway through, Shireen and Sali returned from their errands, and she took the cordless up to her bedroom and closed the door. By then, she was no longer angry, but she hadn't yet worked out exactly how she felt. When the call was over, she lay on her bed and stared at the ceiling.

That last day with Anahita on the beach in Montauk came to her. The wind and the roar of the waves, the defiance in Ana's eyes when Mitra challenged her to end her affair. *I don't see it that way, Mitra. It's not like that, Mitra.*

Aden in his shop, the shock of him, so different from what Mitra had imagined. *Ana played a role for you. She was afraid to lose your respect.*

And Olga on the other end of the line that

last time they talked. *Do not make of yourself an island.*

She went into her bathroom and splashed water on her face. In the mirror, she saw her flushed olive skin and an ugly scowl she recognized. She *was* like her father. Judgmental, arrogant, queen of the double standard, a know-it-all fool. Lucky for her, Nezam had reined in her worst tendencies this time. Anahita had been the one who'd always done that. In her subtle ways, she pulled Mitra back from bullying everyone into doing what she was sure was best for them. What a lot of work she was.

And yet, she knew they loved her. Nezam and Libby. Parviz and Golnaz. Shireen and Olga. It wouldn't be the last time she and Nezam quarreled, but also not the last time they joked and cried and remembered. The accident may have fractured their little family, but not shattered it. All these years, she'd held on to them, despite her separation from the Jahani clan. She'd held on because she loved them back, and now that Ana and the children were gone, now that Shireen was here, her tie to them felt all the more frayed. The idea that her desire to keep them in her life might, in fact, push them away — as Yusef's hubris and domi-

nance had — moved her to tears. She
couldn't let that happen.

CHAPTER 29

Jafar's apartment was dark save for the flickering of the television set. Yusef shut the door behind him and was struck by the stink of cologne, sweat, and moldering fast food. Kareem? Did he no longer live in the swanky building where he'd sublet a studio from a maternal relative? The sound of an action film confirmed it: the boy lived here now — until he could find someone else to cadge from.

Kareem peeked around the corner into the hallway. "Uncle," he said warily. "Is anything wrong?"

Nausea struck Yusef at the sight of his nephew. Rage too: heat rising into his chest and throat, sweat beading on the back of his neck. He'd come here to confront Jafar with what his son had done to Anahita. He hadn't expected Kareem. But this was no time for emotion. A hothead was a stupid head. He exhaled slowly and willed himself

570

to speak in his usual sardonic tone, "Why would anything be wrong?" he asked. "I am visiting."

"But . . . it's evening."

"I don't turn into a pumpkin at dark," Yusef said in English. He knew the reference was somehow incorrect, but the meaning came across. It was funny how English expressions often came more easily to him now than Farsi ones. And why not? He'd lived in America almost three times longer than he'd lived in Iran.

"Happy New Year," Kareem said, pretending deference. Yusef didn't reply; it was almost February. The boy looked especially disheveled with his long hair sticking in oily strands around his neck and unshaven jaw. He stood in dirty stockinged feet, dressed in an extra baggy sweat suit made of the shiny material that had become popular with the TV video musicians. By God, Yusef suddenly realized, he was no boy; he was a middle-aged man — filthy outside and in.

The main room was a mess. No wonder Jafar insisted on a housekeeper twice a week. A blind man needs predictable order, and this was the opposite of that. There was garbage everywhere: wadded-up tissues and candy wrappers, jumbo plastic soda cups, abandoned shoes next to fallen sofa cushions, a worn blanket bunched up on the couch, half-empty chips bags next to bowls of encrusted dip, a lampshade askew. Like a strong wind had blown through. And yet the air was stale.

"It's stifling in here," Yusef said, his lip curling in disgust as he moved toward the window.

Kareem was either oblivious to the disorder or too proud to apologize for it. Probably the latter — his passive aggression a way of showing disrespect. Jafar in his recliner seemed half-asleep, but then Yusef saw the bottle of scotch next to him, the empty tumbler. So this was how they managed the evenings. A blind man confined to one spot and an indolent son who couldn't be bothered with tending to him. On the floor next to the recliner was a portable plastic urinal, half-full. Another lazy-son contrivance.

Yusef cracked the window to let the evening air in. "It's cold," Jafar whined.

"Put a blanket over your father," Yusef said.

"Who's that?" Jafar slurred. "Yusef?"

There was no need to respond. Jafar's head lolled as soon as Kareem covered him. Yusef wondered if the boy had given his father a sedative on top of the alcohol. Pity niggled at him, but he quashed it.

"Can I offer you some tea, Uncle?" Kareem asked in that softened voice he used to ward off the severity of a looming interrogation about an uncompleted or insufficiently completed task. So common, so predictable. He was useless. Worse than useless, Yusef now knew. But he was family. What a lousy excuse. Yusef could only blame himself.

"No tea. Nothing." He flicked on the light and Kareem squinted, then hunched his shoulders and retracted his neck like a turtle. It was fake, of course, this display of submissiveness. All these years the kid had played him for a fool. And he was a fool. His daughter had suffered for it dearly. He snatched the TV remote from the coffee table and pressed the off button. His hand shook.

Kareem must've noticed. "Has something happened, Uncle?"

Not *Have I done something wrong, Uncle?* Not *Are you angry with me, Uncle?* He never admitted to failure; he simply reached for his dossier of excuses and blamed someone else. If that didn't work, he resorted to quiet remorse: *I misunderstood, misheard, thought you meant thus-and-such.* Never *I'm sorry.* Never *I'll do better next time.* But also never

573

a hair's width of anger or frustration or offense; no response that a person could grab on to and wrestle with. He acquiesced. Or at least that was what Yusef had always thought. This meek and stupid boy — was he capable of forcing himself on anyone?

Yes. Yusef had sworn to himself that he wouldn't entertain any doubt about the truth of what Mitra had written. Once over the initial shock of Mitra's letter, he'd forced himself to examine the past for clues — physical markings on Ana or suspicious situations he'd ignored — but all he came up with was a sadness he remembered feeling when Anahita reached puberty and stopped nuzzling him; she'd been the most delightfully demonstrative child, the opposite of Mitra. In fact, he realized, Anahita in adulthood recoiled from his fatherly touch. And there it was: not puberty, not natural; the clue he hadn't seen, was too ignorant to see, too busy with his newfound hegemony as family savior to see. He'd been a weak, despicable father.

He went to the window, looked out. To calm himself, he tried to focus on what was happening on the street below: cars moving slowly in search of parking spaces, a woman walking her dog, a family sitting around a table in the building across the way. Lives go on. People seem untroubled, but all have secrets and pain. He knew this, had always known it. But he'd let it burrow into a corner of his mind, forgotten and buried by the false notion that he was above and beyond such fates. He remembered when this shit-boy and his shit-father came to ask for his daughter's hand — she was only sixteen! He'd spoken privately to Ana, asked her if she was attracted to Kareem. It was a difficult conversation. She was mortified; her guilt must have been tremendous. She could barely respond to his questions, and when she did, she could only shed tears. He'd allowed himself to presume she was simply too innocent to speak of such things, and he let her go. He knew now that she must have concluded that he wasn't against such a match between first cousins, though he agreed with the Western contention that such a match was genetically dangerous and he would never have approved it. He'd prolonged her torture — this boy's hands roving and groping her body. He would give his life if he could go back and beat Kareem senseless. What he needed to do now was the least he *could* do in memory of his dead daughter. He turned to face Kareem.

"I know what you did to my Anahita."

Kareem frowned quizzically.

"Yes, I expected you to feign ignorance."

Kareem tilted his head and chuckled nervously. "Uncle, I really don't know what —"

"Shut up. You are filth." Yusef leaned forward. "Your denials are as useless to me as your useless lying life."

Ah, yes: a flicker of anger reddened Kareem's face. His lips tightened.

Yusef stared at his nephew as if he intended to impart a secret. "This is the last time I want to see your face. You have no job and no family. Make one move to solicit sympathy from *anyone* and I'll tell them all what you did."

As expected, Kareem's expression turned angry. What an ugly man he was! He took a step back, raked his oily hair into a knot, and let loose. "You ruined my life, Uncle. You ruined Anahita's life too, by marrying her to that Bijan character. He never loved her like I did. I loved her since we were children!"

"You were *not* children together. *Seven years* separated you. When she was nine, you were sixteen! You molested her."

Kareem cackled. "Believe what you want. We came together naturally; we were drawn to one another, and I did *not* molest her. A stupid American concept. I preserved her.

She was a virgin until she met that nobody Bijan."

"And you're a somebody? Bijan provided very nicely for my daughter. He gave me two beautiful grandchildren. You can barely follow through on a punch list. Your fiancée left you because you ran through her dowry in Atlantic City on roulette and whores. Yes, she told me you'd treated her badly, but I did nothing so people wouldn't talk, so our family name wouldn't be muddied."

"You should've thought of the family, Uncle, when I asked for Anahita's hand and you said she was too young. If you'd betrothed us then, we would've waited two years until she was eighteen and then our family would've been *strengthened*. I held out for that. Why do you think I never married myself? You ruined it for me. I couldn't love another woman. When I got engaged to Laleh, it was because she reminded me of Anahita, but then she was nothing like Anahita, always telling me what to do, always disappointed in me, wanting a different kind of man."

"She wanted a man; a man of any sort, but a man."

Kareem snorted and turned his back, walked across the room. "You know nothing, Uncle. Anahita and I were meant for

577

each other. We had a pact; we loved each other. You destroyed what we could've had. She would be alive today if you hadn't given her to that Bijan."

"You stupid, stupid boy! I didn't *give* her to him. She *begged* me to let her marry him. She didn't want you. Ever. You disgusted her. She would've done anything to escape you."

"That's a lie! You think you know everything, but you know nothing. Just because of the Revolution, you became our patriarch, but you weren't bred for it and you aren't good at it. If we'd remained in Iran, the scepter would've passed to one of the other uncles, and he would've ordered you to allow the marriage."

"Don't be stupid. I wouldn't have lived in Iran. I fled Iran to make a life for myself *here,* without the family that considered me of no consequence."

"Exactly. And you are of no consequence." Kareem wore a triumphant expression. Perhaps, Yusef thought, he'd said one of his nasty thoughts out loud for the first time in his life. It didn't matter. The words had ricocheted off Yusef like thrown sand.

"I'm done with you, boy." He reached for his coat and hat.

"Fine. I don't need you. I have my father's

shares in the company."

"Your father no longer has his shares. I have sold the company to Manny Hourian. See if he'll hire you. He knows you're useless."

Kareem couldn't hide his shock; his mouth was open. "How can you do this to your family? We're your blood. You will lose the love and respect of everyone."

Yusef allowed himself a dramatic chuckle. "You all played me like a *santoor,* plucking my strings into a melody for your own pleasure. There was never love and respect. Everything we ever shared means *pooch,* or as they say in America, zilch. Yes, zilch." He shrugged his coat on. Kareem had moved closer to his father, and the silence that came from that area of the room was deafening, or maybe Yusef could only hear his own thoughts. He felt as if he'd left them already — the same feeling he'd had when he boarded the plane in Tehran for the US forty some-odd years ago; a sense of anticipation and dread, of freedom and loneliness. But it was the *right* feeling, and it had been missing from his life. He'd come to America so long ago to reinvent himself, but the Revolution and its consequences had pulled him back, this *family* had pulled him back. Well, no more.

He went to Jafar's chair and half sat on the arm. "Brother, can you hear me? I have an important thing to tell you. I have arranged for you to move from this apartment in a month's time."

Jafar opened his eyes and grunted. "What? Where? Why?"

"The building is no longer mine. I have sold it."

Kareem said, "My father can't move in his condition. He can't get used to a new place. We'll stay here."

"There is no 'we,' Kareem. Your father needs assistance. You don't."

"I am his assistance."

"Don't make jokes. I have reserved a space for him at Woodcliff Manor."

Jafar gasped. "I will not go to one of those places!"

"It will be best for you. There is no other choice."

Jafar felt for Yusef's sleeve and tugged. "Let me come to live with you, brother. That big house, it is empty. I will even stay in the servant room. In the evenings, we will keep one another company."

"I am renting the house out until Shireen decides what she wishes to do."

"But where will you live?"

"I am leaving this place."

"Leaving? To where? You have gone crazy!"

"No, brother. I have become sane."

Jafar's unseeing eyes darted wildly. He lifted his neck from the chair. "But my son, where is he to go?"

"Your son will need to take care of himself for once in his life."

Yusef stood and walked down the hallway to the door. As he reached for the handle, Kareem called out to him. "You've brought humiliation to the whole family! Everyone will be laughing at us!"

Yusef didn't care. What people would say, what they would think, how they would talk, how he would be remembered. All their fake pleasantries and phony gestures of respect, he'd believed them all. Only a very few had been genuine. Nezam. Nezam especially. And he'd thrown him away! He'd discarded all those who'd been true to him. Who'd been true to themselves.

He stepped into the hallway and let the door close behind him. Oh, how he wished more than ever that his daughter were alive, if only to hold her close and tell her he was sorry. The scent of her was all around him, what she smelled like always, as a child and as an adult, to him anyway: like sugar, like the sweet scent of that fluffy pink candy at the amusement parks.

THE BIRD OF WISDOM

In the time of our history when a harmless boy named Amadou was slaughtered by police in New York, and when China banned all opposition groups, there was a man deep in the labyrinth of Evin Prison whose only wish was to hear of his daughter's freedom.

In this place, information traveled like a vapor, in quiet centimeters. Some time ago — the man had lost sense of time — news came that the reformist government would seek justice for the Writers who had been strangled and stabbed and poisoned and bludgeoned, their bodies strewn and then discovered and then neatly buried in the Cemetery of Zahra's Heaven. The Assassins — rogue agents and Chain-Makers of murdered bodies — would stand trial before the nation.

The man was not fooled. The Assassins took orders from the Righteous Patriarchs of the shadow theocracy. Nothing would change. He turned his gaze inward, hid the victims in the folds of his heart, and allowed himself a thimbleful of tears. He understood that the Tehran Spring was over, that it had been scorched by Summer, murdered by Autumn, and now buried by Winter.

When the vapor brought a message from the old Russian woman that his daughter was free, he rejoiced and silently toasted his oily tea at the walls of his cell. It was all that mattered, she was all that mattered.

He hoped he had nurtured her long enough, that she perceived all that he valued: the lure of Telling and the delirium of Remembering, the addiction of Uncovering and the liberation of Testimony. He hoped she would write the stories of the people who had been taken, which was the story of herself.

Lying on the dirty blanket that was his bed, he imagined the sound of her pen scratching on paper, and he was lulled to sleep. He dreamt of the mythical simorgh's radiant wings beckoning him. Nestled in its loving talons, he rose above the earth to see the feline shape of his homeland, the two seas that kiss her north and south shores, the desert plateau and the mountain ranges that guard it. The Bird of Wisdom then flew him beyond the fortress of his hijacked country to soar over the wide-open earth — the dry countries and the small countries, the forests and the borderless ocean — to hover for a moment above the island city where the citizens would resurrect his daughter's true name, and where she could begin anew, never again in Silence.

EPILOGUE

The rains came to the Bay Area with a vengeance in February, causing floods north of the city and mudslides along the coastal highway. The water rushed down Liberty Street past Mitra's house like a river. It was a time to hunker down, which didn't suit Mitra at all.

After her tempestuous conversation with Nezam about Olga and Zoya, she'd thrown herself into her work, determined to complete her two restoration projects, but also to avoid contemplating all the issues the conversation had brought to light. Getting out of her head was achievable at the job sites, but now that an El Niño had descended, she was tied to her home office, managing subcontractors by phone, adding up costs and tracking shipments, going over punch lists with Carlos. Every task felt labored, and though she hid her distress, the nearness of Shireen reminded her of

585

those who were not here. She felt herself losing the connection with her cousin and Libby, her aunt and uncle, and therefore with Anahita and the children.

Diversion came when the rain lashed at the windows and gushed from the downspouts, giving Mitra an excuse to pull on her rain gear and tramp outside to unclog a gutter or put sandbags at the garage door. When the wind gusts turned trees and bushes into pop-up clowns and the local news showed enormous downed trees in the suburbs, cresting rivers up north, and snow to the eaves in the Sierra, Shireen was alarmed. "This normal, Mitra-joon?" Mitra laughed and set them to the task of placing candles and lanterns and flashlights in every room for when the power went out, launching Shireen into stories of her childhood and kerosene lamps.

Finally, the string of violent storms passed, the steady rain settled in, and Mitra got back to work. The more she tried to revive her old routines, the more she felt unsatisfied and unmoored. She remembered the dark months after the accident when she would suddenly emerge from a spell of numbness in a panic about money and idle projects. These were brief episodes, like coming up for air in an ocean of no feeling, no thought, no past or future. Since the One Year, she'd entered the shallows of that ocean, the shore ahead unfamiliar and beyond that, the landscape nebulous. Had she thought her life would eventually return to what it was before the accident? That, over time, her grief would diminish to a low-grade melancholia? She must have. A simpleton's expectation, she realized now. A tragedy didn't stand alone; it was one in a connected sequence, like a chain, each link steered by the one before. She'd always been clear-headed about what came next in her life, always proud that her desires were steady and definable. But maybe that was the problem. She'd long ago assumed that she'd figured everything out.

Eventually, the houses were done. The Victorian in the Castro and the Craftsman's bungalow in Sausalito looked nothing like the "tear-downs" she'd bought nearly three years before. She had her realtor draw up the papers to put them on the market as soon as possible. Selling a house she'd restored always broke her heart a little, but not this time. And when her realtor asked her what she had in mind for her next project, Mitra realized she'd stopped scouting for possibilities months ago.

■ ■ ■

When Shireen announced that Golnaz was coming for a week's visit, Mitra's spirits lifted, but she was also nervous. She wondered how much Nezam had told his mother about her hissy fit over the Zoya situation. Just the thought of revisiting that episode with her aunt turned her face warm with humiliation. She still avoided Olga's phone calls with Shireen for the same reason. What would they talk about? Mitra's stupidity?

As was her way, Golnaz arrived with clear intentions. "Rest and relaxation," she said, looking sallow and thin in her uncharacteristic sweatpants and flannel shirt. Serious conversation was obviously not on the agenda. Only facials, massages, body wraps, whole-body threading, restaurant meals, siestas — *like civilized people* — and ice cream every night. Relieved, Mitra agreed readily to the ice cream, but used work as an excuse to bow out of the rest, glad she hadn't yet told Shireen that the houses were on the market.

When Golnaz and Shireen weren't out getting their bodies tended to or taking their siestas, they rooted themselves at the kitchen table. Mitra, in her office, was comforted by the murmur of their gossipy voices as she sifted through pages of listings sent over by her realtor. Sali couldn't get enough of the sisters, and found reasons to quietly hover near them, little Jack in a bundle slung around her waist, as they drank tea after tea at the kitchen table and spoke in Farsi about everything and nothing. They indulged the baby generously, saving more serious conversations for when Sali was at school or off with Julian.

Despite their intention to remain friends, both Mitra and Julian made subtle efforts not to run into each other. Not surprising, Mitra finally concluded. Just because she'd willed it didn't make it realistic. At night, alone in her bedroom, she sometimes missed him next to her, and this intensified after Golnaz's arrival. Mitra had prepared the downstairs apartment for her visit, had it deep-cleaned and outfitted with new linens, flowers, and bath salts. Another wrong-headed move. The sisters naturally shared Shireen's bed; she and Ana would have done the same. Had Mitra thought to deprive her mother of what she, herself, couldn't have? Shireen had lost a child and two grandchildren; the least she deserved was a living sister.

There were times when Mitra recognized the rhythm and cadence of sorrow in her mother's and aunt's voices, and she wanted to spin away. These exchanges were short, mere allusions now to all the stories and memories that had been recounted over and over in detail. The dead belonged to their collective subconscious now, the stories about them indelible. Ana and Nikku and Nina were moving into the past. To Mitra, it felt treacherous, and she would reach for a gift Golnaz had brought her about Persian gardens. The photographs were stunning, the historical and architectural details fascinating. Mitra had studied the subject long ago, but only cursorily. Those were the days when she didn't want to have much to do with her parent's culture, which prized opaque symbolism excessively. The harder a person had to work to discover hidden meanings, the higher its value. It was why Mitra had turned to simplicity and realism, beauty for the eye, not meant to be pondered.

But now, she was drawn to the ancient garden formula — the geometry of its four quadrants and four water channels representing the natural elements of the world, the sacred plants and courtyards that enhanced its symmetry, and the high walls that enclosed it all, a safe paradise on earth. For the first time in a while, she sketched. Not houses, not floor plans, but gardens. Though she used only a pencil, her visuals were radiant with color. Hundreds of leafy greens, pink and yellow roses, white oleander fifteen feet high, jasmine and purple trumpet vines woven through lattices, mini-orchards of apricot and pear and pomegranate. She was reminded of her uncle Jafar's garden in Tehran's foothills, and thus was reminded of all the gardens her mother's generation talked about with longing. Strangely, she felt it too.

In the evenings after their dinners of bread and cheese and herbs were cleared, Mitra joined her mother and aunt at the kitchen table for ice cream, cards, and backgammon. She'd forgotten the comfort and pleasure of congregating like this, or she'd chosen to forget. There was a lot of teasing and feigned outrage over Shireen's luck and Golnaz's killer instinct. As usual, Mitra never won a match, and she didn't mind as long as the sisters didn't try to throw a game. Laced through second helpings of chocolate chip were opinions, advice, and snippets of news about the others: Nezam's happy obsession with human rights law; Libby's refusal to wean Katy; Golnaz's joy at not having seen Yusef, or anyone else in the Jahani family, since before Christmas.

Studying her fan of cards, Mitra wondered about the letter she'd sent her father. She hadn't expected a response, but she would've liked to know his reaction. She remembered feeling similarly after telling him about her operation all those years ago: she would've liked to witness the effect — his humiliation and frustration, maybe even his redemption. The thought shocked her. Both times she'd acted for Ana's sake, hadn't she? Her father's redemption was foolish fantasy, a remnant of the love and camaraderie they'd had before Mitra grew a mind of her own. But had she subconsciously hoped to coerce her father into changing? It was what she'd tried with everyone, and what had failed with everyone.

On the last night of Golnaz's stay, Mitra found Jezebel fast asleep in her closet, curled up on top of the still-unopened box Aden had sent. Mitra took it as a reprimand for her neglect, bent over and pulled the package out, sending the cat scurrying. She peeled off layers of cardboard and padding to reveal a polished mahogany jewelry chest. She sat cross-legged before it. One by one, she opened the skinny drawers, peered at the sparkling pieces nestled in brown felt, her body vibrating with wonder and admiration. Not pity. She'd always felt pity, but now, she felt Anahita's power.

She dragged the canvas out, pulled off the brown wrapping, and leaned the painting against the wall. Standing back, she saw that Aden had done more than simply replicate the original photo of the four of them. Their poses were the same, but none of them were looking into the camera. It was as if Aden had gone back in time to the seconds before Bijan took the shot, when they were all cracking up over his joke about someone farting. They leaned and pressed into one another, attempting self-control. It was a cameo shot that had never been taken, a shot that revealed all that they'd meant to one another. But there was more. Aden had subtly rendered pieces of Ana's turquoise jewelry into the painting. A delicate bracelet around Nina's wrist, a pendant resting on Ana's chest, earrings glittering against Mitra's hair. Like a *Highlights* hidden picture puzzle. A piece in the polka dots of Nina's blouse, in the stitching on Nikku's belt, in Ana's curls, in the shadow between shoulders and elbows.

Aden, she whispered. He'd been so patient and discreet, had elevated Mitra's suffering above his own, and had given her the Anahita she'd been too blind and arrogant to see. Such gifts were worth more than blood ties. How long had she kept him waiting for her gratitude and solace?

She found the pendant Ana was wearing in the painting — a single oval stone set in a silver-winged sun disk — and clutched it in her palm. She hadn't felt this close to Ana since her death. She slid the chain over her head, let the jewel rest between her breasts. She didn't have to look in the mirror to know that she could never wear it. As Olga once said, *Jewelry not for rebel girls like you, Mitra. Look like joke making.* But the pendant, Mitra realized, would look amazing on her mother.

Shireen begged off going to the airport to drop Golnaz off. She was already crying and didn't want to cry more, especially in public. The sisters hugged and kissed each other's necks and cheeks for so long that Sali was sobbing quietly when they finally separated. In the car, Golnaz promised Mitra she'd be back again soon, maybe next month, maybe with Parviz this time, maybe with Zoya. It was the first time Golnaz had mentioned Zoya by name, but it rolled off her tongue as if Mitra knew the whole story.

For a second, she worried that her aunt had prepared a lecture for these last twenty minutes of her stay. But Golnaz added, "Zoya's eager to visit Berkeley, where her parents studied in the seventies." Her tone was sober, as if Zoya was an ordinary student free from trauma, and Mitra thought, well, whose life was free from trauma?

"It'll be nice to finally meet her," said Mitra. Golnaz smiled and extracted a tin of Altoids from her purse.

The rain was steady, but much lighter than it had been since Golnaz had arrived. As they neared the airport at the southern edge of the city, a jagged patch of blue sky spit out a rainbow that impressed Golnaz. Mitra had grown used to this between-storms phenomenon, and she directed Golnaz to scan the sky for more prisms, which she did successfully. "What a lovely place you live, darling," she said wistfully.

Golnaz wouldn't let Mitra park and see her to the gate, and at the curb, she refused help toting her bag to the ticket counter. Golnaz pulled Mitra in for an embrace, then held her cheeks and stared into her face. "Thank you . . ." Golnaz's lips trembled, and Mitra was unnerved by the sudden and rare show of emotion. "Thank you for," she choked out, her eyes brimming, "for saving my sister." Mitra raised her eyebrows, confounded, and Golnaz brought her forehead in to touch Mitra's, then abruptly let go, turned, and disappeared through the revolving door.

Mitra swayed slightly, unblinking. Her aunt's mint-leaf breath hung in the air. For the first time in a long while, she felt herself rooted, solid. A car horn honked, the over-gelled driver eager for Mitra's space. She thought about flipping him off. *Wow, when was the last time I had an urge to do that?* It made her want to laugh, not for the funniness of it, but for the sudden giggly way she felt. She got into her car, feeling every part of the seat touch her body, awakening her skin.

Saved, her aunt had said.

A lovely thing to say. Perhaps a true thing, but not entirely. Shireen had also saved Mitra. They'd saved each other. And there had been no strategy or coercion or manipulation. There had been only mutual need.

She smiled, put the car in gear, and cranked up the volume on "Hotel California." The patch of blue sky had expanded, turning the landscape an emerald green. Mitra knew it was only a respite, a breath between storms. She scanned for rainbows.

Why not sunbow? Olga had asked after Mitra pantomimed the arc of a bow and Olga found the Farsi word. *Because you need the rain for it to happen,* was Mitra's cocky retort. She winced at the memory of her fourteen-year-old self, exasperated by Olga's preoccupation with bilingual vocabulary. *Need the sun, too,* Olga had finally said, her raspy voice now crystal clear in Mitra's ear. She'd been right. The Farsi word translated to an "arc of colors," which, Mitra had to reluctantly admit, was smarter. She felt her throat swell as she heard Olga's big-mouthed, infectious cackle. Her chest filled with yearning. She pulled off the freeway, stopped alongside the glistening Bay, and reached for her phone.

ACKNOWLEDGMENTS

During the course of writing this book, I lost three women who meant the world to me. Each of their lives — the way they lived and the way they didn't — inspired and informed parts of this story. Unfading gratitude to my mother, Iman Khosrowshahi, née Faith Lita Knobel, who patiently and lovingly listened to early drafts through years of illness, recovery, and relapse; to Kathi Kamen Goldmark, whose presence I still feel whenever writing in a café, and whose friendship was as pure as sunlight; and to Asya Levai, the inspiration for "Olga," who died in Tehran in 2014, dashing our hopes that we would see one another again.

This book would not have survived its long journey to publication without the tough love and unwavering heart of my brilliant agent, Laurie Liss. I am forever indebted to my private editor Joy Johannessen, who read through over a thousand pages, pointed to Version Two, and never lost faith, even when I did. So much gratitude to my editor, John Scognamiglio, for championing this book without hesitation, and for treating it with care and respect.

Once a novel is written, it must find a house in which to live and grow. If the novelist is lucky, that house becomes a welcoming, nurturing, and well-run home. I'm very lucky. Thank you to my Kensington family, especially Steve Zacharius and Adam Zacharius, Lynn Cully, Kristine Noble, Joyce Kaplan, Carly Sommerstein, Vida Engstrand, Michelle Addo, Matt Johnson, and Jackie Dinas.

My infinite appreciation to the people who read my words, listened to my frustrations, calmed my anxieties, advised me, drank my tea, fed me, yelled at me, laughed and cried and kvetched with me, lectured me, teased me, and held me: Rabih Alameddine, Anita Amirrezvani, Ozi Badiey, Naseem Badiey, Carol Hodges Balodis, Rosaleen Bertolino, Karen Bjorneby, Louann Brizendine, Sylvia Brownrigg, Riki Carignan, Jeanne Carstensen, Roya Chadab, Jane Ciabattari, Joshua Citrak, Cindy Dunne, Ladonna Fasig, Audrey Ferber, Cynthia Gentry, Molly Giles, Sheila Gordon, Susan Ito,

Scott James, Lauren John, Guy Johnson, Farimah Justus, Yukari Kane, Juliette Kelley, Deborah Kirk, Laura Osio Khosrowshahi, Lili Khosrowshahi, Alice Kleeman, Lee Kravetz, Shana Mahaffey, Carol Markson, Kirsten Menger-Anderson, Diana Miller, Marjaneh Moghimi, Blair Moser, Kate Moses, Randi Murray, John McMurtrie, Janis Cooke Newman, Gina Nahai, Peggy Orenstein, Elaine Petrocelli, Nahid Rachlin, Ethel Rohan, Elizabeth Rosner, Roxana Saberi, Mariam Safinia, Jacqueline Shapiro, Ellen Sussman, Laura Secor, Lisa See, Lalita Tademy, Amy Tan, Cameron Tuttle, Ayelet Waldman, Susan Wels, and Marsha Williams.

Special gratitude to my daily Surveillance Writing Companions for keeping me in the chair, and to the writing communities that have nurtured my mental and social health: Hedgebrook, The Community of Writers, The Castro Writers Cooperative, The San Francisco Writers Grotto, and Word-of-Mouth Bay Area.

Deep love and gratitude to my father, Nasrollah Khosrowshahi, for every story he ever told me, for showing me how a person can change and soften over decades but still remain infuriatingly the same, and for letting me make fun of his accent at every turn. To my siblings — Marcene, Kevin, and Cameron — thank you for loving me and for pretending to put up with my unsolicited advice. Shout out to my niece, Roxanna Hedayati, for her unique and amazing artist's eye.

Thank you to my badass organizational genius daughter-in-law, Hilary, and to my precious son, Darian, who shows his devotion in so many ways and who never lets me give up. Finally, to my husband, Shahram Shirazi, who has known me and protected me and annoyed me since we met as children: I could not have persisted without you.

■ ■ ■ ■

READING GROUP GUIDE: IN THE TIME OF OUR HISTORY

■ ■ ■ ■

ABOUT THIS GUIDE

The suggested questions are included to enhance your group's reading of Susanne Pari's *In the Time of Our History*!

DISCUSSION QUESTIONS

1. *In the Time of Our History* tells the story of a secular and educated immigrant family, most of whose members have resettled in the United States because of a Revolution that gave rise to a brutal regime in Iran. Can you imagine yourself in a similar situation? How do you think you would cope with exile and migration to a foreign country? Many of the Jahanis cling to old traditions in order to retain a sense of belonging. Which beliefs and norms would you try to preserve?

2. Mitra and Anahita are first generation Americans, while the rest of the Jahanis are immigrants. What are some of the ways the sisters are different from the others, and do you think the presence of the extended family in their lives influenced their personalities and choices?

3. Mitra and Anahita's childhood relationship was strained, as many sibling relationships are. As adults, however, they have a strong and loving bond. Do you think this would have been the case if Mitra had not discovered Kareem molesting Anahita?

4. Child sexual abuse in families is widespread across ethnic, cultural, and socioeconomic lines. Each incident is unique, and each victim is affected uniquely. In what ways do you think Anahita's trauma played a role in her decision to pursue a relationship with Aden? How do you think the story would have been different if Anahita hadn't kept so many secrets from Mitra?

5. Revelation and growth is a theme for many of this novel's characters. Could you relate to Shireen's journey away from stalwart wife toward independent woman? If Anahita and the children hadn't died, do you think Shireen would have taken this path?

6. The romance between Mitra and Julian is complex. While their devotion to each other may run true and deep, there are obstacles that stand in the way of a future

for them together. Do you think these obstacles could have been overcome?

7. Both Salimeh and Zoya are refugees. How are they similar? How are they different? If they wound up on your doorstep, would you help one or both or neither?

8. Yusef is depicted mostly as a ruthless and narcissistic patriarch, not to mention a cold and unfaithful husband. And yet, he also has a traumatic history. Did this history of trauma excuse any of his behavior? And does he achieve some redemption in your mind in the end?

9. Since the 1979 Islamic Revolution and the US Embassy Hostage Crisis, Iran and its society have been closed to most Americans. *In the Time of Our History* gives us a peek into that world through several characters' eyes. Were you surprised by the unconventional shape of Olga's life? Were you sympathetic to Zoya's plight? Could you relate to Golnaz's discomfort in visiting her birth country? Did reading *In the Time of Our History* alter your view of Iran and/or Iranians?

10. Autocracies survive when they can

control the substance and flow of information to their citizens. This requires a ruthless vigilance to silence intellectuals and creatives. Have you ever been in a situation where you were afraid of writing or saying something you believed?

ABOUT THE AUTHOR

Susanne Pari is an Iranian-American novelist, journalist, essayist, and book reviewer. Born in New Jersey to an Iranian father and an American mother, she grew up both in the United States and Iran until the 1979 Islamic Revolution forced her family into permanent exile. Since then, her writing has focused on stories of displacement and belonging, of identity and assimilation, of trauma and resilience. Her first novel, *The Fortune Catcher,* has been translated into six languages and her nonfiction writing has appeared in the *New York Times Sunday Magazine, Christian Science Monitor, Boston Globe, San Francisco Chronicle,* National Public Radio, and Medium. A former program director for Book Expo, she is a member of the National Book Critics Circle, the Author's Guild, the San Francisco Writers' Grotto, and the Castro Writers' Cooperative. She serves on the board of the Lakota Children's Enrichment Writing Project and is an alumna of the Hedgebrook Writing Residency. She blogs occasionally for the Center for Iranian Diaspora Studies and divides her time between Northern California and New York. Visit her online at SusannePari.com.